Stone River

Stone River

Keeper of the Keys

Wilma Styles

Grateful Steps
Asheville, North Carolina

Grateful Steps Foundation
Crest Mountain
30 Ben Lippen School Road #107
Asheville, North Carolina 28806

Library of Congress Control Number 2020946080

Styles, Wilma
Stone River:
Keeper of the Keys
Cover photograph by Kiselev Andrey Valerevich
Photograph on dedication page
is from author's personal collection
ISBN 978-1-945714-47-4 Paperback

Printed in the United States of America
at Lightning Source

FIRST EDITION

www.gratefulsteps.org

to my granddaughter, Kaylee

I dedicate *Stone River*, to my beautiful granddaughter, Kaylee Stanaland. I love you, Kaylee, and want you to know how very proud I am of you and your many writing abilities.
(See you later alligator!)
Love you!

ALSO BY WILMA STYLES

When I'm in His Presence

Angels of the Ages

Forbidden Heart

Joy on the Mountain

Contents

CONTENTS

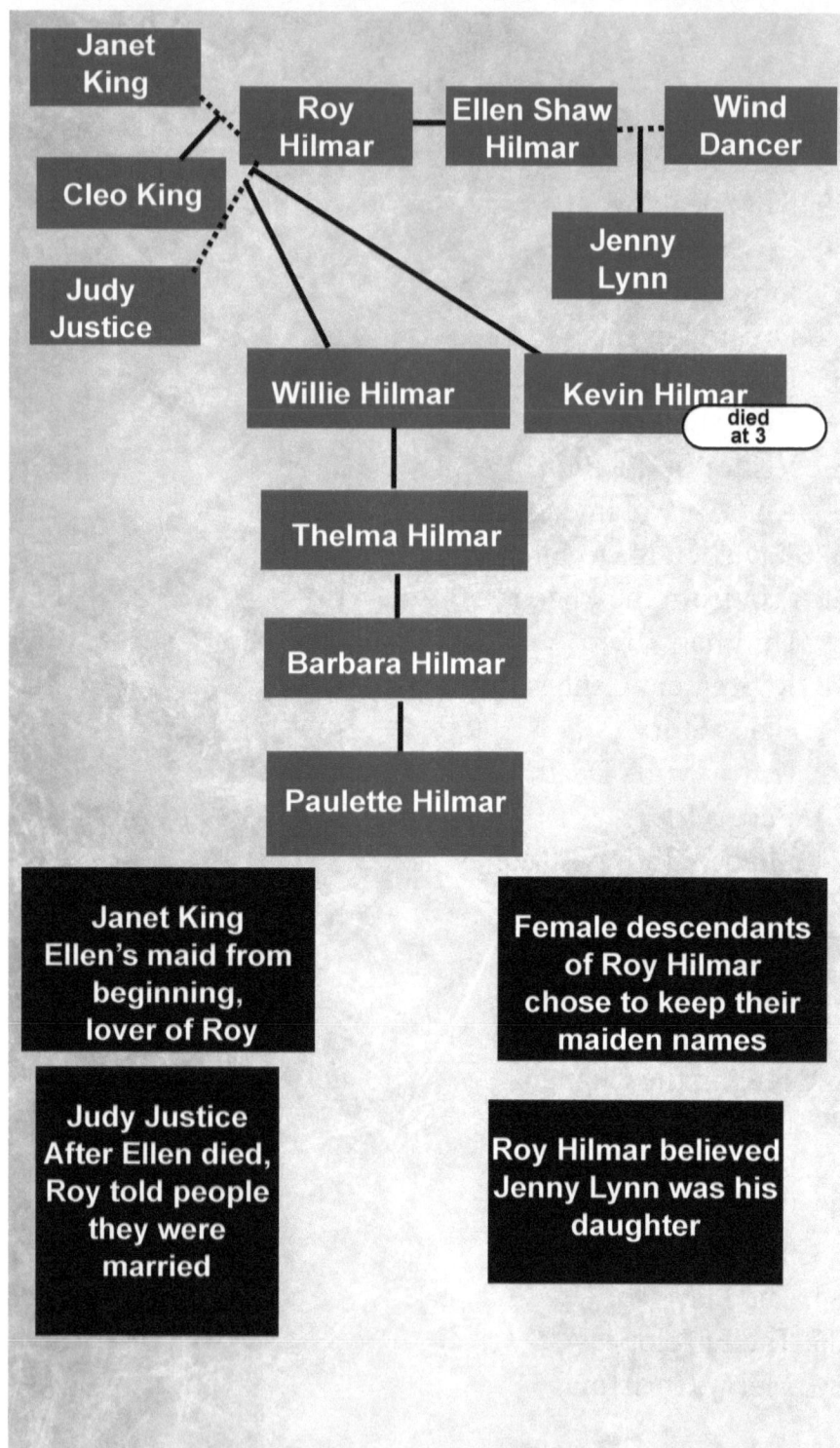

Janet King
Cleo King
Judy Justice

Roy Hilmar — Ellen Shaw Hilmar ⋯ Wind Dancer

Jenny Lynn

Willie Hilmar   Kevin Hilmar
died at 3

Thelma Hilmar

Barbara Hilmar

Paulette Hilmar

Janet King
Ellen's maid from beginning,
lover of Roy

Female descendants
of Roy Hilmar
chose to keep their
maiden names

Judy Justice
After Ellen died,
Roy told people
they were
married

Roy Hilmar believed
Jenny Lynn was his
daughter

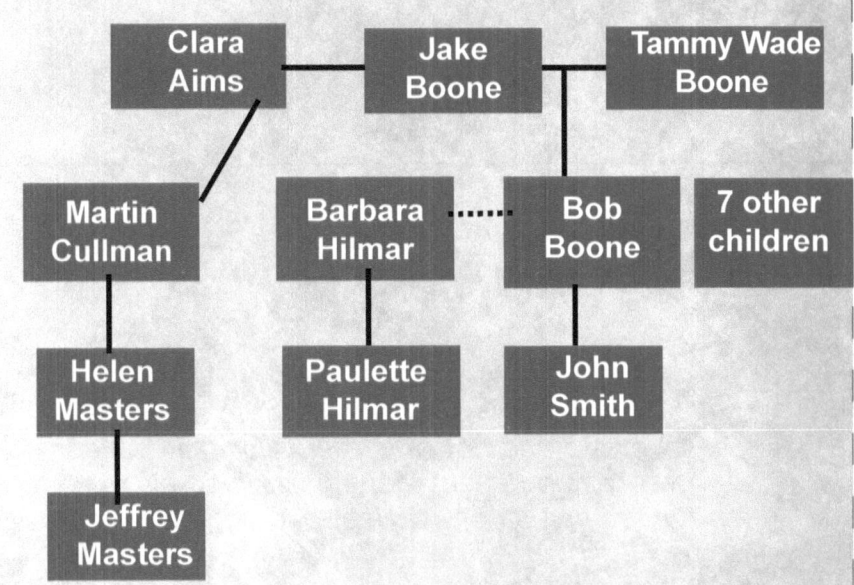

Other Characters:

Kaylee Shell   Teacher and private investigator, Jeffrey Master's fiancée
Adam James   Grounds keeper
Kitty Snow   Tara Wallace's mother
Dotty Sams   Guardian of the house
Moving Cloud   Brother of Wind Dancer

Students
Eddie Boone
Betty Moore
Charlie LittleHawk
Lori Chandler
Kyle Jones
Joshua Coats

Teachers and Other Stone River Individuals

Nick Long   principal (wife Donna Long, school secretary)
Rick Owens   teacher
Tara Wallace   teacher
Tim Dodd   Mayor of Stone River

"Why would my mother take time to write all these letters and not mail them?" Martin asked.

After reading each one, Martin fixed his eyes on Kaylee and said, "Kaylee, darling, will you do something for me?"

"Of course, Martin. You know I will."

He took the letters in his shaking hands and handed them to her. "Kaylee, are you ready to take on your first case as a private investigator?"

"Martin, you know I can't wait. What do you have in mind for me?"

"Kaylee, honey, it's time for you to go North Dakota . . . to Stone River."

Prologue

Wiping sweat from her face and trying to moderate her breathing, Kaylee turned her head and listened for the faint voice she thought she heard in her dream. Instead of a voice, she heard what sounded like someone crying in the distance. As she focused on the sound, it became clear. It was a woman crying. Recalling what Lola Barnes had said about hearing a woman crying, Kaylee kicked free from the twisted sheets and grabbed her robe from the chair.

She tried to turn on the lamp, but it wouldn't come on. *The power must be out*, she thought. Holding her hands in front of her, she hurried across the dark room to the wall switch, desperately wanting the lights on. She flipped the switch up and down several times, but to no avail. Kaylee leaned her back against the wall and took a couple of deep breaths. The low crying, she heard had now turned into low moans and then into loud wailing.

Kaylee wanted to go down the hall and see if there was a woman on the staircase, yet her legs felt so weak. "Kaylee calm down," she said aloud to herself as she put her hand to her mouth and blew her breath through her fingers. "Great heavenly days! What if it's . . . Ellen?" Unnerved, she flipped the light switch several times . . . still nothing.

Not having an idea where a candle or a flashlight was, she moved to the hallway. Putting her hand to the cold wall, she moved cautiously in the darkness toward the foyer. The weeping grew louder as she neared the staircase. Nearing the foyer, she paused to catch her breath before making the turn that put her at the bottom of the stairs. Kaylee gradually raised her eyes, gasped and stumbled backward.

Halfway up the stairs, a pale blue light shimmered around a tall, slender woman. Her head was bowed. In one hand, she held a wrinkled piece of paper to her stomach and the other hand, she held over her face. The mysterious woman continued to weep. Unhurriedly, she moved her hand from her face as though suddenly aware of Kaylee's presence. She slowly raised her head and fixed her eyes on Kaylee. Breathing escaped Kaylee as she stared into the face of Ellen Hilmar. Ellen's emerald green eyes looked as though she had cried an ocean of tears.

Chapter One
A New Job

Kaylee leaned her head back on the pillow the stewardess had given her. She gasped as the plane taxied for takeoff. Turning her head to the right, she glanced one last time at the man who stood with his hand pressed against the window at Gate 12-B. The plane paused and then shot forward down the runway. Kaylee put her open hand to the window as her body pushed back from the force of the plane. Even though the plane was totally out of sight of the terminal, Kaylee continued to press her hand against the glass. It wasn't until the pilot announced they would be flying at thirty-two thousand feet, that she removed her hand slowly to her lap.

Kaylee had lived in Cary, North Carolina, a small rural area outside Raleigh, North Carolina, for most of her life. A recent graduate of Duke University, she wanted to go to work immediately and make good use of her teaching degree. She had also worked hard and received her private investigation license like her father. Growing up she loved helping her Dad work on his cases sometimes. He was so proud that his only child wanted to follow in his footsteps. Her Mother was also thrilled that Kaylee had gotten her teaching degree, like her. Kaylee had applied and was accepted for a teaching position at Fair Mount High School in Stone River, North Dakota. Not knowing anyone there, she felt apprehensive about starting a new career so far away from home. She gently touched a small scar on her right cheek and closed her eyes.

"Are you all right?" the woman sitting beside her asked quietly.

Kaylee promptly opened her eyes and replied, "Yes . . . yes, I'm fine."

The woman chuckled. "I thought maybe this was your first flight," she said. "I remember the first time I flew. I was so scared I couldn't breathe for most of the trip. I might add, it wasn't a short flight. I was going from Seattle to Dallas. I was so dizzy from the lack of oxygen getting to my brain I almost passed out when I stood to get off the plane!"

Kaylee wanted to be left alone, but not wanting to hurt the woman's feelings, she smiled on occasion and nodded but talked very little. To her dismay, the silence only peaked her neighbor's quizzical ambition.

The stranger shook her head. "I'm sorry, I haven't introduced myself." She extended her hand to Kaylee. "I'm Shannon Morris."

Kaylee smiled and shook her hand. "I'm Kaylee Shell."

Shannon nudged her arm and teased, "You wouldn't happen to be one of the heirs of the Shell Oil Company, would you?"

As Kaylee observed the stewardess pointing to where the oxygen mask was located, she answered, "No, I'm afraid not."

"Where are you headed, Kaylee?"

"Stone River, North Dakota. I've taken a teaching position at Fair Mount High School."

"Hum, you're going to Lakota territory."

Looking at Shannon, Kaylee responded, "It does have a vivid history of the Lakota Indian. It's my understanding that almost no Lakota live in Stone River."

"I'm not talking about the town. I'm talking about the territory that stretches beyond the town. Several Lakota still occupy the land allotted them by the government." Shannon squinted and asked, "Do you have family in Stone River?"

"No."

"Where did you say you were from?"

"I didn't say, but I'm from Raleigh, North Carolina. I drove to Charlotte to get a nonstop flight."

"Raleigh? How in the world did you make a connection to teach at Stone River, North Dakota?"

"Actually, I'm from a small town outside of Raleigh called Cary. I applied through the University. A few days later, I received an acceptance from Fair Mount, took it, and, as they say, 'the rest is history'."

"Where did you go to school in North Carolina?"

"Duke University."

Shannon giggled. "You're a graduate from Duke and you're going to teach at Fair Mount? The entire school only has only three hundred students."

"Yes, I know. I'm sure you're referring to the money aspect, but money isn't everything. I want to make a difference in a place many choose to ignore because of the money."

Shannon tensed her brows. "Money isn't an issue at Fair Mount."

"Really?" Kaylee replied. "Nicolas Long, the principal of Fair Mount indicated . . ."

"Hum. A trust fund to last way into the future was set up years ago by the founding fathers, Jake Boone and Roy Hilmar. You'll see their names attached to almost everything in Stone River. Did a teacher retire or something? I thought their staff was totally adequate."

"I understand one of the teachers quit suddenly. My application was at the top of the stack. So, how is it that you know so much about Fair Mount?"

"I'm in computer sales for a major corporation. Our company just donated all new computers a couple of weeks ago for none other than Fair Mount High School! Tell me, Kaylee, what are the odds of two people meeting on a plane, both having connections with a small high school in Stone River?"

Kaylee chuckled as she pulled at her scarf. "Almost impossible!" she said. "Will I be seeing you at the school?"

"Not likely. I help build the computers to meet the schools' needs. Someone else sees to the installation. That will be John Smith. I told him his name sounded like a cheap motel alias. I must warn you, he's very handsome in a rugged sort of way. To top it off, he isn't married. Are you married, Kaylee?"

"No."

"I'll put in a word for you if you'd like."

"Thanks, but no."

"If you change your mind, let me know."

"I don't think so," Kaylee remarked as she reached down to retrieve her iPad from her carry-on bag.

"Who knows, maybe you'll meet Mr. Right in Stone River. What kind of men do you prefer?" Shannon questioned, as if she were taking notes.

The stewardess saved Kaylee as she announced dinner was about to be served. After dinner, Kaylee put on her headphones and leaned back to take a nap. She wasn't really sleepy but felt a desperate need for peace and quiet. She closed her eyes and finally relaxed.

After drinking three small bottles of Jack Daniels, Shannon leaned her seat back and in seconds, Kaylee could hear the rumble of snores over the peaceful tunes of her classical piano music.

The plane was due to land in Fargo at 11:45 p.m. Terra Wallace, a teacher at Fair Mount, was to meet Kaylee at the airport. Nicolas Long, the principal, had told her about an old estate scheduled for renovation in the spring that was located on the outskirts of town. The estate was willed to the town after the original owner's daughter passed away. Before the renovation took place, the city council voted to rent the house for a six-month period. The school was a short distance from the estate, which was a plus. Nicolas emailed her a couple of photos of the rooms. The rent was unbelievably inexpensive. So, Kaylee signed the lease and sent the deposit along with the first and last month's rent.

Shannon slept until the captain announced the plane would be landing in five minutes.

Shannon leaned forward, and yawned. "My goodness. I should have settled for only one of those little bottles. Kaylee, I'm sorry we didn't get to visit longer."

"No apology necessary."

"Good luck on your new job. The people I've worked with at the high school are exceptionally nice, like you. I think you'll make quite an impression at Stone River."

"Thank you, Shannon. It's been a real pleasure meeting you."

Kaylee withdrew a small bag from the overhead compartment and made her way to the front of the plane. Once she retrieved her luggage, she strolled out the main doors, pulling her suitcases behind her.

Chapter Two

Meeting Terra

The cool October night was as clear as Kaylee had ever remembered. This night was different somehow. The moon looked fuller, the stars brighter and the sky clearer.

Her stare was broken when someone called her name. She turned to find a slim, middle-aged woman with short brown hair, large green eyes and narrow lips. "Excuse me. Are you Kaylee Shell?"

Kaylee grinned. "Yes . . . yes, I am. You must be Terra Wallace."

Terra extended her hand confidently. "The one and only! For him to have only seen your photo, Principal Long's description of you was perfect. If I may quote him, he said, 'Miss Shell is a lovely 26-year-old with long, auburn hair, fair skin and rosy cheeks. She has a tall, slim frame; squared shoulders; full lips; a beautiful smile; and her Southern drawl is charming.'"

Kaylee blushed. "He's very flattering."

Terra crossed her arms. "I think he summed you up nicely."

"Thank you."

Terra looked to the sky. "I see the beauty of the North Dakota nights has captivated you as it still does me after all these years."

"It's almost hypnotic," Kaylee said.

Terra insisted Kaylee stay the night with her due to the late hour. Kaylee felt comfortable with her offer and politely accepted.

Terra lived a half-mile away from the school. Terra showed Kaylee her room and a bath and then they changed into their robes, and slippers. Afterward, they settled down in the living room to get better acquainted.

Sipping her tea, Terra stated, "I understand you've leased the Hilmar Estate."

Kaylee sat her cup on the saucer. "Yes. The pictures Mr. Long sent were lovely. I must confess, the rent sealed it for me."

"The city council wanted someone in the house so they could make a little money from the rent rather than let it sit empty and gather cobwebs!"

"I gather the house is very large?" Kaylee said. "I only rented most of the first floor."

"Thirty rooms is quite large, and its furnishings are all basically the same as they were when Roy and Ellen moved into their home in 1884. Roy Hilmar and Jake Boone, his partner, were the founders of Stone River. I personally think Roy and his partner were crooks."

"How do you mean?" Kaylee asked.

"I mean Roy Hilmar took gold from the Lakota. He hired men to kill the buffalo for their hides, not caring that the buffalo were the main source of the Lakota food, clothing and housing. He fenced the pastureland

8

and didn't allow the Lakota to feed their animals, which pushed them out of their safety zone to find pasture. I hate people who make their money at the expense of others."

"It sounds as though Mr. Hilmar and Mr. Boone were a pair of darling men," Kaylee sarcastically added with a cough.

Terra set her tea on the table. "I'm sorry I spouted off. That could have waited. I don't want to make a bad first impression!"

Kaylee shook her head and exclaimed, "You haven't! You sound like a person who cares about the treatment of others, especially the Lakota."

Terra smiled. "I do have Lakota blood flowing in my veins. My great-great-grandfather, Swift Eagle, was a full-blooded Lakota and the chief of the tribe of Lakota who made their home at what is called the "Bend." However, it was the chief after my grandfather, Black Bear, that Roy Hilmar constantly fought against."

Kaylee frowned. "At that time, weren't there more Indians in the area than there were white men?"

"Yes. Nevertheless, Black Bear didn't want to massacre the white men because news about soldiers herding the Cherokee Indians from their homeland to Oklahoma had spread. The Little Big Horn had been fought. After that battle came a massive number of soldiers. Treaties were drawn up for the Lakota to sign. If the chiefs signed, the government would force them from their land to what was called the Great Sioux Reservation. This prevented Black Bear from doing what he wanted to do, which was to kill Roy Hilmar and Jake

Boone. He feared doing so would cause an uprising and the soldiers would end up wiping out his tribe." Terra paused. "Let's end our history class for now."

"Good idea." Kaylee said. "Are you married, Terra?"

"No. Well, I was. My husband passed away three years ago. We didn't have children, so here I am alone. My mother does come to visit once a month."

"Does she live here in Stone River?"

"No. She chooses to live at the Bend. It's the place where my father grew up. I've tried to get her to move to town where I could at least watch after her, but she won't hear of it."

"She sounds very interesting," Kaylee mentioned with a smile.

"Believe me, she is. She still thinks the cavalry is going to attack any day now. She's 80 years old, yet acts 30."

Kaylee eagerly asked, "Terra, would you tell me about the kids at Fair Mount?"

"Sure. They're a good group of kids. Of course, like all schools, you have the four or five rebels. Fair Mount is no different. Good teachers."

Terra fixed her eyes on Kaylee and frowned. "With your credentials, why would you come across the United States to a dinky little town like Stone River to teach?"

"I want to make a difference."

Terra stood and excused herself. Kaylee took a deep breath and blew it out. Exhaustion kicked in. When Terra returned, Kaylee glanced at her watch.

Terra smiled. "Please forgive my rudeness, Kaylee. I forgot you're still operating on Eastern Time. Can I get you anything before you retire?"

"No, and thank you for your hospitality. I'm just very tired."

Terra nodded.

Kaylee raised her exhausted body from the chair and took a hot shower. Afterward, she snuggled in the soft bed. After glancing over a few notes, her concentration was broken as images of a man at the Raleigh Airport filled her mind. Kaylee pulled tissue from a box on the nightstand, wiped her tears and turned the light off. When her tears finally stopped, Kaylee's hand released the tear-filled Kleenex to the floor.

Kaylee whined, "Why am I crying? What's wrong with me? This is so unlike me at all."

Chapter Three

A Letter

The first of October had brought a cold chill to the morning air. A few mountains and a lot of rolling knolls surrounded Stone River. Hardly any colorful leaves remained on the trees, and the knolls were all but brown with stubble.

Kaylee moaned and blinked her eyes in an attempt to see the wall clock near the door. The night had passed swiftly and most of the morning. It was ten forty-five. After making the bed, Kaylee took an aged envelope from her purse, opened it and read it once again. The date at the top of the page read August 18, 1899. She pondered the words of the letter.

> *My darling Jake,*
> *Time could never take away the love I have for you.*
> *I still feel your gentle touch. I wonder if you have found*
> *another to fill my void. I wish I could have told you—*

Kaylee closed her eyes and remembered her visit with Martin Cullman before she left for Stone River. It had been eighty years since Martin Cullman's mother, Clara Aims, had passed away. He was now 89 years old and knew, as an only child, it would be up to him to go through his mother's things while he was still able. Martin had one daughter, Judy Masters, whom he saw only twice a year due to her work. Her son, Jeffrey, Kaylee's fiancé, was very close to his grandfather, but Kaylee was Martin's best friend. It was Kaylee who encouraged Martin to go through the attic of the old farmhouse and see what inheritance his mother had left him. Martin's father had stored all his mother's possessions in the roof space after her death. After his father died, the house had been empty. Martin had not been in the loft of his grandparents' home since that time.

Kaylee recalled that it was on a cool spring day after taking Martin to the doctor that she had convinced her old friend it was time to check out the attic of the country house. Martin agreed, "Yes, today on the way home is a perfect time for the undertaking." Kaylee approved and left the city for the fifteen-mile ride to a small rural area called Cary.

Martin was silent as they pulled onto a narrow dirt driveway that led them to the aged, white, two-story farmhouse that was in need of a coat of paint. Kaylee turned the engine off and helped Martin from the car.

She looked around the yard. "I sure love this old place, Martin."

"Me, too. I see Jim Harper has been taking good care of the grounds. I should have asked someone to come clean the house before our visit."

"The grounds look great, and I'm sure the house will be fine."

"I hope we will be able to endure the dust. I know how your allergies act up around dust sometimes."

Kaylee held to Martin's arm as they ascended the old, gray, plank steps onto the porch.

Kaylee nodded toward the swing. "Would you like to sit in the porch swing for a moment?"

Martin smiled. "Yes . . . yes, I would." He briefly held Kaylee's hand and sat down.

Kaylee watched as he glided his fingers across the wood on the arm of the swing.

He closed his eyes as he pushed back and forth. He moaned and said, "My mother used to bring me to visit my grandparents when I was just a young boy. We sat in this swing and she told me lots of things. I wish I could go back just for one moment to hear her voice again. I would love to be able to recall some of her stories. The only thing I can remember her telling me is, 'There is a grand house and a swing that hangs in an old oak tree out back where all the kids played.'"

"Martin, you're sharing something new with me right now. I have never heard you tell that about the grand house and swing before."

Martin shook his head. "Actually, the memory just came to me while I was sitting here."

Kaylee took his hands and helped him from the swing. "Martin, we are going to have a wonderful adventure today. I am so excited to get to see your mother's personal things. Everyone who knew her says she was such an elegant lady."

After a smile and a deep breath, Martin said, "She was so beautiful and always smelled like roses. In the spring, I always went to her flower garden out front just to smell the roses. It was hard to tell the difference if I was hugging Mom or smelling the roses she had planted in her garden."

Upon entering the house, Martin squeezed Kaylee's hand. "My, my," Martin said. "Nothing has changed in this house for as long as I can remember." He looked at the old family photos on the mantle. He picked up a photo of his mother, gently touched the glass with his fingertips and wiped the dust away. "Do you think I look like my mother?" he said as he handed Kaylee the picture.

Kaylee chuckled. "Yes, I do, Martin! When you were younger, the resemblance is striking. Very handsome, I might add."

Martin blushed. "Thank you, Miss Shell." He took a deep breath and blew it out. "I guess we better get started."

As they neared the attic door, Martin paused and wiped his upper lip. He was going to take the key for the door from his pocket but was instantly hindered. His hands had begun to shake.

"Martin, are you okay?" Kaylee asked, as she took his hands in hers.

His hands steadied at her touch. He looked at them, then to Kaylee. "Yes . . . yes, I'm fine. Just a little anxious I think." His eyes darted around the area as he took the old skeleton key from his pocket and handed it to Kaylee.

"Martin, we can come back another time, if you wish. We don't have to do this today."

He faced Kaylee and blurted out, "No! It's time . . . it's time I tell you."

Kaylee touched his arm. "Okay, Martin. I've never seen you like this before. You look a little pale. I don't want you getting all stressed out over this."

Martin's weak eyes stared out at Kaylee from under his white furrowed brows. His grim expression quickly turned to a tight-lipped grin. "I'm fine, now. Let's just get this done."

Kaylee turned the key, nudged against the time-worn door, looked at him and smiled. "Are you sure you're ready?"

Martin nodded and at the same time, took hold of Kaylee's arm. "I don't know why I acted the way," he said. "I just did . . . or why I have waited so long to do this. Good golly, if I had waited much longer, old age and death would have relieved me of my duties all together. Still, standing here, my emotions are working overtime. One part of me is saying, *Go on, you old fool, and get this over with.* The other part of me is saying, *Once you go up those stairs, you and Kaylee will never be the same again.* Because of the last sentiment, I feel a bit hesitant. You know me, Kaylee. I am not one to procrastinate, and yet here I am 89 and still haven't gone up those stairs yet."

Kaylee looked up the steps. "I don't have a clue why you feel so strongly about going through your mom's belongings, or why you feel it will affect you and me in such a profound manner. I love you, Martin. You may not know why you haven't already completed this task years ago, but look at it this way, if you had done this a long time ago, I wouldn't have the pleasure of assisting you today."

Kaylee took Martin's hand and cautiously ascended the eight screeching steps that led them to a large, dusty room. After a moment of glancing around the area to see where to start first, Martin and Kaylee opened a cedar wardrobe and began looking at Clara's beautiful dresses. After seeing so many wonderful things and thinking they were almost through, Martin raised his hand and pointed toward something near the back of the room. As they drew near the shadowy area, they saw it was an antique trunk that was partially hidden with a long, black coat covered in dust. Kaylee cleared the top of the trunk. She got a chair for Martin and placed in front of the chest. After sitting, Martin put his leathered hand on the chest, paused and looked at Kaylee. With tears in his eyes, he said, "I haven't seen this trunk since I was a little boy. I had almost forgotten how beautiful it is. Mama used to let me take a look inside here every once in a while and see what she had added to her treasures. Sometimes, she would let me find a place inside to put her keepsake."

Kaylee patted his shoulder. "Let's take a look inside. You want too?"

A quick nod of his head gave Kaylee permission to open the lid for him. Tears ran down his cheeks as he gently touched a beautiful brush and mirror set on the top tray. Beaded combs of different colors, small clutch purses and hats with feathers and veils lined the top layers in the chest. Underneath the top layers, was his mother's wedding dress—a long, white, satin gown. It was overlaid with fine lace and arrayed with long puffed sleeves and an extended row of small, pearl buttons that ran down the back of the dress.

Kaylee held the dress up for Martin to see. "It's stunning, Martin."

Martin took a handkerchief from his pocket and dried his tears as Kaylee folded the dress, turned and laid it aside. When Kaylee turned to face Martin, she noticed that he had removed a small colorful crocheted spread from the trunk and laid it across his lap. He didn't respond at first when she spoke his name. His stare was fixed on the corner of the trunk. Upon removing the spread, Martin had seen a large stack of envelopes tied together with a pale pink ribbon. He motioned for Kaylee to get them for him. He held them a moment and then slowly untied the bow. As he looked at each envelope, Kaylee could see the confusion on his face. She too was baffled when she saw that each letter was addressed to the same man, Jake Boone, in Stone River, North Dakota.

Terra knocked lightly on her door. Kaylee hurriedly ended her reverie, put the letter back in her purse, pulled her robe together and rushed to open the door. Terra apologized for disturbing her.

"I never sleep this late," Kaylee moaned.

"Now that you're rested, are you hungry?"

Kaylee put her hand on her stomach. "I'm starved," she replied.

"Good! Principal Long wants to take us to lunch. Jim and Mary Farley own Beef Eaters, the best and only steak house in town. I confess I'm a very frequent visitor. It's quite nice! I think you'll like it. May I suggest you wear something warm?"

Kaylee slipped her jeans on and a white turtleneck. She brushed her auburn hair, allowing it to hang loosely on her shoulders.

"We need to be going," Terra called.

"I'll be right there," Kaylee replied, as she put on her black suede jacket.

Chapter Four
High School Staff

*K*aylee surveyed what she could see of Stone River as she got into the car.

"The town is charming. It looks like a Norman Rockwell painting! Modern, yet maintains the character of the Old West."

"It is beautiful here," Terra said. "When the winter snow starts, it really looks like a painter's canvas."

Almost as fast as they pulled from the driveway, Terra was parking. An aroma hovered over Beef Eaters. A rustic, plank porch; a foyer filled with Western memorabilia; and country music playing loudly set the stage for what would prove to be a memorable first day.

A bar was centered in the extensive room and was surrounded by three large-screen televisions. As the hostess led them past the bar, Kaylee saw a tall man in the far corner stand and wave toward them. Terra responded with a wave. As they approached the table, they saw another man and two women stand to greet them. The man, who waved, smiled and firmly shook Kaylee's hand. "You must be Kaylee Shell."

Kaylee nodded. "Yes, and you must be Nicolas Long."

"That's me. It's a pleasure to finally meet you." He pointed to the woman beside him. "This is my wife, Donna, and this is Shelby Pole, one of our tenth-grade teachers." Turning to the right, he nodded toward a gentleman. "This is our Biology teacher, Ricky Owens."

Ricky gently squeezed her hand. "I insist you call me Rick."

Kaylee smiled and cut her eyes to her hand Rick continued to hold. At her look, he swiftly released her hand. "I'm sorry. I'm just a little surprised. I didn't expect someone of your caliber."

Donna nudged Rick's arm and laughed aloud. "Oh lord, Rick. Why don't you say you didn't expect Miss Shell to be so pretty?"

With a moan, Rick confessed, "I didn't expect anyone half as pretty as you."

Nick said, "As you can tell, Miss Shell, Rick is a bachelor."

Rick cleared his throat. "Kaylee, I understand that you're single."

"You understand right," she replied, as she lifted a menu into her view.

The waitress approached the group, looked at Kaylee and said, "You must be our new teacher!"

"Yes, I am. It would appear word really gets around here in Stone River!"

The waitress chuckled. "Kaylee, you'll learn fast there are very few secrets in this town."

"She's right," Donna added. "Everybody in town practically knows how many times a week Nick and I make love!"

19

Nick's eyes widened, and his jaw dropped open. "My god, Donna! What kind of thing is that to say to our new teacher?"

Trying to break the embarrassing moment for Nick, Kaylee said, "That's okay. I grew up in a small town, so I know what Donna's talking about."

The waitress interrupted, "Kaylee, I'm Alice Gray. I hope your stay in Stone River will be a good one."

"Thank you, Alice."

Alice took a pad from her apron pocket. "Are you ready to order?"

After dinner, Nick wanted to show Kaylee around the high school. Kaylee closely observed the people she would be working with. Nick's salt and pepper hair was thinning. He was about thirty pounds overweight and stood about six feet tall. His eyes were narrow and complexion rough.

Donna was five' six" and she, too, was a little overweight. Her short, blond hair was highlighted, her brows were arched, and her lips were thin.

Shelby, on the other hand, was short, thin and very domineering. Her hair was white, skin fair, eyes blue, lips full, and cheeks rosy. A smile would have improved Shelby's appearance.

Rick was five' eleven" and had a great build. His Western attire looked as though he was headed for a rodeo. His smile displayed perfect teeth and cute dimples as he grinned at Kaylee and squinted his large, dark brown eyes. All in all, he was easy to look at, and he knew it.

Fair Mount High School was compiled of red brick with black trim. The white tile floors were polished to perfection, and the clean smell in the hall and rooms was very welcoming. Kaylee followed Nick and Shelby into her medium-sized classroom filled with seventeen metal desks. Her older, wood desk sat to the side of a large blackboard. One side of the room was filled with sizeable roll-out windows with off-white blinds and a clear view of the flagpole and the tree line. After her tour, Kaylee wanted to see where she would be living.

During the brief drive through town, Kaylee noticed almost everything carried the name Hilmar or Boone.

Terra explained the Boone and Hilmar clans took a monopoly on everything, and it hadn't changed after all the years.

Kaylee's eyes widened as Terra's car followed Nick's through a tall, black, iron gate and up a winding drive that led to a three-story, gray stucco house that resembled an English castle. Kaylee hopped out of the car and stood looking up at the beautiful home adorned with statues, a tower room and everything needed to perfect a colossal estate.

A magnificent, covered archway connected with a cobblestone circular driveway, and a splendid, sculptured, four-tier water fountain stood erect in the midst of lavish gardens that surrounded the grounds near the home. Kaylee was astonished at the breathtaking sight. The pictures she had received via email didn't resemble what her eyes were beholding, and the house appeared to need no renovation.

A magnificent gazebo with extensive carvings sat in the midst of a circle of oak trees. Most of the leaves had fallen from the oaks, but the ones that remained were radiant with color. Inside the gazebo, a swing moved slightly from the arousing northern wind. Kaylee could hardly wait to see inside the massive house she would call home.

"My, my", Kaylee said, "this surely isn't the place I saw in the pictures, is it?"

Nick spoke up. "Yes. I think you'll recognize it better when we get inside."

Terra abruptly said, "Before we go inside, I want you to meet Adam James."

Kaylee hadn't noticed a young man had joined them with her bags in hand. She had to fight the urge to swoon as she looked into his large blue eyes that gazed directly into hers. She turned her head to keep from being obvious that his dark, lashed stare had captivated her.

He nodded and grinned. "It's a pleasure to meet you, Miss Shell."

"And you, Mr. James," Kaylee said, trying not to be obvious about how taken she was with his striking good looks.

Terra frowned, "Kaylee, I'm sorry, I forgot to tell you Adam is the reason the grounds look so good. He lives in one of the caretaker's houses out back."

Kaylee frowned. There had been no mention of other dwellings on the estate. However, after seeing the house and gardens, she wasn't surprised.

Nick stepped forward. "Let me apologize, Miss Shell. I should have given you more details."

Kaylee insisted that everyone call her Kaylee. "There's no need to apologize. I'm thrilled with the low rent and astounded at the grandeur."

Nick slapped his hands together. "Well then, enough said. Let's take a look at your new home."

Once through the dark oak double doors, Kaylee noticed the wide, escalating staircase accented with a royal blue runner.

Adam waited for instructions on where to put Kaylee's bags.

"Adam," Nick said, "Miss Shell, I mean Kaylee, will be staying on the lower level only."

Adam turned his eyes to Kaylee, then to Nick. "Where shall I put her bags?" he asked.

Nick pointed toward a long hall. "Put Kaylee in the green room, which has its own bath.

Donna looked at the ceiling. "You know, Kaylee, sometimes old houses like this one can be very drafty, especially in the winter. The wind in these parts can be furious." She smiled at Kaylee. "You'll hear all kinds of creepy sounds. Don't let it bother you. It will be the wind. I'm telling you now so you won't be startled when it happens."

Shelby shook her head and tightened her lips. "Donna, you just managed to paint the perfect picture of a haunted mansion for Kaylee!" Shelby faced Kaylee. "She's only teasing, honey."

"All kidding aside," Rick said. "Our winters are bone chilling. The wind is terrible. Adam takes care of the electrical needs of the house. The wiring is old and may act up on occasion, but Adam's here if you need him."

When Adam came from the bedroom, Rick asked him, "You did check the furnace last week, didn't you, Adam?"

"Yes, sir."

"Good, the furnace is like me . . . old."

23

Chapter Five
Hilmar Estate

Kaylee smiled as they entered the grand room. The tall walls were covered with silk wallpaper bordered with wide, sculptured crown molding. The center of the ceiling held the most beautiful crystal chandelier she had ever seen. There were magnificent mahogany antiques, and brightly colored, wool area rugs crowned the polished, dark oak floors. Kaylee jerked when a towering grandfather clock began to chime.

Terra smiled and placed her hand on the side of the clock. "This is my favorite piece in the whole house. Isn't it gorgeous?"

Kaylee moved closer and stared at the face of the clock. The clock's face was mother of pearl. It displayed a big smile. The lips were laid with rubies, and teeth were perfect white pearls. The eyes were two, large, black onyx stones. The jaw line was prominent and the small neck was surrounded by sapphires.

"It's amazing! I've never seen anything like it," Kaylee said.

"Nor will you," Rick added. "Old Man Hilmar had the clock especially designed in Germany. The face is eerie and speaks of his lack of sense!"

"You only wish you had the money that clock cost," Shelby said. "It's an awesome piece and you know it."

Rick frowned and asked Kaylee her opinion.

"I think it's enchanting. Look at the eyes. It's as though a real person is staring back at you."

"That's because they are," Terra said. "Mr. Hilmar had his daughter's likeness fashioned into the face of the clock."

"How unique," Kaylee said as she surveyed the large room.

Tall windows arrayed with blue, velvet drapes, gold piping, lacey white sheers, as well as a padded window settee, added to Kaylee's awe.

Nick cleared his throat. "Kaylee, dear, Donna and I have to be going." He took a business card from his pocket and handed it to her. "Here's my number if you need anything. Terra will show you around and help you get settled. Is there anything I can do for you before we go?"

"Yes. I need to buy a car."

Rick bowed his head. "At your service, Miss Shell. My father owns the Ford dealership in town. I'll fix you up with a good car at a good price."

Shelby growled comically. "Spoken like a true salesman, Rick."

"Thanks, Shelby, for recognizing a professional. We usually close at three o'clock on Saturday, but for you I'll give a private showing."

"That would be great."

"Terra," Rick said, "when Kaylee gets settled, bring her down to the lot."

"Until Monday?" Nick said. "It's a pleasure to have you aboard, Kaylee.

At the lot later, A hunter green Explorer caught Kaylee's eye right away. After a test drive, she decided to take it.

***

When Terra left, Kaylee took a moment to fully appreciate the luxury she would be occupying for the next six months. Wanting to unpack, Kaylee walked down the hall toward her bedroom. She paused as an eerie feeling swept over her. Rapidly turning, she saw Adam standing at the end of the hall.

"Adam, you scared me."

He gradually approached her. "I'm sorry. I've finished my chores and wanted to make sure you didn't need anything before I left."

"You're leaving?"

"Yes." He smiled shyly.

Awkwardly, Kaylee asked, "You live in the caretaker's house, right?"

"I do."

"I'll see you later," Kaylee said.

"You will see me later, but not tonight. On Saturday, I like to ride out to Coyote Canyon, visit my friends and maybe camp out."

"That sounds like fun." Kaylee said.

"It is. Maybe I can take you there one day," he added, as his eyes focused on hers.

"Sure, maybe."

Adam grinned and turned to leave.

Kaylee briefly added, "Thank you for your help."

Adam nodded. "No problem. That's what I'm here for! Goodnight, Kaylee."

"Goodnight," she said. Her heart pounded as his tender stare sent a warm sensation through her body, unlike anything she had ever experienced.

Thus far it had been a day filled with surprise. The house and Adam caught her unaware. "Kaylee Shell!" she groaned. "What's wrong with you? You barely say hello to Adam, and you're all but praying for a trip to Coyote Canyon. Get a grip and remember why you're here." She looked at her watch and moaned. The day had passed so fast. "Oh my, I forgot to call Martin." She found a phone and hoped for a dial tone. "Thank goodness," she said and dialed the number.

A man's voice growled before she could say hello. "Miss Shell, you were supposed to have called me an hour ago!"

"I'm sorry, Martin. I had to wait until everyone left."

His tone lightened after hearing Kaylee's voice. "I'm so sorry I snapped. I was worried about you. So, tell me, how was your trip?"

"Good. I met a woman on the plane who has a connection with Fair Mount High School."

"Who?" he asked in a stern voice.

"Her name is Shannon Morris."

Martin groaned. "Maybe I shouldn't have asked you to investigate a bunch of old letters. I'm old and a nervous wreck! I love you like a daughter. I would hate to feel that I took advantage of you because you have a private investigator license."

"Martin, you didn't take advantage of anything. After reading your mother's letters, I had to come . . . even though this will be my first case as an investigator. Doing my first case for you is very gratifying."

"I don't know why I feel so worried about it."

"There's no need to worry. This isn't the kind of case you need to worry about. You be sure and tell Jeffrey. I'll call him tomorrow."

"I will, dear. Sorry for snapping when I answered the phone."

"Nothing to worry about. I'll talk to you tomorrow. Now get some sleep."

After unpacking, Kaylee took a hot shower. Feeling chilled after the shower, she pulled her terrycloth robe together and tied the sash tightly around her.

An uneasy feeling caused Kaylee's stomach to tighten. She surveyed the room but saw nothing. Breathing a sigh of relief, she dried and brushed her hair. "I need some rest!" she moaned.

Chapter Six

Unexpected Guest

*T*he sound of a car door slamming caused Kaylee to abruptly sit up in the bed. *Dang!* she thought. *What time is it, and who in the world would be visiting on Sunday morning?*

Kaylee hurried to the window and looked out. A black GMC pickup truck was parked out front with a young girl standing beside it. Kaylee grabbed her robe, hastened to run her fingers through her hair and rinsed with mouthwash. She wet a washcloth and rubbed her face as she made her way to the door. Stopping abruptly, she tossed the washcloth behind a chair that sat nearby. After a deep breath, she opened the door.

A pretty girl with long, straight, blond hair wearing large, silver, hoop earrings smiled, "Hello! I'm Betty Moore. I . . . I hope I didn't wake you."

"That's okay."

"I'm a senior at Fair Mount High School. I wanted to come by and welcome you to Stone River."

"Thank you, Betty. I'm Kaylee Shell."

"I know. Gosh, you look so young."

"I'll treasure the compliment. Won't you come in?"

Betty's facial expression prompted Kaylee to ask, "Is something wrong?"

Betty grinned and replied, "Yeah, I'm shocked! No one's ever asked me to come inside before! I've visited here several times hoping to get inside, but was never invited."

Kaylee frowned. "Why is that?"

"I don't know. Maybe they were afraid one of the Hilmar ghosts would come out of a closet and reveal the dark mysteries that have seeped into the walls. They surely don't want me to know their secrets."

"Well, I don't believe in ghosts, but why don't you come in and check for yourself?"

Betty's gasped as she walked past Kaylee into the foyer. "Oh, my gosh! This is too cool. If this place were mine, I would want to show it off to everyone." Betty winked at Kaylee. "What's it like upstairs?"

"I haven't been upstairs. I only rented the downstairs."

"Are you saying you're not going to explore the island? You're going to stay on the beach front never knowing what treasures surround you?"

"I'm afraid so. I paid for the lower lever, not a grand tour. Would you like to join me for a soda?"

"Yeah, thanks." Betty smiled as she observed the room. She followed Kaylee to the kitchen and watched her pour her Coke. Afterward, she took the drink and followed Kaylee back to the living room. Kaylee handed Betty a coaster and asked, "Did you say you're a senior at Fairmount?"

Betty sipped her drink. "Yes. I'm glad we have a new history teacher. Miss Barnes was awful. She was one of the rudest people on the face of the earth. I confess, I didn't care for her at all."

"Does she live in Stone River?"

"Oh, no. She left Stone River. I heard you're single, is that right?"

"Yes."

Betty raised one eyebrow. "Hum, is that by choice?"

Kaylee sat her glass down, smiled and said, "Absolutely!"

Betty stood. "That's good. I didn't think someone as pretty as you are would have any problem finding a husband."

Kaylee noticed her guest glancing toward the window. She turned to see what Betty was looking at. Before she could ask, Betty anxiously said, "I've got to go. Thanks for the drink and welcome to Stone River."

"You're leaving so soon?"

"Yeah."

Again, Kaylee looked out the window. "Can you tell me whose car that is?"

"Right now, I wish I couldn't, but I can. It's Thelma Hilmar. She's a real bitch. I mean witch. I've got to get out of here."

Hurrying past Kaylee, Betty attempted to get in her truck before Thelma could get out of her car. Betty jumped in her truck, but before she could get it started, the woman stopped at her window. Kaylee couldn't hear what she was saying to Betty, but from the woman's facial expressions and the fact that she was pointing toward the gate, she could tell it wasn't a friendly chat.

At that moment, it dawned on Kaylee that the woman's name was Hilmar. She instantly straightened her robe as Thelma Hilmar walked toward the door. Her stern face and fast-paced walk caused Kaylee's mind to fill with wonder. Why was Thelma Hilmar coming to visit, and was that her usual demeanor? Kaylee hoped it was a one-time thing; otherwise she might ought to run out the back door.

Kaylee pushed open the door as Thelma marched up the steps. Kaylee mustered up a smile and greeted, "Good morning."

Thelma frowned and pushed her coat sleeve up far enough to look at her watch. "According to my watch, morning has passed. Nonetheless, I'm Thelma Hilmar. I take it you're Kaylee Shell."

"Yes, I am."

"I suppose Betty already introduced me."

Feeling awkward, Kaylee replied, "When I saw you coming up my drive, Betty did say you were Thelma Hilmar, but only after I asked."

Thelma's eyes narrowed as she tilted her head to the side. "Your drive? This isn't your drive. This is my drive and my house."

"I didn't mean it was literally mine."

"I don't want Betty Moore or her friends in my house. They're a bunch of riffraff that will steal you blind if you blink your eyes."

"I'm a little confused," Kaylee said. "I thought the estate belonged to the town."

Thelma growled. "It's mine. They stole it from my mother, and I will have it back."

Thelma went on and on, but Kaylee heard only part of what she was ranting about. Kaylee had a strange feeling as she stared at Thelma. Thelma Hilmar wasn't all that attractive, yet her high cheek bones, straight nose and round eyes were well structured. Her hair was cut short and frosted to help conceal the gray. Her shoulders were square, and her posture, straight. She was about twenty-five pounds overweight.

Kaylee had to make herself get in on the conversation and at least give some kind of response to Thelma's raving.

"You said, it was stolen from you?"

"I didn't stutter, Miss Shell. I may as well tell you up front. Everyone you've met thus far has told you how happy they are that you're here. Well I'm not! If the truth were known, they're not either. Don't look for me to accommodate you in any way during you short stay."

"Just a minute, Mrs. Hilmar. I don't know what your quarrel is with the town, but I'm not the town, and I signed a lease for six months. I'll be here until the end of my lease."

Thelma snarled, "Oh, you will, will you? I'll see about that." She stomped out the door.

Wanting some understanding, Kaylee called Nicolas Long. He apologized and swore that Thelma's mental elevator didn't go to the top floor. He explained that Willie Hilmar knew Thelma would sell the place before she was cold in the grave. Willie wanted the place to be a landmark for the town. Nick assured her Thelma wouldn't bother her again. However, Nick agreed with Thelma about Betty staying away from the house.

Chapter Seven
Total Confusion

*A*fter hanging up, Kaylee fell back into the overstuffed chair that sat near the bay window, closed her eyes and sighed, hoping to get the image of Thelma Hilmar out of her mind. The woman's squinting eyes and harsh tone had left an uneasy feeling in the pit of Kaylee's stomach. Regardless of what Nick said, Kaylee feared this would not be a one-time occurrence with Thelma.

Suddenly, Kaylee's eyes sprang open. Moving to the edge of the chair, she listened closely to the faint sound of music. Where was it coming from? Perhaps Adam returned home early and it was coming from his house. She hurriedly dressed while her much needed pot of coffee was brewing.

The air was cool. Kaylee put a sweater on, poured a cup of coffee and stepped outside. As she sipped her coffee, her eyes surveyed the vast lawn and gardens that surrounded the house. The music was no longer playing, but her curiosity about the grand estate had peaked. She was having a hard time believing that Nick had somehow steered clear of showing or telling her how elaborate the house and grounds were. Why not showcase the property and get the kind of rent that would warrant living in such a place?

Kaylee made her way to the backside of the home. Two medium sized houses sat on either side of the fenced backyard, and a large, closed gate sat at a distance behind them. The gate opened to a wide dirt road that led to a large, red barn and manicured stables. Beyond the stables, miles of white picket fencing surrounded the pastures and training grounds for the horses.

Kaylee didn't see Adam's vehicle at either driveway. Gradually, she made her way to the front porch of one of the houses. Feeling uncomfortable, yet, wanting to take a peek through one of the windows, she put her face to the glass. At once another set of eyes emerged from the other side of the glass and stared directly into Kaylee's. Kaylee stumbled backward and screamed at the top of her voice. She sprinted off the porch and was briskly making her way back to the house, when a voice called out, "Miss Shell? Miss Shell?"

Her heart pounding, Kaylee slowed down and immediately looked back to see a woman standing on the porch. Again, the woman called out, "Are you Miss Shell?"

Trying to control her breathing enough to reply, Kaylee managed a trembling, "Yes, I am."

The woman came from the porch toward Kaylee. "I'm Dotty Sams. I didn't mean to scare you."

Managing a nervous chuckle, along with blushing cheeks, Kaylee replied, "You have no idea how awkward I feel right now. I mean, about peering into your window."

"Don't be embarrassed. If I were you, I would have done the same thing."

Kaylee tried to explain. "I didn't realize anyone other than Adam lived on the grounds."

Dotty frowned. "You mean Principal Long didn't inform you about the housekeeper?"

Kaylee rubbed the back of her neck. "A . . . a housekeeper?"

"Unless someone has fired me—and I'm sure they haven't—I'm still the housekeeper."

"No . . . no one mentioned a housekeeper."

"I could tell by your expression no one had. I've lived on the Hilmar Estate forever. I worked for Willie Hilmar and her daughter, Thelma, who lived here until after the will was read. It stated that Stone River was to inherit the Estate with stipulations: not Thelma, nor her descendants. Tim Dobbs, the mayor of Stone River, had the unpleasant task of informing Thelma. Needless to say, Thelma wasn't going to stand for any such jargon. She was all but cut out of the will along with her children. I think a meager $400,000 was all she received from the enormous estate. Thelma, of course, had money of her own she acquired while her mother was alive, so she wasn't left destitute.

"My paydays have continued weekly, and I do what I'm paid to do. So, what time do you like your breakfast served?"

Kaylee squinted and shook her head. "I . . . I don't understand. Why wasn't I told about any of this?"

"Maybe you had better ask Mr. Long about that."

"Are you married?" Kaylee asked.

"A widow. My husband passed several years ago."

"I'm so sorry."

"No matter. You still haven't answered my question."

Kaylee paused. "Forgive me, what was the question?"

"What time would you like breakfast and what types of food do you prefer?"

"Thanks, but I rarely eat before noon through the week. However, the weekend is a different story. On Saturdays I like French toast with lots of butter. Sunday, I prefer Frosted Flakes with fruit."

"Sounds fine," Dotty said with a pleasant smile, "but if you change your mind and want something through the week, just let me know,"

"I will, thank you, Dotty." Kaylee glanced toward the other house and asked, "Is Adam your neighbor?"

"Yes, and a good one. He's friendly and will assist you in any way possible."

Kaylee told her new acquaintance goodbye and turned to go back to the house, then stopped, looking back.

"Is there something else, Miss Shell?" Dotty called to her.

Kaylee faced Dotty. "I heard your music playing earlier, and I just wondered who the artist was. The tune sounded like a CD I have."

Dotty frowned and shook her head. "No, Miss, it wasn't my music you heard. I haven't played any this morning."

"Are you sure?"

Dotty tilted her head. "I would know if I had been listening to music or not."

"Of course. It's just I clearly heard music playing and there isn't another house close enough . . . I'm sorry. Have a good day."

"And you, Miss Shell."

Kaylee went back home and glanced around the grand room. She heard music, but where was it coming from? She locked the front door and went to the bedroom. Sitting in bed, she took some papers from her briefcase and laid them on the pillow. She was unable to focus on anything but the man at the Raleigh airport. "Jeffrey," she said softly.

Chapter Eight

Guarding Emotions

That afternoon, Kaylee drove around the town and surrounding area. The need to visit the grocery store was at the top of her list. Coke was always a necessity for Kaylee. It was also nice to know she had something to offer for a drink should someone else come for a visit. After her quick purchases, she drove toward home.

When Kaylee arrived at the Hilmar Estate, Adam appeared unexpectedly from the side of the house and helped carry the groceries inside.

Kaylee thanked him and asked, "Did you have a nice visit at the Canyon?"

Adam smiled. "It was tremendous, as always!"

Kaylee took the food from the bags. Adam's blue eyes were so alluring, stirring Kaylee's emotions to the point of feeling awkward. Besides, Jeffrey was her love.

Adam took a couple of cans of soup from a bag and laughed. "You and I have something in common."

Kaylee looked up. "What would that be?"

"We both like chicken noodle soup," he replied comically.

"Chicken Noodle is my favorite. I like to drink it from a cup and sometimes dip a peanut butter sandwich in the cup, let the sandwich soak, and then gobble it down."

"Are you kidding me?" Adam asked.

"About what?"

"The way you eat your soup!"

"Why would I kid about my soup?"

"I'm just surprised because that's the exact way I eat my soup. We have more in common than I thought."

The last thing to be put away was the milk, and as he closed the refrigerator door, Adam faced Kaylee. "I guess I'll be going if there's nothing else I can help you with."

Kaylee thought a second and then asked, "Adam, would you like to have a cup of soup with me? I haven't eaten today and frankly, I'm starving!"

His face lit up. "I don't want you to go to any sort of trouble."

"It's no trouble. I'll just make two of everything." She shrugged her petite shoulders and grinned.

"Only if you'll let me help."

Kaylee warmed the soup, and Adam made the peanut butter sandwiches. After being seated, Kaylee mentioned, "I met Dotty Sams this morning."

Adam dipped his sandwich. "Yeah, Dotty is a nice woman and a hard worker too."

"Is there anyone other than you and Dotty who live on the estate?"

"No, we're it. There used to be a good-sized staff, but after Willie Hilmar died and Thelma was evicted, there was no need for a large staff."

Kaylee lowered her head, and there was a moment of silence.

"Is something troubling you?" Adam asked.

"Actually, yes. I'm surprised Nick Long neglected to tell me about you or Dotty. He sent a couple of pictures of the inside of the house, but nothing more. I'm stunned at the rent. They could rent this place for fifty times what they're charging me. Of course, I'm thrilled, but I don't understand it."

"Maybe he wanted to surprise you."

Kaylee sipped her soup and said, "You're right. I'll just take full advantage of everything while I can."

Adam spoke softly as his eyes caught hers. "Do that. I mean, take full advantage of what's being offered to you."

Kaylee momentarily looked away and tapped her fingers against the table.

"Do I make you nervous, Kaylee?"

She stopped tapping her figures and put her hands in her lap. "No . . . no why would you ask that?"

Adam shook his head. "Hum, maybe it's me, but I feel like you have a problem looking at me. I hope I don't make you feel uncomfortable."

Kaylee made herself look into Adam's eyes. "Heavens, no. You don't make me feel uncomfortable. I'm sorry if I've left that impression. I do have a lot on my mind including starting my new job tomorrow." Kaylee sighed. "I must also confess that being away from home is a bit uncomfortable."

"Don't think me forward," Adam said, "but, do you have a boyfriend back in North Carolina?"

"Yes. Jeffrey and I have been dating for two years now. He'll be coming for a visit soon."

Adam wiped his mouth. "Jeffrey is a very lucky man." He washed his cup and put it in the dish drainer. "Thank you for the soup and sandwich."

Kaylee stood.

Adam nodded. "If you need me, call."

"Thank you, Adam. Hope you have a good night."

"Goodnight Kaylee. I hope your first day of school will prove to be a good one."

Kaylee was up before dawn. She had been too anxious to sleep. Wanting to look just right, she took outfit after outfit from her closet and held it to her chest, hoping to find the perfect, first-day look.

Before leaving for school, she stopped in front of the mirror on the way out and took one last look at her hair. She thought of pinning it up but decided to let it lie loose on her shoulders.

Chapter Nine

First Day of School

Kaylee arrived early, wanting to be in her classroom before anyone arrived. She had rehearsed how she would greet her class.

Terra knocked quietly on the door and then opened it. Kaylee promptly stood. "Hi, Kaylee," Terra said. "I thought I would drop by and say welcome."

"Thanks, Terra."

Rick immediately opened the door behind her and said, "Good morning, ladies. Wow, you look wonderful, Kaylee. All these 18-year-old boys will think they've died and gone to heaven. I can tell you I never had one teacher who looked like you when I was in school."

Kaylee smiled. "Thank you, Rick."

"If I can be of help, let me know. Got to go, girls."

Nick Long came in immediately after Rick left. "Good morning, Kaylee, Terra."

Terra excused herself and went to class. "Kaylee, can I do anything for you?" Nick asked.

Kaylee folded her arms. "Yes. I met Dotty Sams. You didn't tell me about her."

Nick shrugged. "There's not that much to tell. She's worked on the estate for as long as I can remember. There was a provision made for her in Willie Hilmar's will, that stipulated she stay on the estate as long as she wanted. Her salary was to continue regardless if the house was occupied or not. It was also predetermined that should someone take up residence in the house, Dotty was not to clean only the house, but also to serve as a cook. Therefore, she will serve as your cook, and don't you be shy about telling her what to prepare. She obtains a very handsome salary for the work that she does."

Kaylee glanced at the floor. "Just something that significant should at least be mentioned."

"All due respect, Miss Shell, I don't see the big deal. Look at it as a bonus."

"That I will," Kaylee said.

Kaylee hadn't noticed Betty Moore and another student had entered the classroom. Nick patted Kaylee's forearm and asked, "Is there anything else?"

"No . . . no that's it."

"Okay," he said, as he walked toward the door. "My office is just down the hall should a need arise."

One by one the seventeen desks were filled, and the bell rang. Kaylee stood to greet her students. "Good morning, class. I'm your new history teacher, Kaylee Shell."

As she turned and wrote her name on the blackboard, one of the boys in the back of the class chuckled and remarked, "You sure don't look like any teacher I've ever seen."

Kaylee smiled, put the chalk down and faced the class. "May I ask who made that flattering compliment?"

A tall, slim young man in the back slowly stood. "Miss Shell, I don't mind confessing. I paid you the compliment."

"And what is your name?"

"My name is, Colton Britt."

"Colton, I want to thank you and at the same time let you know that though I may not look like a teacher to you, I am your teacher. You may be seated." Everyone laughed, including Colton.

"Now that I've had the pleasure of meeting Colton, I would like to meet the rest of you. We'll start on the right front row."

After everyone had given their names, Kaylee leaned back on the front of her desk, folded her arms and announced, "This morning, I've learned your names. That's a start; however, over the rest of this school year, I want to know not only your names, but your goals and what I can do in this class to help you achieve your ambitions."

Eddie Dean raised his hand.

"Yes, Eddie."

"Miss Shell, if you don't mind my asking, how can a history class really help achieve my goal as an accountant?"

"That's a good question. I'll answer by saying, there are many types of accountants. Experience reveals to us the locations where each type of accountant is needed. If you plan on staying in Stone River, you first need to know what businesses are here and why they want to be located in Stone River. Second, what's the demand for accounting and how many accountants are here already? If you have several accountants in a small town, you know the demand isn't here. In the South, textile plants and tobacco are a huge commodity. Not so in Stone River. So, if you want to be an accountant for R.J. Reynolds or Philip Morris, you wouldn't send your resume to Stone River."

Taking a deep breath, Kaylee added, "I believe in research, and you'll learn that about me soon enough. I did a lot of research on Stone River and the whole state of North Dakota before I applied for a teaching position here at Fair Mount. I wanted to know about the state's taxes, sales tax, the value of real estate, education programs and state community colleges. I wanted to know how the state was developed and about the Native Americans who were here long before the white man. What resources drew the white man here? I wanted to know the unemployment percentage and about the health care in Stone River. Need I go on?"

Eddie had an I'm-sorry-that-I-ever-asked look on his face. He shook his head and responded, "No, I think you've made your point."

Kaylee smiled and continued, "I love history! History tells me where I came from and under what circumstances. Was it a gilded era or the time of the Great Depression? History works as a preservative. What you do in the time you're allotted here on earth will also affect history. You may be known as another Margaret Mitchell. She wrote only one novel, *Gone with the Wind*; yet, look at the impact it's had on so many people who have read the novel or watched the movie.

Or, we can look at a harsher side of history and see those who have impacted our lives with their murdering, stealing, lying and corruption. People who have touched our souls. For instance, some say that Jesus is our Savior. Some say Buddha, others Mohammad. Some believe that they're their own savior."

Kaylee chuckled and added, "I know that I've gone above and beyond making my point. I did that for a reason. Knowledge in any field is going to be the springboard to your future, whether you want to be an accountant or an actor. I'm here to see that it does just that. After saying all of that, I want to spend the time in our first class together getting to know you and what your driving ambitions are. Eddie, since you asked the first question, I'll let you go first. What are some of the goals you have for your life later as an accountant?"

For some reason, unknown to Kaylee, everyone laughed. Eddie included. Eddie was tall and lanky with brown hair cut short around his neck, yet long on top. His dark eyes, narrow lips, dimple in his right cheek and a huge smile made a cute package.

He focused on a young girl at her desk and began, "My goal, besides marrying and producing many offspring with my beloved Betty—"

Betty stood. Her mouth fell open as she put her hands on her hips and ranted, "Eddie Dean, you're crazy! You're not going to spawn me every few minutes and have twenty kids. I thought I made it plain that we would have two children only, and here you are announcing that we're going to raise a Maw and Paw Kettle brood. Get a grip, sweetie pie!" She turned toward Kaylee, and as her voice became softer, she added, "I'm sorry

Miss Shell, I was traumatized for a moment with that national press release."

Everyone laughed when Eddie said, "That's what I love about that woman. She has the spunk of a small army!" Eddie put his hand on his chest and lowered his head. "I too apologize, Miss Shell, for being overcome with love." Raising his head toward his new teacher, he seriously spoke. "Now, back to your question. My goal is to ride in the Kentucky Derby." Everyone applauded as Eddie did a half-way bow.

Kaylee laughed and commented, "Eddie, I like your humor. Tell me, how tall are you?"

After Eddie revealed he was 6-foot, 1-inch tall, Kaylee added, "That's what I thought. This is where history really comes into play. Jockeys are never six feet tall, nor over one hundred pounds. So, do you have another goal in mind in case Betty and the jockey deal don't work out?"

Eddie leaned back in his chair. "Have mercy, Miss Shell, you just dashed my dreams! But being a man of vision, I have a plan C. I want to own a horse farm and train horses."

"Hurray for plan C," Kaylee said. "Do you have experience in that field?"

"Actually, yes! My parents have dealt with horses all my life."

After listening to several students, one girl stood. Kaylee looked at her name sheet and questioned, "Paulette Boone, what are the goals you've set for your life?"

Paulette's face hardened as she fixed her eyes on Kaylee. "First, let me set the record straight. My name is Paulette Hilmar, not Boone. My father's last name is Boone. However, my mother didn't take his last name. As for my goals," she growled, "I intend to see that my grandmother gets back what belongs to her—the Hilmar Estate and all that goes with it."

At first Kaylee thought Paulette was demonstrating her acting skills. Maybe to be an actress. However, that wasn't the case. Paulette pointed to Kaylee and yelled, "My goal is to get you out of Grandmother's house and see that those who stole it from her go to jail."

In an instant, Kaylee felt numb inside as her heart began to beat rapidly.

A girl sitting beside Paulette pulled at her arm and whispered something to her. She sat down. The girl who had pulled on Paulette's sleeve stood immediately. "I'm Lori Chandler. I have many goals. My main goal is to be an attorney."

Kaylee watched the skinny girl as she nervously played with her fingers and talked a mile a minute. Her eyes scanned the class, whose demeanor had totally changed after Paulette's comments. Kaylee heard Lori's voice but couldn't repeat anything she had mentioned. After class, Kaylee asked Paulette to stay for a moment.

Straight-faced, Paulette snapped, "I need to go to class now."

With a quiet voice, Kaylee spoke. "Paulette, I want to get one thing straight. I will not tolerate outbursts like the one you displayed today. What happened between Stone River and your family isn't my business. As far as living in the house, I'm living there because I signed a six-month lease. I want no hard feelings over things that don't concern me. Can we agree on that?"

"I suppose so. I don't think I have a choice, do I? Is that all?"

Kaylee fixed her eyes on Paulette. "Yes. I hope that is all. You're free to go."

Chapter Ten

Late Call to Martin

After school Rick Owens and Terra came by to see how Kaylee's first day had gone. Kaylee told them about Paulette and wanted to know what her story was.

"I'll sum her story up," Rick replied. "She's nuts like her great-grandfather Roy Hilmar who built the estate."

Terra snapped, "Rick, shut up. Paulette does have an attitude, but she knows only what Thelma tells her—"

"So," Kaylee interrupted, "Thelma Hilmar is her grandmother?"

"Yes," Terra said. "Down deep, Paulette's a good girl."

Rick shook his head to disagree. "You can't go that deep, Terra."

Terra lips narrowed. "You have a tendency to focus on the worst in people."

"No, no, that's not true. Rick said. "I look for good, but there has to be good in order to see it."

Kaylee spoke up. "Listen, I'll just draw my own conclusion. What are you two doing for supper tonight?"

Rick smiled. "I would love to be seen with both you lovely ladies at Beef Eaters tonight. What do you say?"

Terra shook her head. "Sorry, I have a meeting with some parents tonight."

Rick winked at Kaylee. "Has God smiled on me and given me my first dinner date with our beautiful Miss Shell?"

Terra put her coat on. "Kaylee, Rick is full of manure. Give me a call in a couple of hours, Rick."

"Couple of hours!" Rick said. "Who set a time limit?"

Kaylee put her jacket on. "Rick, it's not a date. It's two adults going out for dinner. Nothing more."

Rick grabbed his heart and jokingly cried, "Miss Shell, you have just shattered my dreams."

***

Kaylee had a good time with Rick at dinner. Nick, Donna and Shelby were there and joined them. Rick kept the evening light-hearted while joking about his first date with the teacher of his dreams being invaded by the school faculty.

The evening went longer than Kaylee had intended. Looking at the time while leaving the restaurant, she realized her call to Raleigh was late. She searched through her purse for her cell phone and dialed Martin's number.

The night air was cold. Kaylee turned the heater on low while she waited for Mr. Cullman to answer his phone. Unfortunately, it wasn't a cheery hello, but a snapping, "You were supposed to have called an hour ago. Are you all right?"

"I'm sorry, Mr. Cullman. It took longer at dinner than expected."

"It's just that every time you're late, I panic that something bad has happened to you."

"Martin, nothing is going to happen to me. If I'm late calling, just know that I'm tied up and will call as soon as possible."

"I know. Maybe I'm just an old man who has nothing to do but wait for your call. I'm sorry. I will work on doing better at that. So, tell me, how did things go today?"

"I understand, Martin. Now, about the day's events: according to my roll sheet, there's a Paulette Boone in my history class. However, she let me know clearly that her name was Hilmar, not Boone. She wanted to set the record straight for me that her mother never took the Boone name. She's very bitter and doesn't try to hide it."

"Really? What did she say to you?"

"I asked the whole class what some of their goals in life were, and she strongly replied that her intent was to get me out of the estate and her grandmother back in. She was ranting about wanting the people who were responsible for stealing the Hilmar Estate, to be put in prison."

"Speaking of the name Boone," Martin said, "have you heard anyone say anything about Jake Boone or the two Lakota Indians who disappeared?"

"No, not yet. But I will work on that as soon as possible."

Kaylee paused. "Martin . . ."

"Yes, Kaylee."

"How is Jeffrey?"

"He went to Wilmington on assignment. Kaylee, you promised to concentrate on the investigation while in Stone River. Jeffrey will have to wait until the case is over."

"I know, and I am focused, but I love Jeffrey."

"Kaylee?"

"Yes."

"I'll tell Jeffrey you love and miss him."

"Thank you, Martin. I'll call you on Saturday."

"Take care of yourself."

Chapter Eleven
Missing Jeffrey

*A*s Kaylee hurried up the steps to the door, she paused when she caught the smell of pipe tobacco. She put the key into the lock and looked from left to right before turning it. Who had been, or was, close enough that the sweet odor of pipe tobacco would invade her nostrils? Kaylee hurried in and bolted the door behind her. Breathing a sigh of relief that only lasted until she noted the sweet scent hovered inside the house as well.

"Hello, is someone here?" she called out as she started through the house. After going through each room, she could find no sign that anyone had been there. Perhaps Adam or Dotty had been there while she was away. Finding out would be at the top of her list first thing in the morning, but for now, a hot bath was calling her.

After filling the tub with water and adding lilac bath gel, Kaylee lit four scented candles, put on her favorite piano love songs and placed a mat beside the claw-foot tub. A small wooden table was sitting beside the sink. Kaylee pulled it to the tub. Before undressing, she dashed to the bedroom, grabbed stationary and a pen from her briefcase and placed them on the table. When ready to get into the tub, Kaylee paused and remembered the bottle of red wine she had noticed in the cabinet. She slipped into her robe and hurried to the kitchen.

She paused and looked around the large room filled with white cabinets. The doors of the cabinets were framed with etched glass. Noticing a corner cabinet that contained glasses, she opened the door and found the most beautiful set of goblets she had ever seen. Off to the side, away from the others, sat two tall, diamond-cut crystal wineglasses. Carefully taking one from the cabinet, Kaylee admired its beauty, and seconds later, filled it with wine.

Remembering a few months earlier caused Kaylee to smile. She and Jeffrey had shared the same kind of tub, candles and wine at a private resort in the Blue Ridge Mountains. Continuing her thoughts, she sank into the mound of bubbles. The hot water brought groans and sighs as she relaxed her head against the headrest that fit over the edge of the tub.

After a few moments, Kaylee took the stationary, a clipboard and a pen from the table and began to write.

My Darling Jeffrey,

I miss you more than any words can say. My mind is racing with thoughts of our night at The Three Pines Resort. As my body is relaxing in the warmth of water in a tub and tingling from the tall goblet of exquisite red wine, I feel as though your body is pressed against mine and my head is spinning out of control from the touch of your perfectly shaped lips. I could not stand the thought of your lips never touching mine again. I want desperately to call you, just to hear your voice. Nevertheless, for now, I will hear your tender voice within my heart.

I could tell you how things are going here, yet the overwhelming surge of "I love you" is all that will emerge this night. I pray the same I love you is flowing from your heart to mine, every minute of every day.

I love you, Kaylee.

Kaylee's mind shifted to the stack of old love letters that Martin had found in his mother's trunk, years after she had died. Letters that were written but never mailed. Why were they never mailed to the address in Stone River? The man they were written to would never know the love that Martin's mother Clara held in her heart for him.

The old mansion was drafty like Donna had warned, so right away Kaylee dressed in her flannel pajamas. After blowing the candles out, she started to turn her music off, then decided to let it play until she brushed her teeth. She loved the soothing sound of the piano's romantic tunes. Kaylee had discovered the CD in an old shop outside of Raleigh a few days before she came to Stone River. Although she had never heard any of the songs before buying the CD, she had played it so much she had almost become obsessed with it. The writer of the compositions was unknown according to the title sheet inserted inside the CD case.

Wanting to continue listening to the music, she took the CD to her bedroom and put it into play. After one last sip of wine, Kaylee set the goblet on the nightstand, turned the lamp off, went to the window and pushed the sheers back, letting the night sky reveal itself. Chilled, Kaylee rubbed her arms and continued to stare. The full moon could barely be seen through the indistinct clouds of gray and black that raced across the sky. A small limb from a tree hit against the side of the house directly over Kaylee's bedroom window that looked out across the garden. Squinting, she tried to imagine how dark it would be outside without the many area lights that surrounded the stone fortress.

Just as she started to close the sheer, Kaylee gasped as she leaned forward and watched the light of the moon being swallowed up into the dark clouds. Leaving total darkness across the manicured garden.

Feeling dizzy, Kaylee closed the curtain, telling herself, *The wine must be playing tricks on me.* She started to turn the CD player off but thought, You'll cut off when you're through playing. Hastily climbing into bed, she pulled the covers tight around her chin and immediately fell to sleep.

Later, Kaylee's eyes sprang open as she flung the covers off and shot straight-up in the bed grabbing her chest. The music from her CD was playing so loud it caused the windowpanes to vibrate. "Oh, Lord!" she moaned as she knocked the goblet off the nightstand, shattering it while reaching for the lamp. Scurrying out of bed from the other side, she rushed to turn the music off. Her heart pounded as she looked at the clock. It was five a.m. But how could the CD have played that long? I didn't push the repeat button. How did it turn up so loud? Focusing her stare on the floor, Kaylee knew she had to get the glass up. How would she explain to Dotty how the expensive goblet was shattered? While gathering the glass pieces from the floor, she muttered, "I should have used a paper cup."

Chapter Twelve

Mysterious Music

*K*aylee was too wired to go back to sleep. She started the coffee maker and went to wash her face, hoping it would help clear her head. The water took forever to get warm. While waiting, she put her hair in a ponytail. Finally, the water was warm enough to wash her face and brush her teeth. Afterward, Kaylee put her hand on the handle to turn the water off, but without warning, her body stiffened and her breathing grew shallow. Tilting her head, she listened carefully. Still holding the handle, she managed to turn the water off. Her eyes raced around the room. Catching her breath, she swallowed so hard it hurt. "What's going on here?" she whispered, as the soft sound of piano music flowed from her bedroom. Kaylee moved gradually to her bedroom and unplugged the player just to be sure the music wouldn't play again. Maybe there's a short or something in here. I'll ask Adam to check it, she thought.

Still wary from the music, Kaylee belted out a short scream when someone knocked loudly on the front door.

Relieved after looking out the peek hole, she hurriedly opened the door and asked Adam to come inside.

"I'm sorry if I scared you," Adam said. "I knocked several times."

Kaylee wrinkled her brows. "You said you knocked several times?"

"Yes. Didn't you hear me?"

"No . . . no, I didn't. I had the water running in the bathroom. Maybe that's why."

Adam shrugged. "Maybe so."

"Would you like a cup of coffee? I just made it."

Adam observed Kaylee's appearance and questioned, "Is there something wrong, Miss Shell?"

Kaylee answered as she led the way to the kitchen, "No, why do you ask?"

"You're looking pretty uptight."

Kaylee poured their coffee, and they sat facing each other at the small table in the corner.

"Actually, I didn't rest very well. My CD player has been acting up. I let it play last night when I went to bed. I made sure that the repeat button wasn't on, yet it woke me up blasting at five o'clock this morning. Just before you knocked, it started to mysteriously play again."

Adam sipped his coffee and offered, "You may have a short in the player. I'll check it if you'd like."

Kaylee sighed. "That would be great! I'll fix dinner for you tonight as my way of saying thank you . . . that is, if you don't have other plans."

"I don't have plans and would appreciate the dinner! Are you going to cook or Dotty?"

"What would you recommend?"

Adam smiled and shyly lowered his head. "I think after you work all day, I would allow Dotty to earn her pay. She's an awesome cook, and this would be a perfect time to find that out for yourself."

"Fantastic, Adam! That's what I'll do. I'll create a menu and deliver it before I leave for work."

He grinned at her enthusiasm. "You don't have to do that! Through the week, Dotty comes in and checks this house. Just leave a note on the kitchen counter."

Adam took his cup to the sink, thanked Kaylee for the coffee and said he had to be going. Kaylee walked him to the door. Adam turned to face her. He put his cowboy hat on and said, "I really look forward to our dinner tonight. I'll pick up a bottle of wine. What's your preference? Red or white?"

Briefly looking away to break his stare, she informed softly, "Red . . . red wine is my favorite."

"You seemed very jumpy this morning. Is there something else I can do for you?"

"No, nothing else, thank you! Just take a look at my CD player!"

He nodded. "Until tonight." He turned to walk away.

Kaylee called out, "Adam?"

He turned to face her. "Yes."

"Do . . . do you smoke?"

"No. I never picked up the habit."

"Does Dotty?"

"No. At least, not since I've been working here. Why? Do you need a cigarette?"

"No, I don't smoke. Last night when I came home, I smelled that sweet odor only pipe tobacco acquires. It lingered outside and inside the house."

He shrugged and remarked, "I don't have a clue. Forget smoking for a moment. Check this." Adam blew his breath. "This breath mist says you better bundle up. It's already freezing with no chance of warming."

***

Had it been her imagination, or did she really smell pipe tobacco? What about the music she had heard a few days earlier and the CD last night? How could it all be her imagination? She wasn't one to get antsy over every little thing. Regardless, it was getting late and she didn't want to be tardy for work. She hurriedly wrote a note and menu for Dotty and grabbed the letter she had written Jeffrey. The thought of calling him was overwhelming. Yet, she had promised Martin to focus on her quest. Jeffrey was so different in appearance than Adam. Yet, Adam's blue eyes caused her passion to blaze the same as Jeffrey's dark brown eyes. However, she had known Adam only a few days, but she felt as though she had known him for years. She had known Jeffrey most of her life. This was the first time she had been away from him for any extended amount of time. Jeffrey Holden was 38 years old, 6 foot, 2 inches tall and weighed 200 pounds. His eyes were so dark, like his long black hair he kept pulled back. His medium skin tone, full lips, perfectly rounded eyes and white teeth were the full sum of beauty in Kaylee's eyes.

Their romantic nights together were what Kaylee missed most since she had arrived in Stone River. The affectionate way he would glide his fingertips across her cheek. The gentle way he would hold her face in his strong hands. Kaylee glided her own fingertips across her lips, remembering the passionate touch of his lips to hers. She closed her eyes and touched her ear as she recalled his warm breath while he whispered, "I love you," every night before going home. Hopefully, the time would pass swiftly and she would accomplish her purpose for coming to Stone River. But what if it didn't happen as fast as she hoped? So many questions and thoughts were flooding her mind as she entered her classroom. She was glad to see that Betty Moore and Eddie Dean had arrived already. It was imperative to get her mind off Jeffrey and concentrate on her job.

Chapter Thirteen
Charlie LittleHawk

"Good morning, Miss Shell," Betty said. Eddie hurried to assist Kaylee with her coat.

"Thank you, Eddie. What brings you two out this early? It's forty minutes before class starts."

Eddie patted his heart. "I can't speak for Betty, and I'm sure her reasons would be completely different than mine, but I couldn't wait to see your beautiful face, Miss Shell! It's exciting to come to class, knowing that your eyes won't be burned by a woman that has a . . . a rough look."

Betty groaned. "Dear Lord, Eddie, you're such a flirt. Miss Barnes wasn't that bad. She wasn't pretty, but she wasn't totally ugly either."

Kaylee laughed. "Come on, you two, beauty is in the eye of the beholder."

Eddie nodded. "I agree. We beheld her every morning and her look never changed."

Betty giggled. "I don't know who I'm kidding! She was very ugly and never once did she try to improve herself. Actually, she appeared far worse as time went by."

"That's for sure," Eddie said.

Kaylee thought a second and asked, "Let's put Miss Barnes away. I have a question. Are there any Lakota Indians who attend Fairmount?"

"Yeah," Eddie said. "Charlie LittleHawk. As you can imagine, he used to take quite a bit of teasing over the last name. It just doesn't sound very masculine, if you get my meaning, but he's a good guy."

Betty swooned. "He's sure good looking, Miss Shell."

Eddie nudged her arm. "Hey! I'm standing here."

Betty chuckled. "You big baby. Would you stop with the jealousy?"

Kaylee's jaw dropped. "Are you talking about the Charlie LittleHawk in our class?"

"The one and only," Betty said. "I wish he would ask me out. Just once."

Eddie put his hands on his chest. "You got me, babe. Why would you want Charlie to ask you out?"

"There's something romantic about a Lakota brave."

"Heck, I look more like an Indian than Charlie. That's probably the reason Miss Shell was surprised about him being an Indian." He looked at Kaylee. "Is there a reason you asked, Miss Shell?"

"Actually, there is a reason. I want the class to do a study on the Lakota people. After all, they are the dominant group of Native Americans whose root history is here in Stone River. Nick Long informed me there were a couple of Lakota Indians who attend this school. I was wondering if they were touchy, perhaps on the history side. Do I dare call the Indians a tribe? Some people take offence whether it's history or not."

"Hum," Betty uttered. "Did you say that Mr. Long said there were two Lakotas that attend this school?"

"Yes," Kaylee said, as she leaned back on her desk to relax.

Straight faced, Betty shook her head. "That's how well he knows his students. Charlie is the only Indian in this school. Why am I shocked at Mr. Long's lack of knowledge? You can't believe anything that man says, anyway."

Eddie interrupted her. "Maybe we had better change the subject. I don't want our new teacher to think we're down on our principal."

Before they could continue, more students entered the classroom. Among them was Paulette Hilmar. She walked straight to Kaylee and asked, "May I speak with you, Miss Shell?"

Kaylee had no idea what to expect but nodded to Paulette. They stepped outside the classroom door.

"What is it, Paulette?"

She lowered her head. "I told my grandmother what I said to you yesterday. She had a fit and demanded I apologize to you first thing this morning." Paulette looked up at Kaylee. "So, I'm apologizing. I was out of line. It won't happen again. Even though I reminded grandmother about her visit to the estate when you first moved in."

"Paulette, I accept your apology. No harm done. Thank goodness. We all have to vent at times or our minds would explode."

"I did mean what I said about the one, or ones, going to jail who had anything to do with stealing

Grandmother's estate."

Kaylee stood tall and responded, "If that be the case, they should go to jail. Stealing is still against the law."

"Yeah, but proving it is the hard part."

Before the conversation could go any further, the bell rang. Kaylee saw Rick coming down the hall. She patted Paulette's arm and told her they would talk later. Paulette looked at Rick and then glanced at Kaylee.

Rick put his arm around Paulette's shoulder. "Good morning, Paulette. Were you trying to butter up Miss Shell?"

Paulette didn't respond. She turned and walked back into the classroom.

He winked at Kaylee and smiled. "I dreamt about you last night, Miss Shell. I don't suppose I interrupted your sleep, did I?"

"I'm afraid not." Kaylee laughed as she entered her classroom.

Kaylee observed Charlie all through class. He was a pretty quiet individual, yet seemed to get along fine with his classmates. If he was an Indian, she could never have told by his looks. He had very nice, light brown hair, handsome hazel eyes, a height of around 5-feet 10-inches and a fair complexion. Like everyone else, he wore jeans, a pull-over knit shirt and a black jacket with a lambskin lining. Betty was right. He was a stunning young man. Not only did he have looks, he was an honor student as well. After class, Kaylee asked to speak to him.

In his soft-spoken tone, he responded, "Of course."

Kaylee shared her plan to teach Lakota history and

asked if there would be a problem using certain words. If so, she would change them.

He grinned. "Why would I have a problem with you teaching history? That's what this class is about and what you're about: a history teacher. I'm not that easy to offend."

"Thank you, Charlie."

"No. Thank you, Miss Shell for your thoughtfulness."

"Charlie," she called as he was about to walk out the door.

He turned around. "Yes, Mum."

"Would you mind sharing with me, or with the class, when we begin the study, what you know about your family history?"

"What is it you want to know?"

"Maybe you could share the names of some of your ancestor—where and how they lived and died."

He scratched his neck. "I don't think anything I could tell would be that outstanding."

"It may not be to you, but who knows what someone else might gain from your heritage. Will you consider it?"

"Sure," he said and started down the hallway.

"Thanks, Charlie."

Chapter Fourteen
Dinner Guest

*A*fter school, Terra asked if Kaylee would join her for a potluck dinner.

"I'll take a rain check," Kaylee replied. "I invited Adam to dinner tonight. He's going to take a look at my weird-acting CD player!"

Terra swooned. "Adam!"

"Yes, the caretaker."

"Oh, I know who he is. I'm just surprised, that's all."

"Terra, why don't you come over this weekend? Do you ride horses?" Kaylee asked.

"I do! I think everybody in Stone River rides horses."

"I saw at least three or four horses at the stables. Maybe we could go riding if the weather permits."

"That sounds like fun. I'd love to," Terra said.

"How about noon Saturday?"

"Sounds good to me," Terra said and walked away.

Before leaving the parking lot, Kaylee called Mr. Cullman. He answered the phone before the first ring had completed.

"Kaylee, how are you, dear?"

"I'm doing very well, and you?"

"Doing good, just waiting for your call. Do you have something encouraging to report?"

"Maybe. There's only one Lakota Indian in the school. His name is Charlie LittleHawk.

"Really? Only one?"

"Yes. I told him I wanted to do a study about the Lakota's history. I asked if he would share with the class, information concerning ancestors."

"Good thinking, Kaylee. I can't wait to hear about that story."

Kaylee was silent for a brief moment. "There was something that bothered me last night at the house."

"What was it?"

Kaylee proceeded to tell Mr. Cullman about the music she heard and the about the pipe tobacco smell.

"You watch yourself, Kaylee. I'm not sure exactly what you'll be dealing with."

"I will. Martin, please tell Jeffrey I miss him so very much."

"I will. I look forward to our next call. Goodbye, Kaylee. Take care."

"Goodbye."

The weather was freezing as Kaylee hurried inside, wanting to take a bath and rest awhile before Adam arrived. Upon entering the foyer, she observed Dotty placing two candles on the formal dining room table.

"Dotty, the aroma is breath-taking. Thank you so much for helping out tonight!"

Dotty put her hands on her hips and laughed. "I don't think it's sunk in yet with you, dear!"

Kaylee frowned. "What hasn't sunk in?"

"The fact that I am paid to do this. It's not free."

"You're right. It hasn't sunk in at all. I'm not used to this kind of luxury. Nonetheless, from the smell and looks of things, I could get used to it fast."

As Dotty reached back to align the candles, she said, "Adam said he had to run an errand, but he would be back in plenty of time for dinner."

"I need a thirty-minute nap before freshening up. Will you be here?"

"Yes. I won't make the sauce for the salmon until the last minute. It's better if it's served right away."

"I can't wait to taste it. Adam's been bragging about your cooking."

"That's good to hear. Now you go rest, and I'll wake you."

"Thanks, Dotty." Kaylee paused and then asked, "Dotty, do you smoke?"

"No. I never took up the habit. Why do you ask?"

"Oh, nothing."

"Are you sure?"

"Yes. Thank you."

Dotty woke Kaylee in time to freshen herself before dinner. As Kaylee neared the dining room, she stopped when she heard the faint sound of music. She listened intently to the piano playing as she entered the dining room. A fire crackled from the large, marble fireplace, and lighted candles were scattered throughout the room. Table settings for two were placed at the end of the long, cherry table near the fireplace. The plates were topped with high, stainless steel covers. A silver wine bucket sat between the two place settings, and a refreshing aroma of roses filled the air.

Above the massive fireplace hung a colossal painting of Ellen Hilmar. Kaylee stared at the painting, noticing that the skilled artist was a genius with the stroke of his or her brush. Ellen stood like a queen, her shoulders squared and posture straight. Her hair was piled in curls on top of her head. A gold comb filled with pearls sat like a crown in the center of her head. Her face was so pleasant to view and her large emerald eyes and perfect porcelain cheeks appeared to glow in the amber flame that leaped in the fireplace. She had cherry red lips and a direct stare from her emerald green eyes was captivating. Her long dress, emerald green like her eyes, was made up with a hoop petticoat, tiny waist and long sleeves. This was one of the most elegant designs that Kaylee had ever seen. A long, gold chain with a large pendant that matched the dress's color, rested on top of her amply exposed breast.

Kaylee left the room and found Dotty in the kitchen. She asked Dotty if she had put her CD on in the dining room. Kaylee's shoulders slumped in relief when Dotty said she thought the music would be a delightful touch. Kaylee thanked her, but reminded her the dinner wasn't for romance. It was only a thank-you dinner. Kaylee glanced at her watch and rushed to the bedroom to change.

She put on a silky, black and white pullover with matching slacks. She pinned her hair up in a French twist and pulled her bangs around her face. After spraying her perfume, she paused to sniff the fragrance and frowned, wondering why her perfume smelled strangely of roses as she slid her feet into strapless high heels. She viewed herself in the full-length mirror and wondered why she had chosen an outfit she knew would appear alluring. Before she could change, the doorbell chimed.

A feeling of foolishness filled Kaylee as she journeyed down the hall to the door. She didn't want to give Adam the wrong impression. "Too late now," she thought aloud and opened the door.

The expression on Adam's face said it all.

"Hi Adam! Come in out of the cold."

"My God, Kaylee. You're stunning."

Kaylee put her hand on her stomach and blushed. "I feel as though I'm a bit over-dressed. I think I'll go change."

Adam caught her arm, stopping her. "I'm sorry," Adam said in a concerned tone. "Please don't change. A man in boots and jeans can enjoy the beauty of an elegant woman."

Her eyes caught his stare. He smiled and held up a bottle of red wine.

"Thank you." Kaylee took the wine and walked away.

Adam glanced around the room and smiled. "I must confess that I've never imagined this room with this aura . . . I mean the fireplace and candle light—"

"I have to say it wasn't me that did all of this," Kaylee interrupted. "It was Dotty."

"How about the music?"

"That too was Dotty."

"No matter. Let's just enjoy our dinner."

Chapter Fifteen

Rumors about Ellen

Adam took off his coat, and Kaylee hung it on the coatrack in the grand room. Her handsome visitor was standing in front of the fireplace when she re-entered the dining room.

He touched the marble and said, "This fireplace is gorgeous."

"Yes, it is. Why don't you join me, and we'll have dinner before it gets cold? Dotty mentioned the sauce for the salmon wasn't good unless used right away."

Adam rubbed his hands together. "Salmon, that's my favorite," he said.

Kaylee smiled. "Mine, too. I left a note for Dotty this morning and told her to surprise me. And she most certainly did."

Adam glanced around the room and looked back to Kaylee. "You said that Dotty did the fire, music and candles?"

"Yes. I must say it too was a bit of a surprise."

"Do you think maybe Dotty is trying to play the matchmaker?"

"Maybe so," Kaylee said. She tried to control her breathing as she approached the table where Adam was standing.

Adam pulled her chair out and poured the wine as Kaylee glanced above the fireplace again at Ellen Hilmar. "She was a beautiful woman, wasn't she?"

Adam put the bottle back into the ice bucket and focused on the painting. "That she was. I've looked at that painting a hundred times, and I still feel that she was ahead of her time."

"What do you mean?"

"I mean, the rare beauty she displays. I'm sure she stood apart from all the other women in Stone River. I can't imagine that kind of beauty was commonplace. Rumors have it that Ellen was quite the woman."

Kaylee looked at Adam. "Exactly what does 'quite the woman' mean?"

"Let me be sure and restate that rumors have it. Not anything I know personally. Ellen, had a way with men. Back then, Roy was away for days at a time, and his young wife wasn't a fan of being alone."

"And just 'who' did these 'rumors' say the lucky men were?"

Adam wiped his mouth and put his napkin on the table. "You know, I'm sitting here spreading gossip about a woman who's been dead for years."

Kaylee faced Adam. "I wouldn't call it spreading gossip. We're talking about a very beautiful and prominent woman. In other words, we're having a conversation, not spreading gossip."

Adam tilted his head. "Adequately put." He sipped his wine and then said, "Ellen Hilmar doesn't come remotely close to the radiant woman sitting here in front of me."

Kaylee blushed. Adam gently placed his hand on top of hers. With his head slightly lowered, he looked up through his long lashes and asked softly, "May I have this dance?"

The touch of his hand sent a warm tingle through Kaylee's body. She looked at his hand on hers.

"Dance?" she whispered.

Adam smiled confidently. "Yes, dance. I love the music. Don't you?"

Kaylee paused, then agreed.

Adam took Kaylee's hand and led her to the fireplace. Her heart raced as Adam put his hand on her waist and pulled her close. Oh my, what am I doing? she thought. Was it the wine causing her head to spin or the racing of her heart? Whatever the reason, she knew the dance would have to be a short one.

Kaylee was always in control no matter the situation. Yet, being close to Adam was almost frightening. She felt his hand slowly pull her closer to his warm body. When he pressed his cheek to her temple the song ended, and Kaylee quickly pulled away and refrained from looking back.

"Kaylee, you're a very graceful dancer."

"You, too. It's been a pleasant evening; however, it's getting late. I really need to go over some work for tomorrow."

"You're right. It is getting late. Thank you, for the dinner and the dance."

"I'll get your coat."

Kaylee hurried to the grand room and retrieved Adam's coat from the rack. She paused and held the coat to her and then hastened down the hall to the dining room where he had returned to staring into the fireplace.

"Would you like for me to make sure the fire is out before I go?" Adam asked.

Kaylee wanted to decline his request and tell him to leave while she had the courage to not give-in and ask him to stay. She rapidly replied, "Yes."

Adam put on his coat and stepped outside. A few minutes later, he returned with a bucket. He sprinkled into the coals a powered substance, which instantly killed the fire.

"Hum." Kaylee said. "I can't believe that worked so fast and without an odor. What is it?"

***

Adam faced her. "This is a secret recipe that my grandfather told me about. Now, I better go and let you get your homework done."

He stepped onto the porch, sat the bucket down and turned to find himself gazing into the deepness of Kaylee's stare. He was conscious of her every move, even the slight tightening of her forehead. He stepped into the doorway, gradually leaned forward and ever so gently touched his lips to hers, then pulled away. Stroking his open palm across her cheek, he moved forward and kissed her long and tenderly.

Kaylee was unable to move. Was it not wanting to move that held her?

Adam smiled and unhurriedly raised his head from hers. "Goodnight, Kaylee," he breathed as he glided his fingertip across her lips.

"Good . . . goodnight."

Adam raised his collar around his neck, picked the bucket up and said, "You had better get inside. It's freezing out here."

***

Kaylee watched in silence as Adam stepped from the porch into the yard. Nearing the corner of the house, he turned and hollered, "If you need me, just call."

Kaylee nodded. Closing the large door behind her sent an echo through the splendid house. Stunned, Kaylee turned the lights on, made sure the CD was off and blew out the candles. *What has just taken place?* Her head was spinning with questions. *Why and how could Adam have such an effect on me?* She didn't really know him and to give in to his exhilarating touch had sent her emotions into chaos.

Everything seemed in slow motion as she started down the long hallway. She abruptly stopped and leaned against the wall with her open hand. She began to tremble at the faint sound of the music playing in the dining room. Kaylee found enough strength to get to her bedroom and immediately dialed Adam's number.

"Adam?"

"Yeah, Kaylee? What is it?"

"The . . . the music is playing in the dining room."

"Did you turn it off?"

Gasping, she replied, "Yes . . . yes I did. That's just it, I did!"

"I'll be right there."

Kaylee waited in her room until she heard Adam knock. She hurried to the door and opened it. She could tell Adam could see she was shaken. He took her shoulders in his strong hands. "Kaylee, are you all right?"

"I'm all right. But listen, Adam."

Adam, listened, then looked at Kaylee. "I don't hear anything at all."

Kaylee frowned and lowered her head. "It stopped."

"Let me take a look at the player. I checked it earlier, but who knows?"

Adam made sure the player was all right while Kaylee waited in the foyer. He came back and reported that he didn't see anything wrong with the player, but just to make sure, he had unplugged it. He then suggested that she might want to buy a new one.

"Yes, I will. I feel silly calling you the minute you arrived home."

"Don't feel silly. That's what I'm paid for. I don't suppose this would warrant another dinner would it?"

Kaylee grinned. "We'll see. Thanks, again."

"You're quite welcome. Goodnight."

"Goodnight, Adam," she said, as she closed and locked the door.

Chapter Sixteen

Plans for a Field Trip

The next day at school, Kaylee asked the class how they would like to go on a field trip. The class was more than agreeable.

"Where will the field trip be?" Eddie asked.

"Since I have been preparing for our study on the Lakota Indians, I think a trip to the northern bend of Stone River would be appropriate. I understand a tribe of Lakota made their home at the bend." Kaylee looked at Charlie and asked, "Can you shed any light on this fact, Charlie?"

"Yes. There was a tribe of Lakota Indians who made their home there. Some of my ancestors were among them."

Kaylee slapped her hands together. "That's wonderful. Class, I asked Charlie yesterday if he would help me out on our study of the Lakota who made their home here in Stone River. I'm excited to report that Charlie told me before class that he would be glad to share about his family and tradition. Dakota history will tell us that winter snow will be coming soon, so our trip will be next week. Charlie, if you will meet with me after class, I'll share what I have in mind?"

Charlie nodded.

"I will also be asking for at least three volunteers for this project. If you recall, I asked you to share your goals with me. I did that for a special reason. First, I wanted to see what challenges you will more than likely be facing after you graduate. I took a look at your grade averages. I must say I was totally impressed. Every student in this class has a C + average or above. I'm sure that the three with the C+ average can pull it up to a B+ easily by the next grading period. I will help you do that. We have a wide variety of future occupations in this class. From Eddie wanting to raise and train horses, Kyle wanting to carry on his father's tire business, and Lori wanting to be an attorney, I am very impressed! The fact that Lisa wants to be an author is pretty fabulous! Paulette, I didn't get what occupation you intend to follow. Would you please share that with us?"

Paulette shrugged and shook her head. "I want to be the sheriff of Stone River."

"Hum. What caused your mind to shift in that direction?"

"Too many things to say. I will say, I would never take a bribe. If somebody did something wrong, I would see that person brought to justice."

"As they should be," Kaylee said.

"I'm glad you agree with me on that, Miss Shell."

"Of course."

Kaylee glanced around the class. "Earlier, I mentioned wanting three volunteers to help with our projects. However, I think I've changed my mind about volunteers.

We'll draw names for the three people. I want everyone to write your name on a piece of paper and fold it. Charlie, exclude yourself. You'll be working on this with me regardless. So, if you will take the names up and bring them to the front, please."

Afterward, Kaylee asked Charlie if he would please draw the three names.

Charlie drew Lori Chandler, Lisa Pate and Kyle Jones. The students were looking at each other, wondering what Miss Shell was up to. Kyle raised his hand and asked, "Since I've been chosen, would you mind telling me what I've been chosen for?"

Kyle, like most of the male students, dressed in jeans, cowboy boots and denim shirts. He was tall with a slim frame, hazel eyes, narrow lips and short, dark brown hair.

"Of course, Kyle," Kaylee said. "I'm sure you remember my answer to Eddie's question the other day about what history has to do with everything."

The class's response assured Kaylee that they did. "I mentioned two of the occupations before Charlie drew the names. Lori an attorney, Lisa an author and Kyle a businessman. I want each one of you to think about the history of Stone River. What has impacted the town? Who has impacted the town? I want each student to pick the name of a person you feel is a worthy candidate for us to research. What business has made an impact? Kyle's team will look into the businesses that have made Stone River productive and will find the roots of those businesses.

"Lisa, your team will search the Stone River Archives. I want you to put their findings in story form.

"Lori will be our attorney. She and her team will be responsible for finding an unsolved mystery, comparable to the television show with the same name. After Lori and her team decide on a case they wish to pursue, we will come together, discuss what each team has decided. We will locate the business's root, the person's root history and the crime's root history. You have two days to come up with the assignments. I'm here to help you in any way I can. While you're doing your work, Charlie and I will be going over his Lakota family roots. Do you have any questions?"

Without hesitation, Lori raised her hand.

Kaylee pointed to her and asked, "Yes, Lori."

"Any case? Regardless of what it is?"

"Any case. You can check court records and microfilm, and you can ask your parents and grandparents if they know of any cases that were never solved. In Raleigh, there are several cases that haven't been solved. As a result, they have been filed away in what is called Cold Case Files. I would prefer that you go back to the town's roots and find a case that has been placed in storage. I recommend an older case because of the challenge of searching out the history that surrounds the case. The more up to date the case, the easier it will be to access the history. We don't want that. We want a challenge that will be exciting and a case that will force us to use our imaginations. Lisa, wanting to be an author, will appreciate that. Her group will assist our research by feeding our imaginations when history appears to be blocked. What was going on at that time in history? How did they live? Was life a struggle? Were there times, when perhaps being hungry and no means of finding or buying food played a part in their decision making? I don't have children, but if in that day children were born into such circumstances, it would have to play a big part in how a parent would make decisions. Would they stay here? Would they leave Stone River because of the terrible situations?"

Kaylee faced Kyle. "Kyle, I want you and your group to be in charge of going into the imagination of the people at that time—the individuals who chose to research and find the good and bad choices they made to make his or her business a succeed. After saying all of that, I have a question for you. Do you think you're up to such a challenge? Can we do it?" Kaylee exhaled and then smiled.

The class was so pumped up, Kaylee received a resounding, "Yes!"

Kaylee, held her hand up and said, "Since we have agreed on the matter, we'll have a group meeting at the Hilmar Estate, which is where I'm living . . ." Kaylee looked at Paulette, ". . . for now."

Paulette raised her brows and did a quick nod causing the class to laugh.

"There is one more thing," Kaylee added. "You can tell your parents what we're doing and ask them the questions that I stated earlier; however, our findings will be kept top secret until the end of the study. At that point, I will have a night set aside for all who are interested in attending and hearing the outcome of our quests. Each student will take the stage and present something that their group has learned about Stone River's people, business and history. We will present our findings in a theatrical form, by talking, acting and using the music from the era we chose. In addition, props and costumes, may also be used. Hopefully, we'll make history for a future class to find."

***

After Kaylee had assigned teams to help Lori, Lisa and Kyle, she let them spend the rest of class time in groups discussing their assignments.

The students were so excited. For the first time they had an assignment that actually sounded like fun. She and Charlie discussed the field trip. Charlie would be in charge of finding and telling the history of the Indians who made their home at Stone River Bend.

Chapter Seventeen

The Keys

After school, Terra met Kaylee in the hall. "Miss Shell, I have never seen a more excited group of students than the ones who left your class."

"Yeah, they're pretty motivated."

"Would you like to join me for dinner at Beef Eaters and share your secret?"

"I would love to join you for dinner, but there is no secret." Kaylee laughed as the two women exited the building.

"I'll meet you at Beef Eaters at seven o'clock."

"I look forward to it." Kaylee said as she hopped into her Explorer.

When Kaylee arrived home, Dotty was dusting the grandfather clock.

"Good evening, Miss Shell. I surely hope you had a good day."

"I did, and you?"

"Yes, I did. I dusted the rooms on the upper floors. It's quite a job. The good thing is, I only dust them twice a month."

Kaylee fixed her eyes on the clock. "Rick Owens said the face on the clock was that of Roy and Ellen Hilmar's daughter. Is that right?"

"That's what I've been told."

"The face has a child-like quality. I wonder how old she was when the clock face was made."

"Who knows? You hear so many tales that seem to keep getting bigger and bigger as the years go by. I think people have a tendency to think what they want and push the rest aside."

"Hum," Kaylee said, "you're more than likely right."

Kaylee turned and started down the hall. Dotty called out, "What will you be having for dinner?"

"Oh, I won't be eating in tonight. Terra and I are having dinner at Beef Eaters. By the way, I want to compliment you on the dinner last night. The salmon and sauce were superb. Thank you, very much."

Dotty grinned. "I know Adam enjoyed last night."

"Really? How's that?"

"He told me. He also mentioned how very beautiful you were."

Kaylee chuckled. "I think he thought the fire in the fireplace, candles and music were romantic. I did inform him that it was you alone who went to that extreme."

"He did ask if I was trying to play matchmaker. I'm sorry if I embarrassed you. That definitely wasn't my intention."

Kaylee shook her head. "Dotty, there's nothing to feel sorry about."

Dotty shrugged and added, "Well, I knew you weren't married and neither is Adam. I wasn't sure if you had a boyfriend back home or not; however, I do know Adam isn't dating anyone."

"Thank you, Dotty, but there is someone. His name is Jeffrey. He'll be out for a visit soon."

"I look forward to meeting this Jeffrey," Dotty said. "Now, if you don't need me, I think I'll say goodnight."

"I can't think of anything. Rest well, Dotty. Thank you for everything!"

"Yes, dear. I'll let myself out the back."

Kaylee started past the formal dining room when instantly she felt compelled to stop. She turned and entered the vast room, stared up at the painting of Ellen Hilmar and wondered what she had been like in her day. A woman who lacked for nothing as far as money was concerned. But what about her personal life? Adam had mentioned that she wasn't happy being alone so much. Yet, if she had a daughter, she wouldn't have been alone. Kaylee went to the foyer where the grandfather clock stood and wondered about the face in the clock? Turning her focus back to Ellen's portrait, Kaylee mouthed, "If you're going to annoy my mind, I will find out everything there is to know about you, Mrs. Hilmar."

As Kaylee left the dining room, she paused. From the corner of her eye, she had noticed Dotty's keys lying on a table in the foyer. Dotty had surely forgotten them. Curious, Kaylee picked them up. The irresistible urge to rush up the grand staircase and take a quick peek inside one of the rooms became overpowering. But what if Dotty misses the keys right away and comes back to get them? Before she could decide what to do, a knock on the front door prompted her to hastily put the keys back where she had found them. She blew her breath out and answered the door, thinking Dotty would be standing there. It was Adam.

"Adam!" Kaylee stepped to the side and told him to come in. "May I take your coat?" she asked.

"I only have a minute. I need to go into town and pick up a few supplies for my barren refrigerator."

Kaylee smiled. "I always have a can of chicken noodle soup in the kitchen!"

"Thanks, but I need everything. Dotty asked if I would come by and get her keys before I left for the grocery store."

Kaylee grabbed the keys and handed them to him. "Do you have time for a cup of hot tea before you go?"

Adam nodded with a big grin. "I'll make time."

"Good. Let me take your coat." Adam's cologne was very unusual and the most intoxicating she had ever smelled. After putting his coat on the coat rack, Kaylee called out, "I'll put water on for the tea. Be right back."

"Let me help."

Kaylee held her hand up. "No. I'll be just a minute."

She put water in the teakettle and set it on the burner. After taking two teacups from the cabinet and putting them on a tray, she glanced up at Adam in the foyer. He was looking out the window. The pleasant aroma of his fragrance lingered in her nostrils. He looked exceptional in his tight jeans that rested on top of his shark-skin boots. His black, long-sleeve shirt with white pearl buttons was tucked neatly underneath his black leather belt with an oval-shape silver buckle. The profile of his face looked like a Greek god. Clean-shaven, flawless skin, gleaming white teeth and amazing eyes that were at times hypnotic.

While she remembered the distinctive touch of his lips to hers, the kettle whistled causing her to jerk. Adam joined her and watched as Kaylee poured the water into the cups and placed the tea bags inside the water. She wondered as she walked down the hall with the tray, *Did he catch me staring at him?*

Kaylee led the way to the living room, and Adam took a cup from the tray as he sat down near the window in a wing-back chair. "Did you have a good day, Kaylee?"

She remained standing, facing Adam. "Yes, I did. I'm starting a class project I think the students are thrilled about."

"Really? What's it about?"

"The history of Stone River. The details aren't going to be disclosed until the project is completed, which will be in a couple of months. I may be calling on you for any light you could shed on the topic."

Adam took a sip of his tea and responded, "I'll be happy to help with anything you need, Miss Shell!"

Suddenly he stood, took the last swallow of his tea and placed his cup on the tray. "I better be going."

"I'll get your coat."

Kaylee held his coat and pulled it up over his shoulders. He lowered his head, took her hand and gently kissed the top of it. "Thanks for the tea."

"Any time," she said.

Adam looked down and then into Kaylee's eyes and said warmly, "All day I kept visualizing how beautiful you were last night." He touched his finger-tip to her lips and whispered, "The thought of your kiss . . . Miss

Shell, the sweet sound of your Southern drawl is driving me crazy. With that said, I better be going. Goodnight, beautiful lady."

Kaylee stood spellbound after he closed the door. *What's going on here, Kaylee? Your love is in North Carolina and yet at times, your passion is fully in Stone River. Oh, goodness!* She groaned. *How can someone like Adam not be married or at least have a girlfriend?* Kaylee noticed the clock. It was six-thirty. *Where did the time go so fast?*

She showered, grabbed a long, royal blue sweater and jeans. Once dressed, Kaylee sat on her bed, pulling her sock up, when suddenly she gasped. For an instant, she thought she heard the piano rhapsody echoing lightly through the hallway.

Again, as she brushed her hair, she was positive she heard the music playing in the distance. After putting her cap and her long, black, wool coat on she hurried out the door.

Chapter Eighteen

Adam at Beefeaters

$\mathcal{F}$earing she would be late was a needless worry since Terra wasn't there when she arrived. Beef Eaters was overflowing. Kaylee went inside to put her name on the waiting list. Upon entering, someone called out, "Miss Shell!"

Her eyes scanned the crowded room to find who had called her name. In the step-up area, she noticed Eddie Dean, Betty and Lori waving to her. She wrote her name and told the hostess where she would be. Nearing the table, Kaylee was greeted by a group of her students.

"Miss Shell," Eddie called, "why don't you join us?"

"I would love to, but I'm meeting Terra. However, she hasn't arrived yet."

"We'll make room for Miss Wallace if you want to sit with us," Lori said.

"I'll check with her when she arrives, and if she doesn't mind, we'll join you."

Kaylee put her hands on her hips and grinned. "My goodness, I didn't expect to see most of my class here tonight! What are you all up to?"

"We have been talking about our history project," Betty replied. "I think it's so cool."

"As your teacher, I'm thrilled to hear that."

A familiar voice from behind Kaylee said, "I'm just thankful they don't mind a teacher being within a mile of them when school's out!"

The area was overcrowded, but Kaylee turned and managed to see Principal Long standing behind her. "Oh, hi!"

A busboy cleared a table next to where the students were sitting.

Nick Long promptly shouted across the room, "Hey, Jim, how about turning the music down a notch? It's deafening tonight.

Jim was tending the bar. He waved his hand and shouted, "Don't you know that music keeps me young? But for an old grump like you, I'll sacrifice and turn it down a little."

"You're full of bologna, Jim. All this noise does is speed up your hearing loss. Kaylee, would you take a look around. There's fifteen TVs all playing different songs." As soon as the music lowered, Nick gave a wave of "thank you" to Jim. "So, tell me, Kaylee, are you here alone? If so, you're certainly welcome to join Donna and me."

"Thanks, but I'm meeting Terra."

Nick put his hand on Eddie's shoulder and lightly shook him. "You kids are staying out of trouble, aren't you?"

Eddie threw his hands up in the air and bragged, "You know we are, or else we would be sitting over there at the bar."

"If you were at the bar, I'd tell Jim to stick your heads in those giant speakers and give you full volume." Nick moved his eyes to Kaylee. "Tell me, Kaylee, what kind of project did you assign this bunch that's brought out their extreme enthusiasm? I don't recall ever seeing this many of them out eating in one large group! They don't even sit together like this in the school cafeteria."

Kaylee grinned and replied, "Mr. Long, you'll have to wait and see about our project. Isn't that right, class?" She turned and winked at her students.

Just then, Kaylee heard Terra call her name.

Terra joined the group, exhaled and said, "I'm sorry to make you wait, Kaylee. I had to go and check on Mama."

"That's fine, I've been visiting with Nick and some of my students."

Terra looked at the kids and shook her head. "What is all of this?"

"That was my question," Nick said.

Kaylee shrugged. "It would appear that everybody in Stone River had a hankering to come eat at Beef Eaters tonight."

"It would appear!" Terra said.

Nick placed his hands on Terra's and Kaylee's shoulders. "I better get back to Donna before she comes looking for me. You two have a good evening." He pointed to the students and smiled. "You kids stay out of trouble."

The hostess showed Kaylee and Terra to a table.

After placing their order, Kaylee said, "You mentioned you had to go check on your mother. Is she all right?"

"Yes, she's fine. I wish she would move in with me. I worry about her staying by herself, especially at night. She's just so contrary and set in her ways. If I make a suggestion, she thinks I'm telling her what to do."

Kaylee smiled. "My grandmother was the same way. But, after I mastered the science of letting her think I was doing what she wanted, everything worked out great."

"After you meet my mother, maybe you could give me a few pointers."

"Are we still on for our ride tomorrow?" Kaylee asked.

"Yeah. I'm sure it will be a cold ride, but I'm game if you are."

"That's fine. Didn't you say that your mother lived out at the Bend where some of the Lakota tribes used to make their home?"

"Yes, I did. The tribe lived there before Stone River ever came into anyone's mind."

"Could we ride out and visit your mother tomorrow?"

Terra furrowed her brows and warned, "Yeah, but it's about a half-hour ride. Do you think you're up to it?"

Kaylee nodded. "I do."

"Then we have a plan."

As they were eating, Terra swooned and blurted, "Oh my Lord! Would you look at who is sitting down at the bar?"

Kaylee peered to see whom Terra was drooling over. Her heart practically stopped when she saw it was Adam.

"Hum, if I were you, I couldn't stand knowing he was living out behind my house." Terra leaned toward her and continued, "How do you do it, Kaylee?"

"I know he lives out back, but he's a caretaker for the estate, so it's not uncommon."

Terra shook her head. "What's uncommon is his beautiful face and my gosh . . . his body looks like an Adonis."

Kaylee wiped her mouth and smiled. "Am I detecting feelings toward Adam?"

"I think every single woman and even a few married ones in Stone River have a crush on him."

Kaylee frowned. "Why in the world isn't he married or at least dating?"

"I don't know. It's not because he couldn't have anyone he wants."

"Would you like for me to have you and Adam over to dinner one night?"

A massive smile covered Terra's face. "Yes, I would! Hopefully soon."

"I'll have Dotty fix dinner for us tomorrow night about seven thirty. I'll ask Adam to join us."

Kaylee had to fight the urge to keep from glancing at the bar. Terra was right. Knowing that Adam was sleeping in a small house in her backyard had at times proved to be very unsettling.

As the women were leaving the restaurant, Terra asked, "Kaylee, are we going to speak to Adam before we leave?"

Kaylee glanced at Terra and smiled. "Of course."

"Great" Terra said.

As they were approaching him, Adam stood and laid money on the counter. It wasn't until he was sliding his muscular arms into his coat, that he noticed Kaylee and Terra approaching him. He greeted them with a smile.

"Hi Kaylee, Terra. Don't tell me you've been here and I didn't notice."

Kaylee pointed toward their table and said, "Yeah, we noticed you come inside, but didn't want to embarrass you by doing one of those whistles where you use your fingers!" She felt her heart racing but managed to appear calm.

Adam smiled and shook his head. "How are you, Terra?" he asked.

"Great, thank you! I haven't seen you around the last few days."

"I've been working with the horses and getting everything ready for cold weather. May I walk you ladies to your car?"

Kaylee put her stocking cap on and replied, "That would be nice, don't you think, Terra?"

"Yeah, real nice." Terra smiled.

Before approaching her car, Kaylee stopped and stated, "Adam, is it all right if Terra and I use a couple of the horses tomorrow?"

"Sure!"

"We plan to ride out and visit with Terra's mom."

"Sounds great! What time would you like for me to have the horses ready?"

Kaylee glanced at Terra. "How about nine o'clock?"

"That's fine with me," Terra said.

Adam nodded, "I'll have them ready at nine sharp. I hope it's warmer tomorrow than it was this morning."

They arrived at Terra's car first. Adam opened the door for her.

"Thank you, Adam." She smiled bashfully.

"You're welcome, and be careful going home."

Kaylee spoke up, "Before Terra leaves, I wanted to ask if you have plans for tomorrow night?"

"No, I don't!" Curious, Adam leaned against the car without taking his eyes off Kaylee.

"Good! Would you like to join Terra and me for dinner tomorrow night around seven thirty?"

"I would be honored. Thanks for the invitation!"

"Good," Kaylee said. "We'll see you in the morning."

"Goodnight, Kaylee," Terra said. "I enjoyed our dinner together."

"Me too. Thanks for picking up the tab."

"Anytime."

As Terra drove away, Adam stared at Kaylee.

"My car is over here," she said softly.

Kaylee took the keys from her coat pocket and started to put them in the lock. Adam gently put his hand on top of hers. "Allow me."

"I . . . I think I have it."

He lightly squeezed her hand and whispered in her ear, "You look breathtaking tonight. Beautiful women should never have to unlock their car."

Kaylee released her keys and tried to step back out of the way, only to lean against Adam. She promptly moved to the side. "Excuse me. Everyone is parked so close," she said.

"It is tight, but I don't mind being in a tight place with you."

Kaylee could hardly breathe. Was it the dazzling full moon that was taking her breath away or was it her body brushing against his? He stopped within the shaft of the moon as he turned to give Kaylee her keys. Their eyes met, and she could not break his stare. Adam glided his fingertips down her cheek. One of his arms clutched her tightly to him. She could feel his heart pounding and felt sure he could feel the beating of her heart as well. Abruptly, the sound of footsteps coming from Beef Eaters caused her to jerk away from his touch.

"May I come by tonight?" he said tenderly.

Her insides shaking, she managed to say, "No, no."

"Then I'll see you in the morning."

As soon as she sat in her car, she turned on the ignition and without looking at him, said, "Goodnight."

As the car rolled backward, Kaylee acted as though she didn't hear what else Adam said: "It would be a good night to hold you in my arms."

Chapter Nineteen

A Report to Martin

Later, Kaylee hurried into the house without turning on the lights. As her hand moved to her head, she paused, closed her eyes and then pulled her hat and coat off, letting them fall to the floor. Stunned by her actions toward Adam, she gradually made her way to the overstuffed chair by the window and fell into it. Gripping the arms of the chair, she leaned her head back, closed her eyes and allowed thoughts of Jeffrey to tiptoe into her mind, causing tears to stream down her cheeks.

What's wrong with me? I love you Jeffrey, and yet I tremble at the thought of Adam's touch. Kaylee's insides were in knots. She cried until she could cry no more and then fell into an unintended sleep.

Two hours had passed when suddenly, Kaylee's eyes sprang open. She abruptly gasped, rose to her feet and held to the back of the chair as she listened to the piano music playing low. "Is there a piano in this house I don't know about?" she shouted. The only thing she could move for a moment was her eyes. From where she was standing, the view in front of her was the formal dining room. Ellen Hilmar's portrait was lit with a dim, blue light attached at the top of the antique gold frame. *But who turned on the light?* It had not been on since she had been living in the house.

With her knees weak, she gradually moved toward the painting and the sound of the music. About halfway into the room, she stopped and steadied herself by taking hold of the high-back chairs that were pushed under the table. She stared at the painting. Ellen's eyes seemed to peer down at her. Holding the chair backs as she moved toward the fireplace, Ellen's enchanted eyes seem to follow her every movement. She stopped at the end of the table and put her fingers on her lips, holding her breath. After a moment she made herself breathe as she murmured through her fingers, "The music is coming from the painting."

Moving to the fireplace, Kaylee raised her hand and touched the mantel. Instantly, her hand felt frozen to the cold marble. The ringing of her cell phone broke the concentration and sent a shrill scream from Kaylee's throat. She jerked her hand from the mantel and hurried to the wall to flip on a light switch. Her phone continued to ring as she retrieved it from her handbag. Her mouth was so dry, she could barely wet her lips. "Hello," she said.

Martin's irritated growl greeted Kaylee. "Are you all right? You were supposed to have called me hours ago."

"I'm . . . I'm sorry. I fell asleep."

"You fell asleep? Could you not have called before you went to sleep?"

"I should have. I'm sorry, Martin."

As his tone softened, he stated, "I've been worried sick, not knowing if something had happened to you or not."

"I'm fine. You worry way too much about me. What do you think could possibly happen to me and why?"

"I feel bad that I wanted you to go to Stone River. I was wanting to know about those letters so badly that I didn't consider something might go wrong. It will be my fault, and I would not have you hurt for anything in the world."

"Martin, it would not be you. I wanted to do this and I am doing it. I'm curious about the letters as well. Especially, since I'm here and finding out about Stone River. Now, I can report the class was thrilled about doing the study on Stone River."

"That's good, but have you noticed anything out of the ordinary? Anything at all."

Kaylee paused.

"Kaylee! Kaylee! Are you there?" the voice echoed into her ear.

"Yes, I'm here. There has been something out of the ordinary with music playing at random by itself!"

"What do you mean?"

"I mean it plays without me turning it on, and it's the same songs over and over."

"What kind of songs?"

"It's called Piano Rhapsody. A few weeks before I came to Stone River, I bought the same songs on a CD in Raleigh."

"Are you sure?"

Kaylee elevated her tone, "Of course, I'm sure. This music has awakened me from a sound sleep before. I had Adam, the caretaker, check my player; it was fine. Tonight, the music sounded as though it was coming from the painting of Ellen Hilmar! Don't ask me to explain it; I can't."

"Okay, calm down, Kaylee."

"It's not easy to be calm when weird things are happening!"

"I don't mean to sound unsympathetic, but if you feel threatened, maybe you should come home."

"No! I can handle my job. I'm not leaving Stone River until I finish the job I was sent to do."

"That's my girl. Stay focused. Do you think speaking with Jeffrey will help?"

"Jeffrey's there?"

"Yes. Kaylee, be careful, I mean it."

"I will, Martin."

Kaylee's heart pounded as she waited to hear her love's voice.

"Kaylee?"

"Jeffrey, I have missed you so much."

"I miss you more. How are you doing?"

"I'm fine, except the loneliness I feel without you. I want to hold you so bad it hurts inside."

"I feel your pain. It won't be much longer. I've been watching for a letter from you, but I guess you've been very occupied with school."

"What do you mean? You haven't received any of my letters?"

"No."

"I wonder why."

"I don't know," he replied in a low tone.

"They haven't been returned to me, so if you didn't get them, who did?"

"I'll check at the post office tomorrow. At least I got to hear your voice. That's worth a million letters. I love you, babe."

"I love you, Jeffrey."

Martin picked up the other end of the line. "Call me at the end of next week and give me an update."

"I will."

Kaylee looked around the dining room, noticing there was no music and the light over Ellen's picture wasn't burning. She took her coat and cap from the floor, turned the lights off and returned to her bedroom. Hurriedly, she changed into her pajamas and snuggled under the covers. She seized the extra pillow and held to her chest. The bright red numbers from the alarm clock caused Kaylee to groan. "Four o'clock and Terra is going to be here by nine."

Chapter Twenty

Terra Right on Time

The clock alarm went off at eight a.m. Kaylee tried to sit up fast, but to no avail. Her head felt like a drum someone had been pounding on all night. She kicked the covers back and gradually sat up on the side of the bed. "I've got to get dressed. I hope my jeans will fit over the thermal underwear." She groaned. They fit snugly; however, she managed to tuck in her white, long-sleeve cotton T-shirt. She stared into the mirror. "No makeup today, but lots of lotion," she muttered as she did her hair in a French braid.

The morning sun was a welcome sight through the kitchen window as Kaylee fixed a pot of Hazelnut coffee. She stepped outside to check the temperature while waiting for the coffee to brew. The sky was clear and there was only a slight breeze. She sucked in a couple of deep breaths of the cool air to help clear her mind. Checking her watch, she mumbled, "Ten till nine. I better grab a quick bowl of cereal before Terra gets here." Terra was right on time.

"Good morning, Kaylee."

Kaylee smiled. "Hi, Terra, wow look at you, a genuine cowgirl! I absolutely adore your hat!"

Terra was holding a large shopping bag in her hand, and she raised it to Kaylee and said, "Good, I just happen to have one for you!"

"Really?" Kaylee gleamed as she reached for the bag.

"Yes ma'am, you being from North Carolina, I didn't figure a hat like this would already be hanging in your closet."

Kaylee opened the bag, removed a black suede hat and placed it on her head. "How do I look?"

"It look's great! Go see what you think."

They hurried to the full-length mirror in Kaylee's bedroom. "Wow! I love it." She hugged Terra and then checked the hat again. "You've made my day. Thank you for being so thoughtful."

"I couldn't let you meet my mama without wearing one of these. Remember I told you how she thinks it's still the turn of the century."

"I can't wait to meet her. We better be going. I told Adam we would be there at nine."

Kaylee took one last sip of coffee and locked the door. She stopped abruptly on the top step and hurried back inside.

"Did you forget something?" Terra called out.

"Heavens, yes! I forgot to leave Dotty a time and menu for our dinner tonight," Kaylee answered as she led Terra into the kitchen. "What would you like to eat?" Kaylee asked, as she reached for a pen and paper.

"Surprise me."

"How about a sirloin tip roast and . . . baked or mashed potatoes?"

"Mashed."

"Garden salad?" Kaylee asked without having to look at Terra.

"Yes."

"Sourdough rolls, and cheesecake for dessert?"

"That sounds wonderful. I can't wait."

"Speaking of waiting, Adam is surely wondering where we are!" Kaylee said as she placed the note on the countertop, turned and headed back toward the front door.

Kaylee felt refreshed and eager to get out of the house after the night she had experienced.

At the stables, Adam was petting a beautiful white stallion. He looked at his watch and smiled as they approached.

"I'm so sorry we're late," Kaylee said. "How do you like my hat?"

"I noticed that smart-looking hat right away. You look great."

"Terra gave it to me."

Adam smiled at Terra and complimented, "You have good taste."

"I try."

"I've fed and watered your horses. Terra, you'll be riding the pinto. His name is Windy, And, Kaylee, you'll be riding Thunder. Don't let the name fool you. He's as gentle as a puppy; so is Windy. I put them some snacks in the saddle bags and you can water the horses at the bend."

He helped Terra mount and then Kaylee. "You ladies have a safe trip. By the way, are we still on for dinner tonight?"

"We are. See you at seven thirty," Kaylee called as Terra led the way out of the stable.

The ride was invigorating. The sun was warming the atmosphere, and riding through the open fields, hills and trails was inspirational to both of them. They ran the horses for a while then stopped to let them cool.

"It's so beautiful out here. I can see why your mother doesn't want to move to town."

Terra pushed her hat back and wiped her forehead. "It's pretty but I wouldn't want to live out here. It's too isolated for me."

"Can you imagine how wonderful it must have been for the Lakota braves to ride the open range freely?"

"Of course, I can. Mama tells me the stories that her mom told her and so on. So, I have a pretty good image of what it might have been like."

"I'd love to hear some of those stories."

"I'm sure our visit won't pass without a story being revealed. By the way, where did you learn to ride?"

"My father had this huge work horse that he used around our farm. I rode that horse like he was this beauty I'm riding today." Kaylee leaned forward and rubbed the horse's muscular face.

"You ride very well. I'm surprised."

"Really?"

"Really! We better be going. Mom was going to make brunch for us."

"In that case, let's ride."

At the top of a hill, Terra pulled back on the reins, stopping her horse. In the valley, a meager, white house with a tin roof and a small, covered front porch sat near the river. At the side of the house was a rock chimney with a steady stream of white smoke spiraling and disappearing into the sky.

Terra pointed toward the house. "That's where my mama lives."

"It's not what I had expected at all."

"When the old house got run down, some of the men from town brought the material needed and had a few work days. They fixed the roof, cased the outside and built her the porch. It's funny because the material was all donated and when they brought shingles, instead of tin for a tin roof, mama had a fit. She asked, since they could donate shingles, couldn't they just as well donate tin? By the time she was through making her case, someone left there and was on his way to pick up the tin. She informed them that when it rains, she wanted to hear it and you couldn't hear it on shingles."

"Kitty sounds like my type of woman, one that will say what needs to be said to get the job accomplished," Kaylee said.

"She gets the job done, all right." Terra giggled as they started down the hill.

Chapter Twenty-One

Meeting Kitty Snow

As they neared the yard, a short, thin woman with long, braided white hair came from the house and stood at the top of the steps. She held her hand above her brows to block the sun from her eyes. She wore a pair of brown pants; a white, long-sleeve, thermal underwear shirt; a bulky, unbuttoned, green sweater; a multi-colored apron; and high-top black shoes. Her fair skin was wrinkled and her lips were narrow.

Kaylee and Terra slid off their horses and tied them to the rail around the porch.

"Hi, Mom!" Terra said as she and Kaylee proceeded up the steps and onto the porch.

Kitty looked at Terra. "I thought maybe you girls got lost."

"No, Mama, we didn't get lost. We had a later start then we had planned." Terra stepped to the side and pointed to Kaylee. "Mom, I want you to meet my friend, Kaylee Shell."

Kitty wiped her hand on her apron and extended it to Kaylee. "Kaylee, is it?"

Kaylee nodded her head and replied, "Yes, ma'am!"

"Kaylee, I want you to meet my mom, Kitty Snow."

"I wished she would have told you my Indian name."

Kaylee smiled and asked, "What is your given Indian name?"

"It's Gentle Stream. By the way, dear, welcome to my home."

"It's an honor to be here."

"I made you girls brunch. Let's eat now before it gets cold."

"Mom, why don't you and Kaylee get acquainted while I go feed and water the horses."

"Do you need me to help?" Kaylee asked.

"No, thanks. You can visit with Mom. I'll be back in a few minutes."

Kitty muttered, "Well, you hurry, I don't want the food to get cold." She turned and pointed to a chair and said, "Have a seat."

Kaylee put her hands to her back and slightly groaned, "If you don't mind, I would like to stand for a few minutes."

"I don't mind. Stand as long as you like. So, you're from North Carolina?"

"Yes."

"Terra told me about you."

"I hope it was a good report."

Kitty laughed. "Yeah, it was."

"She's told me a lot about you as well."

Kitty turned her sharp eyes to Kaylee and asked, "What did she tell you? That I should move to town because I'm too old to live out here by myself?"

Kaylee rubbed her hands together and nodded.

"I have every convenience I need. Terra gets all bent out of shape over nothing. I have electric lights and a bathroom. Men from town cut my wood for me every winter. Shoot, I even have a phone. It's not fancy, but who's there to impress? You more than likely thought I had a tin tub to take my baths in and a pot I piss in at night. Is that what you thought, Kaylee?" Kitty laughed and slapped her knee. All at once Kitty added, "You don't have to answer that. I'm just playing with you."

"What you have is fine. I am a little surprised though. I mean, a phone and everything."

Kitty giggled. "Did you see that I have a refrigerator and don't have to put my milk in the spring to keep it cold?"

Kaylee laughed out loud. "Kitty, you're my type of person. I love someone who has a good sense of humor."

"It's a good thing you do; otherwise, you'd want to be leaving before you eat the beans and cornbread, I fixed you girls."

"I hope you're talking about pinto beans."

Kitty laughed. "Is there any other kind?"

"My thoughts exactly."

"Terra mentioned you invited her to supper tonight."

"Yes, I did."

Kitty leaned forward and spoke in a lower tone. "I bet you ain't having pintos and cornbread, are you?"

"No, we're not."

Kitty raised her hand and took hold of one of her braids, shook it, and asked, "How do you like my hairdo, Kaylee?"

Kaylee chuckled, pulled her own braid to the side of her face, copied Kitty and replied, "I like it a lot."

Kitty leaned back in her chair and said "Kaylee Shell, I like you. As a matter of fact, you're the only one of Terra's friends I've met who's not a phony. Even the people who came out here and worked on my house, and even the ones who cut my wood, I wouldn't trust one minute with my eyes closed."

Kaylee frowned. "Why is that?"

Kitty leaned forward and pointed her finger at Kaylee. "It's all a show. One would think it's because I'm an old woman. The good Lord above knows that their service is not because of their good hearts. They do it thinking it will keep me indebted to them. You're new to Stone River, but you'll see what I'm talking about as time goes by, dear. We better change the subject; I hear Terra coming. I don't talk about things like that with her. I let her believe it's because they care so much about her."

Kaylee leaned toward Kitty and asked, "Do you mind if I come again some time to visit you? I would love to hear your stories and just enjoy your delightful company."

"You're welcome here anytime. You may just be the first friend I've had in years. I can see into a person's heart. What do you think about that?"

"I think that's pretty impressive. Tell me, Kitty, what do you see in my heart?"

"I see you're not here for no teaching job. I don't know why you're here yet, but I'll know soon. Now let's pour ourselves something to drink so we don't choke on our beans."

In an instant, Kitty pushed up from her chair and proceeded to the kitchen. Kaylee followed.

"Can I help you with anything?" Kaylee asked as she inhaled the mouthwatering aroma that filled the room.

"Yeah, you can put the beans in that bowl on the table while I take the cornbread out of the oven."

Terra stepped onto the porch, but just before she came inside, Kitty looked at Kaylee and said in a low tone, "Don't tell Terra anything I said to you about the town or the town's people."

"I won't," Kaylee said.

Terra entered laughing. "I fed and watered the horses, and now it's time to feed and water myself." She went to the sink and turned the water on to wash her hands. "Kaylee, has mom been talking your ears off?"

"Yes, and I've enjoyed every minute of it."

"How could she not enjoy my company? We're both wearing braids today." The women laughed.

***

While eating, Kaylee brought up the field trip she had planned for her class. After mentioning they were planning to visit the river bend, Kitty said, "Well, you got your first look at some of the bend today."

"This is the Bend?" Kaylee asked.

Kitty wiped her mouth with the back of her hand. "The actual Bend is about a quarter mile north of here; however, the land here is also a part of it."

"Really?"

"You better make your trip pretty soon. Usually, by Thanksgiving the cold weather sets in and you could freeze out here. Tell me, Kaylee, what's the reason for the field trip out here?"

"Charlie LittleHawk—"

"Yeah, I know Charlie," Kitty interrupted. "He's Lakota, like me."

"Exactly," Kaylee said. "We're going to visit the Bend and have Charlie share about his ancestors. Of course, we're going to do a complete study of the Lakota as a whole. I thought it would be a memorable learning experience to bring the class out to where a tribe had actually made their home. Having Charlie tell his story will add personal touch to our lesson. There were a lot of Lakota, but made up of many tribes. We know about Sitting Bull, Many Horses, Kicking Bear and Crazy Horse, but we don't hear about everyday people. Thus, Charlie LittleHawk's family tree."

Kitty shook her head and laughed. "You better brace yourself for that tree."

Terra turned her eyes to Kitty and said, "Mom, that wasn't a very nice thing to say."

"That's right, it wasn't. I didn't intend for it to be nice. However, Kaylee, I will tell you this much. You won't get bored."

"Mom!"

"Calm down, Terra. I like the way Kaylee is allowing her class to learn."

Terra stood and took her plate to the sink. Kitty looked at Kaylee and winked. As they washed the dishes, Terra commented about the heat and opened the front door.

"Mom, how do you stand this heat? You have a furnace and yet you chose to burn wood. With a furnace you can control the temperature; with wood all you can do is close the damper and wait for the wood to burn down. But not you."

"I'm old and got thin blood. You should know not to come out here wearing layers."

After a short visit, it was time to head back to town. Kaylee shook Kitty's hand and thanked her for the lunch. Terra went to bring the horses from the barn. Kaylee took advantage of the time with Kitty and asked, "What did you mean by the wink earlier?"

"I meant some of Charlie's ancestors had a very colorful background. Dig hard enough and you'll find more than history books will ever tell."

Terra kissed Kitty's cheek. "I love you, Mom. I'll be back out in a couple of days. If you need anything before then, call."

Kaylee held Kitty's hand and thanked her for the great meal and the warm company.

"You come back and visit me again soon, Kaylee. Next time, I'll give you a chew of the best twist tobacco you'll ever taste—"

"Mom, for goodness sake," Terra interrupted. "Kaylee doesn't chew tobacco."

"Well then, it'll be a brand new adventure for her. Right, Kaylee?"

"That's right, Kitty. I've never chewed, but who knows?"

After taking off on their horses, Kaylee and Terra stopped at the top of the ridge, turned and looked back toward the house. Kitty was still standing on the porch. After their wave, she turned and went back inside.

Terra laughed. "My mom is a mess."

"That she is, and I loved her!"

"I am so glad you did."

"Not to be nosy, but how old is your mother?"

116

"She's 80."

"Well, how old are you?"

"I'm 35."

"So, your mother, was 45 when she had you?"

"No. My biological mother died when I was born. My father was killed in a car accident when I was 2. Kitty is really my grandmother and the only mother I've ever known. She definitely spoiled me rotten."

"I'm sorry. I wasn't prying, but I did notice she was an older woman."

"It's okay," Terra said. "Everyone knows she's my grandmother. We better be going. I want to look glorious for our dinner guest tonight."

Chapter Twenty-Two

Dinner with Friends

*I*t was five o'clock when they arrived back at the estate. Dotty was in the kitchen, slicing the cheesecake.

Kaylee stopped at the counter and took a deep breath. "Hi, Dotty. I think I like having you around more every day. Everything smells wonderful."

Dotty grinned. "Thank you. I do my best!"

"Hello, Dotty," Terra said as she entered the kitchen.

Dotty smiled and nodded. "Did you girls have a good ride?" she asked.

"Yes, we did," Terra answered. "Kaylee is an excellent rider."

"Really? How was Kitty?"

Terra chuckled. "She was wide open, if you know what I mean. She really took to Kaylee. I think Kaylee's braids had something to do with it. What do you think, Kaylee?"

"I'm sure it did! Dotty, Terra and I are going to shower and rest a few minutes before sharing your wonderful dinner."

Dotty chuckled. "After that ride, I'm sure you need to rest. I'll have everything ready on time."

"Thanks, Dotty."

Kaylee and Terra turned to leave the kitchen. Dotty called out, "Miss Shell, would you like for me to light the fireplace?"

Kaylee looked at Terra. Terra smiled and nodded. "Yes, that would be nice, Dotty."

Terra showered, took her clothes from a garment bag and laid them across the bed. Kaylee, was brushing her hair when Terra asked, "Which outfit should I wear?"

Kaylee turned to observe. "I think the burgundy will look great."

Terra picked the burgundy sweater up, held it to her chest and frowned. "Do you have any burgundy lipstick?"

Kaylee took a tube of lipstick from her case and handed it to her. "I do. You can have this one. I have two tubes."

"Thank you." Terra's hair was cut short, in the back, with longer, natural curls on top. She applied a handful of mousse and picked a few curls into place. After putting her silver hoop earrings on, she carefully sprayed perfume on her neck. Kaylee couldn't help notice the obvious excitement Terra displayed. Terra turned and asked, "How do I look?"

"Stunning," Kaylee said.

"Stunning enough for Adam to notice?"

"Without a doubt."

Terra put her hands on her hips. "You look quite smashing yourself."

At that moment, Dotty knocked softly on the door. "Miss Shell?"

"Come in, Dotty."

As she entered the room, a bright smile spread across her face. "My goodness, don't you two look nice."

Terra smiled and raised her brows. "Oh, thank you, Dotty."

"Everything's ready, and I just lit the wood in the fireplace."

"Thanks, Dotty, you're absolutely amazing!" Kaylee said. "Would you like to join us for dinner?"

"No, no, I couldn't do that."

"Then at least take a heaping plate with you," Kaylee insisted.

"That I will do. I hope dinner is to your satisfaction."

"The wonderful aroma alone tells me it will be perfect. You have a good night, Dotty." Kaylee said.

After exchanging "goodnights," Dotty left, and the girls headed to the dining room. The gleaming white china glistened from the lights of the chandelier above them. As they admired dinner, Adam's knock on the door caused Terra's body to jerk from her built-up anxiety. Kaylee opened the door. Adam looked gorgeous in his well-fitting Levis, royal blue, buttoned shirt and khaki barn coat. He inhaled the appetizing scent filling the air as he hung his coat on the coat rack. "Good evening, ladies! Not only do you look marvelous, but our meal does too!"

As the three of them indulged in their meal, the conversation was non-stop. Terra's attention diligently remained on Adam throughout every sentence he spoke.

It was near midnight as they finished their wine in the grand room. Adam suddenly stood and announced. "It's getting late. I better be going."

"Me, too." Terra said, as she arose to her feet.

Adam slipped on his coat and assisted Terra with hers. "I'll walk out with you," he said.

Terra went to retrieve her things from the bedroom. Adam instantly turned his attention to Kaylee and said in a soft tone, "You look radiant tonight."

Kaylee smiled and watched as Terra came from the hall with her backpack and bag. Adam carried them to her car. Terra hugged Kaylee and whispered, "My, my, he's awesome. I'll call you tomorrow."

Chapter Twenty-Three
Strange Items

$\mathcal{K}$aylee locked the door after her friends left and hurried to her bedroom. She took her baby blue, flannel pajamas from the closet and started to put them on but suddenly stopped when from the corner of her eye, she observed a petite, silky, black negligee neatly placed on a pink satin hanger. "My goodness," she said, as she ran her fingertips down the front, "I wonder where this came from."

The mysterious gown was draped with a matching, long, antique lace robe. Without hesitation, she tossed the pajamas to the floor, released the negligee from the hanger and slipped it over her head, allowing it to drop to the top of her feet. An uncanny feeling swept over her. Automatically, she reached for an old perfume bottle sitting on her dressing table. Though she had never seen the bottle before, she sprayed it lavishly on her neck and chest. As she sprayed the perfume, the fragrance of fresh-cut roses filled the room. Making her way to a full-length mirror in the corner, she gasped at the view. Although it was her own reflection, somehow, she appeared different and inside she felt so unlike herself.

From the mirror, she caught a glimpse of something shiny lying on the chest of drawers. Moving closer, she noticed it was a gold comb with large white pearls across the top. It was perfectly propped against a porcelain figurine. Without a thought, Kaylee pulled her hair into a twist and reached for the comb. As she held up her hair with her right hand, she pushed the comb through with her left. Carefully, she pulled thin strands of hair down around her neck and face. Gently touching her cheek and neck, she then rested her fingertips on top of her partly exposed breasts. At once, the room began to spin. She closed her eyes, leaned her head back on her shoulders in an attempt to stop the dizziness. Right away, her eyes sprang open upon hearing the mysterious music chiming through the house.

Compelled, Kaylee held her breath and stepped into the hallway. The dark hall was aglow with numerous candles. Feeling barely conscious, she maneuvered her body down the hallway toward the music. Without warning, she was standing underneath Ellen Hilmar's portrait.

During dinner, the fire in the fireplace had almost completely burned out, but now a new batch of wood was stacked and burning brightly. But who had replaced the wood? The candles were glowing as the music played low, resounding through the stillness. Kaylee turned her head and listened to light tapping on the front door. Without hesitation, she hurried to open it. It was Adam. Without speaking, Kaylee stepped aside for Adam to enter.

His eyes fixed on hers. He removed his coat, letting it drop to the floor. He lowered his face to Kaylee's and pressed his lips to hers. Kaylee leaned her head back, allowing Adam to kiss her neck and shoulders. Breathing rapidly, she raised Adam's head and pressed her lips to his as he pulled her body tight.

Kaylee unbuttoned his shirt, exposing his muscled chest. He lifted her and sat her carefully on the table. Gliding his fingertips down her neck, he pulled the narrow straps of her gown off her shoulders. Pausing, he whispered, "I love you, Halo."

Kaylee trembled. "I . . . I . . . I love you, too."

Adam kissed Kaylee passionately one last time and took a step backward from her. Kaylee scrambled to pull her straps up and placed her hand over her mouth in disbelief. Tears welled in her eyes as she whispered, "Adam, I . . . I . . ."

"No, Kaylee. I'm so sorry, I would never take advantage of you."

Kaylee slid off the table and shook her head. "What am I even doing on the table?"

"I put you there," Adam said as he buttoned his shirt. "What's happening to me?" he said. "I can hardly control myself when I'm around you. Tonight, I went to my house and paced like an animal. The thoughts of you intoxicated me. Then, I was standing at your door, but I don't remember walking to your door."

Kaylee placed her hand on her stomach and tried to explain. "This negligee and the comb that you took from my hair isn't mine. The perfume I'm wearing isn't either. I've never seen any of these things before tonight, and yet I didn't question or hesitate to use them when I discovered them in my bedroom." Kaylee pointed at the candles and added, "I didn't light any of those candles or the wood in the fireplace. Adam, I didn't turn the music on." Kaylee exhaled and asked, "What's happening to us?"

Adam ran his fingers through his hair. His voice shaking, he said. "I don't know. I wish I did. I'm so sorry, Kaylee."

"You're sorry, you're sorry! I was the one lying on the table!"

"As a man, I want desperately to make love to you, but this is not me, Kaylee!"

Kaylee lowered her head. "I know your feelings. This is just very unsettling. I confess, I'm a nervous wreck. I've never encountered anything like this. What do I do?" I'm frightened.

"I wish I knew. This may seem awkward, but why don't I sleep on the couch tonight. Maybe it'll help us both get some rest."

She shook her head. "I . . . I don't know."

"Don't worry, I'll stay in here."

She sighed, "You don't mind?"

"Not at all. I'd be glad to."

"Great! I'll get you some blankets and a pillow. I'll be right back."

Adam sat near the window, propped his elbows on his knees and held his face in his hands. Kaylee returned with his bedding and laid them on the sofa. She watched Adam bracing his face with his fingers.

"Adam, are you all right?"

Without looking up, he asked, "How can you get over what just happened that fast? I'm in a daze."

Adam stood and took hold of Kaylee's arms. "Kaylee, I can't explain what took place in the dining room, but I still want to make love to you and hold you all night. Those feelings have nothing to do with what happened in the dining room. Do you feel the same?"

"I have very mixed feelings. If you think I don't still feel your lips touching mine, you're wrong. I may feel safer with you sleeping in my house, but I won't rest as well, knowing that you're in here and . . . I better stop right here and say goodnight."

Chapter Twenty-Four

Lady of the House

The next morning when Kaylee woke, Adam was gone. The blankets were neatly folded on the sofa, and the pillow was on top of them.

Kaylee made her bed and took a shower. When she came from her bathroom, she heard the back door close. She was about to call out to see if perhaps it was Adam. Before she could, Dotty shouted, "Miss Shell, it's Dotty. I didn't want to scare you. I'm going to clean up from last night."

Kaylee hurried down the hall, hoping to remove the bed covers before Dotty saw them. Dotty was holding them in her arms as she came into the living room.

"Did Terra stay over last night? I meant to tell you if you want to have someone stay over you may use the pink room."

"Thank you, Dotty."

While Dotty was clearing the table, Kaylee came into the room, holding the negligee and comb. "Dotty?"

"Yes, Miss Shell."

"Do you know where these came from?"

She looked at them in awe. "No, but they are beautiful. Are they not yours?"

"No. They were in my room, but I haven't a clue as to how they got there."

Dotty shook her head. "I'm sorry, I wish I could help."

"Thank you."

After returning the items to her room, Kaylee took her briefcase and laptop to the grand room to do some work. A short time later, Dotty entered the room. "I'm sorry to disturb you, Miss Shell, but I've finished my chores, and if there's nothing else, I'll be leaving for the day."

"Thank you, Dotty. You go and enjoy your day. I have some work to do."

Dotty smiled. "I'll see you in the morning." She turned to leave

"Dotty?"

"Yes, Miss."

"Did you come into the house at all last night?"

"No, why do you ask?"

"I . . . I just can't figure out where those things came from."

"Trust me, if I had come into the house last night, I wouldn't have left such expensive items!"

Kaylee sighed. "They may have been here all along and I just didn't notice."

"That more than likely explains it. Have a good day, Miss Shell."

"Dotty, you may call me Kaylee. Miss Shell sounds like I'm older than I want to be."

"I call you Miss Shell in respect to your position."

Kaylee frowned. "A teacher is an honorable position and the students do call me Miss Shell, but if I can call you Dotty, you can call me Kaylee."

"You're right. Teaching is an honorable position; however, that's not the position that I respect so much."

"Then what is it?"

"I respect the fact that you're the lady of the house."

Kaylee laughed. "I'm going to live here for only six months!"

"Then for six months, I'll give the respect the position deserves."

"One more thing. Have you seen Adam this morning?" Kaylee asked.

"Yes, he left early and mentioned he was going to visit some friends at the canyon."

"Thank you." Kaylee directed her attention back to her work.

As she penned Jeffrey a letter, she felt awkward and somewhat of a hypocrite. She wanted to call and see if he had received the letters she had sent or even if Martin had a change of heart and given them to him. Mostly, she just wanted to hear his voice filled with the affirmation that he still loved her. Hopefully, that would take her mind off of Adam.

Chapter Twenty-Five
Class Quest

$\mathcal{T}$he next morning at school, the students were ecstatic about the task Kaylee had presented to them.

"Okay, class, I trust you've been working on your assignment. First of all, I want to ask if you came up with a person that you want to analyze."

Betty raised her hand, "Yes, Miss Shell, we did."

"Did everyone agree on this person?"

"We did."

"So, tell me who the person is."

"The founders of Stone River."

Tyler stood and added, "Miss Shell, actually, we wanted to ask if we could possibly look into two people's lives? I'll explain. We wanted to look into our founding father; however, there were two of them, Roy Hilmar and Jake Boone. Being equal partners in creating Stone River, both men were powerful business examples."

Kaylee smiled and nodded her head. "By all means! Feel free to do just that. I would also like to commend you for such a very wise decision. When I first arrived in Stone River, I noticed that almost everything in town sported the names 'Hilmar' or 'Boone,' so I think it would be only appropriate to research the lives of both men." Kaylee wrote the names on the board and then asked, "Lisa, are you and your team ready to dissect the town's history?"

Lisa stood. "We are more than ready."

"Good, we can't wait to hear."

Lisa smiled and returned to her seat.

"Lori?"

Lori stood.

Kaylee crossed her arms and said, "What case have you and your team chosen to investigate?"

"My team and I met at the library and searched as far back as possible on microfilm and discovered several cases. Then, Charlie LittleHawk made a recommendation for us to study that we couldn't locate on microfilm. It occurred in 1871. Actually, the case happened to a couple of Charlie's descendants. Two Lakota Indian brothers disappeared and were never found. Their names were Wind Dancer and Moving Cloud. We have a couple of leads for starters and believe that with determination, we will find the demise of the two braves."

Kaylee clapped her hands and exclaimed, "I applaud each of you. Your choices are excellent, and I can tell you've put a lot of thought toward your choices. We will be taking our field trip to the Bend on Saturday morning. Charlie, do you want to add anything concerning our outing?"

"No, ma'am, except I absolutely can't wait. I feel very excited about what's happening in this class."

Eddie raised his hand. "I want to confess this is the first time in my life that I've really enjoyed coming to school."

Kaylee nodded as she grinned ear-to-ear. "Learning can be fun or boring. It's up to you. If you can find a way to relate or connect to an assignment, then it becomes more intrinsically motivating for you! I want you to have fun while you learn and challenge yourselves to go the extra mile to find facts. Facts will give us the whole story, and most importantly, those facts will give us truth. We'll meet once a week at the Hilmar Mansion and discuss our findings. What is the one thing we're not going to do while working on this project?"

Paulette spoke up, "We're not to discuss our findings or our goal with anyone."

"What are you to say if your family should ask why you're asking about certain things?"

The class answered in unison, "We're studying the town's history."

"I want all leaders to get with your groups and spend some time writing down the questions you're going to be finding answers to. Charlie and I will discuss what he has in mind for our field trip. By the way, class, I'm going to bring hot dogs, chips, potato salad and other goodies. As long as we're going, we may as well have a fire to roast hot dogs and marshmallows. It'll be a nice treat for everyone! Each one of you will be responsible for bringing your own drinks. So far, the weather sounds favorable, and let's pray it stays that way. What day would be good for us to meet at the estate? I'm open for suggestions."

In an instant, Paulette raised her hand. "How about Friday night?"

"Will that be a problem for anyone?" Kaylee surveyed their facial expressions.

Eddie scratched his head and commented, "I have a date Friday night."

Betty frowned at him and stated, "Eddie, everyone knows the date is with me, and I think a visit to the estate will be a delightful evening."

"Is there anyone else that has a conflict with meeting on Friday night?"

Just then, Eddie laughed and added, "Actually, a date at the mansion sounds cool. Is there any hope we could even have a little candlelight during our meeting?"

Kaylee giggled at his creative question and replied, "Hum, I don't think so. However, I promise to ask Dotty to prepare plenty of snacks for you all."

Just then, Nick Long knocked and opened the classroom door. "Pardon the intrusion, Miss Shell, may I speak with you when you can get away?"

"Sure! Class, I'll be right back." Kaylee closed the door and asked, "What can I do for you?"

He grinned in a suspicious manner. "Those kids are thoroughly worked-up about your assignment. I can't recall ever seeing them this excited over schoolwork before!" He paused, and then added, "Would you care to share what you're doing?"

Kaylee stood confidently. "They sure are and I love it, but I can't reveal their assignment. I want it to be a surprise. I think you'll approve, with great pride."

His grin turned horizontal as he cleared his throat. "If there's anything I can help you with, let me know."

"Thank you, but I feel we have everything under our control."

"Donna and I would like to have you over soon."

"I would be honored."

He started to walk away, then turned back and asked, "Is everything going okay at the house?"

"Yes, everything's fine."

"Thelma Hilmar hasn't bothered you again, has she?"

"No, she hasn't."

"Good."

Chapter Twenty-Six
Questions about Jeffrey

That night, Kaylee expected Adam to at least stop by, but he didn't. After calling Mr. Cullman and updating him on what was going on, she asked, "Has Jeffrey received any of my letters yet?"

"I sure hope not because your time is to be spent investigating. Anyway, he's not in right now."

She froze and asked, "He's not? It's almost midnight in North Carolina!"

Mr. Cullman cleared his throat. "He . . . he went out with some friends."

"With friends? What friends?" she demanded.

"Oh, I don't know. I think with Justin, Zack and I'm not sure who else. I think you're investigating the wrong person."

"Martin, I've known you for most of my life, and you know everyone Jeffrey goes out with."

"Now, Kaylee . . ." he began in a calming tone.

"Don't patronize me. One thing you taught me is to never let anyone be condescending to me, so don't. Are you covering up for Jeffrey? Tell me, did Hannah go with him?" There was a moment of silence, and then he softly spoke, "I think you should ask Jeffrey that question."

"No, I think you answered it for me."

"Kaylee! You get your focus back on track. We agreed that your personal life would be on hold until you get back to Raleigh. Did we not?"

Kaylee sighed. "Yes, we did."

"Well, this one time . . . do you want to call Jeffrey tomorrow?"

"You know I will."

"Kaylee, it sounds as though you're doing a wonderful job."

"Thank you, Martin. I'll call you tomorrow."

"Goodnight, dear."

"Goodnight."

After she hung-up, Kaylee closed her eyes and groaned. She had been gone only a month and already Hannah was back on the scene. Hannah had dated Jeffrey throughout high school and his freshman year in college. However, she felt guilty to say anything the way her feelings had grown toward Adam.

Chapter Twenty-Seven
Waitress in Erwin

The next day after school, Kaylee drove by the post office with the intention of mailing Jeffrey a letter. Instead, she continued to drive to Erwin, a small town about twenty miles south of Stone River. She stopped at a small diner for dinner. The quaint café appeared clean but could benefit from some renovation. Her waitress was a very friendly, older woman who was heavy-set with white hair, narrow eyes and full lips. With the writing pad from her pocket and a pencil from behind her ear, she took Kaylee's order. Soon Kaylee observed the waitress exiting the kitchen's swinging door carrying a round wooden tray holding her meal. After placing the plate on the table, she asked, "Are you new in town or just passing through?"

Kaylee smiled. "Only passing through. I live in Stone River. I noticed the diner and decided to stop."

"Stone River is a pretty place." The waitress gleamed as she sat the empty tray on the booth behind her.

"Yes, it is." Kaylee unfolded her cloth napkin and placed it in her lap.

"Where do you live in Stone River? In town or out?"

"I'm just outside of town. I rented a place called the Hilmar Estate."

The woman's face instantly grew dismal.

"What is it?" Kaylee asked with an extremely concerned stare.

The woman's voice was firm as she shook her head back and forth. "I wouldn't step foot in that place."

"Why? It's beautiful." Kaylee leaned back against her seat without taking her eyes off the lady.

"It's beautiful all right. It's also haunted."

"Haunted?" Kaylee's voice had become rather elevated by now.

The waitress nodded and replied in a calmer voice. "Haunted. They say Ellen Hilmar's spirit still rules that house."

"What do you mean?"

"I mean, if weird things start taking place, then you know that she is in the house. It has been mentioned that she had more than one lover in her short life. Roy Hilmar wasn't taking care of his homework, if you know what I mean. When he was away, Ellen found her pleasure elsewhere."

"Really?"

"Yes, that was common knowledge. Didn't anyone bother to tell you about all this before you moved in?"

"No, they didn't." Kaylee crossed her arms and frowned.

"Then again, I'm sure you know how tales get bigger with age."

Kaylee responded in disbelief. "So, you're saying the town's people know about the so-called haunting."

"Yes, dear, every last one of them. Heck, if the people of Erwin have heard about it, you know every individual in Stone River has too. Tell me, has anything weird been going on since you moved there?"

Kaylee lifted her fork from the table and responded, "No . . . no, not that I've noticed."

"Well, Ellen must be pleased with your presence. Otherwise, she would be making life a living hell for you."

"Besides me, has anyone else lived in the house since the town acquired the estate?"

The waitress frowned, shook her head and said, "They didn't tell you about the woman who lived there before you?"

"No." Kaylee leaned forward and focused on the lady's face.

The waitress sighed and asked, "How long have you lived at the estate?"

"A little over a month."

"You wouldn't be a high school teacher, would you?"

"Why, yes I am. Why do you ask?"

"The woman who lived there before you was a teacher. You must be the one they hired to take her place."

Kaylee frowned and put her fork down. "I was told the teacher I replaced had to leave rather abruptly."

"From what I hear, Ellen didn't like her and wanted her out of her house. Put that in your pipe and smoke it a while. Look, Miss, I'm not trying to scare or upset you, but I would be careful if I were you. As a matter of fact, I'd get out of that house and Stone River as soon as possible."

Kaylee swallowed hard. "I don't scare easily, and I'm not leaving the house or Stone River."

As she chuckled, the waitress said, "I'm glad you're that kind of woman. Just keep your eyes open and watch out for the housekeeper while you're there. I heard she is stationed there to keep an eye on the house and aid Ellen when possible."

"You mean Dotty?"

"That's her."

Kaylee closed her eyes for a moment and asked, "What about Adam, the caretaker?"

"I haven't heard about a caretaker. If he lives on the grounds, I'd be careful."

Kaylee thanked the woman for the information, managed to eat a few bits of her beef stew and headed back to Stone River. She felt betrayed on every hand. To think Adam and Dotty might possibly be a part of the conspiracy was hard to accept. Especially Adam.

She shook her head in disbelief as her headlights led her path toward home.

Chapter Twenty-Eight
A Talk with Jeffrey

When she arrived at the estate, Kaylee turned the car engine off and sat in dismay. "Surely, Martin had no clue," she thought aloud. "I'll call and ask."

She was surprised when Jeffrey answered the phone.

"Kaylee sweetheart, how are you?"

In a rather monotone voice, she said, "I'm fine. You answered Martin's phone?"

"He's taking a shower. I'm sure he didn't hear it ring, so I grabbed it."

Kaylee promptly asked, "Have you received any of my letters yet?"

"No, I haven't. I asked grandfather if I had received any mail from you. He said no. When he veers from being honest, his face turns a slight shade of red, and he'll refrain from looking at me. That's exactly what happened when I asked about the mail."

"That old stinker. I'll get him good when I get home because I've mailed you several letters."

In a mild tone, Jeffrey assured her, "I'll be checking some of his hiding places. When I asked, he swiftly responded, 'She promised to stay focused, she can't focus if she's writing and calling you every minute.'"

Kaylee chuckled. "That's so funny. Jeffrey, did Hannah go out with you last night?"

There was a brief silence. "No, she did not."

"Good."

"She went with Zack and me."

Kaylee could feel her cheeks warming with anger. "She came with Zack, but who took her home?"

"Now, Kaylee, what difference does that make?"

Kaylee raised her voice. "Who took her home?"

"I took her home first, then dropped Zack off. Kaylee, what happened with Hannah and me is in the past. I love you and you alone."

In a broken voice, Kaylee said, "I'm sorry, Jeffrey, I do trust you. I just miss and love you so much."

Jeffrey chuckled. "You haven't met some dashing young cowboy in Stone River have you?"

"Yeah, at least four or five of them." She tried to laugh as tears streamed down her cheeks.

"Kaylee, as soon as you get back to Raleigh, we're going on a cruise! I have the place already picked out for us!"

"Oh, Jeffrey, that would be wonderful."

"I love you! Grandfather's informing me it's time to hang up the phone. I'd better go. We'll talk in a couple of days."

Kaylee veered away from what the waitress had said about the woman who had lived in the estate before her and instead gave Martin a brief update of her day at school. With that report, he was well pleased.

Chapter Twenty-Nine
Late Visit from Adam

*K*aylee unlocked the front door and stepped inside. She leaned her back against the door and trembled. How could she be jealous of Hannah when she had been obsessed with Adam? She entered the dining room and stared up at Ellen.

Frustrated she shouted, "I sure hope what I heard tonight was all a myth. I'm here for one reason . . . no two reasons. Number one is Jake Boone, Martin's father. Number two, I will find out what happened to the two Lakota Indians who disappeared over a hundred years ago. It was important enough for Martin's mother to mention them over and over in her practically ancient letters. If your spirit, or whatever, is present within this glorious house, as some say, I would like to ask you to please work with me until my assignment is complete and I'll be on my way." Kaylee groaned. "Here I am talking to a painting of a woman who's been dead for years."

Kaylee started toward the kitchen to pour herself a glass of wine before going to bed. It was then, from the corner of her eye, she noticed a silver tray sitting on the hutch across the room. A beautiful goblet, like the one she had broken, and a vintage bottle of red wine were perfectly arranged on the tray. Who put them there? What the waitress told her about Dotty raced through her mind. Had Dotty, or even Adam, been coming into the house and lighting the fireplace and candles or turning on the music? It was her CD that she kept in her bedroom most of the time. Did someone copy it? Maybe Ellen wanted her to leave her home.

After finishing a glass of wine, Kaylee started to her bedroom when she heard a light tapping on the front door. She grabbed her chest and gasped. "Don't answer it, Kaylee," she thought aloud.

With another knock came the deepness of Adam's voice. "Kaylee, it's Adam. I need to talk to you."

Kaylee rubbed her fingers across her lips. After a deep breath, she opened the door.

Adam removed his hat and said, "I was worried about you."

Without moving her hand from the bronze door handle, she asked, "Why would you need to be worried about me?"

"You didn't come home after school and—"

"What, are you spying on me?" Kaylee interrupted.

"No!"

"Then how do you know if I came home after school or not?"

"Kaylee, listen, I drove out to the canyon the other night. I needed to clear my mind. I'm not the same person since you moved onto the estate. While there, I spoke with Kitty Snow. She wants you to visit her soon.

She mentioned that she saw your heart, whatever that means. I promised to tell you as soon as you got home from work. That's how I knew. Why so harsh?"

She rubbed her temples and closed her tired eyes. "I'm sorry, would you like to come in for a minute?"

To Kaylee's surprise, Adam put his hat on and said, "No thanks, I really better be going."

Kaylee mustered up a phony smile. "Of course, it's getting late."

He nodded, tilted the front of his hat and turned, saying as he left, "Goodnight, Kaylee."

"Goodnight," she said softly as she closed the door.

After pumping herself up to say no to his charm, Kaylee watched Adam simply walk away. "Why do I feel crushed?" Kaylee muttered. "I wanted his kiss and yet I scold Jeffrey about Hannah. Kaylee Shell, you're out of control."

Kaylee went back and looked up at Ellen, "Is it you who's tearing my emotions apart? Tell me, Ellen, what kind of person were you? Did you really have all those lovers? Or was there one special man who supplied all your needs? By the way, while I'm talking to you, I wonder, was it you who put the negligee, comb and perfume in my room? Was it possibly you who lit the candles and fireplace and the one who enjoys my music? I thought I was going to have a connection in Stone River to talk with. You appear to be that connection. Enough said. Goodnight, Ellen."

Chapter Thirty
Reviewing Class Assignments

*E*arly the next morning, Kaylee was awakened only moments before her alarm went off. The oversized wind chimes that hung on the side entrance of the house were loudly clanging together. In an instant, she hopped out of bed, got ready for work and headed out the door. She paused after starting her Explorer and dashed to the side of the house, hoping to catch a glimpse of Adam. His Jeep was already gone. Her thoughts were interrupted when Dotty announced, "Are you looking for something, Miss Shell?"

Kaylee pressed her fingers to her temples. "Dotty, you scared me!"

"I noticed your car was running so . . ."

Kaylee began, "I would love to have a pot of homemade chili for supper, if you don't mind."

Dotty smiled. "I don't mind at all."

"Thanks. Be sure to take some for yourself and some for Adam."

"Will you be dining alone?"

"Yes."

On the way to school, Kaylee was furious because no one had told her about the estate and the fact that Ellen still occupied the massive residence.

Terra was the first to meet Kaylee in the hall. "Hi, Kaylee, do you have time for a quick cup of coffee in the lounge?"

Kaylee looked at her watch. "Yeah, I have about ten minutes."

Kaylee listened to Terra's dreams of Adam. She was thrilled when the ten minutes had ended so she could escape to her classroom.

After the bell rang, Kaylee eagerly greeted her class. Let's begin the morning with reports you have gathered on the history project."

Colton raised his hand, stood and said. "Miss Shell."

"Yes, Colton,"

"Today is my eighteenth birthday!"

"Happy Birthday, Colton. Class, let's lift our voices in song in honor of Colton's birthday."

After hearing the singing, Colton pretended to wipe tears from his eyes and announced, "I'm so touched by your off-key rendition of 'Happy Birthday.' Thanks so much. I love you . . . I just love all of you!"

"Now that we've celebrated Colton's birthday, Tyler, would you give me an update on your team's findings of Roy Hilmar's and Jake Boone's strategies on becoming rich men."

"We found out that Mr. Hilmar and Mr. Boone came to what is now Stone River in the fall of 1864."

"So, they came west together?" Kaylee asked.

"Yes, ma'am. They joined a wagon train that left from, St. Louis, Missouri, on April 1, 1864. They did that in order to arrive at their destination before winter. They weren't wealthy men; however, their wives, Ellen Shaw and Tammy Wade, did have sizable nest eggs. Both women's parents protested and begged their daughters not to marry the men who had absolutely nothing and go to a land they didn't know. They feared they would never see their daughters again."

Tyler continued, "We found several pictures of Ellen but only one of Tammy. I could go on and on, but . . . when they arrived in what is now Stone River, they found a lot of gold, buffalo, horses and green pastures for their cattle. Several families from the wagon train decided to settle here as well. With the money that Ellen and Tammy brought with them, the men hired workers to come here and build this town—from those families and other men as far away as Fort Abraham Lincoln. That's all we have for now."

Kaylee was ecstatic. "Great job! That is so interesting. Lisa, what do you and your team have to report?"

Lisa stood. "Well, Kyle gave some of the history about the wagon-train trip from St. Louis so, I'll not repeat that. I do have the maps, showing the route the wagon train followed. We located a copy of the boundaries that Mr. Hilmar and Jake Boone staked out. One thing we discovered from going over the maps was they actually pushed their boundaries into the Lakota tribe's property at the Bend. Here is a surprise: the exact spot that Jake and Roy stole from the Lakota is the very place we're going to have our field trip! Roy and Jake wanted the gold that was plentiful in the Bend area. The Indians fought to push them back. Many soldiers had already invaded their land. The government had prepared the place that we now know as the great Sioux Reservation. The Lakota wanted their families to remain free. They knew if they continued to fight, they would be wiped out. The government offered the Indians a choice, to sign the treaty or not. If they did, they would be moved to the reservation with the promise of food and protection. If not, they could stay where they were but would more than likely starve to death. The Indians were confident if they gave in and signed the treaty the white men were offering, they would never be free again. Roy and Jake knew about their predicament and took full advantage of it. Knowing the soldiers would intercede for them, they did things to force the Indians to fight. So far, it has been very sad, but that's all we have for now."

Kaylee exhaled. "Very revealing, Lisa! Fantastic job!"

Kaylee nodded to Lori and said, "Lori, I can't wait to hear what your team has to report."

Lori stood and cleared her throat. "I will be honest. The case of the two missing Lakota braves has been extremely interesting. From what we've found so far, the two were brothers. Their names were Wind Dancer and Moving Cloud. Both were in their early 30s, and from what we could gather, they were pretty good looking, too! One day, the brothers went out to scout the land and never came back. With two braves missing, what were the Indians going to do? No white man cared if another Indian died. Every warrior's death would bring the white men a little closer to what they wanted, the land and gold. It would do no good to report it to the soldiers or the new sheriff, Jasper Wills, who had been hired by the Boone/Hilmar

Corporation. Meanwhile, the two men's tribe and family looked everywhere for the brothers, but they were never found. We are going to keep searching, but that's all we have for now."

Kaylee smiled at her students. "I am so proud of you! The facts you've brought out just today are painting a portrait of the people, their individual character and a picture of the wealth of this land. I can hardly wait until Saturday when Charlie adds his information. For now, I want to know what time we can meet on Thursday night? Thursday, because of our field trip on Saturday. How about seven o'clock?"

Eddie said, "I changed my date with Betty to Thursday because I thought we were meeting on Friday."

Kaylee looked quickly at Betty. "Is Thursday all right with you?"

"It's perfect for me, Miss Shell!"

Kaylee slapped her hands together. "Then Thursday it is."

The bell rang and Kaylee called out, "Paulette, may I see you for a moment?"

Paulette picked up her books and walked to Kaylee's desk. "Yes, Miss Shell?"

"Is all of this all right with you? I know you're pretty emotional over the Estate. If it isn't okay with you, we'll hold our meetings in class."

Paulette smiled. "I look forward to meeting at Grandmother's house. I haven't been inside it for a while now. Trust me, Miss Shell, what our class finds out about my family will more than likely be shocking to some people, but not to me. I've heard so many stories, it will be good to hear the truth for once."

"Tell me, Paulette, do you think we'll find shocking things that were never told or old rumors that may have died with time?"

"I'm sure we'll find both. Grandmother candy-coats the truth. Now that she's getting older, the stories are changing again. I fear there are facts that will upset everyone in Stone River."

"Thanks, Paulette, for being so open about your feelings. If they change, let me know."

"Thank you for being so considerate, Miss Shell."

Chapter Thirty-One
Meeting John Smith

*A*fter school, Kaylee was sitting at her desk grading papers when someone knocked and slightly opened the door. Kaylee looked up. "May I help you?"

"Miss Shell?" called a male's voice.

"Yes, I'm Kaylee Shell," she called, as she observed a tall, thin man in his early 40s approaching her. His yellow polo shirt and long, pulled-back auburn hair accented his tanned skin and white teeth. Even the creases down the front of his khaki pants were precision.

He extended his hand. "I'm John Smith."

Kaylee frowned, trying to figure out where she had heard that name. John could tell from her expression she didn't know who he was. "I'm the one Shannon Morris told you about on the plane: the computer man."

Kaylee sighed as she stood. "Of course, now I remember."

His dark brown eyes met hers. "Shannon told me you were pretty, but somehow the picture before me is much clearer."

"Thank you, Mr. Smith!"

"Please, call me John."

"Okay, John. My computer is right over there, if you need to check it out."

John sat down at the computer. "How do you like Stone River, Miss Shell?"

"Please, call me Kaylee and I love Stone River."

John worked on the computer for about ten minutes and stated, "That's about it. If you have any problems call me." John muttered as he wrote his number on a piece of paper, folded it and handed it to Kaylee. "Call me." Terra entered the room, and he instantly added, "I think you'll enjoy this new system."

"I'm sure I will, thank you so much, Mr. Smith." Kaylee tucked the paper in her shirt pocket and didn't think about it again until that night when she was undressing. She changed into her pajamas and headed to the kitchen for a bowl of chili. On the way back to her room, Kaylee stared up at Ellen and said, "I trust you had a good day and will have a good night." She paused, then added, "I wonder what our class will find out about you. Don't worry, Ellen, I'll be as merciful as possible."

Somehow, she had managed to stir clear of allowing Jeffrey to overtake her mind. Adam, however, was a different story. Remembering his tender caress, she touched her shoulder. Slowly moving her fingertips to her neck and her lips, her eyes closed as her body tingled from the memory of his body pressed to hers. Kaylee lay back on the bed and moved restlessly, fighting the urge to call him to come lie with her until morning. Instantly, she sat up, wiping the sweat from her face as the music began to play in the distance.

Frantic, she made her way to the bathroom and held the cold cloth to her face. She gradually raised her eyes and looked in the mirror. Moaning, she wiped a tear from her cheek. "What is going on?" she asked.

In the dining room, Kaylee looked strongly up at Ellen. "You're up to your tricks are you, Mrs. Hilmar?" Kaylee continued to talk to the portrait as she moved to the fireplace. "So, you like my music, do you? Well, hear this, I don't care if it plays all flipping night and day. Especially, since it's my CD and you know I like it." She took hold of the mantel and shouted, "Goodnight, Ellen."

Kaylee slid her hand to the side of the mantel to bring it down, but stopped when her fingertips felt something cold touching them. Her eyes widened and her breath escaped her for a moment. She pushed her hand back and wrapped her fingers around a bronze skeleton key.

"What's this?" Kaylee looked intently at the old key. Slowly fixing her eyes on Ellen, Kaylee mumbled, "Would this be the key to your heart?" Immediately, Kaylee felt the hair on her arms rise as she felt the presence of someone standing nearby.

She turned. No one was there. Yet, she felt confident someone was staring directly at her. Kaylee rubbed her fingers over the key and whispered, "Just where do you fit in this house? I will find out." She looked at Ellen one last time before passing through the doorway. "If you're the one that's doing all of this, please stop for the night," she said softly. "I need some sleep. As far as the music goes, I'm too tired to care, just let it play."

To her surprise, Kaylee slept like a baby.

Chapter Thirty-Two
Kaylee's Contact

The next day, Kaylee arrived at school refreshed, though she now believed an entity was dwelling in the estate. As she walked through the hallway, she was greeted by Nick near her classroom. She listened as he laughed and mentioned something about Donna, but she couldn't focus on what he was saying. His conversation ended with asking her to dine with him and Donna that evening at seven-thirty. Without really thinking about it, she accepted and entered her classroom.

After her junior class had cleared the room, Kaylee was writing on the board when John Smith knocked on the door. She motioned for him to enter.

"Miss Shell?"

"Mr. Smith. How are you?"

"I'm fine."

"Did you need to check something on the computer?"

He stopped in front of her desk and spoke low, "I thought you would call me last night."

Kaylee frowned and asked, "Really?"

"Yes."

"Please, refresh my memory as to why." She said.

He leaned a tad toward her and whispered, "I'm your contact."

Feeling confused, Kaylee tilted her head and asked, "Okay, but, contact for what?"

"For, Mr. Cullman."

Kaylee asked, "Oh that's why you said call me?"

"Yes. I figured Terra may have sidetracked you."

"She did. The phone number you gave me..."

He interrupted. "That's my cell number."

While they were talking, some of the students came into the room.

"Call me later," John said. "If you have any problems, I should be here another couple of weeks."

"I will and thank you. Please pardon my scattered thoughts. I'm just taking in so many new things right now."

"Of course, after a few days you will be good as new." He nodded and left the classroom.

Betty smiled at Kaylee as she passed her desk. "He is so good looking, rugged and what about those brown eyes? I would check him out if I were you."

Kaylee smiled. "Handsome, but not really my type," she said.

Betty raised her brows and muttered, "You'll check him out. I can see it in your eyes."

At lunch, Nick informed Kaylee their dinner plans would have to be postponed. Something had suddenly come up and he and Donna would be out of town until Friday.

Chapter Thirty-Three

Light Left On

Kaylee waited until nine o'clock to call John, hoping Adam would drop by, but he didn't.

Finally, she called John, eager to hear what he had to say. Kaylee wanted to know more about the mansion and the woman who had rented the house before her.

When he answered the phone, he groaned in a low voice, "Hello."

"Is this John Smith?" she asked.

He cleared his throat a couple times. "Yes . . . Kaylee?"

"Yes, did I call too late?"

"No, I just fell asleep while watching television. I'm glad you called. I spoke with Martin earlier, and he asked if we had made contact. I told him I thought you would call me tonight."

Kaylee felt a little uneasy about opening her thoughts to a stranger. "Tell me, John, what am I supposed to share with you?"

"I'm here to see to your well-being and to provide any services that you might need. How are things going for you thus far?"

Kaylee wanted to keep things to a minimum, so she only shared about the student's investigation on Stone River's history. Afterward, she assured him that she would be in touch.

***

Kaylee turned the lamp off and pulled up the covers under her arms, hoping for some much needed sleep. However, her thoughts were so numerous, sleep evaded her.

The silence was broken by the large wind chimes that hung on the side porch. Strong winds had picked up, blowing the chimes profusely.

Recalling the half-bottle of red wine from a couple of nights earlier, she got up and started down the hall, pausing when she observed a dim, blue light emanating from the dining room, a light she was becoming very familiar with since its brightness emitted from the top of Ellen Hilmar's portrait.

After a couple of deep breaths, Kaylee found herself walking to the entrance of the grand room. Ellen's eyes appeared to follow her as she moved close to the fireplace. Kaylee gasped as a breeze filled the room, causing the hand-painted globes on the chandelier to vibrate.

Kaylee fixed her eyes on Ellen's and demanded, "Is it you who's doing all of this? What is it you want?" She rubbed her face and moaned. "How crazy am I becoming? I'm talking to you like you're hearing every word I say. You're just a painting and nothing more. But since I'm on a roll, I'll inform you of another thing that bothers me. For some odd reason, I'm starting to feel totally calm and relaxed in this house. Before, I was practically shaking out of my shoes."

Recalling the key she had found a couple of nights before, Kaylee placed her fingertips on the chilled stone and glided them down the mantel until she felt the cool metal. She locked her fingers around the key and brought it to the pale light and stared at it. Suddenly, she held the key toward the painting and said, "I bet, like the key itself, it unlocks something ancient. Am I right?"

Instantly, Kaylee found herself looking toward the magnificent staircase that was barely visible in the blue light. Carrying the key, she gradually moved up each wooden step to the second level of the house for the first time. Upstairs she ran her hand against the wall, searching for a light switch. Finding one, she flicked it on. Feeling extremely nervous, she wiped the corners of her mouth and moved toward the first door.

After steadying her hand, she pushed the key into the lock, but the key wouldn't turn. Instantly, she shifted her eyes from left to right. An eerie feeling swept over her, as though someone was watching her every move. After a deep breath, she hurried to the next door. It too did not open. She continued down the hall, trying the key in every lock to no avail. Just as she pushed the key into the last door, her body jerked at what sounded like a knock on the door downstairs. Her hand trembled as she pulled the key from the lock and dropped it in her robe pocket and hurried down the stairs.

Stopping at the bottom of the stairs to catch her breath, she waited to see if there would be another knock. The grandfather clock chimed; it was 3:15 a.m.

Her mind raced. Who could be knocking in the middle of the night? Kaylee gasped when a louder knock echoed through the foyer. This time a voice called out, "Kaylee, it's Adam."

Kaylee exhaled a sigh of relief and opened the door. "Adam! What is it?

Adam removed his hat and softly said, "I need to talk with you."

Kaylee pulled her robe together. "Can't it wait until morning?"

Adam's brows tightened. "No, it can't! May I please come in?"

Kaylee hesitated for a brief moment. "Okay." Kaylee pointed toward the living room. "Would you like to sit?"

Adam looked at the portrait and then the staircase. Kaylee swallowed hard, realizing she had forgotten to turn the light off at the top of the stairs.

Kaylee started to the grand room, but paused and asked, "What's so important that it has to be said at three thirty in the morning?"

Adam placed his hand on his hip and snapped, "From the looks of things, I didn't wake you from a restful sleep."

Kaylee instantly turned to face him. Through squinted eyes, she surveyed his stern face as her lips tightened.

Adam hit his hat against his leg. "Look, Kaylee, it doesn't matter to me what you do in this house; however, Dotty is a different story. I felt you should be aware of that. What if it would have been her at the door instead of me? She would have seen the light at the top of the stairs. Besides that, she reports to the town council on occasion about what goes on here at the estate."

Kaylee's face muscles tensed as she stared at Adam. "Only Dotty?" she asked in a suspicious tone.

His eyes squinted. "What does that mean?"

Kaylee pointed at him. "It means exactly what I just asked, Adam. Do you report to the town council?"

"Yes . . . yes, I do report to them . . . if I need something out of the ordinary for the Estate and to pick up my paycheck once every two weeks. So, tell me, Kaylee, what did you mean the other night asking if I was spying on you, too? Where did that come from?"

Kaylee lowered her head. "Maybe we better talk. Let's sit," she offered as they entered the grand room.

Chapter Thirty-Four

Previous Teacher

Adam nestled back in the overstuffed chair and stared at Kaylee sitting across from him. "Kaylee, there are some weird things going on lately. The most bizarre of all is that I seem to be right in the middle of everything."

"What do you mean?" she asked.

"I mean it's not like me to do bizarre things." Adam ran his fingers through his hair as his tone of voice weakened a bit. "I'm obsessed with you. Night and day, you rule my mind. It's as though I've known you for a very, very long time. I look for every opportunity to spend just one more minute with you. I can smell your perfume all the time. No matter what I'm doing, I can feel your soft body pressed against mine. Tell me, Kaylee, how weird is that?"

Kaylee leaned back as her eyes grew wide. "Is that the way you felt over the other poor woman that lived here before me?"

"No! The other woman was nice, but I rarely saw her. She only lived here for a short while and left without notifying anybody."

Kaylee turned toward Adam and asked, "She didn't even tell the school that she was leaving?"

"No. As far as I know, she actually left in the middle of the night!"

"Do you know where she was from or where she may have gone after she left Stone River?" Kaylee questioned.

He shook his head. "I don't have a clue."

Kaylee massaged her temples as she stared at him. "Tell me, Adam, why didn't anyone tell me about that teacher?"

Adam shook his head. "I don't know. What difference does it make?"

"There's some kind of cover-up going on in this town concerning this estate!"

"If there is a cover-up, I know nothing about it, but I will tell you, Tim Dodd told me not to say anything about the woman. Since I'm not one to do everything I'm told, I'll tell you she was a young woman and her name was Lola Barnes. She said her family lived in Albany, New York." Adam looked toward the dining room, squinted and said, "Did you turn the light on over that picture?"

Kaylee looked at the painting and muttered softly, "No . . . no, I didn't."

"So, there have been some unusual things going on."

Kaylee confessed, "Yes, there have been many things." Kaylee lowered her eyes, then faced Adam. "I pray I can trust you, Adam. Right now, I'm afraid to trust anyone."

"I feel the same way!" Adam said. "I need to trust someone, and I want that someone to be you."

Kaylee got up from the chair and walked to the dining room. "I'm going to be honest with you, Adam. I . . . I continue to find little things like this lying around." Kaylee took the key from her robe pocket and held it out to Adam.

He ran his fingers across the top of it. "An old key?"

"Yes. I found it on the mantel under Ellen's portrait. Tonight, before you knocked, I found myself going up the stairs and trying to open each door with it. Tell me, Adam, why is every door on the second level locked? What's inside the rooms? I'm going to find out."

Adam took hold of Kaylee's shoulders and said, "Don't let Dotty catch you. She is the keeper of this house, and I mean that literally."

Kaylee's eyes met Adam's.

"Kaylee, I have to know, do you think of me at night when you're curled up in your bed? Are all your dreams of me? I can hardly sleep for thinking about you. I wake up in a sweat, breathless as though I've run for miles to get to you. Do you have those same feelings about me? Tell me, Kaylee, do you?"

Trembling, Kaylee said, "Do I think of you? Tonight, I couldn't sleep. Many things filled my mind, yet you overrode them all. I could feel your fingertips on my shoulders and the warmth of your breath as your lips neared mine. I could feel your strong hand pulling me so close to you I could hardly breathe. I didn't dream about you, I felt you while I was wide-awake. Yet, my heart loves another."

Adam's raised his brows in surprise. "You . . . you have a boyfriend? I thought you were . . . ah . . . I didn't know."

Kaylee threw her hands up and explained, "That's just it. Having a boyfriend makes this all the more confusing. When I came to Stone River, no one could have ever convinced me that I would have given another man a second glance. I've gone way past the glancing stage with you and the memories of Jeffrey are beginning to get cloudy."

Adam sighed. "His name is Jeffrey?"

"Yes. Jeffrey and I have been together for a very long time."

"Kaylee, what's going on here? You were talking about secrets a few minutes ago. It sounds as though you have your own treasure chest of secrets. When were you going to tell me about Jeffrey? Forget Jeffrey! Why did you really come to Stone River?"

Kaylee played with her fingers. "Please, promise me what I'm about to tell you will be in strictest confidence."

"Of course, I won't say anything! I'm not a fool."

Chapter Thirty-Five
Kaylee Explains Mission

*K*aylee took a deep breath and began, "I work for a man who lives in Raleigh. His name is Martin Cullman. Jeffrey is his grandson. Mr. Cullman sent me here on assignment."

"Assignment?" Adam frowned. "Do you work for the CIA or something? What kind of assignment?"

"Let me explain," Kaylee insisted. "Martin wanted me to investigate two things. One is the disappearance of two Lakota Indians—"

Adam interrupted, "Two Lakota Indians! What Indians?"

Kaylee scratched her temple and responded, "Oh, this isn't a recent case. This one goes all the way back to the late 1800s. Roy Hilmar and Jake Boone had hired someone who came out on the wagon train with them to be the sheriff of Stone River. My understanding is that there were two deputies also. Roy and Jake fought against a tribe of Lakota who made their home at what is now called the Bend."

"That's out where Kitty Snow lives," Adam said.

"Exactly. My senior class is going out to the Bend for a field trip Saturday morning, weather permitting, to discuss some of the events. Charlie LittleHawk is going to tell us about some of his ancestors who made their home at the Bend in that time period."

Kaylee continued to share what the rest of her class's quest consisted of and her plans for exposing their finds when the mission was finished.

Adam rubbed his chin. "Well, I guess I don't know you at all. So, what does any of this have to do with this Mr. Cullman?"

"That is the other reason I'm here. Martin Cullman thinks he's possibly Jake Boone's son."

Adam's eyes widened. "Are you talking about the Jake Boone who partnered with Roy Hilmar and created Stone River?"

Kaylee nodded. "Yes. Martin's mother died when he was 8. His father, Bob Cullman, whom his mother married after moving to North Carolina, never spoke of his mother's past. Bob sent Martin to the finest boarding schools. When Martin finished college, he went to live at his father's estate in Raleigh. He was a professor at Duke University until he retired at 70 years old.

"His father passed away in 1963 at 97 years old. At his father's death, Martin, being an only child, inherited everything, which included the farm that Bob's mother and father owned. Martin loved to go to the farm when he was a young boy and stay with his grandparents in the summer. Although his father died in 1963, Martin had never gone through his grandparent's belongings. Bob had left the house untouched after his parent's deaths. Even the furniture hadn't been moved. Martin decided, with my help, and my urging, that he should at least take a look in the attic. He knew his father had also stored several boxes and a couple of trunks that belonged to his mother in that loft. What we found caused Martin to arrange my trip to Stone River just a few weeks later.

"I went with him to the house one day, but when we got there, he decided not to even go inside. Maria, Martin's only child and the mother of my boyfriend, Jeffrey, compelled him to go back and at least look through what was stored there. Since Martin's daughter was away so much with her job, she asked Martin to take Jeffrey or me to help him with the task. Jeffrey had to go to Wilmington for a few days, so I assisted Martin.

"Martin was still hesitant to go inside the house the second time. When we started to unlock the attic door, he became visibly shaken. Before we went upstairs, he said, 'I feel when we go up those steps, it will change you and me forever.' We looked without success through what I thought was almost everything, when Martin saw what appeared to be an old trunk that was covered with a black wool coat. He stared at the trunk for several minutes before he would even touch it. I asked if he wanted me to open it. He nodded for me to go ahead.

"When I opened the trunk, we found his mother's wedding dress, jewelry and a brush and comb set. In the bottom of the trunk, there was a large stack of old letters that had never been mailed. We opened the letters, which were all written by his mother to a Jake Boone in Stone River, North Dakota. In the letters, she told him how much she loved and missed him. Clara then proceeded to tell Jake that she was going to have his baby. She said, 'With the money you gave me, I will see that your baby will want for nothing.'

"His mother dated every letter. One of the letters was written on the baby's birthday, which was the same day that Martin was born. His thoughts were in utter confusion."

Adam exhaled. "You . . . you really mean . . . that Jake Boone might be . . . Martin's daddy?"

Kaylee nodded. "Yes. Martin decided that if he was going to find out whether this Jake Boone indeed was his father, he'd better do it soon. The reason being, Martin had just turned 89 years old."

"That would be a totally, inconceivable discovery."

"That's for sure," Kaylee said. "In several of the letters, his mother also wrote about two Lakota Indians who had mysteriously disappeared. For some reason, the disappearance of the two Indians stuck in Martin's mind. As a matter of fact, he wanted me to find out about the Indians as much as he wanted to find out if Jake Boone was his father.

"It was obvious that it bore on his mother's mind because she mentioned the Indians being murdered a number of times. In one letter she said, 'I wonder if the law might have brought Roy to justice for murdering them.' Then she boldly declared, 'I hope Roy burns in hell for not only murdering the Indians, but also for stealing Jake's gold.'"

"Give me a minute, Kaylee," Adam said. "This is a lot to take in!"

"I know, but I want you to know all this, Adam."

"Please, don't misunderstand, I want to know. It's just a little overwhelming. Please continue. I want to hear every word."

"I was told that Roy cheated Jake out of a fortune of gold. Although they were partners, Roy was the one who handled the books and business while Jake saw to the manual labor. When Jake found out that Roy was stealing from him, he confronted Roy. Of course, Roy denied the whole thing and Jake, being slow where business was concerned, backed away from his charge.

"Clara wrote about Roy sending Jake and his men several times to clear the Indians out of the Bend area. Jake would always end up feeling sorry for them and did not complete the task. One of the Indians of that tribe was named Wind Dancer, and his brother was named Moving Cloud.

"Wind Dancer was second in command of the tribe. His father, Black Bear, was the chief. The Lakota tribe wanted to maintain peace because of the many soldiers who had already moved into the area. They were tricking the chiefs into signing a treaty that would force them to live on the Sioux Reservation. The chiefs had a choice whether to sign or not. And not all the Indians signed the treaty—Black Bear, being one of them who decided not to sign but to stay on their land."

"Yes," Adam said. "I knew that Black Bear didn't sign the treaty."

Kaylee stood and stretched her back. She groaned, sat down and continued, "The bad thing that came with making that decision was more abuse than they could have possibly imagined. Yet, the cause for most of the abuse wasn't the soldiers. It was Roy

Hilmar and Jake Boone. They made Black Bear and his tribe's lives a living hell. Black Bear didn't want to draw attention to him or his people. So, his tribe took lots of cruel abuse in order to stay on the land that was home to them.

"Roy Hilmar obviously didn't care about the Indians. He wanted their land at the Bend, where a vast amount of the gold was located. Clara's letter said, 'Roy himself went out to deal with the Lakota at the Bend. If Jake couldn't kill them, he would.'

"It was soon after when Black Bear's sons disappeared. Black Bear didn't see Roy kill his two sons, but he knew he did. Wanting to try and live by the white man's laws, he rode into Stone River and confronted the sheriff, accusing Roy of murdering his sons. Of course, the sheriff wasn't going to turn on the man who paid his salary. So, nothing was ever done."

Adam leaned back in his chair. "So, Roy owned the local sheriff?"

"It would appear so," Kaylee said. "I was to come to Stone River as a teacher, which I am, and while here, to try to find out anything I could out about Jake Boone and the demise of Wind Dancer and Moving Cloud. Mr. Cullman arranged everything for me. He didn't have to wait long before a teaching position came open, which aligned with the Hilmar Estate coming open and for rent. Knowing now that the former teacher had been living here at the estate, I understand the timing.

"Martin had no clue that Ellen Hilmar, herself, might still be occupying the house, which I'm beginning to believe is true. There was no mention of the Hilmars having a daughter. Speaking of Jenny, no one has mentioned her except the day I moved into the house. Rick and Terra said something about the cost of having the face of the clock designed. Adam, do you know what happened to her?"

Adam leaned back in his chair and raked his fingers through his hair. "I was told Jenny Lynn died when she was 6. Some say she died when her horse threw her and it broke her neck. I've also heard her death was mysterious. I don't think anyone knows exactly what happened to her. About the clock, the story goes that Roy was so grief stricken about Jenny he was determined to frame her face in time. He said, 'Her time on earth was so short that I am going to bring Jenny Lynn and time together.' Thus, the clock."

Kaylee shook her head. "How can someone be so gentle in one sense and so cruel in another?"

Adam shrugged. "I can't answer that, but I would like to ask you a question."

"Sure."

Adam anxiously tapped his finger on the arm of the chair. "Are you a teacher or a private investigator? What is your professional title?"

Kaylee managed a slight grin. "I'm both. I graduated with honors in both fields. My credentials, however, didn't prepare me for a haunted house."

Adam squinted in disbelief. "Does Jeffrey mind you being here? Especially, if there's a possibility of you being hurt."

Kaylee shrugged. "I chose to come here. I'm sure Jeffrey cares, but this was my decision."

"Did Jeffrey . . .?"

172

"Did Jeffrey what?" Kaylee asked.

Not clear on things, Adam shook his head and muttered, "Nothing."

Kaylee yawned and rubbed her face. "I'm so tired." She looked at the clock. "Oh my, it's five thirty."

Adam stood. "I'm sorry for keeping you up."

Kaylee patted Adam's chest. "Don't be sorry. Thanks for warning me about the light visible at the top of the stairs. I'm tired physically, but I'm relieved for you to know why I'm here. I will admit, I'm stunned how some things just seem to be falling into place. Like my students uncovering so many details about the people I'm here to investigate. Martin is so concerned that I may be hurt by someone or something."

Adam stroked her cheek. "I can't imagine anyone being against you." He tenderly kissed her forehead, her temples and her lips. As his mouth closed over hers, she put her arms around his neck, drawing him nearer still. There was such intensity in the way he pressed his lips to hers. He held her so tight, anticipating her movements. She pulled closer, inhaling sharply. Adam's breathing intensified as he caught her mouth in a firm, passionate kiss.

"Adam . . ." she murmured against the pressure of his lips, reaching up to feel the thick column of his neck and the silkiness of his hair. He answered, but she couldn't understand his words. She didn't need to. Her body and mind were being consumed with a longing she had never experienced with such infatuation. She kissed him back with an unbridled passion.

Adam picked her up and carried her down the hall to the bedroom. Kaylee unbuttoned his shirt, pulled it from his shoulders and dropped it to the floor. Adam ravished her with kisses as he removed her robe. He picked her up and gently laid her on the bed. Her heart pounded as he covered her with his muscled body. Gasps of passion filled the room.

Chapter Thirty-Six

Dotty Finds Out about the Meeting

𝒯he sound of someone closing the kitchen door stopped their passion from being fulfilled. Kaylee gave a short gasp when Dotty called out, "Miss Shell, it's Dotty." Panic filled Kaylee's eyes as she quickly put her robe on and straightened her hair.

"Adam, I'll keep her in the kitchen. You go out the side door."

Adam grabbed her shoulders and kissed her one last time. Kaylee hurried down the hall. Kaylee's breath stopped when she saw Adam's coat on the floor. She grabbed the coat, raced to her room and threw it in her closet.

"Miss Shell," Dotty called out louder still.

"Yes, Dotty, I'll be right there." Kaylee took a deep breath, hurried down the hall and cut her eyes at the portrait. The light over the painting was no longer burning. Breathing a sigh of relief, Kaylee proceeded into the kitchen.

Dotty was taking eggs from the refrigerator.

"No, no, Dotty, there's no need to fix breakfast. I'm not hungry."

Dotty glanced at Kaylee and said, "I thought maybe you would be hungry. I was up early this morning and saw lights on in the house."

Kaylee shrugged. "I had some work I needed to finish before class this morning."

Dotty pointed toward the coffee maker. "Would you like a cup of coffee or a glass of juice?"

All of a sudden, Kaylee remembered the light at the top of the stairs. How could she possibly go up the stairs without Dotty hearing her? Kaylee massaged the back of her neck. "Coffee would be wonderful. Thank you, Dotty."

Dotty moved toward the counter, "I'll put it on right away," she said. "You look a bit pale. Are you all right, Miss Shell?"

"Yes, I'm just a little tired."

"Will you be eating in tonight?"

Kaylee nervously tapped the counter with her finger. "I'm glad you asked. I would like for you to make another large pot of chili just like the one you made before. It was great!"

"Will you be having guests?" Dotty asked, as she poured the water into the coffee pot.

Kaylee chuckled. "Yes! My senior class is having a meeting here tonight—"

Dotty turned like lightning and interrupted, "Excuse me, Miss Shell, but do you really think that's a good idea? I mean the house is filled with priceless antiques."

Kaylee tilted her head and frowned. "There are a lot of antiques, but most of them are big pieces and not something that will fit in a coat pocket. Besides, I trust my guests are not a bunch of thieves."

Dotty cleared her throat. "I surely didn't mean that in a bad way. It's just I'm responsible for this house and its contents."

Straight faced, Kaylee replied, "Trust me, Dotty. I'll see that nothing is lifted or broken. The meeting will be at seven. We'll have our chili in the kitchen."

Dotty tightened her lips. "Yes, Miss Shell," she muttered, "would you like for me to prepare a dessert?"

"No, thank you. I'll pick up ice cream sandwiches on the way home."

Dotty took a cup from the cabinet, filled it with coffee and placed on the counter beside Kaylee. "As you wish, madam." She then turned to leave the room.

Kaylee called out, "Dotty, there is one more thing."

Dotty looked back across her shoulder at Kaylee. "Yes, Miss Shell?"

I have a request. "When I'm home, I would appreciate your knocking and allow me to answer the door before entering the house."

Dotty lips tightened. "I'm sorry if I haven't pleased you."

"It isn't that you haven't pleased me. I know you make a point of calling out when you enter the house, but a knock from now on will be expected. Sometimes, I'm in the shower and don't hear you call out. There are times I'm asleep. It's just something that I, being from the South, have been taught all my life: knock before entering."

"I really don't think it has anything to do with where or how you're raised, North or South," Dotty said. "It has to do with the fact I've never had to knock, and therefore, I don't. However, from now on, I will try and remember to do so."

In a calmer tone, Kaylee said, "Dotty, I'm not trying to hurt your feelings. I really appreciate all you do for me."

Dotty's brows tightened. "For you? I don't do it for you. I do it for the mistress of the house."

Unsure of what Dotty meant by the comment, Kaylee concluded, "At any rate, thank you in advance for everything."

Dotty sighed. "If you're not wanting breakfast, I think I'll wait until later to straighten the house." Dotty put her sweater on and quickly left.

Kaylee breathed a sigh of relief and raced up the stairs to turn the light off. Kaylee could tell Dotty was upset, but narrow escapes like the one she and Adam had just encountered could not be tolerated. She didn't want to be caught in an embarrassing situation and left with trying to explain it.

Chapter Thirty-Seven

Rick and Dotty Agree

Kaylee's adrenaline raced as she hurried to get ready for work. After locking the door, she remembered Adam's coat. "Oh Lord!" she muttered, hurrying to her room to retrieve the coat and put it in her car.

Kaylee's mind filled with thoughts of Adam as she pulled into the school parking lot. After taking the keys from the ignition, she leaned her head forward, resting it on the steering wheel. "Kaylee, what's wrong with you?" she whispered. "Why couldn't I control myself with Adam?"

A tap on the window caused her to jump. Thankful it was Terra, Kaylee managed a smile. When she opened the door, Terra patted her shoulder and said, "Kaylee, you look exhausted."

Kaylee stretched and replied, "I didn't sleep very well last night. I had a lot on my mind. You know, when you're dog tired and realize that sleep time is slipping away and if you don't get to sleep, the alarm is going to go off telling you your sleep time is over."

"Yeah! Lately a hunk by the name of Adam has managed to keep me awake," Terra swooned. "When you last spoke with him, did he happen to mention my name?"

Kaylee giggled. "No, but I've barely seen him since the night we all had dinner together."

Terra put her hand on her hip. "Really?" she said.

"Yes, really," Kaylee said, as she got out of her Explorer. "He doesn't just hang out at the house all the time. Usually he doesn't come around unless he needs something."

The bell rang and Terra hurried down the hall to her classroom.

Kaylee hadn't noticed Rick until he spoke. "Good morning, Kaylee."

"Good morning."

He moved close. "I don't suppose you had wild passionate dreams about me last night, did you?"

Kaylee crossed her arms. "I'm afraid not."

Rick stopped, put his hand on Kaylee's arm and said, "I hear your class is having a meeting at your place tonight."

"Yes, the students are all excited."

Rick's sober look prompted Kaylee to ask, "Is something wrong?"

Rick shrugged. "I'm not sure having the meeting at the Estate is a good idea."

"That's strange," Kaylee muttered. "Dotty said the same thing. Why is that?"

Rick replied, "I just don't think it's a good idea."

Kaylee squinted. "Now, Rick, if you feel that strongly about it, there has to be a reason. What is it?"

Rick sighed. "I'm not sure having Paulette in the house is a good idea. She has some pigheaded thoughts about the mansion being her grandmother's. I just don't want to stir the pot, if you get my meaning."

Kaylee patted his arm and responded, "Thanks for warning me, Rick, but Paulette and I have already worked all that out, and she's happy about the meeting being there."

Rick tightened his lips and, with a low-pitched voice filled with sudden irritation, growled, "You may think you have everything under control, but you don't. The Hilmars are looking for any good cause to get back into that house, and it's not going to happen!"

Kaylee furrowed her brows. "First of all, what is it that you think I don't have under control? Secondly, our meeting at the estate isn't going to stir anything. As far as the Hilmar's, wanting to take the Estate back is none of my concern. I have a senior class that is exceptionally well behaved; yet, because I want to have a meeting at my home, people are all concerned. Explain your thoughts to me, or I'm going to class."

Rick put his face close to hers. "Be careful, Kaylee. You don't want to upset the wrong people."

Kaylee demanded, "Who are the wrong people, Rick? So, I can stay out of their way."

"Just be careful." Rick turned and walked down the hall.

Chapter Thirty-Eight
Kaylee's Request for John

When her senior class arrived, Kaylee glanced across the room for a moment. Many questions raced through her mind. Everyone stared at Kaylee, waiting for her to speak. After a moment, she stood in front of her desk, crossed her arms and began, "I need to ask each one of you if you agree with the method of the examination of Stone River's history and people. If you have a problem with it, now's the time to speak up. This method isn't set in stone. There are many different ways we can explore this assignment—"

Charlie interrupted and insisted on taking a private written vote. Kaylee agreed. The vote was unanimous to continue their pursuit as planned.

After school, Kaylee stopped on the way home to buy ice cream sandwiches. She ran into John Smith in the store parking lot. They chatted for a moment, and John asked, "Do you need anything?"

Kaylee was hesitant to answer.

"Kaylee, please don't be afraid to trust me."

Kaylee itched her nose and explained, "Trust doesn't come easy, John."

John helped Kaylee put her package in her car as he spoke quietly. "I'll start by saying that you're causing quite a stir with you class project. Working in the school does have its advantages. You hear everything—parents and teachers talking about their children, parents asking questions the teacher doesn't want to answer. I would be careful around Nick Long. I overheard his secretary say Nick got a call from the main man, whoever that is, and he demanded to see him right away. It had something to do with the new history teacher. The man doesn't live in Stone River, even though he somehow runs the town. He calls his orders into the town council and they jump like rabbits to obey his command. The fact the call was about you proves you've penetrated the beehive and the drones are beginning to stir in order to protect their domain.

"You see, Kaylee, I can be of help if you'll allow me to do so. I better be going. Of course, I could always have the good people of Stone River, who are more than likely watching us right now, think I find you very attractive and was asking you out to dinner."

Ignoring John's comment about taking her to dinner, Kaylee moaned, "You're right John. I should allow you to help me. There is something you can do for me."

"Good. What is it?"

Kaylee put her hand on his upper arm. "I would like for you to ask one of the teachers out."

John frowned. "Who and why?"

"Her name is Terra Wallace. She's pretty and fun to be around. She has her eye on Adam, but I need you to distract her for me. Pay her some attention. Ask her out or whatever you need to do."

John paused for a brief moment and said, "Oh, yes, I know who she is. May I ask the reason for the distraction?"

"I don't know how much she knows about whatever is going on. She's tight with the group that took me to the Estate when I first arrived. As a matter of fact, she picked me up at the airport. I need time with my students, and I can't do anything if she wants to start hanging at the house every day, hoping Adam will show up." Kaylee paused and rubbed her forehead. "That sounds so crude."

"Is that the only reason?" John asked.

"What other reason could there be?"

"Perhaps you want Adam's attention. Guard your emotions, Kaylee."

Kaylee closed her eyes. "I shouldn't have said even that much."

When Kaylee started to walk away, John touched her shoulder and said, "Please don't feel that way. If you need me any time, please call."

Kaylee glanced at him briefly. "I will. Thanks."

Chapter Thirty-Nine
Admiring Ellen's Beauty

Kaylee hurried home to prepare for the meeting. The aroma of Dotty's chili filled the house. Dotty had set a long folding table near the breakfast nook and put place settings on the bar as well.

It was dark by six o'clock and the wind was beginning to pick up. Kaylee passed by the dining room, stopped and backed up. She looked at the portrait of Ellen and said, "Ellen, I hope you don't mind having guests tonight, and by the way, the meeting won't be held in the kitchen, but in here, so you may be a part."

Kaylee had just lit the fireplace and finished bringing everything from the kitchen and setting the grand table when she heard someone knocking. She hurried to answer it, anticipating one of her students, but to her surprise it was Adam.

Kaylee smiled at Adam and asked him to come in. The moment he closed the door, he took her in his arms and kissed her long and fervently.

She pushed him back. "We can't. It's time for my class to be arriving."

"I've wanted so desperately to see you. I couldn't think of anything but you all day. Your lips and—"

Kaylee interrupted, "You need to go before anyone else arrives. By the way, I put your coat in my car. I parked at the side entrance. If you don't mind, go out the side, get your coat and lock the car door, please. And thank you."

Adam took her in his arms and touched his lips to hers, stroked her cheek and stared into her eyes. The stare was broken when they heard a car door close.

Trembling, Kaylee pushed him away and whispered, "Go, hurry."

Adam hurried down the hall and went out the side door. Kaylee opened the front door to greet her first guests, Betty and Eddie.

Betty looked around room and laughed aloud. "It sure feels good to be invited inside the mansion and not be thrown out!"

Kaylee asked Betty to be in charge of the coats and to put them on her bed. After everyone had arrived and was seated, Kaylee, Charlie and Paulette served the chili. The atmosphere was very relaxed. The students were laughing and kidding each other. Kyle, flirting with Paulette, winked at her and said, "Paulette, you would make a beautiful bride and we could make beautiful babies together and you could serve me chili every day. What do you say?"

Paulette punched his arm. "I say no, leave me alone, or I'll be spit in your chili." She put her arm around Charlie and said, "Now here's a real man. Charlie, you can serve me chili anytime."

Charlie chuckled. "It would be my pleasure."

Kaylee stood and crossed her arms. "Boys and girls, we're not here to play boyfriend, girlfriend. We're here for a meeting that I want to start right away. If everyone is through eating, let's take our dishes to the kitchen and gather back here at the table."

***

When Kaylee came back to the dining room, Sara Frank was staring up at Ellen's portrait. Kaylee came up beside her and asked, "Sara, what do you think of the mistress of this grand estate, Ellen Hilmar?"

"Wow! she's beautiful."

"That she is."

Paulette joined them. "Do either of you think I favor my great-grandmother?"

Sara smiled. "Not really," she said.

Kaylee patted Sara's shoulder. "Let's get started. We have a lot to cover tonight, and I don't want to rush through your findings."

When everyone was seated, Kaylee slapped her hands together and said, "Kyle, tonight, I would like for you and your group to get us started. Do you have anything new concerning the business end, regarding Roy Hilmar and Jake Boone. And I want to know if any of you have encountered negative responses from the people you've questioned about the subject."

Kyle began, "I can speak for my group by saying the only one who has reported anything that was sort of negative is Margie."

Kaylee nodded at Margie. "Okay, Margie, would you tell us any questions you ask that brought an unfavorable response?"

Rubbing her hands together, Margie said, "My mother said, 'You need to keep your nose out of the past.' I told her that it couldn't be a history class without the past. It's the past that makes our history."

Everyone applauded. "Great answer!" Kaylee said. "How did she respond to your thought?"

Margie placed her hands on the table. "I know this sounds weird, but after saying that, she kissed the top of my head and said, 'I know, sweetheart.'"

"Thank you, Margie. By the way, class, if anyone appears to be uncomfortable with a question you ask or they make you feel uncomfortable in any way, back off. With that said, I would love to hear any favorable replies to your questions?"

Kyle spoke up. "Miss Shell, my team has some favorable comebacks as well."

Kaylee nodded. "By all means, share."

Kyle cleared his throat and began. "I asked my grandmother if she knew anything about Roy and Jake, and she said, 'What I do know isn't great, but I will share it anyway.'

"It was interesting to learn that Roy and Jake first found gold at the River Bend. Their biggest problem with the gold was the Lakota lived almost on top of the gold. The big challenge was getting the Lakota to move so they could get access to the gold. Another thing we found out, almost right away, was that Roy and Jake wanted to establish many kinds of businesses in Stone River. They brought men and families to the area from all around to help with the building of the town. They hired three crews to build three buildings at the same time. A trading post, a sheriff's office and a hotel. The hotel was unimaginatively called Stone River Hotel. Stories have it that Roy, not Jake, had women brought in from various places and used the upper rooms of the hotel for a, pardon my crudeness, ladies, and you too, Paulette, for a whorehouse. Mom said, 'You better call it a brothel.' But for some reason it didn't fit. I just happen to think you all are old enough to hear the hard truth about it."

Paulette smirked playfully. "You'd better watch who you're picking on, Kyle." She pointed to Ellen's portrait. "My great-grandmother is watching. I don't think she'd like you talking trash around me."

Kyle winked at her. "Paulette, you took me wrong. I happen to love women who are high-spirited, and so did your great-grandfather. I would like to add, Ben found out from his neighbor that Jake was against bringing in the ladies of the evening to town and so was Jake's wife. Ellen, on the other hand, gave it her full support.

"The next three buildings to go up were Stone River Bank, Hilmar/Boone General Store and Hilmar/Boone Blacksmith and Metal works. Roy and Jake made a ton of money off the government in all those areas. They had the biggest blacksmith business in most of the western states. There were several Army posts and hundreds of soldiers in the surrounding areas, and they all brought their blacksmith needs to Jake and Roy. Their business grew so fast that two or three days a week, blacksmiths were sent out to the forts to work. In the meantime, Roy and Ellen began to build their dream home. You can look around at this house and see the massive wealth they were accumulating. Until our next gathering, that pretty well covers all we have for now."

Chapter Forty

Jake and Tammy's Estate

Kaylee stood and applauded. "Great job, Kyle's group! Awesome job! Lisa, I can't wait to hear what you and your team have to offer. Since your group is in charge of finding historical events, answer me this, we hear a lot about the Hilmar Estate, but what about Jake and Tammy Boone? Did they have a grand estate as well?"

Lisa looked through a couple of papers. "Yes, Miss Shell, they did have a grand estate. It was built on the west end of Stone River. From what we have gathered, Ellen and Tammy made house building and decorating a competition. If one bought a grand chandelier, the other had to have one a little bigger. They were both so rich by then, Roy and Jake allowed them to do as they pleased when it came to decorating the estates. Someone said, that Ellen often reminded Roy, 'It was my money that brought us west and got us started.' Tammy wasn't that way. From what we've been able to gather, she was a strong support to Jake in every way.

"There was one thing in which Tammy had the upper hand on Ellen, and that was having children. Tammy had eight children and Ellen only had one. It appears, Roy was away weeks, sometimes months at a time on business. Jake was home every night. I guess that explains that."

Kaylee asked, "Do you know what happened to the Boone's house? I haven't heard anyone mention the Boone's Estate at all."

Lisa continued, "After the birth of their eighth child, Tammy wanted to go back East and visit her aging mother and father and maybe bring them back with her to Stone River. Jake didn't like the idea of her making the trip without him; however, at her urging he agreed. While Tammy and the kids were away, the house mysteriously burned down. Everything was lost. With no house to come back to, Tammy's parents asked her to leave the children with them until she and Jake could get another house built. Upon completion, they would take, not a wagon train, but the newly made railway system and bring the children home and take a look at Stone River. The travel time would be much shorter and safer. Tammy agreed. From Saint Louis, she took the train all the way to Fort Abraham, and from there she took a stage on to Stone River.

"The irony is, Tammy had somehow forgotten how long it took to build and furnish the first mansion when she agreed to leave the children. On top of everything, there were so many hang ups with the rebuilding of the house. Two years passed and the house still wasn't complete. Tammy and Jake began to quarrel because everything was taking so long. She wanted the children back, but so did Jake. It was while they were building the house, Jake discovered Roy had not been honest with him in his handling of their money.

"Jake confronted Roy, who firmly denied any misdealings with the money. Tammy demanded to see the books. Roy hadn't listed but the first two years of their labor.

"Tammy could plainly see in those two years alone that Roy had taken a fortune from Jake. She was furious and wanted to take what they had and move back East. But Jake wouldn't hear of leaving the town he loved and had help build. Tammy could have cared less about staying in Stone River. She told Jake that she was going back East to get the kids, but she never returned. Jake received a letter from her two months later, which told of her decision not to come back to Stone River. Jake, willing to give her and the children up instead of departing his beloved Stone River, sent money to Tammy and the kids. He continued to send enough money so his family could live comfortably for the rest of all their days. He never saw Tammy or his children again. Jake never finished the house that he and Tammy had started to rebuild, but years later, as Stone River grew, the town council, led by Roy Hilmar, bought the place from Jake and completed it. Today it's our court/city building."

"What happened to Jake when his wife and children didn't return?" Kaylee asked.

Lisa raised her brows and said, "He never remarried, but tales floated around town that he often visited a young woman by the name of Clara Aims. She had come west, against her wishes, with her husband,

Brett Aims. He died suddenly of a heart attack a few months after arriving in Stone River. Clara was quite a bit younger than Jake. Because of the age difference, they had some strong disagreements. Even though they loved each other with a passion, Clara wanted to go back East. She missed her family. Jake loved her so much that he granted her wishes and sent her home with a handsome amount of his fortune. I might add that she was from a small town in North Carolina called Green River. Do you know the place, Miss Shell?"

Kaylee squinted. "Yes, I do. It's about ninety miles East of Raleigh. What happened to Jake after Clara went back East?"

"He was devastated. He never remarried or courted another woman. He died here in Stone River in 1923."

Eddie slapped his hands together. "What did you say? Courted? He never courted another woman? How do you court someone? Take them to trial or what?"

Everyone laughed.

Lisa frowned. "For your information, Eddie, I used that particular word because it fit the era we're talking about."

Acting like a hillbilly, Eddie put his arm around Betty. "Well, heck, does that mean me and you are courting, honey?"

Betty tilted her head and blinked her eyes. "Well, I reckon it does."

Kaylee laughed. "Okay, you two, let's get back on track. I am very eager to hear from Lori's team."

Chapter Forty-One

Wind Dancer

Lori stood and faced her team. "I want to start by thanking my team for all the hard work they've put into this assignment. It's really been a challenge, but so much fun. We've gone in a hundred different directions to find anything about the disappearance of the two Lakota Indians. So glad to report, we have found a few things that are pretty interesting.

"First, Paulette's grandmother, Thelma, told Paulette that Willie had told her on many occasions about a very handsome Lakota brave Ellen had met by the name of Wind Dancer. Even the servants talked about his beauty. Thelma said, 'His long black hair flowed in the wind as he rode his Appaloosa across the plains, and he was unusually tall for a Lakota brave. He wore an eagle claw necklace that he never removed. The necklace showed he was a gifted man and a mighty hunter. He had two sons. His wife died when giving birth to the second son. He never remarried, which was very unusual, because the Lakota took great pride in family and having many babies.' Paulette's grandfather said, 'That Black Bear named his first son Wind Dancer because even at 2 years old, his son danced with a passion and screamed like an eagle as he danced.'

"Moving Cloud, Wind Dancer's brother, was totally different. He was of a short stature and had the features of his people. He was married and had five children, long black hair that he braided, rode a black horse and kept a red ring painted around one of the horse's eyes. It seems we have just started to paint a picture of the two braves, but that sums it up for tonight. Hope to have more next time."

Kaylee smiled. "I am so impressed with the determination you all have displayed. With that kind of persistence, nothing will stop you from doing anything you set your mind to. I can hardly wait to hear what Charlie has to share on Saturday at the Bend."

Kaylee looked at her watch. "It's nine thirty and time has slipped away so fast. I have thoroughly enjoyed our meeting tonight. Before you go, I want you to stand and give yourselves a big hand. Great job, everybody."

After the applause, Kaylee ordered, "It's time to go home, everyone. Get some rest and be ready for our outing tomorrow. Be careful going home."

Eddie put his arm around Betty, laughed and said, "Did we have a fun date or what?"

Betty thought a moment. "Yeah! This is our best date ever."

Eddie frowned and mumbled, "I don't think I'd go that far. I mean, we had a good time but I can see it being better. Imagine me and you alone under a full moon snuggling close on a cold night."

Paulette shook her head. "I would imagine being alone with you on a cold night would be about the same as standing in a snow drift."

Eddie pinched her cheeks. "Paulette, you will never find out if you don't start giving me some respect."

Charlie put his arm around Paulette's shoulder. "Do you need a lift home?"

"No thanks, Charlie. I brought my car."

***

Kaylee walked out and said goodbye to everyone, at least she thought everyone had left. After closing the door, she was surprised to find Paulette standing in front of the fireplace staring up at Ellen. Kaylee joined her. "Ellen looks like a queen, doesn't she?"

Paulette rubbed her forearm. "Without a doubt. I look at her and wonder if half of the things I've heard about her are true."

"Are they things you want to believe?"

"Yes and no."

Kaylee put her hand on Paulette's shoulder. "Do you want to sit a while and talk about it?"

"Yeah, if you don't mind, I think I do."

Paulette stared at Ellen and asked Kaylee, "Did anyone tell you about Lola Barnes?"

"Lola Barnes? The name sounds familiar."

"She was our teacher before you came. She also lived here at the Estate."

"Really?"

"Yes."

Kaylee took a sip of tea. "Paulette, do you know why everyone is so closed mouth about Lola? I was also surprised to find out that Dotty and Adam live out back. I didn't find out about them until I arrived in Stone River."

Paulette put her hands in her jeans pocket. "Miss Shell, the town council consists of a bunch of evil men and women. Nick Long and Donna included."

In a serious manner, Kaylee asked, "I need to know, is Rick Owens on the town council?"

"Not to the degree as Nick and Donna are. When you say town council, you're more than likely thinking about a few men and a couple of women. That's not the case in the Stone River council. It's made up of about twenty top families, yet run by someone no one ever sees."

"Do you know who that someone is?"

"No, I don't because I'm not a part of the secret circle," Paulette muttered. "They made sure Grandmother and myself weren't a part. They pay themselves from the mass of money my great-grandmother, Willie Hilmar, left the town. I don't understand it, Kaylee. May I call you Kaylee?"

"Please do!" Kaylee said. "Why would your great-grandmother leave her fortune to the town instead of to Thelma and you? As I understand it, Thelma was her only child."

Paulette shook her head. "That's the trillion-dollar question. Someone in the council must have had something on her, or the family. Otherwise, she would have never cut her own daughter practically out of her will."

"I'm curious, Paulette, what is the Estate worth . . . if you don't mind my asking?"

Paulette shrugged. "Gosh! I don't know exactly, but at least a billion dollars."

"My heavens!" Kaylee gasped. "No wonder you're so upset."

"But, Kaylee, it's not just about the money. It's that someone stole it from us. There has to be a reason my great-grandmother would do that. Grandmother Thelma said, 'Grandmother Willie hated the council.' If that's true, then explain the whopping gift she gave them."

"Do you think Thelma may know the reason?"

"No, she doesn't. I've asked many times." Paulette looked at Ellen and said, "Grandmother Ellen, what do you think about someone other than your flesh and blood living in your grand home?"

Kaylee thought a moment and asked, "Were you going to say something else about Lola Barnes a moment ago?"

Paulette pressed her fingertips to her temples. "Boy, did I get sidetracked! I was going to say Lola left in the middle of the night. She had only been in the house a short while, and she began to complain that weird things were going on. Nothing outlandish at first, but little things, like music playing randomly. She said pounding sounds would wake her in the middle of the night. The last thing I heard she said was something about getting up one night to get a drink of water. When she came from the kitchen to the hall, she felt like someone was staring at her with such intensity, she began to tremble. She wanted to run out the front door, but for a few moments her feet wouldn't move.

"When she looked up, she said she saw the woman in the painting standing on the staircase just staring at her. Here's the part that broke my heart. She said, 'The woman began to cry uncontrollably and then disappeared, yet the sobbing sounds filled the house.' Lola said she was unable to sleep. A couple of days later, she left without telling anyone."

"Who did Lola tell about the things that were going on in the house?"

"At first, she told the council. However, when they gave the impression that Lola was nuts, she told Grandmother Thelma."

Kaylee tapped her lip with her finger. "What was Thelma's reaction?"

Paulette looked at Ellen. "She feels as I do. Grandmother Ellen had many secrets. What the secrets are, I don't know and Grandmother only knows bits and pieces. Let me add, if she knows something, she's never told me. I feel sure that Grandma Willie knew but wanted to protect the precious Hilmar name, which was top priority to her. Even if it meant giving the estate to a bunch of thieves. In order for Willie to give the Estate to someone other than her family, there must have been something substantial to carry that kind of persuasion. What was uncovered tonight is appalling. Roy was cheating his own partner when there was plenty for them both. One of the first three buildings built in Stone River was used for a whorehouse, and Great-grandpa Roy's dealings with the Indians were scandalous. These are things that a senior class could find out without too much trouble. God only knows what else will be discovered."

Kaylee put her hand on Paulette's. "Everything will work out for you in the end. I just feel it."

Paulette tilted her head. "How do you know? What do you mean you just feel it?"

Kaylee shrugged. "I guess I'm trying to encourage you. When you don't know what to say, you come up with whatever to sooth the person's emotions."

Paulette and Kaylee stood. Paulette walked over to the portrait. "Kaylee," she said, "has anything out of the ordinary been going on in the house since you've moved in?"

Kaylee didn't want to upset Paulette or give herself away, so she said no.

Paulette faced Kaylee. "I'm thrilled that we're doing the quest into Stone River's history. Now, I have to go home and get some rest before our big day tomorrow."

Chapter Forty-Two
Paulette's Last Name

$\mathcal{K}$aylee walked Paulette to the door. "Paulette, before you go, may I ask you a question?"

Paulette put her long, wool overcoat on. "Sure."

"The first day of school, I asked everyone to tell me their names. On my sheet, your name was Paulette Boone. You corrected me and told me that your name wasn't Boone, but Hilmar. Would you clear that up for me?"

As Paulette put on her gloves, she explained, "The report tonight that Jake never saw his children again was correct, but after his death, a couple of his children came to Stone River to bury their father. One of Jake's sons, Bob, made many trips to Stone River over the next several years. Bob and my mother had a wild fling, and I was the result. When my mother, Barbara, was seven months pregnant, Bob went back East and never returned. Mother died when I was 2. Grandma Thelma said, "Your mom grieved herself to death over a man that could have cared less about her." Why couldn't she have focused all those thoughts on me, her baby? I don't know Bob Boone, but I hate him with a passion for leaving my mother. I was so young when she died, I don't even have one memory of her."

"I'm so sorry, Paulette."

"Just as well, I guess I turned out just fine, thanks to Grandma Thelma."

Kaylee frowned. "Paulette, this may be the worst timing in the world, but may I ask one more question?"

Paulette shrugged. "Of course, why not? I seem to be on a roll talking tonight about all this chatter."

Kaylee's gaze intensified. "If Roy and Ellen had only one child and she died at age 6, how is it that Willie Hilmar, being married, carried on the Hilmar name . . . unless she married a Hilmar? Otherwise, Roy would need a son to do that."

Paulette massaged the back of her neck. "After Grandma Ellen's death, Roy had two more children by another woman. Her name was Judy Justice. Roy didn't marry her, but he did live with her until she died. Roy fathered a son and a daughter with Judy. Their son, Kevin, died at 3 years old of scarlet fever. Willie, his daughter and sole heir of Roy's estate, was my great-grandmother. She married Buster Hall but never took his last name and never gave her daughter, Thelma, his last name. She carried the Hilmar name with a pride that was unyielding. And why not, after all, Roy Hilmar and Jake Boone, both my grandfathers, built Stone River."

Kaylee took a deep breath and blew it out. "Good heavens, it sounds like a Peyton Place."

Paulette frowned. "I don't know about a Peyton Place, but I do know you have to think fast to keep up with all this mess. I don't know why I shared all of this with you tonight. I'm sure most of this won't come out in the class' report, yet for some reason I wanted you know." Paulette turned to leave, stopped and said quietly, "Miss Shell, if by chance you see Grandma Ellen, would you tell her that I love her? Even though, I never met her, I still love her."

"Of course, I will."

Tears welled in Paulette's eyes as she turned and walked to her car.

Kaylee watched as Paulette drove away, and then she went inside, only to find herself gazing up at Ellen. Her mind swirled with even more questions that had been planted by Paulette. Questions that left her more determined to find the answers. She was going to call Martin, but changed her mind . . . not tonight. Thoughts of Adam raced through her mind as she snuggled her pillow. Wanting to call and not doing so was a struggle, yet she knew she had to get some past-due sleep.

Chapter Forty-Three

Meeting at Nick Long's Office

The night passed swiftly, and the alarm clock sounded. Kaylee woke feeling like the night before had been a dream. Neither Dotty nor Adam had knocked and Martin hadn't called. Kaylee was so excited that the night's sleep had left her refreshed and ready to face the day. As she entered the school, the first person she saw was Nick Long, who wanted to see her in his office, right away.

"Sit down, Kaylee. I had Helen bring you a hot cup of coffee."

"Thank you, but to what do I owe this visit and a cup of coffee?"

"As you know, I had to go out of town a few days ago and meet with some people connected with the school. With all new teachers, of course, they want to know how they are doing and what they are doing in the order of the teaching curriculum of Fair Mount High School. They asked how you were doing. I told them about your class project and study of Stone River's history. They were a little concerned that you weren't using the regular study guide that our school uses. So, they wanted me to pass a message to you from them."

"What exactly is the message?" Kaylee asked.

"It's a very simple message. They said, "She needs to stay in the bounds of our teaching agenda."

Kaylee tilted her head and held back the urge to get in Nick's face. "Just what does that mean? Stay in the bounds of the school's teaching agenda?"

"I think it's very clear what the point is. Use your history books and remain in your classroom to do so and stop bothering people with all the questions your students are asking. Answer the questions you have from the history book."

Kaylee stood and held to the desk. "Nick, I want you to explain to me what the big deal is about a history lesson. You know as well as I do, teaching takes on many forms. So, what if I challenge my students to go outside the normal confines of the classroom to find answers? Who would know more about the history than many of the seniors who live here in Stone River? The trip to the Bend, Saturday, is nothing more than a field trip to explore Native American territory."

"I'm only saying what I was told to say, Miss Shell. It doesn't mean that I agree or disagree with their decision; nevertheless, I have to do as I'm told since they are my bosses. There will be no field trip on Saturday. If for no other reason, to appease the council."

Kaylee's frustration peaked. "Then maybe, I need to meet with the so-called council and explain in person the way I have chosen to study the town's history. By the way, Nick, my teaching of the guidelines is perfectly in bounds."

Nick stood and growled, "Kaylee, you need to consider carefully what I've just told you."

Kaylee leaned toward him, tightened her lips and said, "Is that a threat, Nick?"

Nick slapped his desk. "No, just a warning. If you teach at Fair Mount, you have rules to follow, and I don't make those rules. Do I make myself clear?"

"Nick, I will not be pushed around as long as I am doing nothing to deserve it, and I'm not. Now, if you'll excuse me, I need to get to class."

"No, Miss Shell, I have a better idea! Why don't you take the day off to consider what I've told you? Anticipating your negative response, I had a sub come in to teach your class today."

Kaylee frowned and snapped, "What's really going on, Nick? Is the council afraid of what we may find?"

"Take the day off, Miss Shell. Maybe you'll feel better Monday."

Kaylee left the office so aggravated her head was pounding. She thought of finding one of the students and telling what had happened. As she exited the building, she was elated when she saw Charlie LittleHawk walking through the parking lot. She told him what had happened. He insisted on taking the trip to the Bend regardless of what Nick thought. Kaylee assured him they were going, even if she had to say they went as friends for a cookout. Charlie agreed to spread the word to the others, and they would meet at the Bend at ten o'clock Saturday morning.

Chapter Forty-Four
Seeing Kaylee's Heart

*A*fter leaving the school, Kaylee started to drive home, but with all her sudden thoughts centered on Kitty Snow, she turned her vehicle around and headed for the Bend. Adam's message from Kitty about seeing Kaylee's heart, filled her with anticipation— eager to hear if indeed Kitty's prophesy would match her circumstances.

Kitty was standing on the porch when Kaylee arrived. She was wearing black cowboy boots with her pants stuffed inside. Kaylee grinned when she noticed instead of a blouse with her pants, she was wearing a blue dress with a white bulky knit sweater. Her long, white braids hung over her shoulders. Kitty was thrilled to see Kaylee and wasted no time with chitchat. After entering the house, Kitty poured them a cup of fresh brewed coffee. In the living room, Kitty set the cups down, looked at Kaylee, slapped her hands together and laughed aloud. Kaylee had braided her hair while Kitty got the coffee. Kitty held the arms of her screaking rocking chair and carefully sat down.

"I must admit I'm a big fan your hair style, Kaylee Shell! We're about as stylish as it gets here at the Bend. However, I know you didn't come here this time of day to hear me compliment you on our hair-do . . . or talk about the stylish dress I'm wearing with my pants. So, tell me what's on your mind?"

Kaylee smiled. "First, let me say, I think your pretty white hair and your beautiful blue dress look wonderful!"

Kitty took a sip of coffee and leaned toward Kaylee. "Thank you, Miss Shell. Now, let's get to it. What is it you really want to say?" She pointed her long skinny finger at Kaylee. "I'm an old woman, but I have been blessed with a load of wisdom! I told you when you were here with Terra, you weren't here for just a teaching position." Kitty squinted her narrow eyes. "Do you remember that?" she asked.

Hanging on every word, Kaylee nodded. "Very vividly. I also remember you told me you could use that wisdom to see a person's heart. According to Adam's message, you saw my heart."

Kitty smiled and slapped her hands together. "Oh, I saw your heart all right. I want you to know if there is anything that I can do to help with your quest, I am available."

Kaylee tilted her head. "Thank you, Kitty. The first thing you can help me with is telling me what you saw in my heart."

Kitty leaned back and began to rock. "I saw that you were sent her to expose the evil that's ruled Stone River, even before it was Stone River."

"What do you mean expose?" Kaylee asked.

"You're a teacher; you should know. It means you're here to uncover and make known the corruption that formed Stone River. Someone sent you here. You didn't come on your own. I'm not completely clear as to what you're here to find, yet, I do know it has something to do with Roy Hilmar, Jake Boone and the two Lakota Indians who disappeared over a hundred years ago. Am I right?"

Kaylee paused and nodded. "You're right. How do you know that?"

"Sometimes, my gift of seeing things amazes me."

"You mean, like seeing in a dream or something?"

Kitty shook her head. "No, it's not a dream! A vision is something you see when you're wide awake. For example, I saw you running across a large open range. You weren't sure where you were going, yet you knew you had to get there. It was freezing cold, and the wind was blowing so hard against you, you could barely keep your pace up. Suddenly, you froze and looked helplessly about the terrain. I could feel your heart pounding when you realized you had come to the edge of a cliff. The place I saw was near the north pasture, which just happens to be on the Hilmar land."

Kaylee's brows tightened. "Did you happen to see why I was running?"

"You were trying to beat time. I also saw you in the Hilmar house. You had an old skeleton key in your hand and were desperately trying to find what the key would unlock."

Kitty's knowing about the key made Kaylee a believer. She rubbed her forehead. "Did you see anything else?" Kaylee asked.

Kitty carefully picked up the coffee cup and smiled. "Let me take a sip of coffee. My throat feels a little dry today. You drink your coffee while it's hot. Nothing tastes worse to me than cold coffee."

Kaylee took a sip and held her cup with both hands.

Kitty set her cup down and frowned. "Now, where was I? You asked if I saw anything else. Is that the right place?" Kaylee nodded and Kitty continued. "I saw a woman in the house. She was standing on the stairs desperately crying. I haven't seen why she was crying yet, but I did see her suddenly stop crying. She looked around and turned to go up the stairs. Before she reached the top step, she vanished."

Kaylee stared at Kitty. "I don't know what to say."

Kitty leaned toward Kaylee. "Tell me if I'm right or wrong so far."

Kaylee set her cup down. "I don't know about every word you said, but I do know about the old skeleton key. I found it one night by accident on the fireplace mantel."

Kitty moved to the edge of her seat. "Have I told you enough for you to trust me with what you're undertaking here in Stone River?"

"Yes . . . yes, you have."

Kitty furrowed her brows and snapped, "Then tell me the rest of your story."

Kaylee shared her mission with Kitty.

Kitty fixed her eyes on Kaylee's and smiled. "You forgot to tell me about Jeffrey."

Kaylee's mouth dropped open. "How do you know about Jeffrey?"

"I just know! Who is he?"

"He's my . . . my boyfriend. Martin is Jeffrey's grandfather."

Kitty took a deep breath and blew it out slowly. "This Martin is a character. He is hiding your love letters that you have mailed to your boyfriend. He's not reading the letters but putting them in a small hidden drawer under his desk and locking it."

Kaylee gasped. "You're right! Jeffrey hasn't received any of the letters I've written."

Kitty laughed out loud. "Well, trust me, they're locked up under Martin's desk. Tell Martin you know he's not giving Jeffrey your letters. Then tell him where he's hiding them and you want them given to Jeffrey right away."

Kaylee stood and put her hand on her hip. "I'll call Martin tonight and make sure I share your message about the letters. I would love to be there to see his face when I tell him."

Kaylee went back to town more confused than ever. She really didn't believe in psychics, yet, how could Kitty possibly know all those things? Especially about the letters. Jeffrey would burn every letter without even opening one them, if he knew about Adam. Wanting to see Adam had all but taken over her mind. The thought of his touch sent a fire through her body. The need to clear her mind was vital. So, tonight all she wanted to do was go home and get some sleep.

Chapter Forty-Five

A Forced Day Off

*D*otty was feather dusting in the dining room when Kaylee arrived home.

"Miss Shell, what are you doing home so early?"

Kaylee put her purse and keys on the table, took off her coat and flopped into the closest chair. "I'm taking a forced day off. What do you think about that, Dotty?"

Dotty frowned. "A forced day off? Whatever do you mean?"

"I mean, Nick Long and the school board insisted I take the day off and consider how I'm teaching my history class."

"What difference would that make to them? Unless you're doing something erratic that they consider totally out of line."

"Out of line with what?" Kaylee snapped. "It's over the field trip and the study we're doing on the history of Stone River. For goodness sake! One would think they would praise the fact that the students are learning about their home town."

Dotty placed the duster on the mantel. "That's utterly ridiculous."

Kaylee massaged her temples. "Right now, all I want to do is go into a slumber mode. I'm so tired! Will you be here much longer, Dotty?"

"About five more minutes. Shall I fix you something to eat when you get up?"

Kaylee loosened the braids from her hair and shook it out. "No, thank you. I'll open a can of soup or something."

Dotty tightened her lips to keep from laughing. "It would appear that you've been with Kitty Snow today."

Kaylee pointed to her hair. "I suppose the braids were a dead give-away."

Dotty nodded and took the feather duster and began dusting the bottom of Ellen's portrait.

"Dotty, have you seen Adam today?"

Without facing Kaylee, she said. "Yes. He said he was riding out to the north range for a while. Do you need something?"

Kaylee lowered her head and sighed. "No. I'll get him to check it tomorrow."

"As you wish, Miss Shell."

Kaylee could hardly wait to get into her flannel pajamas and robe. She put her hands in the pockets of her robe and stopped when her fingers touched the key she had found on the mantel. She pulled it from her pocket and looked at it. "How in the world did Kitty Snow know about you?" Kaylee shrugged her shoulders, put the key back in her pocket and yawned. "I'll try and figure it out later. Right now, my bed is calling my name."

Chapter Forty-Six

Forgotten Keys

A couple of hours had passed. Kaylee groaned and stretched as she sat up on the edge of the bed and slid her feet into her slippers. She listened to see if perhaps Dotty was still in the house. She wasn't.

After opening a can of soup and getting a glass of milk, Kaylee went to the grand room and sat in the big chair that faced the dining room. Holding the mug of soup with both hands, she turned it up and took a sip. When she lowered her hands, something on the dining room table caught her eye. She quickly set the soup down and hurried to the table to see if a true miracle had taken place. She could not believe her eyes. Dotty had forgotten her guarded treasure, the keys to the house. After glancing around the room, Kaylee picked the ring of keys up and held them in the air. Every key was numbered and told which door each key went to. Kaylee rushed to the kitchen and looked out the window to see if Dotty's car was there. It was gone.

She squeezed the keys tightly in her hand and raced up the stairs. Her heart pounded as she opened the first door. It was like stepping back in time, just as she had imagined it would be. The room was filled with antiques and the walls were filled with exquisite landscape paintings and tapestries. But no portraits. Each room was filled with the same kind of things.

At the end of the hall, Kaylee opened the last door on the second floor. When she opened the door, a cold chill came from the room. She gasped. "This is surely Jenny Lynn's room," she said breathlessly. The size of the room was twice that of the other bedrooms she had opened.

On one side of the room, there was an oak rocking chair. A large bay window with a pink satin, cushioned settee accented the long pink drapes that were crowned with three layers of pink and white valences. Light pink, silk wallpaper filled with small white parasols covered the tall walls. Detailed, wide, white molding bordered the massive room.

A full-size bed with a scalloped pink and white lace canopy sat majestically across the room from the bay window. A large, gold-scrolled bench covered with light pink satin and small parasols that matched the wallpaper, sat at the foot of the bed. A rocking horse, brightly colored like one seen on a carousel, sat near a toy chest. The top of the chest was lined with an array of dolls.

A large, oak wardrobe sat off to the side, behind the horse. A dresser with an oval shaped mirror and scrolled bench, a smaller version of the one at the foot of the bed, sat near a smaller window. Kaylee gently touched her fingertips to a silver comb and brush set that was on the dresser. She took a quick breath and blew it out as she stared at a full-size painting of a beautiful young girl.

The girl was standing in front of the rocking horse. Her long, dark hair lay in soft curls off her shoulders onto a tea-length, emerald green dress with a wide, white lace collar. A small, white ribbon was pinned to the right side of her hair. Her white tights, black leather shoes and white lace gloves were magnificent. In her left hand was a white parasol with a ruffled edge. Her small hand gripped the handle. The long silver tip rested against the dark, oak hardwood floors. Kaylee shifted her stare to the girl's beautiful face. She had fair skin and large, dark eyes, with a dimple in her left cheek. It was obvious the dimple wasn't from a smile, as her face displayed a somber expression.

Kaylee gently touched the canvas. She trembled as a sudden sadness seized her. She continued to look at the painting of Jenny Lynn. Such a beautiful little girl who died so young. No chance of ever knowing the love of a husband or the joy of having her own child.

"What are you doing in here?" a voice shouted from the doorway.

Kaylee jumped and screamed out. "Oh thunder, Dotty, you scared me half to death."

"You have no business in here. Give me my keys and get out!"

Shaking from her scare, Kaylee handed her the keys and left the room.

Dotty slammed the door and growled, "I'll have to report you to the town council for this."

Kaylee frowned. "Why, because I was curious? I can't imagine anyone living here and not being curious to know what the rest of the house is like. It's magnificent."

Dotty furrowed her brows. "You paid for the bottom level. Nothing more." Dotty turned and started down the hall.

Kaylee shouted, "And just what is the council going to say about you being so careless with the keys? Are they going to pat you on the back for that?"

Dotty stopped and faced Kaylee. Her lips tightened. "You're right. I'm responsible for the keys, not the council. Lucky for you. This time, I won't say anything, but I'll see this doesn't happen again."

"Dotty, I'm sorry."

Dotty walked away without speaking.

Kaylee went down the stairs, her mind filled with the beautiful room she had just seen. She went into the dining room and looked up at Ellen's portrait. "I'm so sorry about your little girl, Ellen. I can't comprehend the thoughts of losing a child." Kaylee shook her head. "Here I am again talking to a painting. What is wrong with me?" She sighed and said, "Ellen, I sure wish I knew what the rest of the house looks like. Really, I'd like to know what this key unlocks, since it's the only key I have." She held the key up. "Can you help me, Ellen?"

Kaylee almost threw the key in the air when someone knocked on the door. She put the key in her pocket and hurried to see who it was, hoping it was Adam. To her surprise, it was Dotty.

"Dotty, what a surprise!"

"May I come in?"

"Of course, come . . . come in."

Dotty looked down and back to Kaylee, "I just wanted to say, I'm sorry for the way I snapped at you. I was way out of line."

"No . . . no, I was out of line. I shouldn't have been so snoopy."

"Anyways," Dotty said softly, "I don't want to have any hard feelings between us."

Kaylee patted her arm. "No hard feelings at all. Would you like to sit for a while? I'll pour us a glass of iced tea."

"No, thank you. I'd better be going. I'm meeting with someone. Maybe another time."

"Yes, I'd like that a lot. I'll see you tomorrow. Goodnight, Dotty."

Chapter Forty-Seven
Was She Dreaming?

Kaylee was stunned by Dotty's apology. "I sure wasn't expecting that from Dotty," she said, as she walked to the back of the house and looked out the window, eager to see if Adam had come home. There were no signs that he had, so she went inside and ran a hot bath.

Kaylee pinned her hair up, lit several candles and poured a glass of red wine. She turned her piano rhapsody on and sank into a mound of bubbles. Wanting her mind to relax, she sipped her wine and rested her head on a small satin pillow that draped across the rim of the claw foot tub and closed her eyes. With her body and mind relaxed, she listened to the music until it felt as though it became a part of her. Before long, she drifted off to sleep. In the distance, she thought she heard someone call her name. Was she dreaming? Instantly, her body ached with desire. Her breathing became moans as she moved her head from side to side trying desperately to wake up.

She panted as she felt her lover's warm breath on her neck. Sheer ecstasy surged through her body. Her head was spinning with passion. She groaned loudly as she struggled to wake from what felt so real.

In an instant, Kaylee eyes sprang open as her hands seized the side of the tub and she struggled to push herself upright. Blinking and disoriented, she tried to make out the pounding sounds. She stepped out of the tub in a panic as she touched her lips. Was it a dream? If so, how could she could still feel the warmth on her lips from her dream lover's touch? Guiding her fingers to her robe draped on the back of the chair that sat beside the tub, she pulled it to her, put it on and looked in the mirror. Her breath escaped her when she saw her lips were red and slightly swollen from the passion she had dreamed of only moments earlier. Kaylee held her stare. She took a couple of steps back, shocked at what she saw and was still feeling even though she was wide awake. Frantically, her eyes searched the room. If it wasn't a dream, where was the phantom that had left her trembling in fear . . . and fulfillment? A scream stuck in her throat when she heard the pounding sound again. She realized the beating sound was someone knocking on the front door. She felt as though she was gliding down the hallway. She paused a brief moment, leaning against the wall to steady her body. Another knock, this time even louder, forced her to hurry and open the door.

"Adam," she said apprehensively.

He could see she was trembling. Stepping inside, he closed the door and turned the lock. For a long moment they stared into each other's eyes. Kaylee's heart pounded in a strange, uneven rhythm. Without speaking, Adam removed his coat and hat, tossing them to the side. Kaylee remained silent as he moved closer. His blue eyes fixed on hers, he held his stare for a long moment. He then took her in his arms and held her tightly to his body. As he held her, Adam whispered, "I love you, I need you. It has been so long since I've held you. I've missed you so very much!"

She held her breath until his lips touched hers.

After a moment, she pushed him back. "Adam, we can't do this right now. I . . . I really need to talk to you. Now."

Adam loosened his arms and agreed with her. Kaylee fixed them a cup of hot tea. In the dim light of the dining room, Kaylee sat her cup on the table. Adam slid his fingertips down Kaylee's long silky hair and pushed a strand from her face. "I love you! I love you! I love you! From the moment I first laid eyes on you, I've loved you."

"Adam, I love you too. But . . . we need to talk. I'm not really sure what I'm going to say, but I really need to talk to you."

"I agree." Adam said. "I just don't know how to put into words what I really want to say either."

Kaylee stood and looked up at Ellen.

Adam joined Kaylee, put his arm around her waist and said, "Kaylee Shell, what kind of hold do you have over me? All of this is too strange. It's to a point, I don't know how to handle it."

Kaylee faced him. "Strange doesn't come close to describing what happened to me just before you arrived."

"What happened?"

Kaylee looked at Ellen as she tried to explain, "I . . . I was taking a bubble bath and . . . and I don't know, I . . . I think I was dreaming, but then again, I'm not sure that I was. Kaylee pressed her fingertips to her temple. "While taking a bath, I . . . I felt as though someone was touching me . . . making love to me."

Adam's squinted, "What do you mean?"

Frantic, Kaylee put her hand over her mouth and tears rolled down her cheeks.

Adam pulled her close to him. "Shhh! Baby, are you okay?"

Kaylee pushed away from his arms and snapped, "No, I'm not okay! Someone or something made love to me while I was in the bath tub."

Totally confused, Adam frowned and asked, "What are you talking about?"

Kaylee pointed at him and shouted, "I'm telling you, something made love to me while I was bathing. Was it a dream or not, I don't know! At first, I thought I was dreaming; then everything became so real. Then I heard a pounding sound, like someone was beating the inside of an empty barrel, which turned out to be you knocking. I managed to get out of the tub . . ." Kaylee swallowed hard and continued, "As I put on my robe, I looked in the mirror, my lips were red from someone's or something's kisses. I could feel his touch on my body."

Adam ran his fingers through his hair and blew his breath out.

Kaylee put her hand on his arm. "When I opened the door and you were standing there, I could only wonder if it was you who touched me." Kaylee shifted her eyes to Adam's and said softly, "I'm not the kind of girl who just sleeps around. But, when you're here, it's as though I have no control over my emotions. The minute I see you, I'm a mess."

Kaylee closed her eyes and lowered her head. "Adam, I . . . I know this house is haunted; otherwise, what am I to blame my actions on? I know this may sound corny coming from an adult, but will you forgive me, Adam?"

Adam pulled a chair out for Kaylee and held her arm until she was seated. Then he sat down beside her. For a brief moment, they sat in silence staring at each other, then at Ellen. Adam reached across the table and put his warm hand on top of Kaylee's. "It doesn't sound corny at all, and there's nothing to forgive. If anything, I'm the one who should apologize to you. You said, 'I feel I have no control.' I'm a grown man, and I confess neither do I have control. There's a lot of weird things going on, and they're multiplying so fast, I can hardly keep up.

"Speaking of weird things," Adam said, "this morning, I was compelled to ride out to the north range. I ended up at Coyote Canyon. That's where I told you I have some friends whom I like to go visit. The truth is, about three weeks before you came to Stone River, I felt drawn to that end of the property. I would go out there and sit for hours, looking off into the canyon. I don't know why or what I was looking for. Tonight, while I was sitting there, I could feel, indeed hear you calling me. I couldn't wait to get to your arms. It wasn't just wanting to make love to a woman, I wanted you forever."

Kaylee groaned, "Adam, do you remember what you said to me a few minutes ago while you were holding me?"

Adam shrugged and shook his head. "No, what?"

"You said, that you love me, need me, and it had been so long since you had touched me."

Adam rubbed the back of his neck. "I did say that because I felt that with all my heart."

"Why did you say it that way. You were with me last night."

Adam shook his head. "I don't know why. I just don't know."

Chapter Forty-Eight
Vague Reasoning

This is all so crazy," Kaylee said. "But while I'm in a talking mood, I may as well tell you what else happened today that made no sense. Nick Long made me take off today. When I got home, I was hungry and went to the kitchen to fix a cup of chicken soup, hoping it would calm my stomach. I took my soup to the big chair that looks directly into the dining room. I took a sip of the warm soup, and when I lowered my cup, something caught my attention on the table. I was stunned. Dotty had left her keys. I couldn't get up fast enough to get my hands on them. I grabbed them and went to the second floor as fast as my legs would run up the stairs. I looked through a few rooms, and then I opened the door to what surely is Jenny Lynn's room. Dotty caught me while I was in Jenny Lynn's room. She scared me so badly. She yelled and told me to get out of the room. She sneered and said she would have to tell the town council."

"Wait a minute," Adam said. "Let's back up a moment. Did you say Nick Long made you take the day off?"

Kaylee sat down while she explained Nick's vague reasoning about not taking her class to the Bend.

"Well . . . are you going to take the trip tomorrow?" Adam asked.

"Are you kidding! I wouldn't miss it for anything. They'll not order me around like a robot." Kaylee told him about her visit with Kitty Snow. "I don't know how she knew any of those things she told me, but what she said was very accurate."

Kaylee put her hand on Adam's. "Adam, is there a way you might possibly get your hands on Dotty's keys? It's imperative. I must see the other rooms."

Adam rubbed the back of his neck. "That's a pretty tall order."

"I know it's a tall order, but she'll be watching me, no doubt about that."

Adam frowned. "If I agree to try and do this virtually impossible favor for you, I want to know what is it you're looking for?"

"That's just it. I don't know what I'm looking for. Adam, have you been in any of the rooms on the third floor?"

"I've been in some of the rooms but not all of them."

Kaylee groaned. "Did the Hilmar's have their bedroom on the third floor? I didn't see anything I would associate as the master suite on the second floor, nor have I seen a master suite on the first floor."

Adam thought a moment. "Have you been in all the rooms on the first floor?"

"All but one and it's locked. What's in that room, do you know?"

"I think it's Mr. Hilmar's office/bedroom combination. I've heard there were times he and Ellen didn't share the same bed. On the other hand, it wasn't all that uncommon then or now, for people of their status to have separate bedrooms. But I'm not sure."

"You know what's really strange?" Kaylee pointed to the portrait of Ellen. "Here is an awesome painting of Ellen, and I saw one of Jenny Lynn in her bedroom, but I haven't seen one of Roy or any other members of the family. Why is that?"

"All the family portraits were taken down and stored on the third floor, except the ones of Ellen and Jenny Lynn. Why they were taken down, I don't know. Dotty had to let me in a one of the rooms to check a vent when the furnace went out. That room was filled with large portraits sitting around on the floor. All of them were covered with sheets or large pieces of material. I asked what the paintings were, and she said they were the Hilmar family portraits."

Kaylee tapped her lips and muttered, "I don't get it! Why . . . why, would they be taken down? In every grand estate, the walls are filled with the family's portraits."

"I asked Dotty why they had been taken down," Adam said. "Dotty said, 'Before Willie Hilmar died, she told her staff to take them all down except for the portraits of Ellen and Jenny Lynn.'"

Kaylee stood and put her hands on her hips. "That's so eccentric. Why would she take her father's painting down and leave up the one of Jenny, her half-sister, and the one of Ellen, her stepmother?"

"That I don't know. The strange thing about leaving up those two particular paintings is Willie never knew or even saw either of those two. On the other hand, she had the portraits of her grandparents; her mother,

Judy Justice; her only daughter, Thelma; and her granddaughter, Barbara, all stored. There is no way I can make sense of any of this."

Kaylee eyes widened. "Adam, I have to have those keys. Will you please help me?"

Adam stood and faced her. "Yeah . . . yeah, I think I will, or at least try. You know I can't promise."

Kaylee grabbed his shoulders. "Thank you, Adam, for even trying! One other thing, I would like for you to take me to Coyote Canyon very soon."

"Awesome!" Adam smiled. "Since you moved into the house, I've felt you riding with me to the Canyon every time I've gone there. We'll ride out one day next week."

Kaylee playfully ran her fingers down Adam's chest. "Would you like to journey to the third floor with me? Just to get the feel of it?"

Adam took her hand and kissed her fingers. "Yes, Miss Shell, I would."

At the bottom of the steps, Kaylee pulled up her robe so she wouldn't trip and led the way up the stairs. At the top, Kaylee looked around the polished mahogany banister that made a large circle. To the right, a hallway led to four rooms. Kaylee sighed and asked, "Do you know what all these rooms are?"

"Mostly bedrooms." Adam smiled, took Kaylee's hand and led her to one of the four doors in the hall. "This room contains one of the most elaborate libraries I've ever seen. The room is huge and breathtaking. It has a substantial marble fireplace, mahogany walls, and a mosaic ceiling that displays the heavens and heavenly beings. There's a spiral staircase that takes you up to a circle walkway. That's where all the books are put on display. If you don't go up the steps, you don't read any of the books. Not one book is in the lower part of room."

Kaylee listened intently as he described the room. She heard him speaking but didn't comprehend a word he was saying. All she could do at the moment was enjoy his rugged good looks. The desire to be close to him was overwhelming.

Adam stopped talking when he noticed her stare. Without speaking, he responded and the third-floor hallway served their unyielding obsession as the piano rhapsody piped through the house.

As they came down the stairs, the grandfather clock chimed. It was three in the morning.

Kaylee put her arms around Adam's waist. "I don't want you to go," she said.

"I don't want to go, but heaven help us if Dotty were to find me here."

Kaylee whined, "I asked her to knock and allow me to answer the door before she came in. She told me she would."

"I know, but what if she forgets?"

"You're right, that would be a disaster."

Adam hugged Kaylee. "I love you."

"I love you. I can't wait until I see you again."

Adam held her face in his hands, gently kissed her warm lips, said goodnight and left.

Chapter Forty-Nine

The Invitation

*K*aylee set the alarm clock, climbed into bed and snuggled one of her pillows. As a rule, her thoughts would have been of Jeffrey, but for the past few days, Adam had all but blotted Jeffrey from her memory. Kaylee fell asleep as the music continued to softly play.

The alarm sounded. Kaylee sat up, stretched her arms over her head and groaned loudly. Squinting, she looked toward the window. Rays of sunlight filled the room. She listened closely but didn't hear the music that had been playing when she had gone to sleep. After dressing, she made a pot of coffee and loaded the car with food for the outing. As she closed the back of the Explorer, Kaylee saw Dotty walking toward her.

"Good morning, Miss Shell."

"Good morning, Dotty."

Dotty pulled her sweater together and asked, "You're heading out pretty early, aren't you?"

"Yes. Today is our class field trip."

Dotty crossed her arms. "So, you're going?"

"Of course, I am. Why wouldn't I?"

"I thought . . . oh, nothing."

Kaylee paused, then asked, "Dotty, would you like to ride with me?"

She sighed and put her hand on her chest. "Me? You would want me to go?"

"Yeah. We'll have a great time. Come with me. You'll love it."

"I . . . I . . . I don't know what to say."

"Say yes."

To Kaylee's surprise, Dotty accepted the invitation.

Dotty appeared elated. "Are you sure you have time for me to get my things?"

"Of course."

Dotty turned and asked, "Do I need to bring any food or drinks? I buy drinks by the case. You wouldn't believe how many I have in my pantry."

"A couple of extra drinks would be good."

Dotty chuckled and hurried toward her house. Kaylee pulled up the Explorer to Dotty's house and was standing on the porch when Adam came from his house.

He put his hat on and shouted, "Good morning, Miss Shell."

Kaylee smiled and waved. "Good morning, Adam. I trust you slept well."

He winked. "I slept like a baby. Have you come to visit Dotty?"

Kaylee smiled. "No. I'm waiting on Dotty."

"Waiting?"

"Yes. She's riding with me."

Adam gasped. "What did you say?"

"Dotty is going with me today."

Adam tilted his head. "Are you kidding?"

"No, I'm not."

At that moment Dotty came from her house. The excitement on her face radiated. "Adam," she said, "I'm going on a field trip with Kaylee. Why don't you join us?"

"Yeah, that's a great idea, Dotty," Kaylee said. "Come with us, Adam. It will be so fun."

"I . . . I tell you what. I'll saddle Black Beauty and join you guys in a little while."

Kaylee waved to Adam as they left the driveway.

Dotty actually laughed and talked almost all the way to the Bend.

When they arrived, Charlie was already there. He had a mound of wood ready to light for the marshmallows and hot dogs roast. He was sitting on a blanket with his legs crossed, Indian style, with his head and hands raised toward the sky. Kaylee loved his brown moccasin boots with fringe down the side and his white shirt with a small brown design and full sleeves.

Before speaking, Kaylee and Dotty paused and waited for him to stand. After a moment, Charlie stood and hurried to assist the women. He gave Kaylee a fast hug and apologized immediately, if he was out of line for doing so.

"I've been so excited about our meeting today," he said, as he took the folding table from the back of the Explorer. He smiled at Dotty. "I'm so glad you came."

Dotty glanced around the area and smiled. "Yes, me too."

By the time they unloaded everything, the other students had arrived. Kaylee called the meeting to order. She smiled, noticing that everyone was sitting on blankets with their legs crossed like Charlie. Two of the girls had their hair in braids and some of the others had feathers dangling in their hair.

Betty stood and took a couple of feathers from her bag. "Miss Shell, Dotty, I have feathers for your hair. You two are going to look glorious."

Lori helped Dotty with her feathers. Betty proceeded to braid Kaylee's hair and put a feather, that was attached to a thin piece of leather, on the right side of her head. Afterward, Betty asked Dotty and Kaylee to stand. Charlie came from behind them and placed a beaded necklace around Dotty's neck. He faced Kaylee, took an eagle claw necklace from his neck and placed it around hers. "For you, Santo. Santo is your name in the Lakota language. Which means Brave Warrior."

It wasn't until then that Kaylee noticed all the students had on beaded necklaces. She looked down and touched the eagle claw. "I . . . I feel at a loss for words. What a surprise! I trust the day will be filled with many more surprises. Thank you all, so much! I'm really moved by the fact that you've dressed the part. I'm a little embarrassed I didn't think of it myself. I want to add that I'm thrilled Dotty came with me today. Adam, will be joining us a little later." Kaylee took a deep breath and blew it out. "I can sense an awesome presence in this place. I have anticipated what Charlie has to share with us today. So, without further ado, I'll ask Charlie to come and communicate to us what's on his heart."

Kaylee sat on her blanket beside Dotty and crossed her legs. To her surprise, Dotty followed suit. She glanced at Kaylee and smiled.

Charlie stood and looked at everyone. He raised his arms to the sky and said, "Great Eagle, look down on us today. Guide our thoughts and open our hearts to receive what you would have us know."

For a moment, he stood with his shoulders back, his arms by his side and his head to the sky. Then he faced the class and said, "Today we have gathered on hallowed ground. Many of my people died here. Many were forced from here to a land they did not know. But not all was sad here. Many babies were born here, grew here and died of an old age here. In this place, if you'll listen with your spirit, you can hear the laughter around the camp and the sound of horses coming and going out of the campsite. If you'll look with your spirit, you'll see fathers teaching their sons to make bows and arrows—showing them how to pull the bow back with just the right amount of tension, so when released, it will hit the target the brave has aimed for. You'll see mothers teaching their daughters how to grind corn into powder and mix it with water to fry corn cakes, and how to skin the buffalo and dry the hide. You will also see the demise of my people, when the white man and soldiers entered our land, not satisfied to share the land but demanding all of it for themselves.

"My Great-great-grandfather Black Bear was a mighty brave and the chief of the Lakota Indians who made their homes here where we have gathered today. He was a just and fair man—a loving man and a man of principles. He was a man who wanted the best for his people. We have gathered and shared a portion of my family's history in our groups, but there are a couple of things I want to share that hasn't been brought out."

"We can't wait!" Kaylee said.

Charlie smiled and continued, "As we know, Black Bear had two sons who disappeared—Wind Dancer and Moving Cloud. But we haven't been told the story about Wind Dancer and Ellen Hilmar."

Upon hearing Charlie say Wind Dancer and Ellen Hilmar in the same sentence, Kaylee's breath escaped her for a moment. Not wanting to miss one word, she listened intently, as Charlie continued, "My grandmother told me that Wind Dancer was out riding one day when he heard a woman screaming. He rode toward the screams, which took him to the open range. He saw a woman riding as fast as she could toward Snake Falls. Four Sioux Indians were riding behind her and surely meant her bodily harm. Wind Dancer drew his bow and killed one of the Sioux. The others stopped when they saw it was Wind Dancer and rode away. The woman was hysterical. Wind Dancer caught up with her, stopped her horse and pulled her out of her saddle to the ground. She fought him like a wild animal. Finally, he got on top of her and pinned her hands to the ground. He held her until she stopped fighting and realized that he wasn't going to hurt her. She saw the dead Indian and knew that Wind Dancer had saved her life. That was the day Wind Dancer met Ellen Hilmar."

Charlie noticed all the girls giggling and saying how romantic his story was. Charlie smiled and said, "Ladies, if I may continue."

"Wind Dancer thought Ellen was the most beautiful woman he had ever seen. He named her Halo, meaning, Angel Face. In his eyes, she looked like a goddess from heaven."

Charlie told many stories about his family, but Kaylee's concentration swayed in one direction. Wind Dancer and Ellen Hilmar. After Charlie had finished his talk, he gave Colton a ceremonial drum. Colton beat the drum, and Charlie did a celebration dance that had been passed down from generation to generation. Adam arrived in time to see the last part of the dance.

Chapter Fifty

Lost Money

When Charlie was seated, Kaylee thanked him for sharing his family stories with the group. Kaylee clapped her hands together and said, "I am so thrilled about our gathering today. I have been anticipating how magical today would surely be! Thus far it has exceeded all my expectations. After Charlie's riveting stories about his family, the Lakota people and the intriguing story about Wind Dancer and Ellen Hilmar, I can't wait to hear from our groups. So, if everyone is ready, I'll ask Tyler and his team if they have any new findings to report today."

Tyler stood. "Just being here today with my classmates, Dotty, Adam and you, Miss Shell has exploded a natural adrenaline rush that I can't explain and I love it! My team has worked so hard. We tried to get a glimpse of the old bank records but were unable to do so as of yet. We want to try and find the net worth of Jake and Roy at their deaths."

Paulette raised her hand. "Tyler, I have some info I can share if you and Miss Shell don't mind."

Kaylee looked at Tyler, who was quick to agree to hear anything new.

"What I have comes from Grandma Thelma. She wasn't sure about Jake Boone, but at his death in 1926, Roy Hilmar was a millionaire hundreds of times over. That doesn't include the funds he and Jake set aside for the upkeep of Stone River. That was his personal pocket change. That is according to only some of the documents Grandma Thelma has in her possession."

"Wow!" Kaylee said. "That's a tremendous amount of money back in that day. I can't even imagine how much that would be in today's money . . . my goodness."

Tyler spoke up, "Though we didn't find out about the finances, we did find that Willie Hilmar employed a staff of almost a hundred people to take care of the ranch, grounds and house when she inherited the Estate. That would take a chunk of change to make payroll. That's it for now, but at our next meeting, we hope to have something awesome."

Lisa raised her hand, "I know I haven't been called on yet, but do you mind if my team goes next?

"Of course not, go ahead." Kaylee said.

"While we are talking about finances, my team did find out something about the financial worth of Jake Boone. This info came from a very reliable source. He said, 'Jake had an estimated worth of $400 million. However, when Jake died, the books had been altered and showed only $125 million.' As Paulette said before, 'That didn't include the funds set aside for the town.'"

"Lisa," Kaylee said, "can you tell us who your source is and how he or she came by that information?"

"Sure. Ken Trent. His father, Raymond, was Jake Boone and Roy Hilmar's accountant."

Kaylee put her fingers to her temples. "So, you're saying Jake Boone was $275 million short, according to his accountant? My question is what kind of an accountant would allow that kind of money to get away from him? Who would have the authority to have access to the accountant's books, other than the accountant himself?"

Lisa spoke up, "Roy Hilmar and his live-in girlfriend, Judy Justice."

Lori asked, "Could Jake have taken it out and sent it to his wife, Tammy, and his children, or to Clara Aims? I understand that Jake sent quite a fortune to Clara Aims after she moved back East."

Lisa spoke up, "This deduction of money was made after Clara went back East. It shows the withdrawal, but no name was signed to show who took the money. To me, it had to be someone who had enough power to just take the money out and perhaps pay a chunk of money for the silence of someone who might have knowledge of that person's dishonesty."

"But, wouldn't Jake have known?" Kaylee asked. "After all, it was his money that's missing, not Roy's."

"If that were the case," Lisa said, "it would have been the only time Jake ever took money out without signing it out. The records verify that."

"How about the accountant himself?" Eddie asked.

Lisa sighed. "I don't think the accountant took it. For one thing, he would have to give an account to Roy Hilmar. Roy kept a vigil over those books. Jake, on the other hand, rarely checked anything." He paused, ". .

. unless the accountant may have taken a payoff. With that thought, I'll say that's all we have for now."

Kaylee clapped her hands. "This is all so exciting! Thank you, Lisa's team. Great job! Tyler, I want you and your group to continue seeking out facts about the money that disappeared from Jake's account. At our next meeting, we'll discuss it again. For now, due to time, I am eager to hear what Lori and her crew have to report on the two Indians who disappeared?"

Lori stood and shrugged. "Miss Shell, we haven't had any luck at all. It's as though they disappeared into thin air, never to be found."

Catching everyone by surprise, Charlie spoke up. "I don't accept that. There have to be clues, and I want us to work and find out what happened. Ever since Miss Shell gave us our assignments to explore and find the true history of Stone River, I've felt an excitement like I've never known. I feel justice crying out in my spirit for my ancestors. I've prayed and asked the God of heaven to reveal to us the truth about what happened, whether good or bad. It's going to happen, and we're getting so close. We have to dig deeper. We have to."

Kaylee looked at the class and raised her hand. "Ok, how many agree with Charlie that we're going to find the truth and share it with the town—whether, good or bad. Let me see your hands."

Every hand went up, including Adam's and Dotty's. Kaylee asked the class to stand, join hands, make a circle around the mound of wood and allow their spirits to connect. They held hands and stood silently for a few moments. Afterward, Kaylee asked Charlie to light the fire while the others got the hot dogs and marshmallows.

Chapter Fifty-One
The Challenge

While everyone was eating, Colton asked, "Miss Shell, may I ask a question?"

"Of course, Colton, what's on your mind?"

"Why would Mr. Long pressure you about the way you teach our class and make you take a day off? I don't understand any of that."

"I don't understand it either." She glanced at Adam and then back at the class. "Since I moved to Stone River, there have been many things I don't understand. If you recall my first day at Fair Mount, I put before you a challenge to uncover the truth about Stone River and Stone River's founders. That challenge has brought us a long way. We all have personal challenges that we face daily. I feel Nick Long has challenged me. But a challenge is not necessarily a bad thing. If we allow it, our challenges can and will make us strong. How many of you agree with me?"

Every hand went up.

Kaylee nodded her head. "I was thinking about our two couples, Roy and Ellen Hilmar and Jake and Tammy

Boone. From what we've learned thus far, Jake was a man of character.

"Roy, challenged Jake by ordering him to kill the Indians who lived here at the Bend. Jake wouldn't do it. The challenge put Jake to the test, and it revealed that Jake had a conscience. He couldn't take a life just because he was ordered to do so by his partner. Roy, on the other hand, seemed to have no problem with killing the Lakota or anyone else who tried to stand in his way. Tammy and Ellen were also very different. One—"

Before Kaylee could finish her statement, Paulette raised her hand. "Miss Shell, may I say something?"

"Please do, Paulette."

Paulette lowered her head, then looked around the fire at everyone. "When we were holding hands in the circle, I felt such a close connection and a sense that what we are doing is right. Our challenge is to know the truth. I too want to know the truth, whether good or bad. Even though Roy and Jake were both my great-grandfathers, I still want to know the truth. My Grandmother Thelma, I'm sure, could shed some light on our questions. Before Grandma Willie died, she gave Thelma no indication that she was giving the town her estate. I, like Charlie, want to see justice done. Besides, I really believe the truth will set you free."

Kaylee smiled, "You're so right, Paulette. Thank you for your input. Thanks to all of you for your input."

Adam had chores to do and needed to go. Kaylee walked with him to his horse. "What do you think of my class?"

"I think they're pretty remarkable, like their teacher. Can I come over later for a private lesson?"

"I can't wait. I love you," she said softly.

"I love you, too. See you later."

When Kaylee came back to the campfire, Betty stood beside her and teased, "I think I saw a few sparks going up . . . and not from the campfire but between you and Adam."

"He's a really nice guy," Kaylee responded.

Betty grinned and shook her head. "Bologna! He's sexy, and please try not to act as though you haven't noticed. Shoot, every woman in Stone River has fantasized about Adam at one time or another, me included. Here's the thing: Adam is very nice to everybody, yet he doesn't go beyond that. So, to see the chemistry between you two is really cool. I'll be pulling for you, Miss Shell."

"Should I thank you for that?"

"Yeah. I've got enough pull to take the fillings right out of Eddie's teeth."

"Okay, but by all means, pull for me."

After putting out the fire and loading the Explorer, everyone headed home. Kaylee was amazed at Dotty. She had laughed and talked with the kids like she was a kid herself.

"Dotty," Kaylee said, "I'm glad you came today."

"Me too. I must say, I surprised myself by agreeing to come. Those kids are so nice, polite and full of fun. They're taking the investigation of Stone River seriously. I may as well go ahead and say the way you're handling the quest has stirred their excitement and mine too."

"Thank you, Dotty. Speaking of the investigation, can you share anything about Roy and Jake that would help us out?"

"That, I'll have to think about."

"Please do, Dotty. I have a very big request."

Dotty looked straight ahead. "And what would that request be?"

Kaylee took a deep breath and said, "Will you please allow me to see a portrait of Roy Hilmar? I would so appreciate being able to put a face to one of the men our class is studying."

Dotty thought a moment. "I'm the housekeeper. You being a teacher, I'm sure you know the definition of 'keeper.' It means guardian. As guardian, I must be careful who I allow inside my post. Though very cautious, I think just this one time couldn't hurt." Dotty exhaled. "Okay," she said, "I'll show you the room where the paintings are stored."

Kaylee was ecstatic. She patted Dotty's arm. "Thank you so much, Dotty. I know I'm more than likely pushing my luck, but would you mind telling me why the paintings were taken down? It's driving me nuts."

"That, I can't talk about. I swore to Willie Hilmar that what she told me would be in strictest confidence."

"I understand," Kaylee said. "A promise is a promise. However, I really need to ask you one more thing."

"You are very assertive, Miss Shell." Dotty paused a moment, then nodded for Kaylee to go ahead.

"Is . . . is the house haunted by Ellen Hilmar spirit?"

Dotty turned her sharp eyes to Kaylee. "Why would you ask me such a thing?"

"Because I . . . I . . ."

Dotty frowned. "Because you what?"

"Nothing, just nothing. I shouldn't have asked."

"Miss Shell, if the house were indeed haunted, you most certainly would not have to ask me. You would know. Believe me, you would know."

Dotty had little to say the rest of the way back to the Estate. It was obvious Kaylee had hit a subject Dotty wasn't going to talk about.

Chapter Fifty-Two

View the Paintings

As Kaylee opened the door, her heart raced when she heard the piano music playing. She knew it wasn't playing when she left that morning.

Dotty looked at Kaylee. "Did you forget to turn your music off before you left?"

"I must have," Kaylee said, not wanting Dotty to ask any questions.

Dotty led Kaylee up the staircase to the third floor. She went to the second door on the left, glanced at Kaylee and proceeded to open the door. When Kaylee stepped just inside the large room, she remembered what Adam had said about the room being filled with paintings that were all covered. Dotty pointed to a full-sized painting that stood on an easel near a tall window and said, "You'll find Mr. Hilmar's portrait right there."

Kaylee stood in front of the sheeted painting for a moment, anticipating what the man she had heard so much about would look like. As Dotty pulled the sheet away, Kaylee stood in awe. She shifted her eyes to Dotty and back to the canvas.

"Wow," Kaylee said. She was amazed at Roy's rugged good looks. He stood tall, his shoulders squared and one arm propped on a burgundy wing back chair. He had the look of royalty. His medium-length, light brown hair was parted almost in the middle and pushed behind his ears. Full dark brown eyebrows crowned his hazel eyes. A generous mustache topped his narrow lips. His light brown suit was the exact color of his hair. His jacket unbuttoned, exposed a matching vest that fit snugly over a high-collar, white shirt and a dark brown tie. Precision-creased slacks rested on top of his brown and black laced-up shoes. One of the most elaborate gold and diamond rings Kaylee had ever seen rested on his left hand.

After a moment, Dotty walked over and took hold of the sheet. "I'll help you cover it," she said.

As they were putting the sheet back over the painting, Kaylee spoke up, "In this room, is there a painting of Roy, Ellen and Jenny Lynn together?"

Dotty appeared uneasy, yet she raised her chin and led Kaylee to another large painting. "This was painted a couple of months before Jenny Lynn passed away," Dotty said.

Kaylee felt speechless as she looked at the family together. Roy was sitting in an over-stuffed chair with Jenny Lynn sitting on his knee. Ellen stood beside the chair with her hand placed on Roy's shoulder. The visual of the three of them together gave Kaylee a different sense of what the family might have been like.

Dotty helped cover the painting. "You may as well take a look at Willie Hilmar while we're here," she said. "I'm sure you were going to ask."

"Dotty, you're reading my mind," Kaylee said with a half-way grin.

The likeness of Willie to her father was astounding. Willie was sitting in a high-back, dark blue chair with her hands folded and resting in her lap. Her posture was tall and straight, and her pink lips were without expression. The brown hair was the same as her father's. Her long hair was done up, revealing her long, thin neck and allowed the perfect look for the high-collared, light blue dress she was wearing.

A striking, light blue topaz oval brooch was anchored in the center of her collar that was trimmed with small white lace. Her large, round hazel eyes stared across the room like an elite guard. On her left hand was an elaborate diamond ring. On her right hand a large, white pearl stood high in a wide, lace gold setting. Kaylee mumbled, "You can sure tell that Thelma is her daughter."

"Yes, you can!"

After looking at some of the other paintings, Kaylee turned to Dotty. "This is all so strange. These portraits are exquisite, and the frames are excellent. To hide them away like this, makes no sense."

"They are not exactly hidden," Dotty said.

Kaylee's jaw dropped open. "What? Not hidden away? They're upstairs, under sheets, in a locked room where no one can possibly see them. Some may call it stored, but I call it hidden. They should be gracing the walls of this magnificent house."

Before Dotty could respond, they heard someone knock at the front door. Dotty tossed the sheet over the painting and ordered, "Come on, let's get out of here."

They raced down the stairs. "Good evening, Miss Shell," Dotty said as she hurried out the kitchen door.

"You don't have to leave, Dotty."

"I must go."

"Thank you, Dotty."

Chapter Fifty-Three

Music

*K*aylee inhaled and blew her breath out, trying to settle her breathing before opening the door. The knock had now progressed to pounding and prompted Kaylee to hurry and answer it. To her surprise, Thelma Hilmar stood there with her lips tight and eyes squinted and nose in the air.

Thelma pulled at the tail of her jacket. "Well, it's about time. I thought I was going to have to knock the door down."

"Mrs. Hilmar, what a surprise."

"I bet it's a surprise, Miss Shell. I need to talk with you." Thelma raised her head even higher and then said in a much lower tone, "If you don't mind, that is."

Kaylee stepped aside and told her to come in. The instant Thelma stepped inside, her eyes widened. For a moment, she froze, unable to move anything but her aged, shaking hand that she placed on her chest. Her knees weakened. She staggered. Kaylee grabbed her arm and helped her to a chair in the dining room.

"Thelma, are you all right? Can I get you some water or a cold cloth?"

"No," she said faintly. Thelma turned her eyes to Ellen's portrait. She held her stare for a brief moment, then despairingly turned to Kaylee and asked, "Where . . . where is that music coming from?"

Kaylee had forgotten all about the music that was playing when she and Dotty entered the house. "It's a CD I bought before I moved here. Why do you ask with such intensity?"

Thelma tightened her fist and growled, "Don't lie to me, Kaylee Shell!"

Kaylee glared. "Lie to you about what?"

"About that music!" she shouted.

Kaylee sternly stated, "Just a minute, Thelma. I don't appreciate you accusing me of lying over a CD. And I don't appreciate your tone either. Now, if you want to tell me what's going on here, I'll be glad to listen; otherwise, I'm going to ask you to leave."

Thelma held to the table and carefully stood. It was evident she was shaken by the music she had obviously heard before. Gradually, Thelma moved to the mantle and fixed her stare on Ellen. She wrinkled her nose as she sniffed the air. Kaylee watched her without speaking.

"Do you smell that?"

"Smell what?" Kaylee asked.

"Nothing! Nothing!" Turning to face Kaylee, Thelma squeezed her eyes shut and shook her head sharply. The brief silence was interrupted by the squeaking sound of the double doors opening. Kaylee turned to see Paulette standing in the doorway. A gust of cold air swept through the door, causing Paulette to stagger. Kaylee motioned for her to hurry inside and close the door.

Stepping forward she said, "Grandma, Boyd told me he thought you came here. I came to take you home, okay?"

Thelma seized the back of a chair. Her voice was low, and each word she spoke was an effort.

Thelma shook her head and said, "She's here . . . she's here. Ellen is still here. But, why shouldn't she be? She never left, you know. Oh, her body left but not her spirit."

Paulette eased toward her. "Please, let me take you home, Grandma."

Thelma's face twisted. She swallowed hard and glared at Kaylee. "What are you trying to do? Why did you come here? I haven't heard that music since I was a little girl. Mama said it was Ellen's favorite. She had a wind-up music box that opened and a man and woman were dancing on what looked like water. Mama said Ellen would play it for hours and stare out the third-floor window toward the open range."

Paulette turned her eyes to Kaylee and again asked Thelma if she was ready to go home.

"Why should I go home?" Thelma growled. "Is Miss Shell tired of my company?" She frowned at Kaylee. "Are you, Miss Shell?"

Stunned, by Thelma's actions and by the things she had said about Ellen, Kaylee shrugged. "Thelma, as a matter of fact, I'm not tired of your company at all. I'm glad you stopped by. Would you and Paulette like to sit for a while? I'll make us a cup of hot tea."

"Maybe another time," Paulette said. "I really need to get her home."

Thelma squinted at Paulette. "I know when I want to go home and it's not now." She looked around the room. "I love this house. I grew up in this house. I thought I would live in it until I died, and Paulette would live here after me."

Kaylee asked, "Thelma, you said you haven't heard that music since you were a little girl. Was there a reason you stopped hearing the music?"

Thelma recalled, "I was 10 years old the last time I heard the music playing in this house. For some reason, Mother had the parlor locked away where Ellen kept the music box, as if it were pure gold or something. I should have had the right at least to see my grandmother's things, but I was forbidden."

"Thelma, I have an idea. Do you want to ask Dotty to open the parlor and let you see the music box again?"

Thelma tilted her head and chuckled. "That's a splendid thought, but I fear the council would all fall over with heart attacks if Dotty allowed me or anyone in the upper portion of the house, or in Grandpa Hilmar's office here on the first floor."

Kaylee itched her nose. "Thelma, after your mother passed away, didn't you have the keys that would open the door to the parlor?"

"No!" Thelma snapped, "I didn't! The only one in control of the keys is Dotty. Mother made that law through her will. Of course, I was dumbfounded when the will was read and I found that out."

"I don't understand," Kaylee said. "Are you saying the council doesn't have a set of keys to the house?

I thought they had a key to the front door the day I moved in."

Thelma pointed at Kaylee. "Only to certain rooms! The parlor, the room where the paintings are stored, Grandpa Roy's office, the tower room, Jenny and Ellen's bedrooms are off limits to everybody, even to them."

Kaylee sighed. "Then if you can, help me understand what is going to happen to the keys when Dotty dies?"

"After Dotty dies, the keys and the estate go to a name that's been sealed, not to be opened until, as Dotty puts it, her work here is through."

"You don't know who that person is?"

"No!" Thelma groaned, "I hate mother for doing me this way. My mother and I never really got along that well, but I never dreamt she would take everything away from me except for a small cash settlement. That's to say, small for the size of the estate."

Curious, Kaylee asked, "If you don't mind my asking, why didn't you and your mother get along?"

"Hum!" Thelma said. "I never felt compelled to guard the Hilmar name. She, on the other hand, was a fanatic about it. She promised Roy no matter what her personal feelings were, she would honor his wishes and not allow anything to touch the Hilmar name. Before Grandpa died, he evidently confessed some terrible thing to Mother. She never told me what he said, but whatever it was, it pushed mother to take the family portraits down. That is, except Ellen's and Jenny Lynn's. I pressed her daily to tell me what Grandpa told her, but her mouth was locked like a vault when it came to that subject. Mother did some strange things as a result of Grandpa's deathbed repentance. She knew I wouldn't guard the Hilmar name as she did. She resented every question I asked about Grandpa. I argued with her about the way things were run here at the Estate, everything being cloaked in secrecy. I told her that when it was mine, there would be no secrets. Mother had the final word on the subject, and I was ousted. I never could have imagined it would come to that."

"Who's the attorney that drew up the will?"

Thelma explained, "In Grandpa Roy's case, there was no attorney. He drew up his own will and sealed it until his death. Of course, there were witnesses. One was Mother and the other was his constant companion and accountant, Raymond Kent. No one outside those two saw what was in Grandpa Roy's will. At his death, Mother brought an attorney from back East to read the will. After the legal work was finished, he went back home to Boston. Mother had the same attorney present when she drew up her will. She had a portion of the will that was read to me and to the leading member of the council. Like Roy, she too sealed an envelope that was to be opened, not at her death but at Dotty's death."

Stunned by what she had just heard, Paulette held her hands up and shouted, "Wait a minute! Did you just say when Dotty dies the keys and the Estate go to someone else. Is that right?"

Thelma lowered her head. "I've said too much. I didn't mean to say that."

Paulette roared, "But is it true? Is it, Grandma?"

"I'm sorry, dear."

Paulette raged "Why didn't you just tell me? All the times you've heard me go on and on about bringing to justice the ones who stole the estate from Grandma

Willie, you never said one word. It doesn't matter if they're brought to justice or not. We still won't get the estate. Is that right?"

Thelma nodded.

Kaylee felt awkward. She wanted to say something to console Paulette, yet dared not and waited for Thelma to explain.

Thelma stood and faced Paulette. "I didn't want to believe it myself. I've always held out hoping that some way we could fight the will in court when the time came. I've talked to my attorney, and he said the will was legal and binding. Therefore, we can do nothing. I didn't want to dash your hopes by telling you."

"Grandma! You surely didn't think I would never find out, did you?"

"I knew the day would come when you would find out. I just hoped it would be a lot farther down the road. Maybe even after my demise."

Paulette's jaw dropped open. "You would allow that to happen to me. The hurt and shock of losing you wouldn't be enough. I would also have to deal with the devastation of losing the Estate as well."

"I'm so sorry, dear. I thought I was doing the right thing. Maybe I wasn't. I just don't know anymore."

Chapter Fifty-Four
Portraits in Line

*P*aulette lowered her head and went into the living room. Thelma followed after her. She put her hand on Paulette's shoulder as her granddaughter looked out the large window toward the gardens. "Darling, I know how you feel. I couldn't believe it myself, but the thought of telling you and destroying your dreams was worse than having it all taken away from me. I did so want you to have the house and land."

Thelma started back to the dining room where Kaylee was standing. Paulette turned and gave Thelma a quick hug. She walked with her arm around Thelma to the dining room.

"Can you forgive me?" Thelma asked as they walked.

Paulette answered in a calm tone, "Yes, I can. You're more important than anything. I love you, Grandma, and nothing will ever stop that. In a peculiar way, I don't think I'm really that surprised. Down deep, I had this gut feeling that confirmed what you just told me."

They stood by Kaylee. Paulette said, "This makes me more determined than ever to find the truth about

Stone River and my family." She looked at Kaylee. "Any suggestions, Miss Shell?"

"Yes. I want you to continue over the next few days what we're doing tonight. Talk about events and things you recall, and, like our conversation tonight, you'll remember more than you think. When you do, the answers will come."

Thelma took hold of Paulette's arm and grinned. "I think I'm ready to go home, dear."

"Me too, Grandma."

As they neared the door, Thelma stopped, raised her head high and listened to the music. "It's so hard to believe. After all these years, I'm finally hearing the soothing sounds of the music Grandma Ellen cherished."

Thelma looked at Kaylee and said, "By the way, Paulette told me about the class history study of Stone River and about your meeting at the Bend today. She also told me what Charlie LittleHawk had to say about Wind Dancer saving Ellen's life." Thelma fixed her eyes on Kaylee and asked, "Do you believe that story? You know tales have a way of getting bigger every time they're told. But then again, I heard that same story from Mother when I was a little girl. Even so, she was very protective of Ellen's character. She never allowed anything negative to be said about Ellen in her presence, or in this house."

Kaylee watched as Thelma closed her eyes and listened to the music a brief moment.

Thelma opened her eyes. "One day, I overheard Mother talking to Dotty. Dotty said her father drove Ellen to Wind Dancer's arms. Nonetheless, the Hilmar name was to be protected. No matter what the cost." Thelma shook her head. "How could Mother do this to me her only child? It's evident no matter what the cost, included me."

"It's a deep mystery," Kaylee said, "why your mother would sign the estate over to the town, but the town has only partial control and only partial access to the house. To enter a room, Dotty has to open the door and go with them into the room. Only Dotty holds the keys, and at her death it all goes to . . . who knows."

Paulette glanced around the room. "Grandma, why do you think Grandma Willie allowed Ellen and Jenny's portraits to remain on the wall, but not the others?"

"Who in the world knows, dear? There were times mother was so bizarre. Out of the blue, she would tell the housekeepers to let Grandpa Roy in the house. He must have forgotten his key. Grandpa had been dead for years. At times, I would find Mother on the third floor sitting in a chair and staring at the family portraits. She would remove the coverings and line them up. Jenny Lynn's painting was always first in line, then Ellen's. Last in line were always the ones of her, Judy Justice and Roy. There were nights when Mother would get out of bed, hurry down the hall and say that she heard someone crying. I never heard anything. Her behavior grew very strange. At times, I thought maybe she was hearing voices, because she would stand at the bottom of the stairs and talk out loud to no one. If I asked about it, she said she was thinking out loud.

"I was never allowed in the tower room. But I did see it one time. I came up with a plan that worked. I knocked on the door, and when Mother opened it, I rushed in before she could stop me. I told her some off-the-wall story that must have been important enough that she allowed me to stay in the room, but only for a moment. Anyway, she didn't get mad at me for doing so. I must confess that after seeing the rest of the house, I was very disappointed in the room. It wasn't elaborate like the rest of the house. There were only a few pieces of old furniture, a large mirror, an oval rug and a black metal chandelier. After seeing the room, I wanted to know why I hadn't been allowed there. Mother vowed, 'I was afraid you would go out on the balcony and more than likely fall or get hurt.'"

"A tower-room?" Kaylee asked. "How cool is that?"

"Yes. It was cool, but I really didn't want to see the tower room. I wanted to find the hidden room—"

"There's a hidden room?" Kaylee interrupted.

"Yes, and I never could find it. Mother didn't have any idea where it was either. Well, maybe she did and didn't tell me. Although she did say, 'Roy will never tell me where it's located. He said, if the need should ever arise, then he would show me where it is at. Until then, there is no need for you to know.'"

"Thelma, you said your mother told you at times she heard someone crying in the night."

Thelma lowered her head. "She swore to me it was Ellen crying."

"Ellen Hilmar?"

"Yes."

"Why would Ellen be crying?"

"She said, 'If ever a person had something to cry about, it was Ellen.' Mother didn't expound further, no matter how many questions I asked. I came to the point that I thought it was all in her mind." Thelma raised her head and stared at Kaylee. "Have you heard anyone crying in the night?"

Kaylee eyes widened. "No, I haven't."

Thelma squeezed Paulette's arm. "Darling, I'm really tired. Will you take me home?'

"Of course, Grandmother."

Tears welled up in Thelma's eyes as she closed her eyes and listened to the music that continued to play. She grinned and moved her head back and forth to the rhythm. She opened her tear-filled eyes and looked at Kaylee. "It's so good to hear the music again. Goodnight, Miss Shell."

"Thelma, would you please call me Kaylee?"

Thelma gave Kaylee a tight-lipped grin and muttered, "Yes, I think I will, Kaylee. You know I came here to throw a fit on you about the trip to the Bend with the students, but I guess it's true that music 'calms the savage beast.' I would love to have a copy of your CD, if you don't mind. I was always stunned how a small music box could play so loudly you could hear the music all through this big house. Ellen would never tell anyone where the music came from or who had composed or performed the song.

"Why do you think that is?" Kaylee asked.

"Mother said, 'That music belonged to Ellen alone.'"

"How could that be?" Kaylee asked. "I found my CD in Raleigh."

Thelma shrugged. "Yet another piece to the mysterious puzzle."

Paulette looked at Kaylee and smiled. "I look forward to our next group meeting."

Kaylee nodded in agreement, walked them to their car and watched as they drove out of sight.

Chapter Fifty-Five

Surprise call

The late November night was cold. The sky was clear, revealing a half-moon and a sky filled with millions of twinkling stars. Kaylee hurried inside, paused and listened to the music playing. She then turned the furnace up and took one last look at Ellen before turning the lights out. Halfway down the hall, Kaylee paused when she heard a light tapping on the front door. With anticipation, she rushed to the door and asked, "Who is it?"

She smiled when she heard Adam's voice. When she opened the door, Adam had his arms crossed and was stepping from side to side. "It's freezing out here," he said.

Kaylee tilted her head. "Then come in out of the cold, cowboy."

Adam stepped inside and closed the door. Before he pulled his gloves off, he took Kaylee in his arms and kissed her long and slowly. Kaylee responded by locking her arms around his waist and pulling him tightly toward her.

Adam removed his hat and gloves, stroked her cheek and said, "I think it's going to take another kiss before I'm warm enough to let go of my coat."

Kaylee put her hand on the back of his neck and pressed her lips against his. After she kissed him, she unbuttoned his coat, pulled it from his shoulders and allowed her eyes to meet his. She gently tapped the tip of his nose and told him to get comfortable while she got him a cup of hot coffee. They silently sipped their coffee and listened attentively as the music softly played.

Adam took Kaylee's hand. "I came out earlier but saw you had company."

"Yes, I did. It was Thelma Hilmar and Paulette." Kaylee told Adam about their visit and the things Thelma had shared about her family. "Adam, have you ever been in the tower room?"

"Yeah, a couple of times."

Kaylee set her cup on a nearby table. "What was it like?"

Adam raised his shoulders. "After seeing the grandeur of the rest of the house, I'd have to say I agree with Thelma. It's meager by comparison. Don't get me wrong. If you hadn't seen the rest of the house, you would think it was exceptional."

Before Kaylee could respond, her cell phone rang. She closed her eyes and groaned. "It has to be Martin. I haven't called him in a while. He's going to be furious."

Adam sat his cup down by Kaylee's, "Then don't answer it."

"If I don't answer, he'll keep calling until I do."

Kaylee took the phone from her purse, paused and said, "Hello."

Instead of an irate Martin, it was a soft-spoken Jeffrey. "Kaylee."

Her eyes widened as she looked at Adam. "Jeffrey, what a delightful surprise."

"Baby, I can't tell you how much I miss you, and I so desperately want to see you."

Still stunned, Kaylee said softly, "Jeffrey, I'm so surprised. I thought surely it would be Martin screaming, because I haven't called lately."

"You're right, he's furious. He would be more furious if he knew I was calling you now, but I had to at least hear your voice."

Feeling awkward and not wanting Adam to hear their conversation, Kaylee walked gradually toward the dining room. Adam managed to hear her say, "I love you too and want to see you so badly."

He took another sip of coffee and moved closer to Kaylee. When he heard her respond to Jeffrey with the words, "I want you too," he was determined to put an end to her every craving for Jeffrey. He came up behind her and paused, allowing his eyes to move up and down her shapely body. Adam put his arm around her tiny waist, pulled her against his vigorous body and smelled her perfumed hair. Kaylee tried to pull away, but he only tightened his hold and moved his warm lips down the side of her face and neck. Trying to talk normally proved to be impossible. Her breathing intensified, causing Jeffrey to ask if she was okay.

"Yes . . . yes, I'm fine. It's just very warm in here." Again, Kaylee tried to break free from Adam's hold but could not. With one hand, he held her body against him and used his other hand to pull her hair behind her ear. He pressed closer to her as he ravished her neck and shoulder with kisses. Kaylee squirmed, but the force of his body pressing hers was too robust. Kaylee uttered a sigh of relief when Jeffrey said he had to go. Kaylee was terrified Jeffrey would hear Adam's low moans as his hand delicately massaged her stomach. Her body ached for his touch, yet she was furious that he would do this while she talked with Jeffrey.

"I love you, Jeffrey, and . . ." Kaylee was getting so aggravated, she wanted to scream. "I . . . I want you more than words can say." As she hung up, she pushed loose from Adam's hold. She slapped his face and shouted, "What do you think you're doing? I love Jeffrey, not you, and don't you ever forget that!"

Kaylee tried to walk past him, but his hand reached out and his fingers circled her upper arm. Gasping at the pressure against her flesh, she tried to pull away but he only held more tightly and drew her toward him. She frowned and tightened her lips and struggled to get loose.

Adam muttered through gritted teeth, "No man could ever love you as I do. And don't you forget that." Adam pulled her tightly against his muscled body and kissed her powerfully. He released his grip, stepped back and said, "Goodnight, Kaylee."

Before he touched the door, Kaylee hurried to grab his arm. "Adam."

He stopped but didn't turn around.

"Adam, please don't go."

He looked over his shoulder at her.

"Don't go. I feel as though my heart will burst if you go out that door."

Adam unhurriedly turned to face her and gazed into her pleading eyes. Kaylee touched his cheek. "I'm so sorry. I didn't mean to yell at you, and I surely did not mean to slap you. It's just . . . I was hearing 'I love you' from Jeffrey and feeling your touch burning like fire on my body. My emotions frighten me when you touch me. I feel as though someone else is in my frame. The wild pleasure you bring alive in me is more than I can withstand. The thing is, I want the wild pleasure over and over again. I can't hardly let you go out the door. I want you with me all the time."

Adam stroked her hair. "I wouldn't have left. I had to feel you and be a part of you. I just needed to know that you didn't want me to go."

Kaylee touched his lips with her finger and glided it down his chin onto the center of his neck. She stepped to him. He kissed her again and again until her mind numbed with a swirling passion that had to be satisfied. They were so entwined with each other, neither had noticed the music had become louder and more dynamic.

After a while, Adam and Kaylee went to the dining room and sat at the end of the table near the fireplace. Adam took Kaylee's hand in his. "I'm so in love with you that it's driving me crazy. You're in every thought and every fiber of my being."

Kaylee rubbed the back of her neck. "I know how you feel. I just don't know what to do about it."

"Why should we do anything? We're adults."

"We're adults all right, but not responsible adults. I know I'm here for a reason and not just for Mr. Cullman. There's so much more going on here. It has something to do with this house and Ellen Hilmar. I just don't know what yet. Tell me, Adam, where do you fit into all of this?"

"I wish I knew the answer to that million-dollar question, but I don't."

Kaylee drummed her fingers on the table. "Since we don't know the answers, let's try and find them. Thelma Hilmar told me, tonight, that Roy Hilmar said there was a secret room in this house but she didn't have a clue where it was and neither did her mom. Roy told Willie that if the need to use the room should ever arise, he would show her then. That, like everything else, makes no sense to me. Why didn't he just show her the room? What's the big secret? What would be in the room that he wouldn't allow anyone to see or even tell anyone where it was located?"

"I totally agree with you," Adam said. "But how do we find out where the secret chamber is?"

Kaylee stood and put her right hand on her hip. "Adam, I need Dotty's keys. That's another thing. Why would Willie make Dotty lord of the keys? She isn't even family. She's only a housekeeper. Then, Willie does the absurd and leaves the estate to the town of Stone River, but only partially. The council can't get into the rooms without Dotty's authority. My question was, 'Who will end up inheriting the estate?' I was told that some unknown person, whose name is sealed up in an envelope and hidden away until Dotty dies, or as Dotty put it, until her work is through."

Adam scratched his temple. "No one knows who the person is including Dotty?"

"That's what she said. She told me when she is ready to leave the estate, the envelope will be opened and the mystery person will get the whole estate, complete with the keys."

Adam shook his head. "So only Willie Hilmar knew who that person will be?"

"Yes."

"You're right, Kaylee. What does Dotty have to do with anything other than being a housekeeper and guarding the keys?"

Kaylee looked at Ellen. "And then there's Ellen, at the beginning of it all." Kaylee shook her head and muttered, "Ellen, if only you could talk, I bet you could fill our ears full of the answers I'm looking for."

Adam stood. "Kaylee, let's give all this a rest for tonight. My tired mind is on overload."

"Sounds like a great idea to me too."

Adam smiled. "Do you have any plans for tomorrow?"

Kaylee put her arms around his waist and pulled him to her. "I don't know. What do you have in mind?"

"I want you to ride out to the canyon with me."

Kaylee grinned. "I'd love to. What time?"

"Around noon. Is that good? But right now, I need to get some rest."

Kaylee's teasing smile caused Adam to want the affection of her lips one more time before leaving.

Chapter Fifty-Six
Willie Hilmar

$\mathcal{T}$he consistent knocking on the kitchen door woke Kaylee. She grabbed her robe and hurried to see who it was. "I'm coming," she shouted. "Dotty, is that you?"

"Yes, Miss Shell."

"Good morning, come in."

"I'm sorry. I didn't mean to wake you."

"No . . . no, that's fine. I was fixing to get up anyway."

Dotty put the coffee on and asked, "Would you like some breakfast?"

Kaylee stretched her shoulders and back. "No thank you, Dotty. I'm just going to have a bagel this morning."

Dotty took a bagel from the package and popped it in the toaster. "Do you have plans for today?"

Kaylee sat at the counter. "Yes, Adam and I are going riding. He wants to take me to see Coyote Canyon. I feel as though I've been there many times, he talks about it so much."

Dotty took the bagel from the toaster and placed it on a saucer. "Would you like butter or cream cheese on your bagel?"

"Cream cheese would be wonderful!"

As Dotty spread cream cheese on the bagel, she said, "It's certainly lovely out there."

"I'm sure it is. Such a beautiful time of the year."

Dotty set the bagel in front of Kaylee. "Miss Shell, did I see Thelma Hilmar here last night?"

Kaylee took a bite of her bagel and moaned. "This is so good, Dotty! And yes, Thelma was here last night. We had quite a visit."

Dotty's face muscles tightened. "I can imagine." She poured Kaylee a cup of coffee. "Without prying, may I ask what she was doing here?"

Kaylee took a napkin from the holder and wiped the corners of her mouth. "You're not prying. As they say down South, she came here to chew me out, but we ended up having a really nice visit." Kaylee could tell that Dotty was eager to know more about their conversation. "Thelma told me some very interesting things about Willie Hilmar."

Dotty's sharp eyes turned immediately to Kaylee. "Really? Like what?"

"Like, you're the only one who has total access to the keys of the estate. I'm curious myself. Why is that, Dotty?"

Dotty took a sip of her coffee, wiped her mouth and said, "Because Willie Hilmar trusted me."

"She trusted you above her own daughter?"

Dotty set her cup on the counter. "I know what you're thinking, and yes, Thelma was nothing but a heartache to Willie. Thelma knew her mother's standards and rebelled against everything Willie stood for. They fought like cats and dogs."

Kaylee propped her elbows on the counter. "Then help me understand. Why didn't Willie leave you the estate and not just the keys?"

Dotty frowned. "Let me make myself clear. My desire isn't to own this estate. It's merely to look after it until . . . until my time here is through."

"Why is the name of the next owner sealed until your work here is through? Why didn't Willie Hilmar just give the estate to the person in the envelope, instead of waiting until your departure? And what if the person named in the envelope dies before you? What then?"

"I don't think that's any of your concern, Miss Shell. If there's nothing else I can do for you, I'll straighten the house."

Kaylee glanced around the room. "I don't think anything is out of place except for my bed, and I'll make it before I leave. Dotty, yesterday you let your hair down and had a good time. You talked, laughed and allowed me to see the portraits."

"Yes, I know. Perhaps that was a mistake."

"Why was it a mistake? What did it hurt? I'm not out to destroy you, this house or the contents. However, all the cloak and dagger actions only peak my curiosity."

Dotty squinted and growled, "Oh, I don't think it's the house that's holding your interest. It's Adam who's here all hours of the night."

"Yes, Dotty, you're right. He's a very handsome man and single. I'm a single woman, so, I don't see the problem."

Dotty grunted, "Hum."

Kaylee put her bagel on the counter and faced Dotty. "Hum what?"

Dotty grabbed her sweater from the counter and put it on. "Oh nothing. You two have a nice ride," she said, as she went out the kitchen door.

Chapter Fifty-Seven
Ride to the Canyon

Kaylee got ready and hurried to the stables. She could see Dotty peering out her window as she went through the gate. Adam had the horses ready when Kaylee entered the stable door. He smiled and grabbed her and kissed her energetically as he pulled her to a large pile of hay in one of the stables. They fell back into the hay. He pulled her on top of him, not allowing her to catch her breath as his lips continued to cover hers. He started to open her coat.

Kaylee seized his hands. "No, Adam, what if someone comes in?"

"There's no need to worry about that! No one is here but Dotty."

"I know. I saw her peeking out the window as I went by. She commented on how you were at the house all hours of the night."

"So what? That's none of her business."

"I would just feel better if we wait until we're sure we won't have visitors."

Adam kissed her forehead. "You know your every wish is my command."

He helped her up and brushed the hay from her back. They mounted their horses and headed toward the canyon. The ride was beautiful. The wind was cool, but the sun was bright. They ran the horses most of the way. Suddenly, Adam pulled back on his horse's bridle.

"What is it?" Kaylee asked.

"We're almost there. It's just ahead." Adam's face grew pale and he nervously licked his lips. He slid off his horse, took the reins and began walking toward the apex of the canyon.

The view from the summit was amazing. The canyon was rocky, but on the other side of the canyon was a slender waterfall flowing down the mountain into the river basin, which was filled with the water of Stone River. There were a few evergreens and oaks along the summit. The grassy fields had turned mostly brown. The roar of Stone River was loud and clear as they stood side by side, looking over the gorge.

Adam lowered his eyes as he stood silently. Kaylee turned to check the horses that were peacefully chomping dry grass along the trail.

"Adam, are you okay? You look a little pale."

He smiled and assured Kaylee all was well. Adam took a blanket for them to sit on from his horse and spread it on the ground. After a few minutes, Kaylee noticed that the color had not returned to his cheeks, nor had he spoken since he sat down. Adam drew his knees to his chest and held them tightly with his arms.

Kaylee managed to stay silent, giving Adam time he perhaps needed to say something. She gently put her hand on his arm. He swallowed hard and stared straight ahead at the falls. At one point he lowered his head, groaned and closed his eyes. After a long period, Kaylee could take no more. She put her hand on his shoulder and said with concern, "Adam."

At first, he didn't acknowledge her.

By then, Kaylee was concerned. "Adam," she shouted, "are you okay?"

Adam raised his head and faced Kaylee. Her breath escaped her as she pushed with all her might to get as far away from him as possible. "Oh, God, help me!" she screamed. Who is the man staring at me? It isn't Adam! Kaylee had never seen this man before. His dark eyes gleamed and his teeth were exceptionally white against his flawless, dark skin. Trembling, Kaylee scooted farther away and attempted to stand. At that point, she was shaking out of control.

She managed to get to her horse. As she mounted, she heard what sounded like Adam's voice calling her name. Too scared to look back, she kicked the horse's ribs causing him to race toward home. For a minute, she didn't hear her name being called. Then suddenly, she heard Adam shouting at her at the top of his voice. He was getting closer. She continued to kick her horse trying to go faster, but the attempt to get away proved to be in vain. He caught up and was now riding beside her. Adam grabbed her horse's bridle, slowing her down.

Frantic, Kaylee bashed him on his back and cheek with the leather strap from her bridle, causing him to slow down. Adam continued to shout out asking what was wrong with her, until she raced over the knoll disappearing from his sight.

Kaylee didn't stop at the stable. She rode the horse to the kitchen door, slid off, rushed inside and locked the door behind her. Frantic, she ran to the front door to make sure it too was locked. Shivering, Kaylee turned, pressed her back against the door, trying to catch her breath and erase the stranger's dark eyes that peered into hers at the canyon. Exhaling, she opened her eyes and was startled to see Dotty hurrying out of her bedroom, down the hall.

"Miss Shell, what's the matter? You look as though you've seen a ghost."

Kaylee progressively pushed away from the door, frowned at her and firmly asked, "What were you doing in my room, Dotty?"

"I put some clean towels in your bathroom."

"You gave me clean towels and linens yesterday." Kaylee tightened her lips and demanded, "What were you doing in my room?"

Dotty nervously pulled at her sweater and said, "I'm sorry, if you think I was snooping. From now on I'll not bother your quarters, for any reason."

Kaylee walked toward her, stopped in front of her and stated, "You know you're not to go into my private quarters, just like I'm not to be upstairs."

"I allowed you to go upstairs."

Kaylee tilted her head and snapped. "Yes, you did. However, they're not your rooms and they don't contain your personal things."

Dotty took a step back. "I said, I'm sorry."

Kaylee put her hands on her hips. "That's not good enough, Dotty. If you want penitence, let me see the tower room."

Dotty gasped and put her hand on her chest. "No! I'll not break my oath to Willie Hilmar. She trusted me to guard this house, and I will do that very thing."

Red faced, Kaylee shouted, "I'm about up to my eyeballs in your honor. I don't care what you promised her."

Before Kaylee could finish her thoughts, Adam pounded on the front door and called out for her to let him in. Dotty turned her eyes to Kaylee and then to the door. When Dotty took a step to go answer the door, Kaylee grabbed her arm. "Don't answer it. I don't want him in this house."

Confused, Dotty stuttered, "Wh-why not?"

"I can't explain it right now."

Adam continued knocking, begging Kaylee to let him come in. Dotty's eyes widened as she looked at Kaylee. "Did something happen at the canyon?"

"Yes," Kaylee said softly, "but I can't talk about it right now."

Dotty sent a shock through Kaylee when she asked, "Did you see Wind Dancer?"

Kaylee stared at Dotty. She didn't have a clue what Dotty was talking about. Adam's pounding on the door had diminished into a light tapping and a low groan.

"Kaylee, please let me in. I need to know what I did for you to run away from me. Kaylee! Kaylee! I love you Kaylee. I need you." Adam began to cry, which was almost more than Kaylee could stand. She put her hand over her mouth and closed her eyes.

Dotty touched Kaylee's arm and quickly pulled her hand back. "Don't turn him away, Kaylee. If you do, you'll kill his spirit."

Kaylee looked at Dotty. Over her shoulder she saw the pale blue light over Ellen's picture was on and the faint sound of the piano rhapsody started playing.

"I'll go out the back way," Dotty said. "Please, please, you must let him in!"

"What's going on, Dotty?"

"I'll explain another day. As soon as I go out the back door, let Adam come in and talk with you." She patted Kaylee's shoulder and hurried toward the kitchen.

Chapter Fifty-Eight
Transformation

*A*dam's cry was so faint she could hardly hear him and the loud knock on the door was now a light tap. More confused than ever, Kaylee bit her lower lip and moved sluggishly toward the faint knock. Bewildered, Kaylee took a deep breath, turned the lock and opened the door. Tears streamed down Adam's face as he shivered in the cold. Adam removed his hat and was gripping the brim. In the moonlight, his silky blond hair glistened. Kaylee stepped back as he raised his head and fixed his eyes on her.

He desperately uttered, "Kaylee my love, my love. My life would be over if you turn me away. Your love possesses me. If your love dies, I die."

She stepped aside and nodded for him to come inside. Still leery, Kaylee closed the door without taking her eyes from Adam. Gradually, Kaylee moved to the entrance of the dining room. Adam reached his hand toward her. Trembling, she stepped back. Adam took a step in her direction, wanting to touch her. Kaylee withdrew. "Don't you dare touch me."

Adam's face muscles tightened. "What's wrong with you? Why did you run away from me?"

Kaylee stood firm. "It wasn't you I ran away from."

"You sure could have fooled me!" Adam cried. "I was with you at the canyon! How can you possibly say it wasn't me you ran away from?" Adam pointed to his face. "Look at this welt on my cheek and the one on my back. You put them there. You, Kaylee!"

Kaylee shouted, "When you looked at me, it wasn't you I saw. I don't know who it was, but it wasn't you."

Adam raised his hands. "I don't know what you're talking about, Kaylee. I need to know what you thought you saw. So, please tell me."

Kaylee pushed her hair back. "It wasn't just what I saw. It was the way you changed from the moment we arrived at the canyon. You were pale as a ghost and wouldn't speak. All you did was lower your head or stare at the waterfall. When you turned to face me, I couldn't breathe for a moment. The face I saw had large dark eyes and tan skin."

Adam exhaled and said, "I swear to you, Kaylee, I don't know what you're talking about. All I know is, I love you and I wouldn't lie to you and God forbid that I would ever think of hurting you. Have I ever given you any reason to doubt me?"

Kaylee lowered her head. "No, you haven't." Kaylee pulled a chair from the table and sat down. She propped her elbows on the table and pressed an open hand to her forehead.

Adam touched her shoulder.

Kaylee pulled away.

"I'm not going to hurt you, Kaylee."

Kaylee was beginning to relax. Adam touched his fingertips to her hair and her shoulder. Calmer still, Kaylee stood, told him to take his coat off and she would get him a cup of hot coffee. Adam asked for a glass of wine instead. She poured them wine as he removed his coat and hung it on the back of the chair beside him.

Kaylee sat across the table from him. After taking a sip of wine, she set the glass down without releasing it. Her eyes connected with Adam's. For a second, she could say nothing. She glanced up at Ellen. "I promise you I've never encountered anything like what's going on here. It's two weeks until Christmas. I . . . I"

"I know your feelings, Kaylee."

"Adam, tell me about your visits to the canyon. What are they like? Are they like the one today?"

Adam took a gulp of wine. "Yes. They're always the same. First, I sit and stare into the canyon, then at the waterfall. The loud roar from the falls sends me into a trance-like state. My mind and body are filled with thoughts of you. I can feel my fingers gliding over your soft body, my lips touching your lips, the smell of your hair. When I leave, I want to come here and make love to you and hold you until my eyes open with the morning light. There's another thing. When I told you, I go there to spend the night with friends, the friends I was speaking of were the Lakotas who had free run on that land until Roy and Jake took it from them. I can feel their spirits, hear their laughter, their children playing and even the neighing of their horses. This all started a couple of months before you moved here. When I first saw you, I was stunned. I had been seeing your face for two months before you even arrived in Stone River."

Kaylee stood and moved to the fireplace. Adam stood behind her. He slipped an open hand on her stomach and pressed his body to hers. Promptly, she knew she had to step away or she wouldn't be able to say no to his, or her, desire. She took his hand and pulled it from her body, stepped back to the table and picked up her wine glass.

Adam ran his fingers through his hair. "We've got to figure this out."

"I know," Kaylee said. "Adam, I need to find that hidden room. I don't know where to look that everyone else hasn't, but I will find that room. I also need to know where the key fits that I found on the mantel." She faced him. "Dotty asked me a very confusing question tonight."

Adam tilted his head. "What did she ask?"

"She asked, if I saw Wind Dancer at the canyon."

"Do what?"

"That was my response. She said she had to go and would explain it later. What would make her ask such a thing? He's been dead over a hundred years. How could I possibly know what he looked like? The only description I've heard is, 'He was a very handsome strong brave with long black hair that blew in the wind as he rode across the fields. He had dark eyes that glistened like the sun dancing on the water and perfect teeth as white as a virgin snow.' I've only heard bits and pieces about Wind Dancer and Ellen. One would think after a while I could put some of the details together and perhaps get some kind of visual, but I haven't yet. Of course, we have the painting of Ellen but . . ."

Adam restlessly glanced around the room, took his last sip of his wine and sat the glass on the table. He raised his eyes to meet Kaylee's. From his stare alone she could feel her breathing intensifying. He moved toward her and lightly touched her cheek with his fingertips, gliding them down to her jaw. Kaylee closed her eyes and moaned. Adam soothingly pushed her hair behind her ear, leaned forward and touched his lips to her ear lobe. His hands held her slender shoulders; ever so gently, he pulled her close, fitting his warm lips over hers with a passion that blotted out her every protest from mind and body alike.

Forgetting everything, Kaylee shivered with desire as her fingers touched his silky blond hair. Adam swept her up in his arms and carried her down the hall to her bedroom.

Gently, he laid her on the bed. An overwhelming ardor passed between them as their bodies came together in a way that Kaylee and Adam had never experienced before. This time, not only were their bodies connected, but their souls were as well. The music amplified, and it too took its place in the immeasurable fascination.

Chapter Fifty-Nine
Not Speaking

*K*aylee's eyes sprang open when she heard a tree limb thump against the side of the house. She sat up in bed and ran her hand over the spot where Adam had laid earlier. She wished he was still by her side. Kaylee turned her head and listened for the music but it had stopped playing. She squinted as a flash of lighting illuminated the dark room, followed by loud claps of thunder. Feeling anxious, yet needing rest, she snuggled in her covers and closed her eyes. By then, the awesome sound of a hard rain had begun to pound against the window, a true antidote for peaceful sleep.

The alarm clock sounded, causing Kaylee's body to jerk. There was little sign that night had indeed ended. Sluggishly, she pulled herself from the bed and moved to the window to look outside. A steady, cold rain continued to fall, but the wind had died down. Dark clouds raced across the sky, blocking the morning light.

Kaylee expected Dotty's early morning knock, but it didn't come. After opening the front door, she grabbed her umbrella from the stand and stepped outside.

Pausing a moment, she remembered the devastating look on Adam's face the night before when she had opened the door. The impulse to forget work and go knock on his door was alluring, but not practical. So, she fought the urge and went to work.

Needing to see a friendly face, she knocked on Terra's door. Terra motioned for her to come in. Kaylee tensed her brows and asked, "Terra, what in the world is going on? Two thirds of the teachers won't even speak to me."

Terra glanced toward the open door, "They're all bent out of shape over your field trip Saturday. Nick told you to stay in the teaching guidelines. Kaylee, why couldn't you have your meeting in your class during school hours? You could have avoided all those hard looks?"

"What in the name of Tom Sawyer is going on here? What is the big deal about going to the Bend, Beef Eaters or H & B's Drug Store? What difference does it make? You'd think I was the first teacher in the world to take a class on a field trip. That makes me so mad, I could spit."

Terra shook her head. "Well please don't. Let me tell you something that will ease your mind for a moment."

"Please do! I need to hear something positive."

Terra propped her elbows on her desk and smiled. "You know John Smith? The computer man?"

"Yes."

"He asked me out Saturday night."

"Really? So, what did you tell him?"

Terra chuckled and said, "Are you kidding? I told him yes."

Kaylee leaned on the desk. "What did you two do?"

"He picked me up at seven and we drove to Pickens. We had dinner and went to a movie."

Kaylee chuckled. "And, what about afterward?"

Terra leaned back and giggled. "That's private."

"Did you guys kiss?"

Terra swooned. "Oh my, yes. His kisses are out of this world."

"Well, well. Are you going to see him again?"

"Yes, I did see him again, last night. I made dinner for us."

Kaylee crossed her arms. "I was going to ask if you liked him, but I think you've already answered my question."

"I like him a lot. He's such a gentleman. And, he asked me out to dinner Tuesday night."

Kaylee squeezed her hand. "I'm so happy for you."

Terra rolled her big eyes. "Me, too."

Rick interrupted their conversation as he entered the room. "Well, look who's all smiles today. Did you get lucky over the weekend, Terra?"

Terra stood and smiled. "One thing for sure, Rick, you'll never know."

He turned his eyes to Kaylee. "Did you have a nice little weenie roast at the Bend, Miss Shell?"

"It was awesome!" Kaylee said. "You should have been there. Of course, when you live under somebody's thumb, it's hard to get away, isn't it?"

Rick raised a brow and growled, "You had better be careful, pretty lady. The Wild West can be brutal."

"I'm sure you're not threatening me, are you, Rick?"

Terra stood and stepped between them. "Rick, I think you had better be going."

Kaylee was furious. "The audacity of that jerk."

"Kaylee, please listen to me. This is no ordinary town, and these aren't ordinary people. If you rub them wrong, they'll make your life a living hell. I know from experience."

Before Kaylee could respond, a couple of students came in. "I want to hear more later, please." Kaylee said, as she left the room.

Chapter Sixty

Circle Meeting

*A*s Kaylee entered her classroom, Betty hurried up
to her and whispered, "Miss Shell, we've got a juicy
bit of information for you. Can we have a circle meeting
this morning?"

Kaylee tilted her head and smiled. "A circle meeting
indeed, how exciting."

Paulette rushed through the door just seconds after
the bell rang. As she passed Kaylee, she grinned. "Sorry
I'm late, Miss Shell."

"No problem."

After the bell rang, the students moved their desks
and made a circle in the center of the floor. Everyone
one was so motivated. Kaylee could hardly wait to hear
what the class had to say. Kaylee paused, when she saw
each student pull their necklaces from the openings of
their shirts.

"Where's your necklace, Miss Shell?" Charlie asked.

Taken by surprise, Kaylee was elated that she had
put her necklace in her purse. The group clapped when
she put it on, sat down and crossed her legs. "All right,

288

you guys, you have my curiosity peaked. Lori, I would like for your group to start and give us some details."

Lori slapped her leg and said, "I am so glad you started with me. I know everyone will love this. There's an old woman by the name of Cleo King who lives at Stone River Retirement Village. I volunteer at the Village two afternoons a week. My dear friend and classmate, Betty, comes out to the Village sometimes and helps me out. Yesterday, I was assigned to Cleo King's ward to help assist in feeding them lunch. Betty was there also to help with the feeding. She assisted Cleo with her lunch. I'll let Betty take it from there."

Betty put her hand on her chest and giggled. "This is so romantic!"

Eddie said, "Betty, told me the story last night. Man, it was all I could do to keep from crying like a baby."

Betty looked at Eddie and declared. "Men are beasts! They wouldn't know romance if it walked up and slugged them."

Eddie held his hand out to her. "Baby, you know I can be a Romeo when I want."

"That is true," Betty said. "However, women have a more sensitive side about them. Now, if I may continue without further interruption, dearest Eddie."

Eddie winked at her. "I'm sorry, baby. Go ahead."

"Thank you. As I was helping Cleo with her lunch, I got to talking with her about school, Miss Shell and the history lesson we're doing on Stone River. When I mentioned, Wind Dancer's name, her eyes lit up like the Fourth of July. Well, you know me, I asked her what that big beautiful smile was about. She said, and I quote, 'What a love story.' I'm always in the mood for a juicy love story. So, I asked what she was talking about. Miss King squinted her pale blue eyes at me like I should know what she was talking about. She said, 'You don't know about the love affair between Wind Dancer and Ellen Hilmar?'

"I almost flipped out, right at the table."

Amazed, Kaylee asked, "How did she know . . . about the affair?"

"That was my first question," Betty said. "Cleo was quick to inform me that she heard the story from her parents. Keep in mind, Cleo is almost 94 years old. She confirmed what we have gathered so far. Ellen wasn't a happily married woman. She played the role of the dutiful wife when needed, but behind the scenes it was a whole different story. Cleo told me that Wind Dancer indeed saved Ellen's life, as we had discussed Saturday. She also verified that Wind Dancer thought Ellen was the most beautiful woman he had ever seen. Cleo said the love affair started the day he saved her life.

"'When Ellen stopped fighting Wind Dancer,' Cleo said, who, according to her story, actually did sit on top of Ellen and hold her down until she realized he wasn't going to hurt her, 'he helped her up and began brushing her clothes off. Ellen asked his name. He told her he was Wind Dancer, son of Black Bear, Chief of the River Bends, Lakota tribe.' Just listen to what happened next. I can hardly stand it."

Eddie chuckled, "Now, baby, you sound like you're getting turned on by all of this Wind Dancer and Ellen stuff."

Betty eyes widened as she looked at Eddie. "That's because I am. Now listen and learn, sweetness."

Everyone laughed. Betty placed her opened hand on her chest. "I'm getting chills just talking about it. Is anyone else feeling the chill, or is it just me?"

The girls promptly agreed. Colton chuckled and asked, "How about you, Miss Shell? Are you a romantic?"

Kaylee rubbed her arms. "I'll let my chills answer that question."

Betty glared at Colton. "If I may continue . . . the moment Wind Dancer told Ellen his name, it happened." Betty paused, put her fingertips to her temples and blinked her eyes repeatedly.

"Betty, come on, what happened?" Lisa asked.

"Their eyes met. Wow! Can you stand this, are you seeing it?" Betty fanned her face with her hand, took a deep breath and slowly blew it out.

Paulette, eager to hear the rest of the story, insisted, "Come on, Betty, we're dying here. What happened next?"

Betty bit her lower lip and continued, "Let me put it this way. It was the same thing that happened with me and Eddie."

Eddie chuckled and proudly said, "Hey, we did have magic, didn't we?"

Betty frowned. "Really? Was that magic? Let me tell you about real magic, sweetheart. Cleo said, 'When Wind Dancer and Ellen's eyes met, it was as though their souls instantly became one. They held that stare for several minutes.'—"

Eddie interrupted, "Come on, Babe! Several minutes?"

Betty frowned. "Look here, fast Eddie. Wind Dancer wasn't in a hurry to get home to watch the eight thousandth episode of *Happy Days*."

"Watch it. There's nothing wrong with *Happy Days*. I know for a fact most of the boys in here watch it."

Betty looked at Kaylee. "Miss Shell, would you please instruct Eddie to zip his mouth? He's ruining the story."

Kaylee nodded her head and said, "Eddie, please let Betty finish her story without further interruption."

Eddie placed his hand on his stomach and bowed his head. "Anything for you, Miss Shell, and my deepest apologies to you, lovely Betty."

"Thank you, Miss Shell. As I was saying, before I was interrupted, "When their eyes met, the connection took place. Still holding their stare, Wind Dancer carefully touched Ellen's cheek with his long, strong fingers and then he leaned forward and kissed her. Can you believe it, he kissed her right after saying hello?"

The girls were giggling and chatting and the boys were shaking their heads. Kaylee, on the other hand, was stunned at what she was hearing.

Betty's raised her brows as her eyes scanned her classmates. "Now, my fellow students, as Paul Harvey would say, here's the rest of the story. Cleo expressed that Ellen made the next move by touching his long, straight, ebony hair. She ran her fingers under his long mane, clamped her hand to the back of his neck and pulled his lips to hers. Ellen's kiss wasn't the kind of kiss you would give your little kid when you put them to bed at night. It was a long, passionate kiss. Wind Dancer, obliged Ellen and right there on the apex of Coyote Canyon, they made wild, sizzling love!"

"My gosh," Eddie gasped. "Miss Shell, may I be excused? I need some fresh air. I'm about to smother . . . nah, I'm just kiddin'."

Everyone was rattling on except Kaylee. She could hardly breathe for real. Her mind raced with the events that had taken place with her and Adam at the canyon. Kaylee recalled Dotty asking if she had seen Wind Dancer at the canyon. Even though her mind was spinning out of control, Kaylee knew she had to get herself together and continue the class.

"Betty," she said, "was that all Cleo told you?"

"No, there's more. Cleo was an ancient treasure chest of information. She said, 'The love affair went on, almost daily.'"

Colton laughed, "Almost daily? How could they not get caught? I would get caught. I know I would."

Eddie rubbed his forehead and asked, "How did he keep up his energy? Forget getting caught. I mean with having to hunt food and stuff like that and still care for his woman."

Betty rolled her eyes. "Eddie, darling. True love produces an energy that never fails and never tires. Now, I'll answer Colton's question."

Eddie grabbed his chest. "Baby, you've hurt me in front of all these fine nobles. I have energy."

Betty squinted at Eddie and continued. "As I was saying, Cleo said Ellen showed Wind Dancer a secret way to enter and exit the house . . . whenever Roy was away."

Kaylee spoke up. "Betty, did I hear you right? A secret way to enter and exit the house?"

"Yes, Miss Shell, I did. Cleo said, 'Wind Dancer came to the house, and they carried the affair on right here in the Hilmar Estate.' Do you believe it? In the Estate!"

Kaylee's mouth was dry as she listened to what Betty was saying. She wanted to get outside and breathe some fresh air, but the need to hear the rest of the story was foremost.

"Well, subsequently, the romance escalated to the point that Ellen's lover would stay overnight in a secret room. Now, keep in mind, Cleo said, 'Roy built the secret room in the house for himself.' I asked Cleo, 'Why did Roy need a hidden room?' She said, 'For his own love affairs.' Cleo said, 'One day, without warning to the workers, Roy stopped work on the house for several weeks. It was then he incorporated the mystery room somewhere amid the construction. When the workers came back to finish the house, they had no idea a room had been added.'"

Paulette looked at Kaylee and said, "Miss Shell, we were talking about the secret passage the other night. It's cool to hear that someone else knows it."

"That's for sure," Kaylee said.

Lori looked at Paulette and asked, "Paulette, did you ever see the secret room?"

"No. Betty called it a mystery room and that's what it appears to be. Even my Grandma Thelma doesn't know where the room is."

"Betty, if you would please continue. I can't wait to hear the rest."

Betty cleared her throat. "The last thing I have to say is, Cleo said, 'Ellen wanted her lover in the house so she could go to him in the night' . . . if her desire should get out of hand.'" Betty giggled. "I'm only teasing. That was my personal thought going on there."

Eddie rubbed his fingers through his hair and smiled. "Do you ever feel that way about me in the night, cupcake?"

Betty leaned her head back. "Oh yes, I do. Every time I watch a Brad Pitt movie before I go to sleep."

Eddie threw his hands up, "Hear this, class, Brad Pitt has nothing going for him that I don't. Except millions of dollars. But before you think me destitute, I'll inform everyone that I have $348.75 in Hilmar/Boone Savings and Trust."

Betty cleared her throat and continued, "Let me make a brief confession about Cleo's story. I threw in the part about Ellen's desire getting out of hand in the middle of the night, only because I know that's the way a woman would feel. The romantic thoughts about the secret room thing is messing with my mind."

Everyone chuckled when Eddie asked, "Honey, you wouldn't have a secret room at your place I could sleep in, would you? Just in case your desire gets out of hand, I can be there to satisfy."

"Yeah, my daddy would put you in a secret chamber and seal the entrance. You, my dear, would never be seen again." Betty put her hands up and said, "Okay, all kidding aside. In conclusion, Cleo said, 'The lovers continued that path until Wind Dancer and his brother, Moving Cloud, went missing."

Paulette was sitting beside Charlie. She nudged his arm and said, "Should we carry on where our ancestors left off?"

He leaned his head to hers and said, "I have no problem with that. Are you talking about at the canyon or at the estate?"

"Well, in order to carry on a tradition, it would have to be experienced in both places. Wouldn't it, Miss Shell?"

Kaylee shook her head. "I think every couple has to make their own love story. If what we've heard here today is true, then that's what Ellen and Wind Dancer did. And here we are, talking about their love affair over a hundred years later. Therefore, let's learn a valuable lesson from this today. Be careful what you leave people to talk about. You may be someone's history lesson one day."

Chapter Sixty-One

John and Terra

$\mathcal{B}$efore Kaylee could ask any questions, Nick Long knocked on the door. Kaylee motioned for him to come in. "Hi, Nick. What can I do for you?"

He surveyed the class and growled, "What is going on here?"

"We're having a history lesson. Would you like to join us?"

"No!" Nick snapped. "But I want to see you in my office before you leave today."

"Yes, sir." Kaylee muttered as he closed the door.

The bell rang. Everyone left, fascinated by what they had learned. On the way out, Paulette stopped and asked, "Miss Shell, do you believe the old woman's story?"

Kaylee sighed. "Yes . . . yes, I do. If it's true, it could explain so many things. Do you believe it's true?"

Paulette looked at her watch. "Without a doubt. I'd better go. See you and don't let Nick Long get to you."

"I won't! Thanks for the words of encouragement, Paulette."

After the last bell, Kaylee gathered her things and started down the hall to Nick's office. She saw John Smith going into the gym, which was located beside the office. She wanted to speak to him and called out to him, as she entered the gym door.

Seeing it was Kaylee, he went to meet her. "Miss Shell, what a nice surprise!"

"Hi. I wanted to say hello and let you know I spoke with Terra."

John nodded. "She's a wonderful woman and fun to be with. I'm glad you wanted me to ask her out. How are things going with you?"

Kaylee shrugged. "I'm not sure about everything, but we've definitely made some progress. I'm on my way, as we speak, for a meeting with Nick. God only knows what that will entail. Have you heard anything about why we are having this meeting?"

"Only that you're on the list. Whatever that means. They want you out of here, Kaylee. You must be getting too close to something important. I would try and rush things along, if I were you."

Kaylee frowned. "Well, I wish I knew what I was getting close to. I'd better be going."

"Miss Shell?"

"Yes."

"Have you called Martin lately?"

Kaylee sighed. "Actually, no! He's left a thousand messages. I just haven't called."

"Maybe you need to." John suddenly changed the subject when he saw Nick standing at the door. "I'll check it first thing in the morning, if that's all right with you."

"That will be fine. Thank you, Mr. Smith."

Kaylee turned and acted startled to see Nick standing there. "Mr. Long, I was on my way to see you."

"Good!"

Kaylee followed him to his office. Nick closed the door behind them. "Have a seat, Miss Shell."

"I prefer to stand, if you don't mind."

"As you like." Nick sat down, leaned back and folded his hands on his stomach. "Kaylee, when you first came Fair Mount, I thought you would be a top-of-the-line person, but now, I'm not so sure."

Kaylee frowned. "So, tell me, Nick, what changed your mind."

Nick leaned forward and placed his elbows on his desk. "I'm going to be straight and to the point. I've had a serious complaint about you."

Kaylee crossed her arms. "Really? By whom?"

"Joshua Coats."

Shocked, Kaylee asked, "The Joshua Coats in my senior history class?"

"Yes."

Kaylee fixed her eyes on Nick. "What kind of a complaint?"

Nick scowled. "One of a very personal nature."

Kaylee put her hand on her hip and snapped, "Enough already. What kind of a complaint?"

"There's no need to get upset if you've done nothing and raising your voice won't change one thing."

Kaylee replied in a softer tone, "What is the nature of the compliant?"

"Joshua said you gave him a ride home last Thursday after school. Is that right?"

Kaylee nodded, "Yes, I did. His car wouldn't start. He asked if I would drop him off at his house on my way home. I said yes."

"He stated that you stopped at the drive-through bridge at the end of town."

Kaylee responded, "Yes! He said he felt sick and asked if I would I mind pulling over."

Nick tapped his finger on his desk. "Then what happened?"

Kaylee leaned toward Nick. "Why don't you tell me, what happened?"

Nick stood and glared at Kaylee. "If you needed a man, why didn't you let Rick take care of you? He's wanted to take you to bed since he first met you."

For a moment, Kaylee was speechless. "Just what are you talking about, Nick?"

"I'm talking about how serious it is to try to seduce one of your students."

A dozen emotions passed across Kaylee's face as she tried to form her words. "Are you . . . are you . . . serious? she asked"

Nick placed his hands on the edge of his desk and stood. He leaned forward and asked, "Do you think I'm joking about something this serious?"

Kaylee cut her stern eyes to Nick. "Why would Joshua say such a thing?"

Nick raised his brows, "Maybe, because it's true."

Kaylee could feel her cheeks warming with anger. "That's a lie, and you know it. Desperation must be kicking in for you to use a student to accomplish your underhanded schemes. Joshua is a quiet young man. He's kind and considers others above himself. Knowing this about him sways me to believe that he would have to be forced by an individual to come up with such pile of crap."

"Pile of crap? We need to work on our vocabulary, Miss Shell. It may be crap to you but to me, and the council, it's fact." Nick straightened his posture and added, "In light of the seriousness of this complaint, we have no choice but to put you on leave. With pay, of course, until we can further investigate this perverted act on a minor. By the way, your leave is effective immediately. I've already scheduled a sub for you. The council will be in touch. Maybe you should contact a good lawyer. You're free to go, for now, Miss Shell."

Kaylee's face muscles tensed. "I'll speak to Joshua about this. Maybe, you had better contact your own lawyer, Nick." She turned to leave.

Nick called out, "By the way, Miss Shell, if this dreadful act should prove to be true, you'll also be evicted from the Hilmar Estate immediately."

Kaylee didn't acknowledge his statement, but promptly left the office. Outraged, she collected her things from her classroom and was about to leave when John knocked and opened the door.

"Miss Shell, if you don't mind, I can take a look at that computer program today."

"Sure. Come in, I'll show you what the program's doing now."

Kaylee sat down and John stood behind her. He mumbled, "I heard what just happened. Maybe you ought to head back to North Carolina while you can."

Kaylee stood. "No! I am not going anywhere!"

"Maybe you're right. Call me later, I'll let you know if I hear anything."

Kaylee got her things and headed for the door. Her stomach was in knots. She walked slowly in the pouring rain to her car. Although she was soaked, she was determined to speak with her accuser before going home. Joshua's mother answered the door but didn't ask her inside out of the rain.

With one hand on her hip, she shouted, "I don't think I have anything to say to you, Miss Shell. Neither does Joshua."

"Mrs. Coats, I don't know why Joshua would say I made advances toward him. I didn't. I do know Nick Long and the council are behind this. I don't understand why."

Mrs. Coats lowered her head. "I think you had better be going." She stepped back and closed the door.

Chapter Sixty-Two

Dream Lover

*T*he ground rumbled from the thunderclaps, and the hard rain continued to fall. Kaylee was freezing by the time she got home. She turned the heat up and hurried to the bathroom to run a hot bath while she undressed.

After slipping into her robe, she took her wet clothes to the laundry room and placed them on hangers to dry. Needing something hot to drink, she put on a pot of coffee and went back to check the bath water. Chilled to the bone, she hurriedly turned her CD on, lit a lilac candle and pinned her hair off her neck. She removed her robe and sank into the mass of bubbles. The water was a bit warmer than usual but felt perfect on Kaylee's cold body.

"Ah!" she said, resting her head on the blue satin pillow that hung over the rim of the claw-footed tub. She closed her eyes. Instantaneously, her eyes sprang open, remembering the night she thought . . . no, the night she knew someone had made love to her while she bathed. Though she saw no one that night, the lover's touch she would never forget. After glancing around the room, she closed her eyes and drifted off to sleep.

After a short while, Kaylee began to move her shapely body in the warm water, trying to open her eyes, but not really. She feared the dream that had returned would end and the stimulating fingers that stroked her body would stop. In her dream, it was Adam's face she saw, not Jeffrey's. It was Adam's kiss that ignited a fire in her core of passion. Kaylee moaned loudly at his massaging touch. Her groans intensified as her body squirmed enthusiastically and as his full warm lips robbed her of her breath. There was a kind of desperation in the way his lips pressed against hers. His strong fingers had stilled against her back, holding her securely to him. Something wasn't right. Realizing this caused her to gasp for air as his lips continued to press hard against hers.

Kaylee's groans were no longer about passion, but fear. Struggling to free her mouth from his was in vain. Her body thrashed trying to wake up and see who had entered her dream. After a long fight to awaken, her eyes sprang open. She wildly searched the room, but again, there was no sign of her mysterious lover.

Kaylee trembled as she scurried from the tub, dried off, grabbed her robe and secured it around her waist. Slowly, her feet took her down the hall, which seemed endless. Stopping at the dining room entrance, Kaylee braced herself against the door, trying to steady her unstable knees. She raised her head, fixing her stare on the pale blue light that shown over Ellen's portrait. She faced Ellen and shouted, "Ellen! What are you doing to me? Is there something you're trying to tell me? If so, start by telling me who just crawled into my bathtub with me and why? Why?"

Her body jerked, breaking her gaze when the grandfather clock chimed. It was already midnight, and exhaustion had overcome her, yet her desire for Adam to come by had peaked to a desperate level. She needed someone to talk with, to calm her fear.

Repeatedly, she mashed the stop button on her CD player, but her attempt to turn the music off was useless. Overwhelmed with anxiety, Kaylee turned the lights out and put her fingertips to the silky wallpaper to help steady herself as she made her way down the hall to her room. Without hesitation, she climbed into bed and pulled the covers tightly around her shoulders.

Sometime during the night, Kaylee eyes sprang open when she heard a tree limb atop her window banging against the side of the house. As she listened, the wind picked up to a hard, steady blow that circled the drafty old house. Kaylee remembered what Donna said about the house creaking and making strange noises when the bone-chilling winds of winter began. At this point, she was beginning to understand what Donna was talking about. With her head pounding, Kaylee turned on her side, pulled the heavy down comforter up over her ears and hoped for sleep. Nightmares tried to edge their way into her mind a she finally dozed off. They succeeded just long enough to prevent any real sleep. The touch of the man who had now twice infiltrated her dreams, lingered like a thick fog on a rainy morning.

Kaylee pressed her fingers to her temples, trying to stop the throbbing that kept perfect rhythm with her pounding heart. She threw off the covers, sat on the edge of the bed, made her way to the bathroom, took a couple of aspirin and went back to bed.

Nothing was making sense. Thoughts of Jeffrey had all but faded. That was inconceivable, until now. Martin had called more than a hundred times, yet she dared not answer her phone. "Kaylee, why don't you call him?" she muttered to herself. Turning from her side to her back, Kaylee folded her hands on her stomach and stared into the darkness. Inconsistent flashes of lightning illuminated the room. At times, she could have sworn she saw the man who had entered her dream while bathing, standing at the foot of her bed. Too tired to fear or fight, she drifted off to sleep.

Chapter Sixty-Three
Joshua's Allegations

Kaylee was awakened by the smell of coffee and cinnamon toast. She put her robe on and headed to the kitchen. Dotty was sitting at the bar, drinking coffee and eating a piece of toast. Kaylee stopped in the doorway.

Dotty smiled and greeted her. "Good morning, Miss Shell. I know you asked me to knock and allow you time to answer the door; however, I thought perhaps with the storm, you may not hear me knock. So, I let myself in." Dotty poured Kaylee a cup of coffee and sat it on the counter. Kaylee felt numb. She yawned and took a sip of coffee.

"Are you okay, Miss Shell?"

Kaylee pushed a strand of hair behind her ear. "Yes. I'm fine. Thanks, for the much- needed coffee and toast."

"You're quite welcome. I . . . I heard what happened to you at school yesterday. I want you to know, I don't agree with it one bit. It's not right."

Kaylee massaged the back of her neck. "No, Dotty, it isn't right. Just like so many other things."

Dotty looked down at her coffee. "I also heard . . . about Joshua's allegations."

"Yeah. That's the worst part of all. I know Joshua wouldn't say those things unless he was backed into a corner that he couldn't get himself out of."

Dotty finished her toast, put her coat on and asked, "Miss Shell, would you like to decorate for Christmas? It's only two weeks away, you know."

Kaylee held her cup with both hands and stared at Dotty. "Who knows, Dotty, I may not be here that long."

Dotty took the house keys from her pocket, looked at Kaylee and laid the keys on the counter. "I'm going into Sioux Falls to check on a friend of mine. I won't be back until tomorrow night around seven. Would you like me to bring you anything?"

Surprise filled Kaylee's eyes. She looked at the keys and then to Dotty. Dotty smiled and said, "It's happening, isn't it?"

Kaylee shrugged, "What's happening?"

Dotty chuckled. "You'll know soon enough. I'll see you tomorrow night."

Kaylee swiftly asked, "Dotty, have you seen Adam?"

"Yes, yesterday morning. He said he was going to ride out to the canyon."

Kaylee lowered her head. "Oh."

"Do you need something, Miss Shell?"

Kaylee shook her head, "No . . . no. You drive carefully."

Dotty opened the door, stepped outside and released the bronze handle, allowing it to shut.

Kaylee called out to her and rushed to the door.

Dotty pushed it open and asked, "What is it, Kaylee?"

She peered at her and said, "Dotty, the other night when Adam was knocking, I was hesitant to let him in. You told me if I didn't let him in, it would kill his spirit. What did you mean by that?"

Dotty responded, "When a person's in love, the only one who can kill that person's spirit is their lover. I really need to go. I'll see you tomorrow night."

Kaylee closed the door and leaned her back against it. *Does Dotty know about me and Adam? Of course, she knows.*

Chapter Sixty-Four
Dotty Left the Keys

*K*aylee's cell phone ringing interrupted her thoughts. She hurried to her bedroom and took the phone from her purse. It was Martin. Pausing for a brief moment, she thought of answering Martin's call but decided not to, placed the phone on the nightstand and dressed.

Kaylee was elated that Dotty had left the house keys for her, although she did wonder why. Whatever the reason, she would take full advantage of the amazing opportunity that had presented itself.

The first key she wanted to find was to Roy Hilmar's office. Looking at the keys, Kaylee was thankful each key was marked. After taking a deep breath, she pushed the key into the lock of the downstairs room and turned it. She shivered with anticipation as she pushed the heavy door open. A mystifying consciousness swept over her as she surveyed the magnificent room lined with beautiful mahogany wood that had darkened with age.

Facing the entrance was a large stone fireplace, framed by two mahogany spiral columns that extended to the molding. Above the mantel was a mosaic medley of the Western era. The domed ceiling was brilliantly framed with a mural of large white clouds and blue sky. In the center of the dome, a rider clothed in red and white rode a white stallion standing on his hind feet.

Roy's vast, oak desk sat across the room facing the wall of books. A vintage pool table was situated directly behind two brown leather French chairs. The hardwood floors gleamed, accented by a decorative hand-woven Lakota patterned rug. The walls displayed trophies of animals' heads hanging in abundance. Roy had spared no expense in building and designing the place where he conducted business. Moving gradually into the room, Kaylee keenly surveyed every nook and cranny. To her surprise there was no bed, as Adam had suggested.

On his desk, a wood frame displayed several pipes. Underneath a substantial buffalo head was an immense gun display locked in a gun cabinet with an etched glass front. Kaylee noticed right away the room was devoid of windows. When she sat down in Roy's high-back, brown leather desk chair, she felt as though he was standing in the room, rebuking her for having the audacity to touch his things.

Kaylee opened one of the drawers. It held a few papers and a small inkbottle. She glanced at the quill pin sitting on the corner of his desk. All the drawers basically contained office supplies. When she tried to open the last drawer at the bottom of the desk, it would not open. Pulling hard to open it proved to be ineffective. It was locked.

She looked through the books that lined the shelves, hoping to find a key on the shelf or between the books.

That too, proved to be a dead end. Feeling desperate, she lifted the corners of the rug in case something might be there. Her mind was set on finding the hidden room. She pushed on everything feasible, expecting to find a quickly moving door that would open at her touch, like in the movies, but nothing happened.

As she moved toward the door, like lightning she turned and fixed her eyes on the desk and the locked drawer. Pausing a moment to think of the locked drawer only heightened her desire to find out what was inside. Kaylee thought about prying the drawer open after all. What would be the worst thing could happen if she did? The council doesn't have access to that room. Therefore, they wouldn't know. "Dotty would be the one to reckon with," she muttered. "Yet she did leave the keys. At any rate, that's a chance I'm willing to take."

Again, she tried shaking and pulling the drawer. Again, it didn't work. So, she went to her room and got a hairpin. She had resorted to a hairpin more than once in her career and it had worked quite nicely. Hopefully, it would work again. It did. Breathing a sigh of relief and filled with anticipation, she carefully pulled the drawer open. At first, all she saw were papers. She thumbed through them.

One group of papers was of particular interest. It contained bank files. One of the sheets displayed several large withdrawals, but no name was signed showing who had withdrawn the money. That is, until she came to the last page. A five-hundred-thousand-dollar withdrawal had been made and signed for by Ellen Hilmar on October 10th, 1888. That wasn't the only surprise Kaylee came across. In the very bottom of the drawer, underneath the files, was a piece of paper that had been crumpled up. After removing it, Kaylee was stunned when she opened the paper. It was a picture of a woman and a young girl. Looking closely, ink had been smeared over their faces, Kaylee realized the picture was of Ellen and Jenny Lynn.

"Why would Roy do this to a photo of his wife and daughter?" she wondered aloud. If you love someone, you put their picture in a place of honor, maybe on your desk. You would not keep it locked in a desk drawer with their faces stained with ink and twisted together.

Before leaving the room, Kaylee returned the picture, closed the drawer and took another tour around the room. Again, she pushed and pulled on everything, hoping to find an entrance to the hidden room or something. The probe for the secret chamber proved to be to no avail, yet the bank records and photo were gold nuggets in her hunt.

She could hardly wait to check the tower room. Before that, she wanted to check the room where the portraits were stored again. For the second time, she checked the paintings one by one, hoping to find any possible linkage to the hidden room, but she found nothing. After that room, she moved to the next room, and the next, but nothing. After checking all the third-floor rooms, except the four rooms off the main hallway, Kaylee sighed and opened the first of the four doors.

It was the large library Adam had told her about. Saying it was magnificent was an understatement. Kaylee went up the spiral stairs to the upper level where the books were shelved. After taking out most of the volumes, checking and pushing on the wall, she was exhausted, yet determined to continue her search. Halfway down the steps, Kaylee stopped when music began to play. By now she had grown used to hearing the moving melody the pianist played with such excellence.

When Kaylee opened the next room, she was immobilized. In the center of the room, she saw a tall, slender mahogany table with a round music box, sculpted of white porcelain, sitting on it. The top was a glorious blue that looked like water. The stem was wound tight, allowing the piano music to echo through the house. In the center of the music box were miniature figurines of a man and a woman dancing around and around. Kaylee's eyes surveyed the round room before going in.

Slowly moving toward the music box, Kaylee trembled at what the woman was wearing. The black gown she had found in her closet was an exact replica. The woman's hair was pinned up and a gold and pearl comb sat like a tiara on top of her head. "Oh God," she moaned.

In front of her she saw a large, rounded-top window with purple velvet drapes. They were outlined with gold tassels and scalloped valances. Matching velvet cushions filled the window seats. To the right of the window was a sculptured mahogany poster bed with a sheer purple canopy. The walls were covered with imported silk, lilac wallpaper. A dressing table and a hutch desk sat to the right of the bed. A book of poems lay open on the desk. Kaylee opened the hutch. There was only stationery and a couple of small poetry books inside.

As she stood in front of the window, she remembered what Thelma had said about Ellen staring out the window across the open range. Kaylee not only saw the open range, but the large, white marble mausoleum that housed the Hilmars' remains. Four significant pillars lined the entrance. A tall black-laced iron fence walled the burial chambers. Kaylee muttered, "Maybe it's time for me to pay my respects to the Hilmars. I'll do that tomorrow morning."

Kaylee opened the massive wardrobe that held Ellen's clothing. As she opened it, the smell of cedar filled the room. Kaylee immediately recognized the emerald green gown Ellen was wearing in the portrait. While the room was way beyond her expectations, there was still no clue that led to the secret chamber . . . if indeed, there was one. Before leaving the room, Kaylee tried to turn the stem on the music box to rewind it, but it was still wound tight.

The tower room was exactly as Thelma had described it. Kaylee felt sure if there was a hidden room, it would be in that room, but not so. After locking up and going down the short hall, Kaylee paused where she and Adam had made love. She hoped he was back from the canyon and would knock on her door any minute, and again she would be in her lover's arms.

Chapter Sixty-Five

Visitor in the Rain

*I*t was late evening when Kaylee finished going through all the rooms. With her stomach growling from hunger, she made a peanut butter and jelly sandwich and poured a glass of milk to drink while the coffee was brewing. She put her food on the breakfast nook. There, she could put her feet up on the bench and rest her aching back against the wall at the same time.

Her eyes danced when she heard a light knock at the kitchen door. Feeling sure it was Adam, she wiped her mouth and hurried to open it. Her smile quickly vanished when she saw it was Joshua. He was soaking wet from rain that had continued to fall for two days. Before she could say anything, Joshua quickly said, "Miss Shell," he muttered with lowered head, "may I talk to you for a moment?"

Kaylee crossed her arms and asked, "Should I invite you in or is someone waiting in the wings to take a picture of you coming into my house and call that evidence?"

"No one knows I'm here."

"How is it no one knows you came out in the middle of the night in a drenching rain?"

Joshua sighed. "Maybe you're right. Maybe . . . maybe, I should just go."

He turned, but Kaylee caught his arm and said, "Please, come in."

He looked at Kaylee and again lowered his eyes.

"Please," she said, "come in and dry off. I'll get you something warm to drink."

He slowly entered, took off his raincoat and hung it on the coat rack near the door. Kaylee gave him a towel to dry off and put water on for hot chocolate.

Joshua sat at the nook without speaking. Kaylee brought their chocolate and set it on the table. She sat down across from Joshua and said, "Do you think it's going to rain all night?"

Joshua anxiously shifted his lowered eyes from left to right and sighed several times. Without warning, he jerked his head up. It caused Kaylee to shudder. His brows tight and his breathing depleted, he seized Kaylee's wrist. Her eyes instantly cut to his. Pleading he said, "You have to know, I didn't mean to hurt you."

Kaylee's eyes went from his to her wrist he was still holding. Swallowing hard, she said, "Joshua, let go of my wrist, and we'll talk about it."

He pulled his hand away and licked his upper lip.

"Drink your chocolate while it's still hot." she said, as she picked her cup up and took a sip. "Okay, Josh, what's so important, that it would bring you out in this flood?"

Joshua spoke in a low broken voice. "What I'm about to tell you, you've got to promise you won't tell anyone."

"Even if it will clear me?" Kaylee asked.

A serious look seized Joshua's face. "They won't let you be cleared."

Kaylee squinted, "What are you talking about?"

"I'm talking about the council. They want you out of Stone River and fast, for some reason."

"I'm listening. What is the reason?"

"Tim Dodd, the mayor of Stone River, came up to me one day after school about a week and a half ago. He said he needed to talk to me alone. I didn't have a clue what about. We went to the school bus area; no one was there. I felt a little nervous, not knowing why he would want to talk to me. He said the new teacher, Kaylee Shell, was causing a problem for the town and the school. That you were going out of the boundaries of Stone River's teaching curriculum, and it would only bring trouble and embarrassment to the town. Then he said you weren't just a teacher, but a private investigator sent here by a Martin Cullman, a man who lived outside Raleigh, North Carolina. They feared you were going to destroy what our founding fathers had built and you were using the class to help do your dirty work. That was your way of picking our minds in order to find whatever you're looking for."

Kaylee was dumbfounded. "Joshua, did Tim Dodd say where he got his information?"

"No."

"What else did he say?"

Joshua rubbed his forehead, "He said he knew my father and mother were three payments behind on our house and the bank would foreclose before the fourth one came due. However, he could see to it that we would be handed the title free and clear if I would cooperate. He knew we couldn't come up with the payments. So, in order to keep the farm, I said I would do whatever he wanted. Please understand, Miss Shell, I did this for Mom and Dad."

Kaylee put her hand on Joshua's arm, "I understand completely. What did he say he wanted you to do?"

"He said he wanted me to act like my car wouldn't start and get you to take me home. I was supposed to feel sick at my stomach by the time we got near the covered bridge and ask you to stop. He had a witness nearby to verify that we were sitting there for about ten minutes. When I asked you if I felt hot, it was so the witness would see you touching me. Then I jumped out of your car like I was getting away from you. Not to throw up. Miss Shell, if they find out I told you, the bank will foreclose on our farm. Please promise me you won't say anything. Please."

Kaylee stood, put her hands on her hips and thought a moment. "All right, Joshua, I won't say anything, but I do need some time. I may need you to play sick for me."

"Anything, Miss Shell. Just let me know."

"Don't worry, I will. What could the council possibly be so afraid of?"

Joshua squinted and asked, "Are you really a private investigator?"

Kaylee sat down and took a sip of her hot chocolate. "Joshua, this time I need you to please keep *my* secret. Promise?"

He nodded. "I promise."

Kaylee leaned toward him. "Josh, it's vital when I say no one can know. Not your mother or father, classmates, Tim Dodd . . . no one."

"I promise!"

"What Tim Dodd told you is mostly true. I am a teacher, but also a private investigator sent here by, Martin Cullman. How Tim Dodd could possibly find that out, I don't know. I am here to look into Jake Boone and Roy Hilmar's lives."

"But why? They've been dead for years."

Kaylee tapped the side of her empty cup. "Martin found some letters that led him to believe Jake Boone is his father."

"Wow!" Joshua groaned. "His father?"

Kaylee pushed the cup aside and propped her elbows on the table. "Do you remember when the class discussed Tammy Boone? How she went back to Missouri but never came back to Stone River?"

"Yeah."

Kaylee leaned back and continued, "Jake took a lover after his wife and children left. That lover was Clara Aims. They never married, but he gave her a good portion of his fortune. Martin Cullman is Clara Aims' son."

"What?"

Kaylee explained, "When Martin's stepfather died, Martin inherited everything. Including his grandparent's home and property. Martin didn't know, but when his mother died, his stepfather stored several of her things in his grandparent's attic in Raleigh. Martin had never even been in the attic, so he had no way of knowing about one of his mother's trunks, which contained many letters addressed to a Jake Boone in Stone River, North Dakota. She talked about a Roy Hilmar who had stolen some of Jake's money. She also asked if Roy had ever been jailed for killing Wind Dancer and Moving Cloud. Clara told her lover the money Jake had given her would ensure his son would never lack for anything. The thing is, she never mailed the letters. Martin has lots of connections. He asked if I would come to Stone River and check out what his mother had written in the letters—to see if the Jake Boone in Stone River was indeed his father."

Joshua frowned and stuttered, "You mean-you mean what the class has found out has clearly been a confirmation?"

"Yes, it most certainly has."

Joshua lowered his eyes and asked, "Were you using the class?"

"Yes and no," Kaylee said. "Yes, because I too wanted to find the information the class has so easily found. No, because, as a teacher, we would have done the study of Stone River regardless of my investigation."

Joshua thought a moment. "Miss Shell, whatever the reason for the study, it's been tremendous. We've all been so excited. I think it's brought out the private investigator in all of us, and we love it."

Kaylee pushed her hair behind her ears. "There's still so much more to all of this. More than I could have ever imagined."

"What do you mean?"

Kaylee stood. "I can't say right now because I'm not sure. I want you to go home before you get caught and questioned about where you've been. Are you sure no one saw you leave your house?"

"Positive. I waited until dark and went out the back. I walked over here so my car wouldn't wake Mom and Dad."

"Thank you so much for coming, Joshua. That took a lot of courage."

Joshua grinned and pulled his necklace from under his shirt and said, "At the Bend, we prayed for truth, good or bad, and we all said amen to it. We were bound together that day, and together we will prevail."

Kaylee pulled her eagle claw from underneath her collar, "That we will, Joshua Coats. That we will."

Chapter Sixty-Six

An Overwhelmed Mind

*T*hat night, Kaylee was restless. Questions flooded her mind. The foremost question being, *Where is Adam? Is he okay? It is late and the weather is terrible. What could he possibly be doing? Is there a secret chamber?* She had pushed and pulled on everything imaginable and nothing moved. *What's up with Dotty leaving the keys? What about the council, Ellen, the music, the overbearing desire to be with Adam, so much more than finding out if Jake Boone was Martin's father? Why couldn't I call Martin?* He was her friend and employer, and yet she couldn't bring herself to call him or her beloved Jeffrey.

The chilling fact that she could feel a mysterious lover who was now invading her thoughts and touching her as she lay there wide-awake in her bed was way beyond anything she could fathom. If all of that wasn't enough, after talking to Joshua, yet another question had entered her mind. *How could the city council have possibly found out about Martin and me?*

Lighting flashed; thunder clapped. Heavy rain swept against Kaylee's high bedroom windows. Her heart pounded; still she managed to drift off to sleep.

In the early morning hours, Kaylee began to toss and turn, entangling herself in the loose-fitting sheets. Her body broke out in a cold sweat, and her breathing was shallow as she continued to thrash about. Kaylee sat up, and frantically her eyes searched the dark room.

Wiping sweat from her face and trying to moderate her breathing, Kaylee turned her head and listened for the faint voice she thought she heard in her dream. Instead of a voice, she heard what sounded like someone crying in the distance. As she focused on the sound, it became clear. It was a woman crying. Recalling what Lola Barnes had said about hearing a woman crying, Kaylee kicked free from the twisted sheets and grabbed her robe from the chair.

She tried to turn on the lamp, but it wouldn't come on. Holding her hands in front of her, she hurried across the dark room to the wall switch, desperately wanting the lights on. She flipped the switch up and down several times, but to no avail. *The power must be out,* she thought. Kaylee leaned her back against the wall and took a couple of deep breaths. The low crying, she heard had now turned into low moans and then into loud wailing.

Kaylee wanted to go down the hall and see if there was a woman on the staircase, yet her legs felt so weak. "Kaylee calm down," she said aloud to herself as she put her hand to her mouth and blew her breath through her fingers. "Great heavenly days! What if it's . . . Ellen?" Unnerved, she flipped the light switch several times . . . still nothing.

Not having an idea where a candle or a flashlight was, she moved to the hallway. Putting her hand to the cold wall, she moved cautiously in the darkness toward the foyer. The weeping grew louder as she neared the staircase. Nearing the foyer, she paused to catch her breath before making the turn that put her at the bottom of the stairs. Kaylee gradually raised her eyes, gasped and stumbled backward.

Halfway up the stairs, a pale blue light shimmered around a tall, slender woman. Her head was bowed. In one hand, she held a wrinkled piece of paper to her stomach and the other hand, she held over her face. The mysterious woman continued to weep. Unhurriedly, she moved her hand from her face as though suddenly aware of Kaylee's presence. She slowly raised her head and fixed her eyes on Kaylee. Breathing stopped as Kaylee stared into the face of Ellen Hilmar. Ellen's emerald green eyes looked as though she had cried an ocean of tears.

What Ellen was wearing was as much of a shock to Kaylee as seeing her. Draped on her shapely frame was a long, black negligee and black lace robe, identical to the one that had mysteriously appeared in her closet. The same one Kaylee had worn when she and Adam made love. Ellen's hair was pinned up with loose stands hanging about her neck and around her face. On top of her head, sitting like a crown, was the gold and pearl comb that Kaylee too had worn in her hair that night with Adam. Around Ellen's neck, was the same gold chain and enormous emerald, resting on the top of her breasts, like the one in her portrait over the fireplace.

Once again, tears began to roll down Ellen's cheeks. The pain in her eyes pierced Kaylee's soul. Feeling vulnerable, Kaylee moaned aloud as Ellen's pain wrapped tightly around her and then released her just as suddenly as it had touched her. Ellen lowered her head and looked at the paper she held. After a few seconds, her fingers relaxed, releasing the paper. Kaylee watched as it shifted side to side and then came to rest on the stairs. Ellen shifted her eyes to Kaylee as she continued to weep softly. Suddenly, Ellen's long, slender fingers took hold of the skirt of her long gown and pulled it from her feet. She turned and began to fade away. She had totally vanished from sight before she went up the first step, although her weeping could be heard as the sound moved up the stairs and then ceased. At that same moment, the lights came on and the piano rhapsody began to play softly. This time, the music carried a sadness that Kaylee hadn't noticed before.

Kaylee's head was spinning as she sluggishly moved up the stairs to the paper Ellen had dropped. The thought of touching the paper after Ellen had held it sent a biting chill through her being; nonetheless, she knew she had to pick it up. After hesitating, Kaylee lowered her head, staring at the paper Ellen held tight just before dropping it. She wiped the corners of her mouth, then proceeded to bend down and take hold of the corner of the crushed paper and pull it up to her. After a brief moment, Kaylee smoothed the paper out. Her eyes widened and her jaw dropped. "How . . . how, could it be?" she panted as she looked at the picture of Ellen and Jenny Lynn. "It's in Roy's desk," she gasped. "I put it back in the desk and locked the drawer. I know I did!"

Kaylee rushed to Roy's office. She fumbled through the keys, trying to find the one that opened the door. Shivering, she managed to push the key into the keyhole and opened the door. She rushed to the desk and unlocked the bottom drawer to see if the picture of Jenny Lynn and Ellen was still there. Stunned by the realization that it wasn't there made Kaylee feel nauseated. With her knees shaking, she sat in Roy's desk chair, leaned back and gazed at the picture Ellen had dropped on the stairs.

"How did she get this picture from the desk?" Kaylee said out loud. "Why did she drop it on the stairs? If it was for me to see, what is it she wants me to know? The faces have been covered with ink, and it was crumpled and locked away in the bottom drawer of Roy's desk. What is it you trying to tell me, Ellen?"

Chapter Sixty-Seven
Kaylee Rants to Ellen

*A*fter locking the office door, Kaylee moved to the dining room and stared at Ellen. "What do you want from me? Believe me, I want to know, but in order to help you, I need to know more. Tell me, Ellen, is there a hidden room?" Kaylee took the key she had found on the mantel and held it up to Ellen. "What mystery will this key unlock? You've more than got my attention. You've scared me half to death!" Kaylee held the picture up. "Why is this picture such a mess? Who did this? Roy? Another thing, Ellen, while I'm too freaking wired up to sleep, what is the connection with the music? It wasn't by accident I found that CD before I moved here was it?"

Kaylee checked the closet for the negligee. To her surprise, it was still hanging in her closet and the comb was still laying on the dressing table. Feeling so uneasy and alone, Kaylee sat in the oversized chair and leaned her head back. She squeezed her eyes shut and pressed her fingers tightly to her temples. To her frustration and dismay, she began to weep as total exhaustion swept over her. Her mind was struggling, trying to remember why she had even come to Stone River. It was supposed to have been a pretty simple task of finding out about Jake Boone and a couple of Indians. However, the investigation had somehow gone awry and everything had centered on Roy Hilmar and his family, to the point Kaylee's focus had totally eluded her. The only thing that remained crystal clear, were her thoughts of Adam.

Kaylee was awaked by the sound of someone knocking. The breaking of daylight was a welcome sight as she quickly dressed and hurried to open the door, hoping it was Adam. To her surprise, no one was there. A cold gust of wind burst through the foyer. Kaylee crossed her arms and rubbed them to keep warm.

Curious, she stepped onto the porch and looked around but didn't see anyone. The rain had softened, and a thin fog hovered over the estate. After stepping inside, she pushed the door closed and locked it. Again, she thought she heard someone knocking . . . at the kitchen door this time. It must be Adam, she thought as she hurried to the kitchen door. No one was there. Kaylee got a coat and umbrella from the rack beside the door and raced out to see if perhaps it had been Adam who had knocked. Not seeing his Jeep didn't stop her from knocking on his door. When he didn't answer, she tried to look through the windows, to no avail.

On the way back to the house, she thought about the mausoleum. Kaylee felt so compelled to go to the vault that she turned and hurried in that direction. As she neared the burial chamber, the fog thickened. With her free hand, she took the keys from her pocket, and looked through them for the one to unlock the tall, black iron gate. Walking toward the entrance, she could hardly believe she was out in the early morning in cold rain and fog to visit a burial place. Four large, white columns graced the wide porch that led the way to tall, dark, double doors covered with carved vines and decorated with elaborate black iron scrolled handles. Kaylee stood the umbrella beside the door, took a deep breath and blew it out, then proceeded to put the key into the lock, paused and then turned it. Scared and not knowing what to expect, she put the keys in her pocket and swallowed hard. Her fingers barely touched the handle and the door became ajar. With great caution, she pushed the creaking door further open and stepped inside.

Just clearing her throat echoed through the vast room. White marble with thin light gray swirls lined the tall walls. A fresco on the ceiling matched the one in Roy Hilmar's office. The main wall was entirely for Roy, Ellen and Jenny Lynn. Between each crypt, large marble columns stood erect. At each end of the wall were full-sized, ivory carvings of a woman standing with her hand on a young girl's shoulder. Solid gold nameplates let Kaylee know Roy had been laid to rest in the center vault. She looked at the black-and-white-checked marble floor.

To the right there was another wall with several vaults. There, Willie Hilmar, her brother Kevin, their mother Judy Justice and Thelma's daughter, Janet, were buried. There was also a place for Thelma who would be the last of the Hilmars to be buried in the chamber. Across the room a gold plaque was on what looked like

yet another vault. There was no name on the plaque,
only the words:

LOVE IS LIKE THE MORNING SUN
GIVING WARMTH TO OUR HEARTS UNTIL THE DAY IS DONE.
THOUGH DARKNESS MAY FALL, AND SHADOWS STAND,
I STILL HOLD TIGHT TO MY TRUE LOVE'S HAND.

Chapter Sixty-Eight
Visit from the Mayor

*B*y the time Kaylee got back to the house, the rain had stopped and the fog had lifted. Blue sky shown sporadically through the fast-moving clouds, and only a light breeze remained. She could hardly wait to put on a pot of coffee and fill her empty stomach with a bowl of Frosted Flakes. After pouring the milk in her cereal, Kaylee went down the hall and into the dining room. She looked at Ellen and shook her head. "Have mercy, Ellen. I wish I could see through your eyes for one solitary minute. Or do I?"

Suddenly, Kaylee halted as the sweet smell of pipe tobacco invaded her nostrils. Her eyes wildly surveyed the room. She turned like lightning to see a man sitting in the chair she had slept in.

"Are you having a morning talk with Ellen?" he asked.

"Who are you and what are you doing in my house?"

"I'm Tim Dodd, the mayor of Stone River. I knocked earlier, and when no one answered, I took the liberty to see if the door was locked. It wasn't, so I came in, anticipating your soon return."

"That's not true! I did lock the door. What are you doing coming into my home when I don't answer the door?"

"The door being unlocked was like an open invitation. Here in Stone River, if you leave your doors unlocked, it's a welcome sign."

"Trust me, Mr. Dodd, I didn't leave my door unlocked, and you don't have an open invitation. Now, tell me what you are doing here or get out!"

His short white hair was full and cut neatly. He was about twenty pounds' overweight and had narrow, hazel eyes and medium lips drawn into a threatening smile. He stood, crossed his arms and moved across the airy room as though he owned the place. Kaylee didn't take her eyes off him.

"I just wanted to come by and say how sorry I am about the misunderstanding at the school. God knows, we need good teachers."

Kaylee's stern voice elevated as she said, "Mr. Dodd, I'm not playing games. I'll ask one last time. What are you doing here?"

Tim looked at the picture of Ellen, turned and said, "Well, I can see you're not one for chit-chat; therefore, I'll cut right to it. I'm here to tell you that you had better keep your nose out of things that don't concern you. I know you were sent here by Martin Cullman to try and dig up some kind of information about him being Jake Boone's only living child."

Kaylee said loudly, "Are you telling me that all of Jake's children are deceased?"

"What kind of private investigator are you, Miss Shell? Everyone knows Jake's last child died a few years back, and no counterfeit child is going to come into Stone River and attempt to take over Jake Boone's fortune."

Thus far, Kaylee had no idea who had inherited Jake's possessions. She assumed that his children or grandchildren had, but the comment made by Tim Dodd had just pointed her in a different direction. "Mr. Dodd, tell me, who has control of Jake's money if not his children or grandchildren?"

He got in her face and snapped, "It's none of your business. If you're not careful, you may find trouble you're not ready to face. Do you understand me?"

Kaylee responded sharply, "No, Mr. Dodd, I don't understand you. Why don't you make it a little clearer to me?"

"I'd hate to see you sent to jail for molesting a minor. If you still don't understand me, maybe that's just what will happen. You're a young, pretty woman. Fifty years in a women's prison could be devastating for you. With the judge being my brother, I'm sure I would have all the influence I need to see to it. Now, do you understand me?"

Kaylee put her hand on her hip. "Yeah, I understand. You just stood there and threatened me."

"Good answer, Miss Shell. I'm glad to see you now appreciate me and the power I have in this town." Tim turned to leave.

Kaylee called out, "What is it that has the so-called 'council' in such a knot? I mean, with all the power you possess, you're bound to know."

Tim frowned and left, slamming the door behind him.

Kaylee sighed and thought aloud, "I think it's time

for me to pay a visit to Cleo King."

Kaylee called Betty and asked when she was going back to the retirement home. Betty said, "Immediately. I will come by and you can follow me."

With it being so close to Christmas, Kaylee decided to take a small gift to Cleo.

Chapter Sixty-Nine
Untimely Chat

$\mathcal{T}$here had been no time to think much about Christmas, although she remembered vividly how she and Jeffrey went shopping and checked out all the wonderful lights in downtown Raleigh. The memories refreshed her thoughts of Jeffrey. She was so thankful for the refreshing as she dialed his number. Anxiously she waited for him to answer. Just as she was about to hang up, someone said, "Hello."

"Jeffrey?"

Her heart sunk when Martin growled, "Why haven't you called me? I've been worried sick about you."

"Martin, please, I don't need this right now."

"Then explain yourself. I'm an old man, and all this stress could cause a heart attack. You could have been dead for all I know."

"I'm not dead. I'm doing fine."

"Then why haven't you answered my calls or at least called me?"

"I . . . I don't know. There has been so much going on here . . ."

"That's your excuse? You don't know?"

"Believe me, Martin, I don't know why I haven't called. Why are you answering Jeffrey's phone?"

"I figured that would be the only way to speak to you. But now that I know you're okay, tell me what's been going on . . . and I want to know everything."

"Martin, I don't know how, but the town council knows about you. Somehow, they also know that I am here in Stone River working for you."

Martin shouted, "How could that be possible—for them to know about you and me? That's it! I want you to come home! And NOW!"

"No! Not now, Martin. I am so close to finding out all the secrets that Clara spoke about in the letters she wrote to Jake Boone. I'm fine. I assure you if anything puts me in danger, I will board a plane and come home."

Martin moaned and said, "Against my better judgment, I am going to say yes to a few more days only because you gave me your word. If danger even comes *near* you, you *will* come home!"

"I do promise you, Martin."

Martin paused and then said, "Although I do agree, it's only until Christmas. Jeffrey and I will still be there in Stone River, as planned . . . not just for a visit, but to bring you home. Do I make myself clear?"

Kaylee quickly agreed, but only to stop the chatter. "Martin, may I speak to Jeffrey?"

"You could, but he's gone to Raleigh, Christmas shopping with friends."

She wanted to ask if those friends included Jeffrey's old girlfriend, but dared not, knowing that Adam had overwhelmed her.

Martin had continued talking and had called her name several times, but Kaylee had not responded.

Realizing this, Kaylee said, "I'm so sorry, Martin, what did you say?"

"I said, are you getting in over your head? If you are, I'll understand. You're more important to me than finding out about some man who may or may not be my father. I'm old, so really it doesn't matter anyway, but you matter a great deal."

"Martin, I love you too, and everything is fine. It's not long until Christmas. I've got to go now. One of my students is knocking at the door. Give Jeffrey my love and the letter's I've written him. You know what I am talking about. The ones you have hidden from him in a small drawer underneath your desk."

Before Martin could respond, Kaylee hung up and turned the phone off. She hurried to answer the door. She was surprised when she saw John Smith standing there instead of Betty. He apologized for not calling before he came.

Kaylee told him that she was expecting someone.

He promptly asked who she was expecting.

Avoiding Betty's name, she said, "Dotty was due back anytime."

John told Kaylee he would only be a minute. "I thought you would have called me by now," he said.

Kaylee massaged her temple, "I've been really busy."

"Have you talked to Martin?"

"Yes, just a moment ago."

"He was pretty upset with you."

"I know. So, how are things going with Terra?"

John smiled. "Going great. I like her a lot."

"Yeah, I think she likes you too."

Kaylee told John about Tim Dodd's visit. "I don't understand how he could possibly know about Martin."

"Maybe someone told him. Have you told anyone?"

Kaylee thought of Adam, but said no."

"How about Dotty?" John asked. "Could she have gone through your things while you were out or picked up on something you might have said? Unintentionally, of course."

Irritated, Kaylee snapped, "There is nothing for Dotty to find, and I've said nothing for her to pick up on."

"I meant no harm by asking."

"I know. I'm just expecting someone, and I don't want you here when that person arrives."

John looked around the room. "I know, but before I go, have you peaked into any of the rooms yet?"

"I'm working on it. Dotty is very protective of the keys to the house."

John looked at his watch. "I better go before your guest arrives. You will call me if anything turns up, won't you?"

Kaylee nodded. "Yes, of course."

Feeling relieved when he left, Kaylee sat on the stairs and tried to think. She trusted no one, including John.

Chapter Seventy

Retirement Center

When Betty arrived, Kaylee got in her car and followed Betty a couple of miles out of town. After turning off the main road and down a couple of twisting side roads, they arrived at Stone River Retirement Home. The setting for the long, one-story, L-shaped white building was a large front lawn, shrubs, walking trails and a fountain. Black shutters framed the tall windows at the entrance. The place was well kept and decorated very nicely. Betty seemed to know everyone they met. She laughed and talked, and she even hugged a couple of the nurses. As she signed in at the nurse's station, she told the nurse named Helen that she had brought Cleo a Christmas present and a visitor.

Helen looked at Kaylee and asked, "What's your friend's name?"

Before Kaylee could answer, Betty said, "Francis Mills. She lives over in Bradford. Her mom and my mom are friends. I told her about Cleo being alone at Christmas. She does a lot of charity work, so I asked if she'd like to come along and meet Cleo. I hope that was okay. I love you nurses and you especially, Helen. Is it all right for Francis to go back with me and say hello and Merry Christmas?"

Betty had charmed Helen to the point she didn't even ask Kaylee for any identification. Helen motioned for them to go on back.

"Why did you tell her my name is Francis Mills?" Kaylee asked.

"Because, Lori's brother heard Tim Dodd say, 'Cleo isn't to have visitors. So, whatever you're going to do, you need to do fast and go out the back way.'"

Before they reached the end of the hall, Helen called out, "Betty."

Betty turned, "Yes, my dear. What can I do for you?"

"I'm sorry, Cleo can't have visitors today."

"Why is that? It's almost Christmas."

"I know. I'm so sorry, Francis, but I just received the orders. Maybe another time."

Kaylee looked at Betty.

"Listen," Betty whispered, "go out the front door and then come around to the back door, which is the door in front of us. I'll watch for you and let you in. Cleo's room is the last room on the right. Hurry."

Kaylee hurried down the hall but slowed down as she passed the nurse's station. She got in her car and drove out of sight. She then circled back to the end of the building. Betty scanned the area and then motioned for her to come to the door. Kaylee rushed through Cleo's door. Betty told Cleo, "Helen said you can't have visitors, but Kaylee wants to hear about Wind Dancer and Ellen so badly."

Betty smiled at Cleo. "I showed them, didn't I, Cleo! Kaylee is here, and you have a visitor."

Cleo was more than ready to cooperate. She fixed her pale blue eyes on Kaylee. "So, you liked the story about Ellen and Wind Dancer?"

"Yes, I did!" Kaylee said. "I liked it so much, I want to hear it again from you."

Cleo chuckled. "You can sure tell you're from the South, with that Southern drawl."

Kaylee held her head high. "Yes, I'm a Southerner, heart and soul."

Cleo was a very slim woman, with delicate white, short hair, narrow eyes, thin lips and high cheekbones. Cleo told the story to Kaylee, who listened intently to every word, hoping for something that would lead to more answers she was seeking. Cleo could tell Kaylee wasn't satisfied with what she had heard. She leaned toward Kaylee. "Okay Kaylee, I can see you want the deeper version of the story."

Kaylee smiled. "Yes, I do, if you don't mind."

"Ask me a question, and I will start from there."

Kaylee leaned back in her chair. "If you don't mind, how is it that your mother knew so much about Ellen and Wind Dancer?"

"Why should I mind? I'm 94 and if I don't tell the story soon, I'll die with it in me."

Betty watched the hall as Cleo continued. "My mother was employed by Ellen Hilmar. She was her personal maid. Ellen shared things with her in confidence. However, after Ellen's death, mother told me everything she knew, and she knew a lot." Cleo took an old photo from her night table and handed it to Kaylee. "That's my mother when she worked at the estate. Roy had a man come and take a picture of all his employees."

"She's beautiful," Kaylee said.

Cleo pointed at Kaylee. "You and me ain't the only ones who thought she was beautiful. She sure was."

"What do you mean?"

"I mean, Roy had a group photo of all the employees that worked at the estate, but he had a separate picture of mother made by herself. There were only two copies of this picture. This copy he gave to my mother and the other he kept for himself."

Kaylee eyes widened. "Are you saying Roy had a personal interest in your mother?"

Cleo shook her head. "Oh, lord, child, that's a whole different story."

"A story I would love to hear," Kaylee said.

"Cleo," Betty said, "have you had your bath today?"

"No, I haven't. They said they would give me one after lunch."

"While you tell Kaylee the rest of the story, I'm going to tell Helen that you want me to give you your bath today. I'm sure they won't mind, and that will allow you and Kaylee more time."

"That's a perfect idea," Cleo said. "Tell her I want you to make my bed too and that I like you better than any of them."

Kaylee put her hand on Cleo's and said, "Thank you, so much."

"Why are you thanking me? I've not told you the story yet."

Kaylee smiled. "I'm just thanking you in advance."

"Let me tell the story, and then you can thank me, if you like. When my mother . . . by the way, her name was Janet . . . was 18 years old, she was hired to work as a maid at the Hilmar Estate. Ellen liked her right away and chose her to be her personal maid. She bought Mother regular clothes to wear instead of uniforms like all the others. Ellen saw that Mom had pretty combs and ribbons for her long chestnut hair." Cleo pointed to the picture. "You see that ribbon in her hair. Ellen bought it for her. And just look at that dress. She looks more like a society woman than a maid. Don't you think?"

"Yes, I do. She's elegant."

Cleo glanced to the door. "I guess I'd better move this story along. Mother said, 'One day Ellen had gone to Grand Rapids to pick out fabric for new drapes in the tower room. That day Roy watched me almost constantly. Even though he had watched me faithfully from the first day I was hired, any time he caught me alone, he would tell me how beautiful I was and how wonderful I would look as the mistress of a grand house like his.' Anyway, that particular day, she was in Ellen's bedroom when Roy came inside the room and closed the door. He had one hand behind his back. Mother said, it scared her half to death when he closed the door, but what was a servant to do?

"After a moment, he called her name and pulled his hand from behind his back. He was holding a red rose bud. He handed it to her and told her to smell it. Mother said, 'I could hardly smell the rose for the sweet aroma of his pipe tobacco.' She hated the smell, but she dared not say a word. He had a collection of pipes. He changed his pipes like a person changes socks . . .

constantly smoking, so there was always that constant sweet odor in the house all the time. She didn't let on and told him the rose smelled glorious. He proceeded to tell her the rose was for her. Poor Mama was scared to death and didn't offer to take the rose. He insisted. When she reached for it, he took her wrist, pulled her to him, kissed her cheek and stepped away."

Chapter Seventy-One
Cleo's Story

*C*leo continued, "After that, Roy brought her gifts all the time. Mother loved it. She was born into a dirt-poor family; and therefore, she was seduced by all his attention and money.

"There was a day when Ellen had gone into town and the other maids were all on the first floor working. Mother was in Ellen's bedroom putting laundry away when she heard the door open. Her first thought was, *Perhaps Ellen has forgotten something because no one comes into my room without permission.* Turning to ask Ellen what she had forgotten, she was startled to see Roy standing with his back against the door staring at her. Up to that point, Roy hadn't done anything except kiss Mama's cheek. This time, the look in Roy's eyes was different. It scared her and even more so when she saw his determined gaze.

"He locked the door and moved toward her. My mom was a virgin and had no idea what to expect. She backed up against the wall. Roy said, 'I want to make love to you.'

"Mother told him, 'I have never been with a man. What if get pregnant?'

"He told her, 'Don't worry about all that. I will take care of you. You will always be my true love.' He did love her and had since the first rose he gave her.

"By the time this happened, Mom had worked there a little over a year. Roy had wanted her all that time, and while Ellen was away, his want was going to become a reality. He put his arms around her waist and pressed his body to hers so tight it hurt her back. He pulled her to the bed, but before she lay down, Roy took roses from a vase on Ellen's dressing table, pulled the petals off and spread them on the bed for her to lie on.

"He unbuttoned the top of her dress, exposing her breasts, and pushed her skirt up to her waist. She was shaking when he pulled his clothes off. She had never seen a naked man before. Of course, being on Ellen's bed—and with all the workers in the house— wasn't the romantic setting she had always dreamed of. When he lay on top of her he stared into her eyes, wrapped his fingers around the back of her neck and crushed his lips to her.

"Then he paused and stared deeply into her eyes. He asked her a strange question."

Eagerly, Kaylee said, "What did he ask?"

"He asked her, 'Do you feel more than frightened?' She told him, 'I am frightened, but the fear doesn't make my wanting you go away.' The fear made her desire grow only stronger. Roy kissed her again. That time she said when his lips touched hers that she forgot to be afraid. She told me, 'I will never forget how excruciating the pain was at first. When I started to cry, he put his lips over mine and kissed me again and again until I responded with the same enthusiastic ecstasy he was experiencing.'"

"My word!" Kaylee said. "He did that in Ellen's bedroom?"

"Yes. Ellen knew Roy visited the whorehouse often, but she didn't know about her bedroom being soiled. But when he started staying away from the hotel, she knew he was finding his pleasure with one of the maids. Ellen confided in Mother all the time. She asked her if she knew which one of the workers Roy was sleeping with. Of course, Mother said she didn't. She felt bad because she loved Ellen and didn't want to hurt her; however, her love for Roy was a different kind of love.

"One day Roy told Mom to meet him in the tower room, not knowing that Ellen was in her sitting room that adjoined it. Ellen heard the moans and groans and listened until the panting had ended. She cracked the door just enough to see who would come from the room. When she saw it was Mother who hurried away down the hall, she confronted Roy, knowing that he would have anyone he wanted, regardless. Roy went into a rage and ended up slapping Ellen. She ran out of the house to the stables, mounted her horse and ran that horse out on the open range as fast as it could run. She knew better than to go out that far alone, but at that point, she didn't care. That set the stage for Ellen and Wind Dancer to meet. Later, Ellen told Mother that she had seen her leaving the tower room and knew it was she that Roy had been sleeping with. However, she no longer cared. She too had a lover. A beautiful Lakota brave whose name was Wind Dancer."

Betty cleared her throat. "This story is about to drive me wild, but you better move it along before Helen decides to check in on you."

"Betty's right," Cleo said. "I better hurry. There's just so much to tell."

"So, Ellen was okay with your mom and her husband being lovers?" Kaylee asked.

"Yes, she was," Cleo said.

"Do you know when Roy found out about Wind Dancer?" Kaylee asked.

"A few months after Ellen met Wind Dancer. Roy had been staying home quite a bit, and of course Mother was the reason. There was a trip that came up that Roy had to attend in California. It had something to do with signing a contract to expand his blacksmith shops to accommodate the many soldiers who had moved west. He would be gone for three weeks. Ellen met with Wind Dancer every day. She slipped him into the house, and he stayed the night with her in her sitting room. Then Mother said, Ellen showed Wind Dancer a route of escape and entrance through a secret passage."

"So, there is a secret chamber?" Kaylee said.

"My mother said so."

"Cleo," Kaylee said, "did she say where the chamber was located?"

Cleo chuckled. "Yes, she did. I think I'm the only living soul who has a clue where it is. If the council knew I had that kind of knowledge, they would have me killed if I didn't tell them. By the way, the things I told Betty, and now you, I haven't told anyone all these years. I was told by my mother to die with it in me and

I almost have. I'm 94 years old. I think that's a long time to keep silent, don't you?"

"Heavens, yes," Kaylee said.

"Let me finish my story before I tell you about the chamber. Ellen got pregnant. She told Mother it was Wind Dancer's baby, but Roy must never know. If you can believe this, Ellen told Mom she could satisfy Roy as much as she liked, but she must keep her secret about Wind Dancer and the baby. Mother swore she would never say anything to Roy, and she didn't.

"Then Roy came home early from his trip to California and caught Ellen with Wind Dancer in her sitting room. He tried to kill Wind Dancer. Wind Dancer was too strong for Roy. He knocked him out and left through the secret passage.

"Roy could do whatever he wanted with whomever he wanted, but the standard for Ellen was different. Mother said he threatened to kill Ellen and Wind Dancer if she saw him again. That night, he not only made love with Mother, he slept with her all night for the first time."

Kaylee leaned close to Cleo and said, "Really?"

"Really! When Ellen began having all the signs of being pregnant, she knew she had to get Roy to make love to her as much as possible. Mom said, 'My heart felt as though it would bust when Ellen called me to come and help with her bath and help her put on a silk, black negligee and a black lace robe that Roy loved. Ellen insisted that Mother brush her hair, pin it up with a gold comb covered with pearls and place a gold and emerald necklace around her neck. To top it off, Mother sprayed rose-smelling perfume from a crystal bottle, all over Ellen's body.

"Even though doing all these things hurt mother, she said, 'Ellen was the most stunning woman I had ever seen. The most painful part of the whole ordeal was having to stand and watch as Ellen, knowing what was going to happen, took a tray with a bottle of red wine and two crystal goblets down the stairs to Roy's room, where he was sleeping.'"

"I don't know your mother," Kaylee said, "but I feel so sorry for her."

"Mother couldn't stand it. She slipped downstairs and listened outside the door to see if she could hear anything from Roy's room. Well, it only took a minute or two and she said when she heard Roy moaning aloud, she had to leave. It was too painful knowing her lover was with another woman, even though it was his wife. I hurt for Mom just telling the story. Anyway, later that night, Roy slipped into Mother's room and made love to her as though nothing had happened with Ellen. He vowed that Mother would always be the love of his life. Ellen went to Roy's room night after night and then suddenly stopped.

"When Roy found out that Ellen was going to have what he thought was his baby, he was elated. He threw the biggest party and invited everyone in Stone River to come. When the baby girl was born, Roy was ecstatic. Ellen chose the baby's first name, Jenny, and Roy gave Jenny her middle name, Lynn. He told Mother that he gave his baby a part of her name. You see Mother's name was Janet Lynn King.

"Ellen began to see Wind Dancer even more. He came to the house when Roy was away and at times when he wasn't.

Kaylee asked, "What happened with your mom when Roy found out about Ellen being pregnant? Did he continue to see her?"

"Roy never stopped carrying on the affair on with my mother." Cleo pointed her finger toward Kaylee. "Something happened when Jenny Lynn had just turned six. Ellen had been taking Jenny out riding with her for a couple of years. One day they rode out to Coyote Canyon, where Ellen and Wind Dancer had first met. Unbeknown to Ellen, Roy was also at the canyon. He had gone out to meet Jake at the falls. He got off his horse and was sitting near the falls while waiting for Jake, when he saw Ellen and Jenny Lynn ride up on the other side of the canyon.

"Before he could call out to them, he saw Wind Dancer and Moving Cloud ride up and get off their horses. That's when he first suspected that maybe Jenny Lynn wasn't his child. Wind Dancer squatted and Jenny ran to him with open arms and Wind Dancer hugged her and lifted her up in his arms. He kissed Ellen on the lips several times and then all three hugged. You know . . . what they call a family hug."

Betty frowned. "Why wouldn't Ellen be smarter than that? I would want to know where Roy was before I met Wind Dancer. Otherwise, it could prove to be very dangerous."

Cleo shook her head. "You're right, Betty. That night, Roy told Mother to meet him in the tower room. She said, 'It was horrible. Roy was outraged and said he was going to kill that dirty savage.' Mom said when he made love to her, he was so rough she could hardly stand him touching her. He ripped her buttons off her blouse, picked her up and threw her on the bed. He came at her like a wild man. Mom said she cried the whole time he was on top of her. He did things to her that she had never imagined. She fought him and begged him to stop. He slapped her across the face and told her to shut up and he would stop when he was through. He took all his rage out on Mother.

"Roy didn't say anything to Ellen about seeing her and Wind Dancer together at the canyon. His plan was to stake out the canyon, and when Wind Dancer came to meet them again, he would kill him. His plan would be that he would have to go out of town for a couple of days, figuring they would meet. Only wanting to kill Wind Dancer, Roy told Mother to delay Ellen if she said anything about taking Jenny Lynn out for a ride.

"Sure enough, Ellen told Mom that she was going for a ride." Cleo laughed. "I try to imagine Mom fainting, which is exactly what she did to delay Ellen. The act must have been good enough, because Ellen had only been gone a few minutes when Roy was back at the estate. Wind Dancer and Moving Cloud were never seen again."

Kaylee, hanging on every word, said, "So, Roy killed Wind Dancer and Moving Cloud?"

Cleo squinted and continued, "Ellen and Jenny Lynn were devastated! Roy, in his cocky manner, asked repeatedly what the problem was. He wanted to know why they were acting as though someone had died. Of course, he always managed to chuckle after asking that question. Ellen knew after a day or two that her lover, the father of her child, wasn't coming back. She went to the tower room day after day and looked out over the open range, watching for Wind Dancer. Black Bear came to the estate one day, wanting to speak to Roy. Roy came to the door with his pistol in hand.

"Black Bear asked, 'What have you done to my sons?'

"'Get off my land or I will shoot you between your eyes!' Roy told him.

Seeing Black Bear riding away from the house, Ellen hurried out the back, got her horse and rode after him. Desperate, she begged him, 'If you see Wind Dancer, someway let me know he is okay.'

"Black Bear wasn't impressed with her concern and told her it was all her fault. He knew Roy had killed his sons and for that he said he prayed her daughter would die as well, not knowing that Jenny was his granddaughter. Black Bear wanted Ellen to know the pain he felt."

Chapter Seventy-Two
Jenny Lind's Death

Cleo excused herself and went to the bathroom. While Cleo was away, Kaylee felt as though her mind was going to explode. She was so taken by what Cleo had said. It explained so much. After Cleo returned, she hurried back into the story. She looked at Kaylee and said, "I'm almost through, Kaylee. Let me see, where was I? After a few weeks, Roy couldn't take not knowing all there was to know about Ellen and Wind Dancer. He came up with a plan to find out just what Jenny knew about the situation. He took Jenny for a ride to the canyon, to the very place where he had seen Ellen, Jenny and Wind Dancer together.

"When they arrived at the canyon, Jenny didn't want to get off her horse. She wanted to go back home. Roy helped her off the horse anyway and asked why she didn't want to take a look at the falls. At first Jenny didn't say anything, but Roy was determined to know what she knew. After a while of answering all Roy's questions, Jenny blurted out, 'Did you kill Wind Dancer?' Roy asked how she knew him. When she didn't reply, he took her by her shoulders and demanded to know how she knew Wind Dancer. Furious, because Jenny wouldn't cooperate, he ranted, shouting that he knew her and Ellen used to meet Wind Dancer at the very place they were standing. Jenny kicked his shin and broke free from his hold and ran. Roy caught her. She fought him, screaming at the top of her voice, asking why he killed her daddy. Roy was enraged, 'I'm your daddy!' Jenny screamed repeatedly that Wind Dancer was her daddy. When Jenny wouldn't stop screaming, Roy lost it. He backhanded her, knocking her down. Her head hit a rock and it killed her."

Betty turned from making the bed and gasped, "Roy killed Jenny Lynn?"

Before Cleo could answer, Kaylee said, "I thought her horse threw her and it broke her neck."

Cleo leaned forward. "Sure, that's what he told everybody, but that wasn't what he told Mama. She said that Roy told her exactly what I told you. Roy vowed to Mama that he didn't mean to kill her, but after hearing Jenny shouting that he wasn't her daddy, his uncontrollable temper got the better of him."

Kaylee put her hand on her stomach. "What kind of an excuse is that? Temper or not, why would someone hit a 6-year old that hard?"

Cleo sighed. "Roy paid dearly for killing Jenny, even though he didn't go to jail. He could hardly live with the nightmares that greeted him night after night when he closed his eyes, hoping for sleep. Ellen went into a depression no one thought she would come out of. Mother said, 'A few weeks after Jenny's death, Ellen sent me into town to pick her up writing supplies. She told me that she was keeping a journal, and if something happened to her, she wanted everyone to know it would be by Roy's hand that it happened. She said she would never forgive him for killing Jenny or Jenny's father. Mother tried to convince her Roy couldn't do such a thing. Ellen made it clear to Mama that there was a time she didn't think he could either, but that was long ago. Then Ellen told Mama, 'I hope Roy never turns on you and the fact he sleeps with you means nothing.' She said, 'One day he will grow tired of you and go on to someone else.'"

"Do you know what happened to the journal?" Kaylee asked.

"Mom said she saw the journal almost every day, but she never got close enough to see what Ellen was writing. A few years later, Ellen died. Roy said that she tripped on her dress tail and fell as she started down the stairs. I don't believe that for one minute. She may have fallen, but it was Roy who pushed her or knocked her down or something. A few months after Ellen's death, Mother got pregnant with me."

Kaylee frowned and shook her head. "Didn't anyone question Ellen's death?"

Cleo cleared her throat. "Who was going to question it? Roy and Jake owned everyone and everything in Stone River. Including the law." Cleo picked the picture of her mother up, shook her head and said, "Mother really thought that with her being pregnant and Ellen dead, she would become Roy's wife, making her the mistress of the Hilmar Estate. What a joke! Of course, Roy said, 'I will love you and our baby as long as I live, but I can't allow a maid to become the mistress of my estate.' For that, he would have to find a lady of means who society would accept. Fact being, on one of his many trips to Atlanta, Roy had met a lady by the name of Judy Justice who came from a money family, and she had already accepted his proposal. Mother was crushed! Roy brought Judy to Stone River to move into the estate, but he never legally married her. He went through all the formalities for appearance sake and to spare Judy the embarrassment of people knowing she was only shacking up with Roy. You see, Roy really did love my mother, and she alone was his one true love."

Cleo sat the picture on the table, pointed at Kaylee and asked, "Did you say you went to the mausoleum this morning?"

"Yes, I did."

Cleo smiled with pride and muttered, "Did you notice a gold plaque on a wall by itself?"

Kaylee nodded. "Yes, but it didn't have a name, it had a poem."

"Hum, my mother wrote that poem and gave it to Roy after I was born. Mama feared she would lose him when Judy came to live at the estate. You see, the real reason Roy wouldn't marry Judy was because he knew it would devastate my mother. Roy made up some god-awful story and told Judy that he couldn't marry her because of his deep love for Ellen. What a joke!

"After Judy moved into the estate, Mother and I moved into one of the houses behind the grand house. Anyway, Mother died one year before Roy. I was 14 years old. Roy grieved after Mother's death like no man

I had ever seen. He told everyone to accommodate my wishes. He said he had Mother cremated. Nothing could have been farther from the truth. He buried her in the Hilmar mausoleum. Even so, Roy couldn't put her name on the plaque. So, he put the poem that mother had written him on it instead."

Kaylee gasped, "My heavens! Your mother is buried in the Hilmar mausoleum?"

"Yeah. Roy wanted her close, even in death." Cleo thought a moment and added, "There is something else that might be of interest to you. Ellen had so many wonderful things, as you can validate by living in her home, but Mother said there was one thing that meant more to Ellen than all the rest. The most eloquent music box that she had ever seen.

"On one of her trips to England to buy paintings for her grand house, Ellen visited a small antique shop. That was where she found the music box and said she felt compelled to buy it. The bottom of the box was detailed with red roses inlaid in white porcelain. The top of the box looked like a pool of pure blue water. Standing in the midst of the water was a man and woman dancing to the most beautiful and enchanting piano music Mother had ever heard. Ellen told her the music box belonged to her and Wind Dancer. They played it every time they were together. It played when they made love, when they cried and when they danced. Ellen constantly reinforced the statement that if anything happened to her, she would never leave the house until Roy was brought to justice. Tell me, Kaylee, have you seen Ellen in the house?"

Kaylee paused and rubbed her upper arms, "Yes! I saw her last night."

"Hum!" Cleo chuckled. "You must be the one she's going to use to bring an end to everything."

Kaylee's eyes widened. "What do you mean?"

Cleo paused a brief moment and fixed her eyes on Kaylee. "Ellen said her spirit would lead the right person to her estate and that person would feel her joy, desire, love, passion, pain and fear. Are you feeling any of those symptoms, Kaylee?"

Avoiding answering her question, Kaylee quickly replied, "There have been a couple of things. Didn't you say that Roy smoked pipes all the time?"

Cleo tilted her head. "Yes, I did."

"Well, I've smelled pipe tobacco several times in the house."

Cleo scratched her chin. "I'm not surprised. Roy also vowed to never leave the estate he built. Of course, to believe that, you'd have to believe in a lot of hard-to-believe things."

"Cleo," Kaylee said, "how is it that you've been taken care of all these years?"

"By my daddy, of course! After Mama died, Roy set up a trust fund for me and had one of the maids assigned to take care of me. She moved into the house behind the estate with me. I'll never forget her. Her name was Dotty Sams."

Kaylee's eyes widened, and her jaw dropped open, "Cleo, what did you say her name was? Did you say, Dotty Sams?"

"Yes! She used to brush my hair every night. Dotty took really good care of me."

Kaylee gasped. "Cleo, there's a Dotty Sams that still works at the estate, but she's no more than 50 years old."

Cleo slapped her leg and laughed, "Miss Shell, I'm sure my Dotty has been dead for years. She was around 50 when I was 14 and I'm 94."

Betty put her hand on her chest. "Are you kidding! That would make Dotty over a 140 years old. If it's the same Dotty but if . . ."

"If what?" Kaylee asked.

Betty had gotten so into the conversation that she failed to hear someone coming down the hall and stopping at Cleo's door. The door flung open. Helen was furious. She ordered Kaylee and Betty, "Get off the premises, or I will call security!"

Kaylee grabbed Cleo's arm and frantically asked. "Cleo, where is the chamber?"

"I . . . I'll . . ." Before Cleo could answer, Helen took hold of Kaylee's arm and pulled her out of the room. Betty jerked open the back door, and they hurried out.

Helen shouted, "I'll see the council hears about this, Betty!"

Chapter Seventy-Three
Betty's Idea

"*I* should have been watching instead of talking," Betty whined.

Kaylee rubbed her arm. "I had to struggle to keep from knocking Helen out when she grabbed my arm like that. But I sure didn't want to give anyone an excuse to have me arrested."

Before getting in her truck, Betty called out, "Kaylee, I have an idea. I'll meet you at the estate."

Upon arriving at the estate, Kaylee noticed right away that Adam still wasn't home.

Inside, Kaylee poured them a Coke as Betty shared her idea. "I will get Cleo out of that nursing home."

Kaylee frowned and said firmly, "No, Betty! Getting me in to see Cleo has already caused you more than enough trouble."

"My gosh, Miss Shell, we learned a wealth of information this morning. The class will be so energized when they hear all of that story. Man, I got a rush that's so incredible. Eddie would love it! Now, if I may continue and at least share the rest of my thought before you say no . . ."

Kaylee nodded. "Okay, I'm sorry. Please continue."

"As I said before, I'll slip in the back way when dinner has ended. That's when the nurses are busy getting the meds for the night. I got the code for the back door from Lori. When it's clear, I'll bring Cleo out the back door that we were tossed out of today and to the estate!"

Kaylee sat her Coke down. "Bring her to the estate?"

"Yes. I'm sure they'll be watching Lori . . ."

Kaylee shook her head. "No way! I won't allow you, or Lori, to jeopardize yourselves like that again. It could be dangerous. No."

Betty put her hands on her hips and shouted, "What do you mean no way? I thought you were the private investigator. You should be telling me this stuff."

Kaylee frowned. "You're right. I should be coming up with a plan, not you. If I were to tell the total truth, I would have to say I fear Tim Dodd will make good on his threat and have me locked away for fifty years."

Betty furrowed her brows. "You talked to Tim Dodd?"

"Yes, this morning before you arrived. He said, 'If you don't abide by our rules, my brother the judge will see to it that you will be an old woman when you get out of prison!'"

Betty threw up her hands. "You let that snake in the grass shake you like that? He's an idiot! You listen to me, Kaylee Shell. Your whole class, not just me, is with you in this investigation. By the way, Joshua called a meeting and told us what happened and why he said what he did against you." Betty pulled her necklace from underneath her sweater and smiled. "When we all made a pact with each other at the Bend, we were serious. We don't take making a vow to each other lightly. Were you serious about the vow we made to find truth, whether good or bad?"

"Well, of course I was."

Betty squinted and ordered, "Then pull your necklace out from under your sweatshirt."

Kaylee connected eyes with Betty and pulled her eagle claw necklace out. "I was as serious as anyone."

Betty slapped her hands together. "All right! Give me five, Miss Shell. I would have been crushed if you didn't have your necklace on."

Kaylee took a sip of her Coke, set the glass down and tapped the counter with her finger. "I want to confess something to you. This is my first case. I probably have come across to you as a substandard investigator. However, in my defense, my training didn't prepare me for the likes of Dotty Sams or Ellen Hilmar."

Betty lightly punched Kaylee's arm. "Stop it, you're a great investigator. I am not saying that you're a Sherlock Holmes yet, but this is your first case? Hey, is the pay good for a P.I.? And if we help you crack this case, do we get a part of your money for our superior help?"

Kaylee hugged Betty. "You guys most certainly do!"

Betty finished her Coke and set the glass in the sink. "Now, since we are officially on the payroll, let's get to work. Miss Shell, I want to hear word for word about this sighting you had last night of Ellen Hilmar."

Betty was ecstatic at the thought of seeing a ghost. Kaylee wanted to be as honest as possible, without telling of the encounters with the lover in her dreams and the passionate love making with Adam.

Betty shook her head and frowned at Kaylee. "You're not telling me everything are you? I can tell from your eyes you're holding back. How can we get truth if you hold back? So, fess up, Miss Shell! My gosh, if you told me about seeing Ellen's ghost what possibly could keep—"

Kaylee blurted out, "How about a ghost making love to you every time you take a bubble bath?"

Betty's jaw dropped open. "Are you kidding me? Don't you be joking around with me, Kaylee Shell. I'm serious."

"So am I."

Kaylee told her about the baths. Betty thought a brief moment and began to laugh.

"What's so funny? I thought you were being serious."

"I am serious. Wow, I was thinking, you have only taken a couple of bubble baths. If that happened every time, I took a bubble bath, I would have taken at least a hundred baths by now and counting." Betty could see Kaylee didn't appreciate her humor. "I'm sorry if I am being insensitive. I'm a teenager. What do you expect? Sometimes my mind gets all crazy, and it's easy for me to joke around. Plus, I've been hanging with Eddie for a while now. I think I'm starting to act like him."

"It's okay, Betty. It's all been just surreal."

Betty squeezed Kaylee's hand. "Another plus, I wasn't the one who experienced the ordeal. As you can plainly see, I don't know what to say, so let's get off that subject. Kaylee, if we can get Cleo out here, she can show you where the secret chamber is."

Kaylee stood, put her hand on her hip and smiled. "That would be excellent, Betty."

Betty stood and clapped her hands together. "Now we're talking!"

Kaylee put her hand on Betty's shoulder. "Promise me you will be careful, and if anything comes up, you get away from that retirement center immediately. No matter what, please call me."

Chapter Seventy-Four
Ellen Withdraws Money

As she was talking to Betty, Kaylee jerked when someone pounded on the front door. She excused herself and hurried to see if it was perhaps that Adam had returned home. To her surprise, it was her whole senior class including Joshua.

Paulette smiled. "I heard we're having a meeting here. Is that right?"

Betty put her arm around Kaylee. "I didn't think you'd mind, so I took the liberty to spread the word that we were meeting here on the way back from visiting Cleo."

Kaylee was so surprised. "Mind? I don't mind at all. I'm thrilled."

Everyone helped bring enough chairs from the kitchen to the dining room, eager to hear what Kaylee had to report. The class was in awe when they heard Cleo's story. The most shocking of all was when the class heard that Kaylee had seen Ellen on the stairs. Paulette stood and looked at Ellen's portrait. "I'm dumbfounded. Grandpa Hilmar killed Jenny?"

Visibly shaken, Charlie took Paulette's hand and reminded her, "Paulette, don't forget, we want truth, good or bad."

Her eyes filled with tears as she looked at Charlie. "He killed Jenny Lynn! A 6-year-old little girl who had her whole life ahead of her. She deserved to live!"

Charlie lifted Paulette's chin with his finger. "He also killed Wind Dancer and Moving Cloud, and according to Cleo, Roy may have killed Ellen also."

Paulette shook her head. "Grandma Thelma will explode when she hears all of this."

Kaylee quickly said, "Due to time, we need to get started with the reports. I want to hear from the groups starting with Kyle's."

Kyle stood and rubbed his hands together. "A couple of us boys went to visit Ken Kent. To refresh everyone's memory, Ken's father was Roy and Jake's accountant. He said, 'Ellen on more than one occasion had taken a big chunk of gold from Roy's account. What she did with it, I don't know. In today's currency it would have come to two hundred twenty million dollars. Jake had set a vast fortune aside and didn't want his children to receive any of it. In his heart, Jake felt crushed that not once, from the time Tammy left him, did any of the children try to contact him or even come to visit him. His thoughts were that if they could not at least try to get in contact with him while he was alive, then they would not enjoy the fruit of his labor after he died. Nonetheless, Jake did send a king's ransom to support his children. He even wrote and sent numerous letters. Yet, not one child ever answered them.'"

Kyle faced Kaylee. "Miss Shell, Ken wanted me to ask if he could meet and talk with you."

"Of course! I would be honored."

Kyle nodded at Eddie who got up and went out the front door. He returned in a couple of minutes with an old man wearing a brown suit covered by a long, brown overcoat and a brown Stetson hat. An aged, black, leather bag was tucked under his arm. Eddie held his arm as they rounded the table to the fireplace. He pulled a chair out for him, took his hat and coat and steadied his arm until he was seated. After Kyle introduced Ken to Kaylee, Eddie looked around the table at his classmates. They all nodded in unison. Eddie took a necklace from his pocket and put it around Ken's neck. "Ken, you have told our group that you want the truth to come out whether good or bad. Is that right?"

The elderly man nodded. "That's right. I'm tired of all the lies and cover-ups."

"Then we are honored to have you as a new member in our group."

Kyle looked at Ken. "As a member of our financial group, will you tell Miss Shell and the class what you have to offer our investigation—"

Kaylee interrupted. "Before you start, Mr. Kent, I want to say that I am so surprised to have you with us in our meeting today. Thank you so much for coming. I'm sure your information will surpass our imaginations. With that said, Mr. Kent, the floor is yours."

In a raspy voice, he began, "I believe the good Lord has allowed me to live long enough to make Jake Boone's wishes known. Jake had an attorney brought to Stone River a couple of years before he died to draw up and witness his last will and testament. As you all know, after Tammy left Jake, he never married again. He did, however, take a woman by the name of Clara Aims to live with him until she decided to go back East. He gave her a large sum of money to take with her. When she left, Jake told the attorney that he felt in his heart that Clara was pregnant with his child. Of course, it was only a gut feeling. He never heard from Clara again. Nonetheless, his love for her never died. It only grew. The records say that when he died, he wanted the $250 million put into a trust for the town council to use, only as needed, to make sure that Stone River flourished. There were only certain amounts of the money that could be used on certain things, such as money to pay the sheriff and needs for the school. Jake was so sure that Clara was pregnant with his child that he gave my father an envelope that contained directions on what to do should Clara's child ever come looking for his, or her, father. Just the other day I called the firm that's holding the envelope and told them that I may need the envelope soon. When I heard that a man thinking Jake Boone was his father had sent Miss Shell to Stone River to find out for sure, I was elated. To hear the man's mother's name was Clara Aims, I must confess, I wept. That aside, my father taught me all he knew about Jake and Roy's finances—"

"Excuse me for interrupting," Kaylee said. "I have two questions. First, who gave you the information about Martin sending me to Stone River?"

Mr. Kent took a note from his shirt pocket and held it up. "This note was under my office door when I went into work last Monday. Someone had written the information about Martin and you."

"I don't suppose it was signed?" Kaylee said.

Ken grinned. "No such luck, Miss Shell."

Kaylee took the note and looked at it. She passed the note around for the students to see.

"My next question, Mr. Kent: Are you saying that Jake had more money than the 250 million dollars he left Stone River when he died?"

"Why, yes, didn't I make myself clear about that?" Ken chuckled. "I could always use my age as an excuse, but instead of excuses I'll just tell you. Jake had not only the $250 million that was showing on the books, but he also had a whopping $125 million put away and held in the event a very lucky offspring should one day come to claim it."

Gasps were heard all around the room. "Ken," Paulette said, "I've known you all my life and have never really asked you about my Grandpa Jake's and Grandpa Roy's money, but since I have you here, may I ask you a question?"

"Of course, Paulette, anything."

"Do you know what happened to the large amounts of money that was taken from Grandpa Roy's account? The records show the withdrawals, but not who withdrew the money."

Ken frowned. "Let me explain it to you by saying, Ellen Hilmar wasn't a poor woman when Roy talked her into moving west. Roy was a different story. Jake and Roy used Ellen and Tammy's money to get everything going, that is until they started to making money. Daddy said, 'Ellen withdrew large amounts of money on different occasions and I'm not talking about chump change.' Ellen felt, had it not been for her money, Roy would have nothing. So, she withdrew not only the money Roy spent when they moved west but withdrew a massive amount of interest from Roy's account for his using her inheritance. What she was going to do with the money, well I can only speculate."

"Then speculate," Paulette said.

"She took the money, anticipating giving it back to the Lakota tribe who lived at the Bend. Wanting Wind Dancer and Moving Cloud's families to be secure. Of course, she hadn't planned on dying so soon. Anyway, Ellen's heart was in the right place. Her dream was that with that money, the Indians could one day rebuild their homes on the land that once belonged to them. Of course, she knew she couldn't give the money to the Indians right away due to circumstances. What she did with the money until that time presented itself, no one knows. After saying that, I'll tell you that Ellen wasn't the only one to take out sizeable sums of money. So did Roy and Willie Hilmar on two or three occasions."

Paulette spoke up, "Grandma Willie withdrew money too?"

"Yes, she did! Her purpose for withdrawing the money, I don't know."

Curious, Charlie stood and asked, "What are we going to do about this information, Miss Shell?"

Kaylee rubbed her forehead. "Before we decide what to do, we need to have all the information possible to make our case. We have a great start, however, there's so much more."

Colton scratched his head. "Why is it that most of our legitimate evidence is coming from our senior adults? Is it possible no one else knows, or it just doesn't matter after all these years?"

Ken glanced at Kaylee. "Miss Shell, if you don't mind, I'll try and answer Colton's question."

"Please do."

"Colton, most stories lose their appeal over time. There are a few people left who know some of the facts about Roy and Jake, but fewer still that care. I know and care because of my father's connections. Had he not been personally connected I would more than likely be in that number who doesn't care because it wouldn't affect me. Only a few of the council are affected by what you and I know, while there are those on the council who benefit from Roy and Jake's money. They keep the story alive to defend their dipping into the resources. Then there is the younger generation like you who want to know the truth about Stone River's history because they've heard so many conflicting stories. While not knowing for sure about anything, most of the people in and around Stone River hold Roy and Jake up like gods. Due to the age of the ones who still know some of the truth, I think Miss Shell's arrival in Stone River couldn't have been timelier. If it weren't being found out now, it could very well die with us. I've always felt the time would come before I died when I would share the truth that I know about the story. And here, I am telling you today."

Ken lifted the antiqued leather case to Kaylee. "Miss Shell, I want you to have my father's records to help you in your fight to bring out the truth. Good or bad."

Kaylee took the case. "I don't know what to say, except thank you, Mr. Kent, for giving us these bank records and sharing your vast knowledge about Roy and Jake."

All the class began to applaud as tears welled up in Ken's eyes. Eddie helped Ken with his coat and hat.

Before leaving the dining room, Ken stopped and for a moment, fixed his eyes on Ellen's painting. "One more thing, Miss Shell. My father said Ellen told him, 'If anything other than old age should end my life, I will never leave this house until justice is poured out on Roy's head. I want everyone to know that it would be Roy's hand that would end my life, in addition to the lives of Wind Dancer, Moving Cloud and my beloved little Jenny.'"

As Ken stood to leave, he looked at Kaylee. "Gather from that what you will, Miss Shell."

Betty looked at Kaylee and whispered, "That's twice today we've heard that!"

Kaylee gave the students time to vent their thoughts on all the new information they had received thus far. The most confusing question being, "Exactly how old is Dotty Sams."

When they were ready to dismiss, everyone joined hands and Charlie led the prayer for truth and justice to prevail over their endeavor to know about Stone River's founders and families. Paulette offered to stay with Kaylee. Kaylee thanked her but insisted that she go home and share what they had learned with Thelma. Charlie put his arm around Paulette's shoulder and said he was glad she wasn't staying. It was a perfect excuse for him to take her home.

Eddie and Betty were going to work on getting Cleo to the estate by nightfall. Before leaving, Betty muttered, "If you need me, call, and I'll be here in five minutes."

Kaylee assured her she would.

Chapter Seventy-Five
The Hidden Room

Wanting to take full advantage of the time she had left with the keys, Kaylee hurried to the tower room and tried, in vain, to find any secret passage. After she looked in Ellen's parlor, she hurried to the room where the paintings were stored and frantically searched over, under and behind everything, with no results.

Frustrated, Kaylee sat down, closed her eyes for a moment and tried to clear her mind enough to refocus. She felt sure if there was a secret passage, it would be in the one of room the council didn't have access to. Maybe, it was in Roy's office. Perhaps, she had overlooked something. At any rate, she was going to look one last time before Dotty returned. She held her hands over her face a few moments, opened her eyes and started to stand when she noticed a fresco painting of Ellen on the far side of the wall. She had looked at it before; however, she had only lifted the sheet that hung over the painting. This time, the covering would come off.

The mural was exquisite. Unlike the other paintings where no one smiled, in this one Ellen's smile was radiant. She wore a long, low-cut, yellow dress and white lace gloves that covered her long slender fingers, fingers that held a long-stemmed red rose. She sported a yellow, wide-brimmed hat with a large white feather on the side. All the other art was done in settings that were recognizable, but not this painting. Inspecting for anything familiar, Kaylee ran her finger across every inch of the mural. Just as she started to back away from the picture, her focus turned to the heart of the rose.

She slowly raised her finger and touched the center of the blood-red rose. When the wall began to move, Kaylee shouted and jumped backward. At the same moment, she heard someone pounding on the front door. By the sound of the loud knocking, the person had been knocking for a while. Kaylee turned her stare back to the wall that had parted, but knew she had to answer the door. It might be Betty and the others with Cleo. She rushed out of the room, closed the door behind her, dashed down the stairs and opened the door.

"Terra! What a surprise. Come in."

Terra managed a superficial smile as she closed the door. "I was beginning to worry. I saw the Explorer and I . . ."

"Yeah, I . . . I was really focused on what I was doing and didn't hear you knocking right away."

Kaylee pointed to the living room and asked Terra to come in and sit down. She didn't want to appear to rush Terra's visit; however, she didn't want her still to be there if the students were successful at confiscating Cleo.

"Kaylee, are you all right? You sound so out of breath."

Kaylee rubbed her cheek. "I'm . . . I'm fine. I was at the other end of the house when I heard you knocking. I'm glad you came by. Is it a social visit or is there something I can help you with?"

Terra did a tight-lipped grin. "I would like to say I stopped by just to have coffee and chat, but there is a reason for my visit."

Kaylee held her breath for a moment, afraid Terra had found out she had asked John to ask her out. A sigh of relief came when Terra said, "I'm here to warn you about the council."

"The council?"

"Yes. They're meeting tonight. If they knew I was here . . . well . . . at any rate, Kaylee, guard yourself. I can't imagine where their information is coming from. Someone close must be passing the information."

"But who?" Kaylee asked.

"I don't know, but it has to be someone close to you. Maybe even one of your students."

Kaylee moved to the edge of her chair. "I don't believe that!"

"Kaylee, things happen when a person is put in a corner. And who knows how anyone will respond?"

"Have you heard any names mentioned that might point to this mysterious informant?"

"No, I haven't, Kaylee. I came here to tell you about the council meeting tonight and . . . and to let you know John told me about you asking him to get me off your back."

"Terra!" Kaylee gasped.

Terra shook her head. "Stop, Kaylee, let me finish. At first, I was furious, but after calming down, I realized Adam wasn't the one for me. First of all, he never showed any signs of interest. He's always polite, as he is to everyone. I want you as my friend more than I need a boyfriend."

Kaylee sighed, "I'm so sorry, Terra." She leaned forward and took Terra's hand. "Thank you for letting me know about the council and John. Why would John tell you that? And when did he tell you?"

"Why, I don't know. When, last night. He said his work in Stone River would be finished by Christmas."

Kaylee frowned. "Really?"

Terra managed a grin. "So, do you like Adam?"

Kaylee raised her brows and nodded. "Yes, I do."

"Does he like you?"

"Yes, he does."

Terra stood. "Since you don't have family here, Mother and I would like for you and Adam to have Christmas with us."

Kaylee hugged her. "Thanks for the invitation. How is your mother?"

"As cantankerous as ever."

"Terra, thanks for coming by. It means so much to me."

Terra opened the door. "If I hear anything else, I'll let you know."

Chapter Seventy-Six
Secret Chamber

*A*s soon as Terra drove out of sight, Kaylee locked the door and hurried up the stairs to examine the opening she had discovered. For a brief moment, she stood at the hidden entrance observing a spiral staircase that led downward. The walls around the winding black metal were formed with stone. Kaylee was surprised to see the chamber had electricity. She grabbed the string that was hanging down, pulled it and noticed the light came on. Anxiously, she wiped the corners of her mouth, grabbed a flashlight just in case and started down the steps. The air was chilly, and a strong musty smell all but burned her nostrils.

Kaylee had no idea where the stairs would lead. Sadly, the light ended at the bottom of the stairs. She shined the flashlight around the small area. Directly in front of her, she saw a dark arched door set in a rock. The musty smell was getting to her so badly, Kaylee pulled the tail of her shirt over her mouth. It was so cold, she wished she had put her coat on but dared not go back to get it because of time.

After a quick glance up the stairs, Kaylee moved with caution to the door, not knowing what she would find on the other side. She took hold of the handle and tried to open the door, but it was stuck. She laid the flashlight down and pushed as hard as she could with no results. Afraid to move, she lowered her shirt tail and shivered as the screeching old door began to slowly open by itself. Backing up, Kaylee stooped down and grabbed the flashlight. Not knowing, yet eager to see what was on the other side of the door, she moved cautiously through the opening, only to find another door. Her eyes frantically surveyed the area and the bronze door in front of her, so different from the old wooden one she had just gone through.

Just touching the freezing metal of the door handle made Kaylee's fingertips completely numb. On top of everything, a breeze had stirred. But where was the draft coming from? As she started to turn the knob, her breath escaped her for a moment when she heard the low, soothing sound of the piano rhapsody playing on the other side of the door. Her heart raced as she gathered her strength and pushed the door enough to expose a dim light coming from the opening. She staggered, but managed to push the door the rest of the way open. In total unbelief, Kaylee trembled as she put her hand to her chest. For a brief moment, she stared at a fire burning in the small, rock fireplace warming the area. But who built the fire, and who lit the candles scattered around the room?

A medium-sized room contained a full-sized poster bed with a bright yellow comforter and a white and yellow sheer canopy. Four pillows, that appeared to have been freshly fluffed, lined the dark cherry headboard. The floor was a dark oak crowned with a brightly colored, hand woven area rug. A small chair and desk sat to the right of the fire. A white-quill pen and a small bottle of black ink sat beside several pieces of white paper. Kaylee frowned as she made her way to the fireplace. On the mantel, in the frolicking shadows of amber flames, a miniature man and woman danced around and around on top of the white porcelain music box as the piano music played. It was identical to the one she had seen upstairs.

Questions overwhelmed her. Were there two music boxes exactly alike? If not, how did it get down the stairs into the secret room and on the mantel? As she observed the room, she wondered aloud, "If Wind Dancer entered the house through a secret passage, there had to be another door or opening to the room. Otherwise, he would have had to enter at the top of the stairs, which meant he would have come through the main house."

Kaylee hastily scanned the walls, knowing her time was short before Dotty returned or the students arrived with Cleo. This time the opening wasn't hard to find. A door, with no knob, blended with the wall and opened with a light touch. Kaylee shined the flashlight into a rock-walled tunnel. The dirt floor and damp walls again emanated a strong musty smell. Kaylee took the chair from the desk and propped it against the door to hold it open, not sure if she would be able to get back in. A few steps into the passageway, Kaylee huffed and spun around, shining the light toward the door. It had closed. The chair was lying on the floor on her side and the light from the room was extinguished. She hurried to the door and pushed; she breathed a sigh of relief when the door did open. This time Kaylee propped the chair against the door in such a way that it would be impossible for it to fall, and with caution she started down the rock-walled passageway.

She went for what seemed a long distance and then came to yet another opening. "Oh, heavens above," she shouted, as her hand seized the ice-cold handle, turned and pushed. Kaylee was stunned when she saw the marble floor. It was the same floor pattern she had seen in the mausoleum earlier. Fully opening the door revealed it was indeed the burial chamber.

A dimly lit chandelier hung in the center of the cathedral ceiling. Holding her breath, Kaylee moved to the front of Roy's vault and glided her fingers over the gold nameplate. Afterward, she followed suit with Jenny Lynn's and Ellen's plaques. Kaylee blew her breath out. "Ellen, what am I looking for?" As she ran her fingers back and forth over Ellen's nameplate, she saw it was different from Roy's and Jenny's, theirs were flat against the crypt, but Ellen's stood slightly out. Guided by fate, Kaylee put her finger to the corner of the gold inscription and pushed down. Amazed, the plaque moved downward, exposing a keyhole underneath it. But where was the key to open it?

Without more thought, Kaylee reached into her pocket and pulled out the old skeleton key she had found on the mantel. Panting, she pushed the key in the keyhole and turned it. "Oh, my goodness," she gasped, when the front of the vault popped open. Her temples pounded as her fingers latched around the handle. After taking a deep breath, Kaylee started to pull the vault handle, then paused. After a moment, she continued to pull, and the vault drawer moved forward. Looking through through the thick glass, Kaylee trembled as her eyes focused on Ellen Hilmar's body. She was even more beautiful than the portrait over the fireplace she had looked at so many times. Ellen looked as though she had just been put into the crypt. Not what Kaylee had expected for someone who had been in the vault for over one hundred years. Kaylee's shaking hand covered her mouth. She was not only stunned by how well-preserved Ellen looked, but at the stacks of one hundred-dollar bills and a massive amount of gold coins stuffed around Ellen's body. Yet, something more seized Kaylee's attention.

Lying on Ellen's stomach was a small, black, leather book. Underneath the book was a medium-sized brown envelope. After managing to compose her unstable hands, Kaylee took the rim of the thick glass and pulled it open. Sure, the smell would be overpowering, she frantically loosened one hand and held it over her nose and mouth. Not smelling anything at first, she took her hand down and sniffed, but to her disbelief the sweet fragrance of roses filled the room. Kaylee's body was totally numb, to the point she had to look to make sure her fingers were connected to the black book and envelope as she carefully removed them from Ellen's stomach.

"You certainly took your time getting here," a calming voice from the shadows said.

Kaylee screamed and jumped back. Her brows tensed as she fixed her eyes on Dotty. Frantic, she shouted, "Dotty, you could have cleared your throat or something. You scared the hound out of me! What are you doing here?"

Stepping out of the dimness, Dotty said in a peaceful tone, "I told you that I'm the keeper of the house, and I feel certain you know by now, Miss Shell. I am sure you know that I am the guardian of the keys as well."

"How did you know I was here?"

Dotty fixed her eyes on Kaylee and said, "I know everything that goes on here at the estate. Nothing escapes me." She took hold of the envelope and slid it from Kaylee's numb fingers. "This is mine!" she said. "You take the journal and read it later."

Kaylee swallowed hard as she gripped the side of the vault. "What's going on here, Dotty?"

"We'll talk about all that later." Dotty pleasantly grinned, looked behind her and said, "Cleo and the others are pulling through the gate as we speak. Now, go before they get to the door."

Kaylee turned to close the vault. Dotty took hold of her arm and assured her she would close the vault. Kaylee stared into Dotty's composed eyes. Dotty said with urgency, "Go quickly."

Kaylee glanced at the book, then to Dotty, and hurried out of the chamber. Upon entering the room, Kaylee removed the chair from the door and paused briefly to view the music box that continued to play. For an instant, she squeezed her eyes shut and could hear the echoing sounds of Dotty's voice telling her, "Go quickly."

Chapter Seventy-Seven

Cleo Comes to the Estate

*K*aylee's heart was racing as she reached the top of the stairs, only to hear someone knocking on the front door. "I'm coming!" she shouted. At the bottom of the steps, she took a couple deep breaths and opened the door. Dotty was right. Betty, Eddie and Lori stood there holding Cleo's arms.

After stepping inside, Cleo staggered, put her hand to her mouth and shivered. Kaylee tried to get her to sit down, but she insisted on going to the dining room. Kaylee had been in such a hurry, she failed to notice the house was aglow with candles. She also failed to notice the white sheets that had covered the paintings upstairs were no longer hiding the family portraits that were now displayed on the walls throughout the house. Also trembling, Kaylee put one hand on her stomach and seized the back of a chair with the other. Her squinted eyes surveyed the foyer, grand room and dining room. "How can it be . . . how?" her stuttering voice cried.

"How can what be?" Betty asked.

Kaylee pointed around the room and said breathlessly, "The paintings. How did the paintings get down the stairs and hung on the walls? I was gone for only a few minutes and no one else was here."

"It's Ellen!" Cleo whispered. "She never left the estate, you know."

Betty vigorously rubbed her arms. "Man, this whole thing is giving me the creeps."

"You're right," Lori said. "Miss Shell told us the paintings were stored, and we were here at the meeting and they were not hanging on the walls."

Eddie stuttered, "Now . . . now ladies. I'm a man and there's no doubt about that, but this is a little out of my league. All this talk of Ellen never leaving, well, we all know she died over one hundred years ago. Am I right?"

Betty patted his cheek. "Honey, yes, she did die a century ago, but only flesh dies, not your spirit."

Eddie was quick to say, "Well, my point is, I know how to fight a man if he attacks, but I'll be the first to confess I don't have a clue how to fight a ghost. So, I guess it's everyone for themselves."

Betty punched his side. "Suck it up and stop being such a baby. If you can't take it, then maybe you'd better leave before things just might get hairy."

"Might get hairy? It's already hairy!"

"Don't worry, Eddie," Cleo said, "Ellen won't bother you. She just wants to avenge her death . . ." Cleo suddenly caught a glimpse of the black book Kaylee was holding. "Where did you get that book?" she asked breathlessly.

Kaylee swallowed hard and then replied, "It's Ellen's journal."

Cleo shook her head. "Are you sure?"

Kaylee nodded. "Yes, I'm sure."

Stunned, Cleo leaned toward Kaylee. "Her journal was black, but does it have a small raised letter 'H' in the lower, right-hand corner?"

Kaylee turned the book over, touched the 'H' and looked at Cleo.

Cleo shook her head in disbelief, "Where in the name of heavens did you find it?"

"That's not important right now."

Ecstatic, Cleo pointed her skinny finger at Kaylee. "You've found the hidden room, haven't you?"

A knock on the door saved Kaylee from having to answer. "I'll be right back," she said.

When Kaylee opened the door, Dotty was standing there with a grin on her face. "Miss Shell, I wanted to let you know I was back from my trip before I turned in for the night."

"Don't leave yet. Come in, I want you to meet someone special."

"I would love to," Dotty said, as she entered and closed the door.

Kaylee watched for Dotty's response when she saw that the paintings were all hanging. The response wasn't the one Kaylee expected. A smile of sheer delight spread across Dotty's face as she glanced around the room. "The house looks spectacular tonight. With all the candles, the painting and the glorious music. Don't you think, Miss Shell?"

It was only after Dotty entered the house that Kaylee noticed that the music was softly playing. Kaylee frowned but said nothing.

"I'm sorry, dear," Dotty said, as she continued to look about the house. "Everything looks so perfect. Now who was it you wanted me to meet?"

Cleo was facing the fireplace when Dotty entered the dining room. After saying hello to the students, Dotty looked toward Cleo and asked, "Miss Shell, is this the guest you wanted me to meet?"

Cleo continued to stare at Ellen's painting. Kaylee stood beside Cleo and said, "Yes, and I would like to add that she is a very special guest. Dotty, I want you to meet Cleo King."

When Cleo didn't turn immediately, Kaylee put her hand on her shoulder. "Cleo, I want you to meet Dotty Sams."

Cleo's body was visibly shaking as she slowly turned to face Dotty.

"Are you okay, Cleo?" Kaylee asked.

"I'm fine," she said as she lifted her eyes to rest on Dotty's face.

Dotty's eyes lit up. "It's a pleasure, Ms. King!"

Cleo placed her hand on her chest and slowly sat down. The look of anguish was quickly replaced with a pleasant, tight-lipped grin and a quick nod of her head. "What a pleasure to see you again, Dotty."

"Have you two met before?" Betty asked.

Cleo continued to stare at Dotty. "Oh, yes, I could never forget Dotty. We go way back."

Dotty, still smiling, slapped her hands together and asked, "Would anyone here care for something to drink?"

"Dotty," Cleo said softly, "how long have you been the keeper of the house now?"

Dotty gently took Cleo's hands. "Not quite long enough, yet, Miss Cleo."

Tears welled up in Cleo's eyes as she whispered, "I remember how you would read to me when I was a young girl. You brushed my hair and soothed me when I cried in the night, wanting to see my mother so desperately."

Eddie, Betty and Lori anxiously looked at each other. Eddie stuttered, What-what-what are you talking about, Cleo? You're ninety-four and Dotty is much younger. How did she brush your hair and read to you when you were a young girl?"

Lori muttered, "That summed up my question."

Cleo looked at Lori. "We all agreed we wanted truth. Well, sometimes you have to look deeper than the surface to know the truth."

"Just how deeply are you looking?" Betty asked.

Cleo clicked her tongue, "Deep enough to see a dear friend."

Betty looked at the book that Kaylee held tightly. "Oh, my goodness, Miss Shell, is that . . . that really Ellen's journal?"

"Yes!"

Eddie scratched his head. "Wow! We need a group meeting fast."

"No, not tonight," Kaylee said. "I want to have a chance to look through the journal first. Besides, it's getting late. We'll set a time for a meeting tomorrow. For now, I want you to go home before they find Cleo missing."

"That may take awhile," Lori said. "We took Mom's mannequin she uses to tailor dresses, put a gray wig on it and put it in Cleo's bed."

"Great idea," Kaylee said. "I want Cleo to go over the journal with me."

Cleo smiled. "I would love to." Cleo took Lori's hand and thanked her for bringing her to the estate. Then she turned to Kaylee and the book she was holding.

Chapter Seventy-Eight
The Journal

*A*fter everyone left, Dotty fixed hot chocolate and served Kaylee and Cleo.

Kaylee stared at Dotty. "I don't know what to say to you."

"Why should you say anything? You and Miss Cleo check the book. I think I'll retire. Cleo, I've prepared the green room for you. It's the room next to Miss Shell's. Goodnight."

"Dotty," Kaylee called out, "did you do all this to the house?"

Dotty raised her head, looked around the room and smiled. "No, Miss Shell, I did not."

Kaylee was stunned. If not Dotty, then who?

Kaylee sat beside Cleo, took a deep breath and opened the book. The pages had slightly yellowed but not enough to dim the eloquent penmanship of the writer.

Kaylee patted Cleo's hand. "Would you like for me to read it out loud?"

"That would be wonderful."

Kaylee lightly touched her fingertips to the first page, which had been hidden away for so many years, and began.

"To the one who is now reading my very personal journal, I want to say, please help me, as I feel my time is short. Thank you in advance for revealing what surely is ahead for me. I do find comfort in knowing that my journal will be protected until the right person comes to assist me. With you reading these pages, I will assume you are that person.

"Saturday, January 30, 1889, 12:34 a.m. I'm sitting at the dining room table near the fireplace. On occasion, the cracking of the fire causes my body to jerk, as though my heart has stopped beating. If not the fire, the strong winds that pound a tree limb against the side of the house. Stone River is known for its howling winds.

"Another Christmas has passed without my darling Jenny Lynn and her father, the love of my life, Wind Dancer. They were both taken from me in a span of three months. How shall I live without them?

"February 3, 2:00 a.m. I can't sleep for crying. My baby, Jenny Lynn, was only 6 years old when she died. She made me laugh and gave me unconditional love. At times, the thought of losing her is unbearable . . . tonight is one of those nights. I questioned God as to why He allowed my darling Jenny to die. Then I realized that such a tragedy would not come from God, but from Satan himself. I miss the many times that she would come and climb into bed with me on rainy nights or just because she wanted to be close to me.

"Her fancy dresses, ribbons and shoes, which were tailored just for her, still hang in her closets. The ruffled petticoats and fur jackets she adored hang like new, never to be worn again and never to be outgrown. The thought of giving them away causes my heart to ache."

Kaylee continued reading, "March 18. It's 1:02 a.m. The clock that bears Jenny's beautiful face has just chimed. Each time I hear the chimes, it's as though a knife pierces my heart.

"Roy has been very moody for the past few days. I'm so thankful he finds his pleasure with Janet. The thought of him touching me makes me nauseous.

"June 2, 1:45 a.m. I had Janet draw me a cool bath. It's so hot tonight. As I sit in this mound of bubbles with my music playing and candles burning, I can feel Wind Dancer's warm breath on my cheek, neck and ears. I feel his full lips pressed against mine, as his strong hands pull his perfect body so tight to mine. I can hardly breathe, until our breathlessness becomes groans of fulfillment. I miss him so very much.

"November 23 12:53 a.m. Lately, all I do is cry. Roy has come to my room the past couple of nights, but I will never unlock my door to him again. I told him to go to Janet or the whorehouse he and Jake built. He screamed that he wanted to have the biggest whore of all, me."

Cleo's sad eyes stared at Kaylee.

"What is it, Cleo?" Kaylee asked.

"I am so angry. My mama loved Roy so much, and he said he loved her, so why is Roy going to Ellen, who hates him, with Mama in the house?"

Kaylee took Cleo's hand. "Because he is a very evil man who is not content with anything or anybody."

Cleo pointed at the page. "All my questions aside for now. Let's read on and see what else Ellen has to say."

"Cleo, look at this next entry! It's not dated like all the other entries."

"I wonder why she didn't date it," Cleo said. "Read on and see if she gives us a reason."

Kaylee continued. "Today as I sit in the tower room, I yearn so desperately to see Wind Dancer riding across the open range, with his shiny, long, black hair flowing in the wind, as he comes to make unhurried love to his Halo."

"Halo?" Kaylee sighed. "I wonder what she means by Halo?"

Cleo leaned back in her chair and said, "How could I have forgotten to tell you about Halo? Halo was Wind Dancer's pet name for Ellen. In the Lakota tongue, it means Angel Face."

"Really?" Kaylee said.

"Did you notice Ellen wrote the same thing about Wind Dancer riding across the range and his hair flowing in the wind, just like Mama told me? Let's read on. I'm anxious to hear what's next."

Kaylee read many such pages, yet it was toward the end of the journal the writing grew more intense. Ellen wrote about Roy not only stealing money from Jake, killing and stealing from the Lakota tribe at the Bend, but she also revealed how very aggressive he had become toward her.

"December 15, 1889. Last night, Roy, in a drunken state, broke my door down and tried to kiss me. I fought him with all my might. My might wasn't enough to stop the brutal rape he imposed upon me. I hate him! As he did every demeaning act possible to me, he shouted that he killed my savage lover and bastard child. I had never heard him say those words about Jenny Lynn before. He boasted that I would be next, and nothing would be done about it. After he satisfied his violent lust and left the house, Janet came, bathed and dressed me and helped me get to bed. Afterward, she sent one of the servants for the doctor.

"Poor Janet loves Roy so. He's incapable of loving anyone but himself. It's strange how he can make love to her, for several years now, and yet won't even consider marrying her. I can only wonder what he will do after I'm out of the way. I fear that time, is fast approaching. All this time I made myself think that killing Jenny Lynn was an accident, but tonight when he called her a bastard child and confessed to taking her life, I wanted to kill him. As he left my room, he muttered, 'I didn't mean to kill her.' Then why did he and how did he? I don't believe a word he says. I could never express with words how much I hate him.

"December 24, 1889, 7:00 a.m. After my morning coffee, I took my journal and rode out to Coyote Canyon where Wind Dancer and I would meet. The need to know where Roy buried him and Moving Cloud is so bad it burns like fire inside my soul. I want to give them a proper burial, but where are they? Moving Cloud was an innocent victim who only came with his brother to watch for us in case some of our men happened by.

"As I sat looking into the canyon, I cried as I remember how devastated my family was the day we joined the wagon train in Missouri heading for North Dakota. They begged me not to follow Roy Hilmar to no man's land. They feared they would never see me again. Were it not for Jenny Lynn and Wind Dancer, my years here would have been nothing more than a living hell.

"Roy has been in an unusually happy mood the last few days. Each year we plan a big party for our workers, servants and their families. Of course, Roy doesn't stop there. He invites almost everyone in Stone River. He and Jake built a ballroom on the outskirts of town to accommodate the event. I was stunned when Roy bought me a beautiful red velvet ball gown to wear to the gala. He hasn't bought me anything in years.

"Cleo, look at this," Kaylee said. "Ellen made another entry that evening of December 24. The first entry was made in the morning and then another one at 6:00 p.m. that evening."

"So, I see," Cleo said. "That's the first time she did that. Maybe she'll explain the reason as you read on."

"December 24, 6:00 p.m. I feel I must log this entry before we leave for the party. I want to add a special word of thanks to the one who's reading my very private thoughts. I don't want you to think that I never cared for Roy. I went against my parents' wishes for me not to marry him, and I married him anyway. They hated him. The thought of a man who had nothing, taking their baby girl from them, was overpowering. I didn't care if he was rich or poor. I thought our love would carry us through any situation that arose. Clearly it did not. I was never enough to please Roy. I gave him everything, including my inheritance. I said that to say that I have taken a vast amount of money from our account and put it away for the Lakota tribe at the Bend. I have explained my plan to Dotty, the main housekeeper and my dearest friend. She will see to my journal, money and the house until . . .

"As I pen these words, my music box is playing beautiful piano music as the man and woman on top of it are swirling around and around on the water. I love that music so much! The same music, Wind Dancer and I danced to, made love to and at times cried to. I . . . I have an eerie premonition that this may very well be my last entry. I know if I should die tonight, it will be by Roy's hand. I don't mind death. I died when Jenny Lynn and Wind Dancer were murdered. Roy Hilmar may kill my body, but my spirit will not leave this house until justice is poured out on his head and until all of Stone River sees him for who he really is. He's an evil man who thinks his murderous acts will never be found out. He's wrong! I need to go now; he's calling me. I want to thank you, in advance, whoever you are for coming to my aid in exposing Roy Hilmar. He is calling me again; I have to go. Thank you for helping me, Ellen Hilmar."

Kaylee slowly raised her eyes to Cleo. "She signed her name like she was ending a letter."

Cleo moaned. "Look at the date. Christmas Eve, 1889. Ellen never made it to the party. She died that night before ever leaving the house. She allegedly tripped and fell down the stairs."

Kaylee stood and fixed her eyes on Ellen. "Such a beautiful woman. Who would have ever thought her life was filled with total chaos?" Kaylee slowly turned and stared at Cleo.

"What is it?" Cleo asked.

Kaylee put her finger to her lips. "Shhh, listen. It sounds like someone crying."

Cleo's eyes widened when she too heard the low sound of someone weeping. Kaylee took hold of Cleo's arm, and they sluggishly made their way to the foyer and looked up the staircase, expecting to see Ellen as before, but saw no one. Kaylee jerked when someone pounded on the front door.

"Who is it?" she called out.

"It's Adam!"

She rushed to open the door and was pulled into Adam's strong embrace. She frantically asked, "Where have you been? I've been worried sick about you."

Adam pushed the door open with his foot, while holding Kaylee's shoulders. He started to say something but hesitated when he saw the paintings hanging on the walls. "It's happening?" Before Kaylee could respond, he stared into her eyes and eagerly added, "I found Wind Dancer's and Moving Cloud's remains."

"What? Where did you find them and how?"

He shrugged. "By divine intervention, I suppose." He glanced past Kaylee at Cleo. "I'm sorry, I didn't know you had company."

"No, no. Adam, this is Cleo King. She's Roy Hilmar's daughter."

Before Cleo could say anything, Dotty came from the grand room and said, "Adam, I'm glad to see you made it home safely." She took Cleo by her arm. "Miss Cleo, why don't I help you to bed? It's been a long time since I've done that."

Cleo nodded and again glanced up the stairs. Kaylee patted her shoulder and said goodnight.

Chapter Seventy-Nine
Feeling the Change

*K*aylee looked at Adam and asked, "Where did you find Wind Dancer and Moving Cloud?"

Adam took Kaylee's shoulders in his strong hands. "I want to tell you when we are sitting down and having a glass of something hot to drink."

"Then we will have to wait because I too found something that has been hidden for a very long time as well."

"What did you find?"

Kaylee took his hand. "Follow me." She could hardly wait to show Adam the secret passageway and bedroom. As they entered the room where the paintings had been stored, Kaylee paused a brief moment and shook her head. Adam too was stunned as he looked at the crumpled sheets lying on the floor that once covered the paintings.

"Wow," Adam breathed.

Kaylee paused and put her hand on his chest. "I found the secret room."

"You . . . you found it?"

"Yes." She pointed toward the side wall where the door had opened earlier.

Adam looked to the opening and back to Kaylee. "Kaylee, have you been down to the room, yet?"

"Yes, come on. I'll show you."

Kaylee's heart raced as they descended the spiral stairs. She stopped at the foot of the steps, glanced at Adam, pushed the screeching door open and went inside. The candles and fire in the fireplace burned as though they had just been lit. Like the candles upstairs, there was no wax dripping, and each candle looked brand new.

At this point, Kaylee wasn't surprised at anything. After all, the mysterious music had hardly stopped playing since she had moved into the estate. Kaylee faced Adam, who was still standing in the doorway. His stare prevented her from moving. Silently, he removed his coat and unbuttoned his shirt, exposing his smooth muscular chest. His enchanting eyes looked at the music box that was playing without end, put his arm around Kaylee's waist and softly said, "Dance with me, Halo."

Her breath escaped her as they began to dance around the room. At times as they danced, Kaylee felt as though she was indeed Ellen and Adam's face and body were truly those of Wind Dancer. They laughed and held tight to each other until Adam stopped and cupped her jaw in his hands and tenderly pressed his lips to hers. At first, his kiss was controlled. So was the way he held her, as though she were a fragile butterfly. Their dance slowed as his kisses deepened. His mouth did not stay still upon hers but roved over her face, eyelids and chin, and traveled along the sensitive softness of her throat.

Kaylee moaned as Adam tugged at the buttons on her blouse until she felt the thin fabric slide off her shoulders. His breathing grew passionate as he gently stroked her body with his fingertips. Her eyes closed and her head leaned back as she cried out from the pleasure of his touch. Adam's hands pulled her tender body snugly against him. He let go only long enough to pick her up and gently lay her on the bed that was covered with red rose petals.

Adam inhaled her perfume as he watched the yearning in her face, as her need for him deepened. In the excitement of becoming one with each other, Adam moaned repeatedly, "I love you."

In the stillness of the afterglow, Adam tenderly squeezed her hand as he stared into her eyes and spoke softly. "I need you more than just tonight. I need you for a lifetime. The last three days without you close to me has driven me insane. Yet, as I sat in the darkness overlooking the canyon, my heart told me that our time together will soon be over."

Kaylee put her fingers to his lips. "True love never dies. How could it possibly be over?"

"You're right." Adam told Kaylee to close her eyes. "I was going to wait, but I can wait no longer." He retrieved his shirt from the floor and took something from the pocket. "Okay, open your eyes."

Kaylee gasped when she saw that Adam held a ring made of brightly colored beads. "This is for me?" she asked.

"You and you alone." He put it on her finger. "Will you marry me, Angel Face?"

Kaylee was so taken by surprise. "I . . . I can't." She tried to get off the bed.

Adam took hold of her arm and cried out, "You can leave Roy."

Kaylee frowned. "What did you say?"

"I mean . . . Jeffrey. If you must go back to Missouri, I mean . . . I mean, North Carolina, I'll go with you."

Kaylee shook her head. "Go with me? Adam, that would never work."

"Then stay in Stone River with me."

Kaylee trembled as she dressed and told Adam to do the same. Compelled, she gently touched the music box. That instant, she sensed something upsetting had taken place in that room between Wind Dancer and Ellen.

"Kaylee."

Adam's appearance had changed from one of fulfillment and joy to sadness. Trying to appear normal, Kaylee picked up the flashlight and started toward the opening. To her surprise, Adam took the light from her and led the way to the mausoleum. Kaylee grabbed his arm, stopping him. "How is it that you knew exactly where to touch that door to make it open? You said you didn't have a clue where the secret place was and yet you went straight to the door."

Adam took Kaylee's hand from his arm and muttered, "I just knew where to go, but I don't know how I knew."

As he entered the mausoleum and looked around, "Now what?" he said.

Kaylee awkwardly pointed to the poem on the nameplate. "Did you know that Cleo's mother is buried here? Roy couldn't put her name on the plate, to avoid a scandal, so he put the poem Janet wrote for him on it."

Adam shook his head, but said nothing.

Kaylee put her hands on her hips and scolded, "All right, Adam, what's this silent treatment? There's more to us than making love every time we are together. Or, is it a man thing that has to be satisfied if we come within touching distance of each other?"

Adam grabbed her shoulders and shouted, "If that's what you think of me, then you don't know me at all. If you did know me, you would know each time I'm with you I want to make love to you because I'm always afraid it will be the last time."

As tears filled her eyes, Kaylee shouted back, "I'm sorry, Adam. I . . . I didn't mean that. You know how I feel about you."

Adam kissed her cheek. "I need to go now."

"Why? I haven't finished showing you everything."

"I'll see them later. Are you all right going back by yourself?"

"Yes, but where are you going?"

"Out the front." He took her hand, looked at the ring and kissed it. "Goodbye, Angel Face."

Chapter Eighty
Release of Emotions

Stunned, Kaylee made her way back to the dining room. As she fixed her eyes on Ellen's portrait, she began to cry. She wanted to run to Adam and shout at the top of her voice that she would stay with him and marry him, yet she didn't. She tightened her fist and shouted at the painting. "What do you want from me? I didn't come here to accommodate you in your mission to ruin Roy Hilmar's good name, and I sure didn't come here to fall in love with a complete stranger. What is it? Do you want me to feel your pain? Well, I do! I've never been so screwed up in all my life. Music playing constantly, fireplaces, candles lighting themselves and never burning out. Paintings that all of a sudden are brought from their hiding place and mounted back on the wall where they should have been all along. And the woman crying her heart out on the stairs. "What's it all about, Ellen? Tell me, what's it all about?"

Kaylee dropped to her knees and began sobbing out of control. She hadn't noticed that Dotty was standing behind her until Dotty put her hand on Kaylee's shoulder.

405

"Kaylee," Dotty said quietly, "come sit with me for a few minutes. If you don't mind."

Through swollen eyes, Kaylee stared at Dotty without speaking.

Dotty tapped the table and stated, "I know you're confused and don't understand all of this right now."

Disgusted, Kaylee cried out, "All of this? Are you kidding me? I don't understand *any* of this. My reason for coming here was Jake Boone, and it's all turned out to be about Roy and Ellen Hilmar."

Dotty patted Kaylee's hand. "Please, try to calm down."

Kaylee jerked her hand away. "Calm down? Calm down? I wish I could calm down. Speaking of calming down, I'm talking to a woman who's been the overseer of this estate since it was built. You explain that to me. Tell me, Dotty, how's that for bringing calm to a person's soul?"

"I realize you need to vent, Kaylee, yet I need you to hear what I have to say. Will you please listen?"

Kaylee threw her hands in the air and ranted, "Great heavenly days, why not, why not? I don't think I have anything to lose, do you?"

Unshaken by Kaylee's release of emotion, Dotty peacefully asked, "When you were in the secret room with Adam, what was your answer when he asked you to marry him?"

Kaylee touched her fingertips to her forehead and asked, "How could you possibly know that?"

"The ring!"

Kaylee held her hand out and looked at the ring.

"Kaylee, what I'm about to say to you may be even more shocking than you've heard thus far. Tonight, it wasn't Adam who asked you to marry him, it was Wind Dancer asking Ellen to marry him and go away with him. The ring on your finger is the one Wind Dancer gave Ellen one night, while in the same room you and Adam were in tonight."

Kaylee closed her eyes, shook her head and questioned, "How do you know it's the same ring?"

"Trust me, Kaylee, it's the same ring. Wind Dancer had wanted Ellen and Jenny to leave Stone River for a long time. Roy had threatened to kill him and had made an attempt to do so, on more than one occasion. He knew Roy meant business. Even so, in his eyes and heart, the need to be with Ellen was greater than his fear of Roy. He told Ellen every time they made love, he feared that would be their last time together."

Kaylee lowered her eyes. "That's exactly what Adam told me tonight."

"I know. That night when Wind Dancer gave Ellen the ring was the last night that Ellen ever saw him. As you said, I've been here at the Hilmar Estate since the beginning. I was the first person hired by Ellen Hilmar, and I'll serve my mistress until my job here is completed."

"When will that be?" Kaylee asked.

"I'll be here until the envelope is turned over to its rightful owner."

"Dotty, what about Martin Cullman? He's the reason I'm here."

"No, no my dear. He is only a small part of why you were sent here."

"What do you mean? Martin is the one who asked me to come here."

Dotty tilted her head and chuckled. "After all you've seen and been through, do you really believe that?"

Kaylee furrowed her brows. "I don't know what to believe. However, the fact remains that Clara Aims did have Jake's son. According to you and Mr. Kent, a fortune now belongs to Martin. So, I'll ask you the same question Charlie asked me. What do I do now with this information?"

Dotty laughed aloud. "You just wait and see. The Christmas Eve party Jake, Roy and Ellen had for the workers and the towns people has continued all these years. Do you remember telling Nick Long you wanted to have a drama that would play out the finding of your quest?"

"Of course, I do!"

"Well, I have connections who have agreed, for a sum of money, to allow you and your senior class to put on the drama you had planned for the end of the school year. I swayed them to believe that they have you scared and right where they want you. They think they have nothing to worry about. I might add, Terra also played a big part in seeing you have the entertainment that night. The night of the big party that Roy, Ellen and Jake always had for the towns people."

"Terra?"

"Terra. She was your connection in Stone River, not John Smith."

Kaylee frowned and asked, "Then who is John Smith?"

"He's Jake Boone's grandson."

"What?"

"He's also over the town council. You see, I didn't tell you everything."

"Well, please do!"

"After Jake's death, his only living son ran Stone River. After his death, the council asked his son, John, if he would come and take charge of the town's affairs. John agreed and did the running of Stone River from Missouri for a while. Then to be closer, he moved to Montana. Don't misunderstand. He has plenty of money from what Jake left Tammy and their children. Right before you moved here, John left Montana and moved to Stone River. You see, there is a clause in Jake's will. It states that if by 12:00 p.m. this Christmas Eve, if Clara Aims' son or daughter doesn't come forward to claim his or her inheritance, the money goes back to his grandchildren. Oh, John would still have control over the money set aside for the town's use, but that money is restricted. Of course, some of the council dip their fingers into the vault on occasion, but they are audited twice a year by the law firm that holds Jake's will. Everything is going to change for Jake and Roy as soon as the clock strikes midnight on Christmas Eve."

Kaylee jumped when someone pounded on the front door. A gruff voice called out, "Kaylee Shell, this is Sheriff Dotson. Open up."

"Let him in," Dotty said.

Kaylee opened the door. Instantly, Sheriff Dotson burst into the room and shouted, "I know Cleo King is here, and you have a part in kidnapping her. So, where is she?"

Dotty came around the corner. When Sheriff Dotson saw her, he turned white as a sheet. "Is there a problem, sheriff?" she asked straight-faced.

He nervously played with his belt buckle. "Yes . . . yes there is. Cleo King. You know, Cleo, don't you?"

Dotty nodded. "You know I do."

"She's disappeared from the retirement home, and we have reason to believe she's here at Miss Shell's request. We came to take her back."

"Yes, Cleo is here," Dotty said. "And she's staying a few days with me. I don't see a problem with that, do you, sheriff?"

The sheriff wiped sweat from his upper lip. "No, no . . . no, there's no problem. I thought Miss Shell had taken her."

Dotty crossed her arms. "Why would Miss Shell take Cleo? Can you tell me why you would even consider a thing like that?"

Sheriff Dotson shook his head. "No . . . no, I can't think of a reason."

Dotty squinted at him. "Is Cleo a prisoner at the retirement home?" she asked.

"Heaven's, no!"

"Then she can go visit anyone she wants, right?"

"Yes . . . yes, she can. She didn't check out, so we assumed she may have been taken by force."

"Oh, come now, sheriff, by force?" Dotty said. "I have one last question for you, Sheriff Dotson. If Cleo had gone and told someone at the facility that she wanted to check out, would they have let her go?"

The sheriff didn't answer the question Dotty asked, but said, "Dotty, you give me your word Cleo is in your care, and I'll be satisfied."

Dotty put her face close to his and sternly stated, "I thought I already told you that she's staying with me."

Sheriff Dotson licked his lips, "Yes . . . yes, I think you did. I'm sorry to disturb you, Miss Shell. Goodnight."

Kaylee stared at Dotty. "Why did he turn so pale when he saw you?"

Dotty shrugged. "Maybe it's because I've known him all his life and he's aged but I haven't. I'd better move Cleo to my house tonight."

Chapter Eighty-One

Changing So Fast

That night Kaylee received a call from Nick Long, telling her that Joshua Coats had reconsidered his complaint, and she was cleared to come back to school the next morning. He said he was sorry to hear she would be leaving Stone River after Christmas. He was quick to add that Dotty and Terra both had mentioned that she would be leaving.

Kaylee stopped and listened for a moment. The music had stopped playing, the candles and fire in the fireplace had gone out and the electric lights had come on. She went to the bathroom, looked at the claw foot tub and decided to take a hot bath before bed. Was the bath really for her to relax her tired muscles or was her passion ignited for her dream lover touch? Whatever the reason, she lit the candles and poured a glass of red wine. To her surprise, she had to push the play button to start the piano rhapsody.

After sinking into the heap of bubbles, she rested her head on the red satin pillow that lay on the rim of the tub. Once she had soaked in the bubbles a long while, Kaylee determined that her lover, whether Adam or Wind Dancer, wasn't going to magically appear. So, confused, she made her way to bed, unsure why everything had suddenly ceased.

A dreadful wind was blowing so hard it caused the tree limb outside her bedroom window to beat against the house with great intensity. With only a dim glow from a small nightlight, Kaylee snuggled under the cover, holding to the ring Adam had given her. Desperately needing sleep and wanting to talk to Adam didn't mix. If things were about to change between them, she wanted to know up front. Therefore, she scurried from the bed, put her long wool coat on over her flannel pajamas and wrapped her scarf around her head. She slipped her boots on and went out the kitchen door to Adam's house.

Kaylee was thankful to see a dim light on in the living room. Winds dashed the heavy rain, soaking Kaylee's pajamas pants and boots. The umbrella proved to be ineffective; therefore, her coat was drenched as well. Without hesitation, she closed the umbrella and propped it against the wall before knocking. After knocking several times, she thought he wasn't going to answer the door. With tears in her eyes she picked up the umbrella, opened it and stepped off the porch. She had taken only a couple of steps when she heard Adam shout her name.

"Kaylee!"

She held her breath for a brief moment and turned to see Adam standing in plaid pajama bottoms and a dark blue robe that was open, revealing his bare chest.

Feeling awkward, she stammered, "Maybe . . . maybe I'd better go. I shouldn't have come this late."

"Nonsense, come inside out of the weather. I was in the shower and didn't hear you knocking for a moment."

Kaylee smiled and hurried to the door. She had never been inside Adam's house before. It was small but very well kept and really quite nice. Adam took her coat and told her to warm herself by the fireplace. Kaylee was surprised to see a handwoven, area rug with a Lakota design in front of the brick, round-top fireplace. Facing the fireplace were two overstuffed, brown recliners. A small lamp table, with the lamp built in, sat between the chairs. As Kaylee warmed up, Adam called from the kitchen and asked if she wanted sugar with her hot tea.

"Yes, please. Two lumps."

He came into the room and sat a small tray on a table and gave Kaylee her tea. "Are you warming up?"

Kaylee took a sip of tea. "Yes, thank you for the tea. I . . . I really shouldn't have come this late."

"Why? I'm glad you came. One reason I'm so glad you came is so I can apologize for the way I left you at the mausoleum. I should never have left you. And, I'm glad you came because you haven't had the pleasure of seeing how a workhand lives."

"I think your house looks great. Small, but great."

"I think my late-night visitor is the most beautiful woman my eyes have ever witnessed." Adam chuckled. "I see you still have my engagement ring on."

Kaylee touched the ring and asked, "Where did you get this ring?"

"I found it with Wind Dancer's remains."

"Oh my, really?"

"Yes."

"Where . . . where did you find his remains?"

"In a cavern as you start down the canyon. I felt such an urgency to go, and when I got there I couldn't leave until I found their bodies. I got to the canyon around noon. It was pouring rain, and so cold, the wind was awful. I had no idea there were so many caverns under the top surface. Kaylee, do you remember I told you when I'm at the canyon, I could see the Indians who lived there? This time I saw more than usual. I saw two men carrying the bodies of Wind Dancer and Moving Cloud to one of the canyons. They tossed them inside a cave and covered them with rocks. That was on my second day there. When I uncovered them, Wind Dancer had a ring, just like this one, on his finger when he died. The ring I gave you was lying beside his hand. When I picked it up, I closed my eyes and saw your beautiful face. I could smell the awesome aroma of your perfume." Adam touched the small scar on her face and said, "I even saw this scar. How did you get this scar anyway?"

Kaylee grinned and blushed. "It's personal."

Adam raised her chin with his finger. "Anything to do with Jeffrey?"

"Everything to do with Jeffrey."

Adam tapped the end of her nose with his finger. "Would you care to expound?"

Kaylee cleared her throat and chuckled. "This is one of those private stories one doesn't usually share, but since you asked . . . a week before I came to Stone River, Jeffrey and I were at his apartment. He had made a candlelight dinner, wanting everything to be special and romantic, knowing I was going away for a while. After dinner, we were having an intimate moment when the bed frame broke and we both hit the floor. On the way down, my face hit the wood frame. It almost gave Jeffrey a heart attack, but all I could do was laugh. Jeffrey insisted I go to the hospital and have it checked. I had to have two stitches! Needless to say, I wasn't fully honest with the doctor about what had happened." Kaylee's smile turned somber. "The day I left Raleigh to come to Stone River, I thought my heart would break. We held each other until I had to board the plane. I can still see Jeffrey standing in the viewing section. Jeffrey held his hand up and pressed his palm against the large window in the viewing area. He held it there until I could no longer see him."

Adam lowered his head, "We're changing, aren't we?"

Kaylee nodded a somber yes.

Adam stroked her cheek with his fingertips. "I don't want a change to take place. I know now that Wind Dancer and Ellen's spirits have brought us together. Not only to bring justice concerning Roy, but also to bring new awareness of what really happened during Stone River's early history. However, for me, it's gone way beyond the history and became very personal. Ellen wanted everyone to know about the love she and Wind Dancer shared and the results of their love. A beautiful little girl named Jenny Lynn. It's a beautiful, passionate love story that will live on in Stone River's history. I feel so honored to be a part of that history."

Adam stroked her hair and asked her to please be seated. She wondered what he was going to do. He pushed the button on the recliner raising her feet up.

Adam sighed. "Your feet are soaking wet!" He squatted, lifted her foot and took her boot off. "Let me be your servant tonight," he whispered. Adam took his T-shirt from the other chair, dried her feet, massaged them and gently stroked them. His long fingers slowly raised her slender foot to his lips, and he kissed them. Kaylee's breathing intensified as she watched Adam's every sensual move.

"Your pajamas are soaked," he whispered as he glided his hands under her shirt, taking hold of the waist of her pants. She exhaled and slightly raised her hips. Adam readily guided the wet pants down her long shapely legs and off her feet. He helped her to her feet. As she removed her wet shirt, Adam got one of his housecoats and helped her put it on. He grabbed a comforter as Kaylee lowered the chair, allowing Adam to move close beside her. His strong hands pulled her shoulders high enough to put his arm around her.

Rain continued to fall as the windows rattled from gusts of wind. Adam spread the comforter over them as they lay in each other's arms in the overstuffed recliner.

"Kaylee, I will always love you."

Kaylee snuggled on Adam's shoulder. "I will always love you as well."

The next morning, Adam awoke to find Kaylee gone from his arms. She left a note on the lampstand.

You are such a sexy man, even when you're sleeping. Love you! Angel Face.

Chapter Eighty-Two
Terra's Surprise

Nick Long and Ricky Owens were the first two people Kaylee ran into at school. They were casual; however, she could sense the undeserved tension that was obvious between them and her. Kaylee knocked lightly on Terra's classroom door. Terra stood and motioned for her to come in.

"Good morning, Terra! I just wanted to say hi."

"I'm glad you did. Hi yourself."

"Terra, why didn't you tell me right away you were my contact in Stone River?"

"Actually, I should have told you sooner than I did."

"Where is John Smith?" Kaylee asked.

"He went out of town but promised to be back before Christmas."

"How is it that Martin made contact with you?"

"Mr. Cullman contacted the school and asked to speak to a senior teacher. I answered the phone. He called me many times before revealing his real reason for calling, which was you. When he felt comfortable and had a background check on me, he told me his reason for sending you here. My pay was $5,000.00. I never cashed the check. After meeting you, I have decided not to cash it. Mr. Cullman loves you very much, Kaylee."

Kaylee said softly, "Dotty said you played a big part in convincing the council to let me back in school. Thank you."

Terra nodded. "You bet. How could you put on the drama of Stone River otherwise? Just watch your back. By the way, I did talk to the council about letting you come back to school, but it was Dotty who had the final say."

The students were thrilled to see Kaylee back in school. She shared almost everything with them. A meeting at the estate was held to decide who would play what parts in the program. It was unanimous that Paulette and Charlie would play Ellen and Wind Dancer. Eddie announced that he and Betty couldn't be trusted to play those parts because there was too much heat between them.

Students were responsible for writing their own lines, finding their costumes and being ready to start practice in two days, with only a week and a half to put everything together.

Though extremely busy getting ready for the play, Kaylee noticed the blue light over Ellen's portrait had not been on in four days, and the music had silenced as well. The hardest change of all was not feeling Adam's loving touch. Working closely with him putting the drama together had been a real challenge. The attraction, though different, was still very much alive.

December 23 had arrived. The stage was set, and the last practice finished. Kaylee's class was so into their parts that it was hard to distinguish acting from reality. When everyone had left the ballroom at the school, Kaylee and Adam took one last look at the stage before locking up.

Adam smiled and boasted, "Well, tomorrow's the big night. I've got a feeling you're going to bring the house down."

"Yeah." Kaylee faced Adam. "Do you want to come by and have some coffee?"

Without delay, Adam replied, "If you hadn't asked, I was going to. I'll lock up and be right there."

As Kaylee entered the house, the candles were lit, the fireplace was burning, and the music was playing once again. On the table near the fireplace, a silver ice bucket held an 1889 bottle of red wine. Two vintage goblets, like the one she had broken, sat beside the ice bucket on a small silver tray. From the corner of her eye, something caught Kaylee's attention. She turned to see the music box on the mantel below Ellen's painting. Piano music echoed through the grand house as the figurines danced on the water.

When she left the dining room, Kaylee grabbed her chest and screamed aloud when she saw Dotty standing behind her. "Glory be, Dotty! Why didn't you clear your throat or something? My heart is about to explode!"

"I'm sorry," Dotty said. "You're right, I should have cleared my throat. I wanted to let you know a change of clothing is on your bed."

"Dotty, you didn't have to do that."

Dotty raised her brows and chuckled. "Oh yes, I did! Enjoy your evening, Miss Shell."

"Dotty? How's Cleo?"

"She is resting. Goodnight, Kaylee."

"Goodnight." Dotty turned to leave.

Kaylee called to her.

"Yes."

Kaylee looked around the room. "Everything's changing so fast."

Dotty sighed and faced Kaylee. "Yes, Kaylee. After tomorrow night, the change will be complete."

"What . . . what about you?"

"My time here as guardian of the house will end as well." Dotty raised her eyes and glanced around the room. "I'm glad. After waiting all these years, I'm tired and ready to go home. However, I'll not be leaving alone."

Kaylee's eyes widened, "What do you mean?"

Dotty pulled her sweater together. "I mean, Cleo told me she was tired as well. I told her she was free to come with me if she wanted. She took me up on the offer."

Kaylee's jaw dropped open. "Does that mean you two are going to die?"

Dotty crossed her arms. "Kaylee, dear, Cleo is 94 years old."

"I know, but . . ."

Dotty laughed. "Miss Shell, you'd better hurry. Adam is on his way. I'll see you in the morning." Dotty clicked her tongue as she wrapped her scarf around her neck. "What a wonderful Christmas Eve it will be! Your guests are going to be here on time, aren't they?"

"Yeah! Their plane should arrive at 3:00 p.m. Terra is going to pick them up and bring them to the gala."

Dotty laughed aloud. "I can hardly wait! Goodnight, Miss Shell."

Chapter Eighty-Three

The Dance

As Kaylee entered her bedroom, she couldn't believe her eyes. Draped across the bed was the black silk negligee, black lace robe and the gold comb. Beside the gown, lay the gorgeous gold and emerald necklace. Without delay, Kaylee dressed and pinned her hair up, leaving long, loose strands around her neck and face. Before leaving the room, she sprayed the rose fragrance over her body.

When Kaylee opened the door, Adam paused and said, "The music and candles. Did you . . .?"

"No, I didn't," Kaylee said.

"You are breathtaking." Gently, he touched her cheek. "May I have this dance, beautiful lady?"

Kaylee took his hand. In the vast foyer, amid the dim glow of candlelight, they swirled around and around to the piano rhapsody that had become such a part of the grand estate. When the dancing stopped, Adam took Kaylee in his arms and carried her to the living room. He sat in the loveseat, holding her close to his muscled body.

Kaylee's warm lips whispered in his ear, "Make love to me."

Adam lowered her head to the pillow and kissed her with all the passion that had been sealed in his heart for this moment. He kissed her face, her neck and her ears. His hands roamed over her as she drew him tightly to her. He couldn't get enough of her and wanted the night to last forever. Adam's gentle touch and Kaylee's willing response were unhurried. Every kiss was prolonged. They feared this would be the last time they would come together with such oneness.

In the afterglow, they danced into the night, failing to notice that Dotty had entered the house. As she drew near the foyer, she gasped and covered her mouth with her hand. Amid the candle's glow, it wasn't Adam and Kaylee whom she saw dancing. It was Wind Dancer and Ellen. After years of waiting, the moment Ellen and Dotty had waited for had finally come. Dotty left without disturbing the couple. Wind Dancer and Ellen spent that night together; however, the cold Christmas Eve morning found Adam and Kaylee in each other's arms.

Few words were spoken the next morning. The change was almost complete. After Adam left, Kaylee asked Dotty if she could use the keys one last time to look through the house. To her surprise, Dotty advised her that the rooms were no longer locked and she was free to explore. Jenny and Ellen's bedrooms would be the first. Afterward, Ellen's sitting room and the tower room. While in the room where the paintings had been stored, Kaylee couldn't resist taking one last look at the secret passageway, which led to the mausoleum. She decided to go down one more time. There Kaylee read the poem again, written on the face stone where Cleo's mother had been laid to rest. As she read the verse, she tried to envision Roy and Janet together, to feel the love he truly must have had for her making her resting place near him. Abruptly, Kaylee's breath escaped her when she felt something push against the back of her head and a low voice growl, "What are we doing, Miss Shell? Bonding with the dead?"

She instantly recognized the voice as that of John Smith. "What are you doing here?"

"I felt sure you would show up here this morning, and my hunch was correct."

"What is it you want from me, John Smith?"

John grabbed her shoulder and turned her around to face him. "Don't be coy with me. You know exactly what I want, Kaylee Shell. I want the money that's in Ellen Hilmar's vault."

"What does that have to do with me? Why don't you take it yourself?"

John's face muscles tightened. "You know I need the key to open the vault."

"Key! What makes you think I have such a key?"

John grabbed her shoulder and shook her.

Kaylee jerked away and shouted, "I know you're Jake Boone's grandson."

John raised a gun to Kaylee's cheek. "Then you know Roy stole a great deal of money from my grandfather."

Kaylee leaned her head away from the pistol. "Yes, I do. I also know the money in the vault belongs to Wind Dancer and Moving Cloud's descendants."

"Do you also know at midnight tonight, Grandfather Jake's millions come back to his grandchildren?"

"Really? I thought the money went to Jake and Clara's child."

"Well, due to a bizarre mishap that's going to take place, Martin Cullman won't make it on time. You see, even if it's one minute after midnight it won't matter who comes forward; it will still go back to the grandchildren."

"How is that you came to be the head man over Stone River?"

"How do you know that?"

Kaylee shouted, "Let me put it this way, the overseer of the estate told me."

"Is that so? You see, Miss Shell, my father was appointed by the law firm that handled my grandfather's estate. After Grandfather and Daddy died, the right was passed to me, his oldest son. My father said, 'Jake had stipulated in his will, since Roy didn't have a son, that my father would be the next in line to take control of Stone River.' Of course, Roy had to agree. Dad was to see the money set aside was used according to Roy's and Grandfather's wishes. Daddy received a handsome salary for being the overseer; even so, the vast estate that belonged to Jake wasn't to be touched. That is, unless a son or a daughter of Clara Aims came forth and proved they're his offspring. Fortunately, the deadline for that to take place is midnight tonight. Who would have thought after all these years, a nobody like you from North Carolina would show up for some old goat wanting to find out if Jake Boone was his father?

What are the odds of that happening just three or four months before the deadline?"

"So, tell me, John, what do you plan to do with me?"

"It depends," John murmured. "Now, where's the key?"

When Kaylee didn't respond fast enough, John cocked the trigger and ordered, "Tell me, or I'll send you to join the Hilmar clan."

"Okay! The key is in my pocket."

Kaylee slowly took the key out and handed it to him. He ordered her to open the vault. She turned the key and pulled the vault out, and instantly turned her eyes to John.

Trembling, John shoved her aside and stared into the glass top. Enraged, he grabbed her arm and shouted, "Where's the money?"

"I-I don't know."

John pushed her against the wall, put the gun under her chin and demanded to know where the money was, or he would kill her. A sudden wind shot through the wall and Dotty was standing behind John with his head in her hands. John turned pale as he struggled to breathe.

Dotty's voice rang out in a tone that Kaylee had never heard. "Drop the gun, or I'll break your neck."

John was so scared he could hardly release the gun.

Holding his neck, Dotty threw him to the floor.

Shaking, John stuttered, "What are you?"

Dotty leaned toward him. "I'm the keeper of the house," she announced. She shifted her eyes to Kaylee and said, "No one messes with the mistress of this house!"

John's widened eyes cut from left to right. "What are you going to do with me?"

Dotty snarled, "That's up to Miss Shell. As for me, I want to put you in one of these vaults and seal it. Perhaps that would give you time to get over your greed, before you suffocate."

Dotty looked at Kaylee, "It's your call, Miss Shell."

Kaylee slapped his chest and demanded, "I want to know about the bizarre mishap that would prevent Martin from making it to the drama on time."

Dotty pointed her finger at him.

John instantly replied, "Okay. After Terra arrives at the airport, I paid a man to slash her tires and to make sure there are no car rentals available. Or whatever it takes to delay their arrival long enough to get Grandfather's money back in the family's hands. I wasn't going to hurt them, only delay them."

"Is that right? Were you really going to hurt me?" Kaylee growled. "After all, you threatened to shoot me!"

John shook his head. "No, I wasn't going to! I only wanted to scare you. Check the gun. There're no bullets in it."

Kaylee checked the gun. Sure enough, it wasn't loaded. Kaylee slapped John on top of his head and laughed. "I hope you enjoy the show tonight, John. Now get out of here."

Kaylee watched as John inched his way to the entrance and ran away.

"Dotty, do you believe that weasel?" With no response, Kaylee turned, but Dotty was gone.

Chapter Eighty-Four
The Play

That night the whole of Stone River turned out to see what Miss Kaylee Shell's Twelfth Grade history class had been up to. Extra seating had been arranged to accommodate everyone. Places of honor were reserved for Cleo King, Ken Kent, Thelma Hilmar and none other than Kitty Snow, who decided to give Terra the Christmas present she had wanted for a long time. She agreed to move to Stone River and live with her daughter.

Right before the lights went down, Kaylee peeked from the side of the curtain one last time. She wanted to make sure Terra had arrived with Jeffrey and Martin. Adam watched from the other side of the stage, as a smile spread across Kaylee's face and she waved to someone in the audience. He knew the wave must be to Jeffrey.

The lights dimmed, and a short overture of the piano rhapsody played. Afterward, Lori adjusted the microphone and read aloud about Jake Boone, Tammy Boone, Roy Hilmar and Ellen Hilmar's decision to join a wagon train that formed in Missouri. Their destination was the lower southern region of North Dakota that would later become Stone River. The curtain slowly opened, and the drama began. With each new act, a new narrator would take the microphone and read. When Betty read the part about Roy murdering Moving Cloud, Wind Dancer, Jenny Lynn and Ellen Hilmar, the audience had to be quieted before the play could continue. Upon hearing the news about Roy being a murderer, Tim Dodd was the first to jump to his feet outraged; the rest of the council followed suit. After everyone finally settled down from the shocking news about Roy, it was time for the final act.

The entire last act was devoted to Ellen and Wind Dancer. The grand hall was darkened, and the curtain opened to a dim blue light and a fog of dry ice that filled the stage floor. The piano rhapsody piped through the hall as Charlie LittleHawk, in ceremonial Lakota Indian attire, came from one side of the stage. From the other side, Paulette Hilmar, in a long, black silk ball gown, with her hair piled high and long strands hanging around her face and neck, glided through the fog toward the center of the stage. The gold and pearl comb was placed like a tiara on her head. The final piece of her attire was Paulette's Great-Great-Grandmother Ellen Hilmar's, gold and emerald necklace resting around her long, slender neck.

As they met in the center of the stage, Charlie put his arm around her waist. Paulette, put her hand on Charlie's shoulder. Their other hands joined and they began to dance and twirl around the stage, swirling the fog about their feet. The dance ended where it began, in the heart of the stage. The pale blue light grew dimmer still. Sighs and gasps were heard throughout the building as Charlie pulled Paulette close to him and their lips met. In awe, everyone stood to their feet in thunderous applause as the curtain came down.

Kaylee looked across the stage at Adam. As their eyes met, memories that were made the night before flooded their minds. The roar of applause and the curtain going up again were all that broke their stare.

Everyone but the council who were appalled by the whole event, was on their feet. After Kaylee and her class took their final bow, Kaylee called Adam to the stage and thanked him for all his hard work in preparation for the play. When Adam hugged and kissed Kaylee's cheek, Jeffrey took notice of how they responded to each other.

Kaylee asked Charlie LittleHawk to step forward. To his surprise, on behalf of Ellen Hilmar, Kaylee presented him with a check that contained a small fortune. It was for him and all the closest descendants of Wind Dancer and Moving Cloud.

For the final touch, Kaylee announced she had a special surprise for the people of Stone River.

Kaylee adjusted the microphone. With tears in her eyes, she said, "It's a great privilege to introduction to Stone River, the son of Jake Boone and Clara Aims, Mr. Martin Cullman."

At the mention of Martin's name, the room immediately filled with groans, sighs and resounding applause with a standing ovation. As Jeffrey accompanied

Martin to the stage, John Smith stood and rushed from the building. The attorneys who handled Jake's estate joined everyone on stage and presented Martin with documents that gave him complete control of his father's wealth. Tears were shed by almost everyone. Of course, the tears shed by the council were for a completely different reason.

After the curtain closed, Jeffrey and Kaylee fell into each other's arms and kissed. Kaylee's eyes opened to meet with Adam's painful stare. When all the students gathered around Kaylee, Jeffrey told her he was going to meet with Martin and the attorneys and would see her back at the estate. Kaylee praised the students and thanked them for everything. After a hug from each student, Kaylee noted that Betty lingered when the others left.

Kaylee embraced her and said softly, "I'll miss you, Betty, more than the rest."

Betty wiped a tear away and asked, "So, you're just going to walk off and leave a hunk like Adam who's so crazy in love with you?"

Kaylee lowered her head. "The reason I came to Stone River is over. I'll never forget Adam, like I'll never forget you."

Betty slapped her hands together and giggled. "I bet you won't ever forget those bubble baths with your dream lover either."

Kaylee laughed quietly. "I'm sure I won't."

Betty nudged Kaylee. "Did you see how Charlie and Paulette put it all in that kiss? Wow! And how they left here arm and arm?

"Yeah, I did! They make a beautiful couple."

Betty pulled her necklace out from under her shirt and asked, "Do you have your necklace?"

With pride, Kaylee pulled her eagle claw from under her sweater. "I wouldn't leave without it."

Betty hugged her one last time and whispered, "I think someone is waiting to see you. I'm out of here. Goodbye, Kaylee Shell!"

After saying goodbye, Kaylee turned to face Adam. He moved close to her and said, "I thought I had better say goodbye tonight. Jeffrey seems like a really nice guy."

Tears welled up in Kaylee's eyes as she gently touched Adam's chest with her fingertips.

He took her hand and kissed it. "I don't want you to go. I love you, Kaylee, and I'll always love you. I would ask you to stay with me, but I don't think I could stand your answer right now."

They held each other a long while. In a broken voice, Adam said, "When I saw Charlie and Paulette dancing, I wished so desperately it could have been you and me."

"I know," she replied.

After a few moments, Kaylee pushed from Adam's embrace. With tears flowing down her face, she moaned loudly, "I love you and I'll never be the same without you. But my place is with Jeffrey."

As Adam wiped his tears, he cried, "I know . . . I know." He grabbed her and they kissed passionately, one last time. As he held her, he whispered in her ear, "I love you, Angel Face." Without delay, he stepped back, put his finger to her lips, turned and hurriedly left the stage.

Chapter Eighty-Five
The Envelope

Unaware that Dotty was watching, Kaylee fell to her knees and sobbed. After a moment, Dotty moved in front of her and gave her a tissue. She gently put her hand on Kaylee's shoulder. "Kaylee," she said. "Love can be so wonderful and so painful."

Kaylee wiped her eyes and blew her nose.

Dotty helped her to her feet. "You've been splendid, Kaylee Shell. Thank you for being obedient to your call."

Kaylee sniffed and whimpered, "I don't dare ask what that means, do I?"

Dotty smiled. "Not unless you really want to know."

Kaylee placed her hand on Dotty's arm, "Yes . . . yes, I do want to know."

Dotty patted Kaylee's hand and explained, "The day before Ellen died, she was very somber. I was worried about her! She went to the tower room, sat in a chair near the large window and stared out that window almost all day. She wouldn't eat or drink anything. When I checked on her, she said she feared something terrible was about to happen to her. Trembling, Ellen seized my hands and said, 'Dotty, if something should happen to me, one day, I want you to know, I will draw the right person to Stone River, and that person will avenge my death.'

"I sat with her for a long while and asked how she would do that. She explained, when the time was right, she would know whom to send. She pointed to the music box and said, 'I will draw the one who loves my music as much as I do.'

"When I heard the music playing after you arrived, I knew Ellen had finally found the right person. You! Ellen told me the person would not only expose Roy for the murderer he really was, but would also draw Wind Dancer back to her arms. You, with Adam's help, did that very thing."

Kaylee was stunned, yet knew she had to go. She explained to Dotty that Terra was taking Jeffrey and Martin back to the estate, and they would be expecting her.

Dotty gently took hold of Kaylee's arm. "Before you go . . ." Dotty took an envelope from her coat pocket and handed it to Kaylee, who looked at the envelope and then at Dotty.

"This belongs to you, Miss Shell."

Kaylee ran her fingers over the brown envelope and stared into Dotty's eyes. "This looks like the envelope that was on Ellen's stomach in the vault."

"That's because it is. The envelope contains two letters. One, by Ellen who wanted her part of the estate to go to the person that she would one day bring to Stone River to avenge the deaths of Jenny, Wind Dancer and herself. Willie Hilmar, who inherited the whole estate after Roy's death, penned the same thoughts as Ellen, word for word. Willie made sure the town council took charge of the estate after her death. Thelma wasn't ready for the responsibility of caring for the property at that time. Willie knew the council would never let it go because of the fortune tied to it. You asked me why Willie had all the portraits in the house taken down except the ones of Ellen and Jenny. I would like to answer that before you leave."

"Please do!"

"Roy confessed everything to Willie before he died. Willie felt the injustice forced on Ellen was greater than anyone should bear. In her mind, by leaving only Jenny and Ellen's portrait up, they alone would be honored in the house. Of course, Willie met and talked often with Ellen at the foot of the stairs."

Kaylee slightly shook her head and tightened her brows as she looked at Dotty and held the envelope up.

Before she could say anything, Dotty said, "That's right. The Hilmar Estate is now totally under your control. You're the new owner and keeper of the house and the keys." Dotty glanced at her watch. "By the way," she said, "the rooms are ready for Mr. Cullman and Jeffrey. I think I'm going home and get some rest tonight."

That night Jeffrey wanted to share Kaylee's bed, but the thoughts of Adam were too strong.

After kissing Kaylee goodnight, Jeffrey asked, "Do I want to know about this Adam, or should I file it under history?"

"Adam is a good friend."

Jeffrey kissed her forehead and muttered, "I could tell by the way he looked at you, that you were *very* good friends. I love you, Kaylee."

"I love you too, Jeffrey. Goodnight."

Kaylee turned the rhapsody on low and climbed into bed. Thoughts of Adam ravished her being. She went to sleep with the memories of his fulfilling touch, his smile and his words, "I love you, Angel Face."

Chapter Eighty-Six
Merry Christmas

The next morning, Kaylee was awakened by the smell of bacon, eggs and fresh brewed coffee. Sluggishly, she entered the kitchen to find Dotty serving Martin and Jeffrey breakfast.

Jeffrey patted the seat beside him, "I saved you a seat." He kissed her forehead and said, "Merry Christmas, my baby!"

She squeezed Martin's hand and wished him a Merry Christmas.

"How about me, Miss Shell?" Adam said, as he entered the kitchen. His smile appeared very chipper. He sat beside Martin, and Dotty put his plate in front of him.

Kaylee's heart pounded as she wished Adam a Merry Christmas as well. He took a bite of his eggs and said, "It's my duty to see that you nice folks don't miss your flight today."

Kaylee reached across the table and squeezed Martin's hand.

He furrowed his brow and said, "I've been meaning to ask, how did you know about Jeffrey's letters?"

Kaylee smiled at Jeffrey. "A very mysterious woman told me," she said. "So, tell us Martin, what are you going to do with all your newly found wealth?"

Martin shook his head. "I'm an old man; therefore, what I don't spend before I die, I'll leave to my daughter and you and Jeffrey." He frowned. "This was never about money. I have money. I just wanted to know about the man in my mother's letters. To me it was very clear that she loved him so much. The mystery that will remain unknown is how she could love him that much and not want to be with him? Or at least mail all those letters she took the time to write him?"

Kaylee glanced at Adam. "Maybe she did want to be with him, but felt for some reason she couldn't."

Martin shook his head. "I read every letter many times and in every one she told him repeatedly that she loved him. She also said, 'Your son is so like him.' Martin added, I just needed to find out first-hand if indeed Jake Boone was my father. I want to thank you, Kaylee, for helping me realize, that, yes, he was."

Kaylee casually turned her eyes to Adam as she said, "It's been a total pleasure, Martin."

Jeffrey lifted his orange juice and announced, "I would like to make a toast." Everyone lifted their glasses. "To the most wonderful grandfather and future wife anyone could ever have. I love you, Grandpa, and I adore you, Kaylee. Merry Christmas."

After breakfast, Kaylee insisted that the men load the bags in her Explorer. As they were putting the luggage in the car, Thelma and Paulette pulled up in front of the estate, parked and hurried inside. "Merry Christmas,

Miss Shell!" Thelma said as she hugged her. "Thank you for all you have done for me, Paulette and Stone River. Please keep in touch with us."

Kaylee smiled. "There is a reason I asked you to come here this morning before I leave. I have a Christmas present for you." Kaylee took the envelope Dotty had given her from her jacket, looked at it, handed it to Thelma and said, "This deed belongs to you and Paulette. Merry Christmas."

Kaylee glanced at Dotty who gave her a tight-lipped grin and nodded.

Thelma and Paulette were beside themselves.

On the way to the airport, Kaylee sat up front with Adam. Her emotions were in chaos, yet she tried to conceal it as best she could. Adam glanced at her hand that rested on the seat. He grinned when he saw the beaded engagement ring still on her finger. Slowly, he inched his hand to hers, slightly touched the ring, then covered her hand with his and held it all the way to the airport. It was hard to carry on a normal conversation, feeling his touch and remembering the passion they had shared.

The men shook hands and said goodbye. Afterward, Jeffrey helped Martin into the terminal, while Kaylee said goodbye to Adam.

"What do you want me to do with your car? Is Dotty going to send it back to Raleigh?"

"No, I had the title put in your name. Something to remember me by."

Adam took hold of her hand. "I don't need a car to remember you. You're burned into my heart, Kaylee Shell. Surely you know that."

Kaylee put her finger to his lips and whispered, "Shhh. I'll never forget our time together in Stone River."

Adam held Kaylee in his arms, fighting to hold his tears back. "I love you! I love you! I love you!" he moaned. Gradually they pulled from each-other's embrace, and Kaylee rushed into the terminal. Before boarding the plane, she turned to connect eyes with Adam one last time. Her window seat in first class allowed her to clearly see the viewing windows inside the airport. The plane slowly taxied down the runway to turn for take-off. Kaylee leaned forward, looking out the glass hoping to see Adam standing at the large panoramic window. As the plane jetted down the runway and Adam came into view, Kaylee's body jerked, suppressing her tears as he pressed his open hand against the glass. She hurriedly pressed hers to the window for him to see in passing. At that moment, she felt as though their hearts were being torn apart. Tears rolled down her cheeks. Knowing that some things are better left unsaid, Jeffrey held tight to her hand to comfort her.

After the captain announced they were free to move around, Kaylee asked Jeffrey to get her carry-on bag from the overhead compartment. She needed tissues and lots of them. Jeffrey accidentally bumped the bag as he handed it to her. A feeling gripped her heart when she heard three or four very familiar piano notes. Trembling, she slowly unzipped the bag to reveal the music box that had belonged to Ellen and Wind Dancer. Lightly touching the small figurines, Adam's fragrance filled her nostrils. Her head was spinning, remembering his touch. At that moment, she knew one day she would return to Stone River.

www.ingramcontent.com/pod-product-compliance
Lightning Source LLC
Chambersburg PA
CBHW020817180626
46814CB00001B/3